FORGOTTEN REALMS®

# SHADOWREALM

## THE TWILIGHT WAR · BOOK III

### PAUL S. KEMP

Wizards
OF THE COAST®

**The Twilight War, Book III**
# SHADOWREALM

Cover art by Raymond Swanland
Map by Todd Gamble
First Printing: December 2008

9 8 7 6 5 4 3 2 1

ISBN: 978-0-7869-4863-5
620-217337400-001-EN

U.S., CANADA,
ASIA, PACIFIC, & LATIN AMERICA
Wizards of the Coast, Inc.
P.O. Box 707
Renton, WA 98057-0707
+1-800-324-6496

EUROPEAN HEADQUARTERS
Hasbro UK Ltd
Caswell Way
Newport, Gwent NP9 0YH
GREAT BRITAIN
Save this address for your records.

Visit our web site at www.wizards.com

For my readers. Thank you.

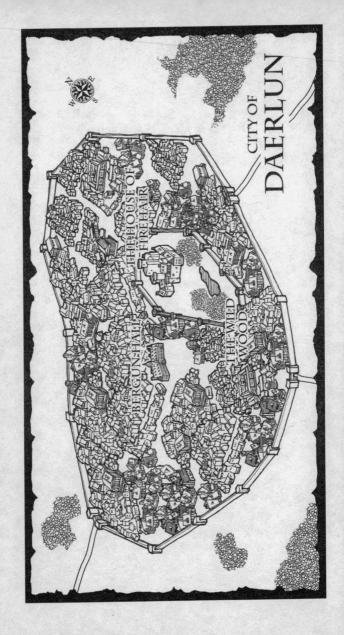

CITY OF
DAERLUN

THE HOUSE OF
FIRE HAIR

BERGUN HALL

THE WEED
WOOD

# CHAPTER ONE

*1 Nightal, The Year of Lightning Storms*
*(1374 DR)*

For hours I pace the dark halls of the Wayrock's temple. The anxious stomps of my boots on stone are the war drums of my battle with myself. Nothing brings peace to the conflict in my head. Nothing illuminates the darkness, dulls the sharp, violent impulses that stab at the walls of my self-restraint. The Shadowwalkers trail me, as furtive as ghosts. I catch only glimpses of them from time to time but I know they are there. Perhaps Cale asked them to watch over me. Perhaps they have taken that charge upon themselves.

Later, I sit in the dining hall of the temple and eat the food the Shadowwalkers set before me. I wonder, for a moment, how Riven gets food to the island, then wonder why I care.

Eating is mechanical, unfeeling, an exercise in

fueling the soulless shell of my body. It brings me no pleasure. Nothing human does, not anymore. The Shadowwalkers see to my needs, my meal, would see to my safety, were it necessary, but say little. They, creatures of darkness themselves, see something in me greater than mere darkness. They see the looming shadow of my father, the black hole of his malice, the dark hint of what I am becoming. I see it in their averted gazes, their quiet words in a language I do not understand. They are not afraid, but they are cautious, seeing in me one past redemption, one whose fall cannot be arrested but whose descent must be controlled lest I pull others down with me.

And perhaps they are correct. I feel myself falling, ever faster, slipping into night.

I consider murdering them, making them martyrs to the cause of being right. They would die, gurgling on blood, but content as they expire in the knowledge that they were correct about me.

"You're right," I say to them, and grin. My fangs poke into my lower lip, draw blood.

Their slanted eyes look puzzled. They speak to one another in their language and the shadows around them swirl in languid arcs.

I need only learn where they sleep, take them unawares, slit throats until I am soaked in blood. . . .

I realize the path my mind has taken, how tightly I am holding my feeding knife. With effort, I put the feet of my thoughts on another path. I bow my head, ashamed at the bloodletting that occurred in my imagination.

My mind moves so seamlessly to evil.

I am afraid.

"I am not a murderer," I whisper to the smooth face of the wooden table, and Nayan and his fellows pretend not to hear the lie.

I am a murderer. I simply have not yet murdered. But I will, given time. The good in me is draining away into the dark hole in my center.

My soul is broken. I am broken.

I am my father's son.

I consider killing myself but lack the will. Hope, for me, has become the hateful tether that keeps me alive. I hope that I can live without doing evil, hope that I can heal before it is too late. But I fear my hope is delusion, that it is only the evil in me preventing suicide until I am fully given over to darkness, when hope will no longer be relevant.

I feel the Shadowwalkers watching me again. Their gazes stir the cup of my guilt, my self-loathing.

"What are you looking at?" I shout at Nayan, at Vyrhas, at the small, dark little men who presume to judge me.

They look away, not out of fear, but out of the human habit of averting the gaze from the dying.

I hate them. I hate myself.

I hate, and little else.

Staring at the walls, at the shadow shrouded men who think me lost, I realize that hope, whether real or illusory, is not reason enough to live. It will not sustain me. Instead I will hold on for another reason—to take revenge for what has been done to me. Rivalen Tanthul and my father, both must be made to pay, to suffer.

For an instant, as with every thought, I wonder which half of me has birthed such a desire. I decide that I do not care. Whether it is a need for justice, vengeance, or simple bloodlust, it is right and I will do it.

I look at my hands—they show more and more red scales every day—and realize I have used my knife to gouge spirals into the wood of the table, lines that circle and circle until they disappear into their own center.

I stab the knife into the spiral, filling it with violence.

Nayan steps across the room in a single stride, emerges from the shadows beside me, puts his hand on my shoulder. His grip is firm, not friendly, and I resist the urge to cut off his fingers.

"You are not well," he says.

I scoff, my eyes still on the table. "No. I am not well."

He will get no more from me and knows it. Shadows curl around him, around me. His grip loosens.

"We are here," he says, his eyes on me.

I nod and he moves away, his expression unreadable.

I know his true concern—he fears I may be a danger to Cale and Riven, the Right and Left hands of Mask. He is right to fear, and once more I want to murder him for being right.

I close my eyes, put my thumb and forefinger on the bridge of my nose, try to find a focus, peace from the swirl of thoughts.

I cannot control my mind. It is an animal free of its cage of conscience.

Tears well in my eyes and I wipe at them furiously, hating my weakness.

I feel a faint twinge deep in my consciousness and it sits me up straight in my chair. It is vaguely familiar. The twinge distills to an ache, then an itch. At first I think it must be a false memory, another symptom of my mental deterioration, but it lingers, not strong, but steady.

I recognize it, then, and it sends a charge into me.

It is the mental emanations of the Source. Distant, faint, but undeniable.

The Shadovar have reawakened it.

The familiar hunger comes over me, another empty hole that I need to fill, this one born of addiction. Surrendering to the need seems fitting and I do not fight it. The mental connection opens and I gasp at its feel. My body shudders.

I sigh, satisfied, for a moment at peace. I wonder how the Netherese keep the Source's damaged consciousness functioning without me.

The question frees a flood of memories. I recall the dark-skinned servant creatures of the Shadovar, the krinth, whose minds I broke, whose consciousnesses I altered, whose minds I turned as brittle as crystal. Useful for a time, but fragile. I remember their wails as I pried away the layers of their simple minds, the blood leaking from their ears. I feel shame, but the shame manifests as a giggle.

The Shadowwalkers eye me, concerned at my outburst. The shadows cloaking them do not hide their mistrust.

"What is it?" Nayan asks in his accented common. He looks as if he might attempt to restrain me.

Contact with the Source reawakens my desire to use my mental powers despite the damage done to my mind by my father, despite the jagged edges of my brain that make the use of mind magic like walking on broken glass. I consider scouring Nayan's mind clean, but resist the impulse.

"It is nothing," I say, but it is not nothing.

I no longer care if using the Source consumes me. With its power, I might yet have my revenge. It will kill me, but I would rather die an addict than live as I am.

Wouldn't I?

The need for revenge grants me certitude.

I will use the Source's power to make Rivalen Tanthul and my father pay.

Then I will die.

Cale, Riven, and Abelar materialized in the darkness on a rise overlooking the Saerbian refugee camp at Lake Veladon. Tents congregated on the shore like fearful penitents. The glow of campfires lit the camp here and there. The reflected light of Selûne's Tears made fireflies on the mirror of the lake's dark water.

Thunder rumbled behind them, in the east, heralding a storm. Rain was coming.

Cale's shadesight cut through the darkness and he saw the nearest team of armed and armored watchmen before they saw him. He hailed them and word that Abelar had returned spread like wildfire through the camp.

A few members of Abelar's company met them, armor chinking, smiles in their eyes. Displaced Saerbians followed more slowly, fear in theirs. Most stared at the shadows around Cale, at the hole in Riven's face where his eye should have been, and spoke in hushed whispers.

Cale's shadow-sharpened hearing caught snippets of their conversations.

"Saved Elden Corrinthal, they say, but what is he? Shadovar?"

"Servant not of Lathander but a dark god . . ."

"Leave off, they are friends . . ."

Regg emerged from the press, his mouth a hard line behind his beard. Battle scars lined the rose of Lathander enameled on his breastplate. His face looked worn, creased with concern. He greeted Abelar with an arm clasp, but greeted Cale and Riven with a nod and an uncertain smile.

"You're well," he said to them all, but with his eyes on Abelar.

Abelar laughed, a single guffaw as coarse as a wood rasp.

Concern wrinkled Regg's brow. "Forrin?"

"Dead," Abelar answered, his voice hollow.

The Saerbians nearby who heard the news raised fists, called Forrin's death deserved. That news, too, would spread quickly.

"Is the war over then, Abelar?" asked a heavyset matron, her graying hair disheveled, her clothing road-stained.

"No, Merdith, it is not." To Regg, Abelar said, "Where is my son?"

"With Jiiris. He fell asleep in your father's arms and we put him in your tent."

Abelar nodded, thanked Regg.

Regg put a hand on Abelar's shoulder. "Whatever happened, Abelar, the Morninglord—"

Abelar shook his head, the gesture as sharp as a blade. "It is night, Regg. No more of Lathander just now."

Regg looked as if Abelar had slapped his face. His arm dropped. Merdith gasped. Some of the other Saerbians nearby overheard Abelar's words, and uncertain, worried mutters moved through the throng.

"Abelar . . ." Regg began.

"Leave it alone, Regg," Riven said, and the softness in his tone surprised Cale. "Just take him to his son."

Regg's face flashed anger but only for a moment before he beat back whatever words he might have said. He started walking.

"Come. Your father will be pleased to see you, Abelar."

"And I him," Abelar said, and Cale thought his voice sounded like that of a man who had not slept in a tenday. "How fare matters here?"

"As it was when you . . . left. Watchmen guard the perimeter. Roen and the men lead patrols of the approaches. But we cannot remain here. If Forrin brings an army . . . I mean, if the army of the overmistress comes. . . ."

"I know."

"Do you?"

Abelar nodded, his eyes focused on some distant point on the water of the lake.

To Cale and Riven, Regg said, "I will see to shelter for you two. Rain is coming."

As if to make his point, thunder shook the sky to the east. Distant lightning lit the clouds. The crowd murmured; some scrambled for the safety of their tents.

Cale shook his head. "Thank you, but unnecessary."

Regg grunted indifference, but Abelar pulled his eyes from the lake, stopped, and faced Cale. "Unnecessary?"

Cale nodded. "We must leave, Abelar. Other matters require our attention. There is . . . much afoot."

He thought of Kesson Rel, Magadon, his promises to Mask and Mephistopheles. Shadows swirled around him, agitated, dark.

Abelar looked stricken. The circles under his eyes seemed drawn with charcoal. He had left more than Forrin's corpse behind in Fairhaven.

"I have started down a path . . ." Abelar said. He looked past Cale to the sky, to the storm, as if there were hope there. Finding none, he trailed off.

"I know," Cale said softly.

Regg put a comforting hand on Abelar's shoulder but said nothing.

Abelar inhaled, straightened up. "There is much to be done here. The bulk of the overmistress's army remains in the field and we are too few to face it. These people need to be led to safety, Selgaunt or Daerlun. There is much afoot here, as well, and I would that you stay. Both of you."

The statement touched Cale. He liked Abelar. Jak would have liked him, too.

"I advise against Selgaunt," he said. "The Hulorn has allied with the Shadovar and is not to be trusted."

"Daerlun, then," Regg said.

"You served the Hulorn, yes?" Abelar said.

"I did, but no longer. The Shadovar have great influence over him now. I think you and your people will not be welcome there."

Abelar considered, nodded. "Daerlun, then. But I repeat my request—stay. Help us. Help . . . me."

In refusing, Cale felt as if he were betraying Abelar, but there was nothing for it. "We will return if we can," he said, and clasped Abelar's hand. "I mean that. As for the path you are on, turn from it. It can be done."

Riven cleared his throat, shifted on his feet.

Abelar's face clouded and he did not release Cale's hand. "How do you know? Did you?"

The shadows around Cale roiled, crawled up Abelar's arm. The question might as well have been a punch. He shook his head.

"No. But my path is different. We're different."

They stared at each other, one once in service to the light and drifting toward darkness, one in service to shadow and just drifting. Thunder growled.

"Perhaps not as different as you think," Abelar said at last and released him.

Cale could say nothing to that.

"I owe you both much," Abelar said, adopting a formal tone. "Thank you for saving my son. You will always be welcomed by the Corrinthals."

Cale decided that the world dealt harshly with men like Jak and Abelar. It killed them or darkened them, but never left them in the light. The realization made him melancholy. He felt Riven's eye on him but ignored it.

"We should see your son before we go," Riven said.

Surprised, Cale turned and looked a question at Riven. Regg, too, seemed taken aback, to judge from his expression.

Abelar appeared unbothered. "Of course. Come."

A light rain started to fall as the men picked their way through the camp. The Saerbian refugees scurried for shelter. Fires sizzled, danced in the wind, expired.

Cale, Riven, and Regg pulled up their hoods. Abelar did not; he seemed to welcome the downpour. Cale knew why, knew too, that rain could not wash away some stains.

Lightning lit the night. Thunder rumbled, lingered, the sky with bloodlung.

They came to a tent near the center of the camp. The soft glow of a lantern leaked intermittently from the wind-whipped tent flap. Regg lifted it for them and they entered.

"I will find your father," Regg said. "It is good to have you back."

Abelar thumped him on the shoulder as he entered the tent.

Elden slept in one corner of the sparsely furnished space, his head poking from a pile of furs and woolens. A red-haired woman in chain mail sat on a small chair near the makeshift bed. She stood when they entered, mail chinking, her face alight.

"Abelar," she said with a smile.

"This is Jiiris," Abelar said, as she crossed the tent. "One of my company. Jiiris, know Erevis Cale and Drasek Riven."

Her gaze move only reluctantly from Abelar. She nodded a greeting to Cale and Riven. Her eyes took them in, the shadows that shrouded Cale, the ghost of a sneer that hung on Riven's face. She had stubborn eyes, a soldier's eyes.

"Thank you for what you did for Elden," she said. "It was noble work."

Her self-assuredness reminded Cale of Brilla, the kitchen mistress of Stormweather Towers. He suspected she would brook no foolery and liked her instantly.

Cale tilted his head in acknowledgment, while Riven sounded almost embarrassed.

"Not sure I've ever heard something I've done spoken of in such a way."

"Perhaps you should do such things more often, then," she chided. To Abelar, she said, "I am pleased to see you returned."

"And I am pleased to return to you, and my son."

She flushed at his words and Cale saw the stubbornness in her eyes give way to affection. She masked it again, and gestured at Elden. "He has awakened twice asking for you. He would like for you to awaken him, I'm sure."

Abelar nodded, though his face fell and colored. He brushed past her, sat on the bed with his back to them. For a time he simply looked upon Elden. He started to touch him twice, recoiled, finally brushed the boy's brow. Elden murmured in his sleep.

For a time no one spoke. The moment was too pure for the pollution of words. Thunder rumbled, rain pattered on the tent, and Elden's hands emerged from the blankets to cradle his father's hand, the hand that had killed Malkur Forrin.

Jiiris daubed her eyes.

In handcant, Riven signaled to Cale, *See.*

Not a question, but a demand.

Cale did not understand.

Father and son held each other in the bubble of the tent, each the satisfaction of the other's need. After a time, Abelar's body shook and it took Cale a moment to understand that he was sobbing. His tears were a confession.

Jiiris looked to Cale, a question in her own tear-streaked face.

Cale did not answer. He did not want to tell her that they had saved the son but lost the father. She would learn that soon enough. Instead, he whispered, "We must go. Help him as you can. We are his friends. Tell him so."

She nodded, pushed through the shadows to touch Cale's hand in gratitude.

Cale and Riven exited the tent, entered the night, the rain. Cale grabbed Riven by the arm, angry for no reason.

"What did you mean in there? When you signed 'see'?"

Riven faced him, eyed Cale's hold on his arm. "I wanted you to see what was happening. Understand it."

Cale released the assassin's arm. "I understood it."

"Did you?" the rain pressed Riven's hair to his skull. "We saved that boy, Cale, but you've been wearing a look on your face like we didn't. Why?"

The shadows around Cale coiled, spun in wide ribbons.

"Don't deny it," Riven said. "I've been killing men for most of my life. So have you. Reading a man's face comes with the work. And I can read you as well as any."

Cale could not articulate his thoughts, the strange detachment he felt, even after saving Elden. He was not himself. Or he was himself and did not like what he was.

"I don't know," he said. "I'm not . . ."

He let the thought die, shook his head.

Riven stepped closer to him. The shadows wrapped them both.

"You lied to Abelar about turning around."

Cale had no answer. He had lied.

"There ain't no turning around, Cale. You know that."

Cale did know it, but he wanted there to be, and he knew that he would tell Abelar the same lie again. He looked into Riven's face and said, "Sometimes we need lies."

Riven stared at him, stepped back, his expression as fixed as that of a golem. Green lightning lined the eastern sky, cast Riven's face in alternating fields of light and shadow. Thunder boomed, once, twice, again, again. He and Riven both turned and the moment was lost.

The distant clouds, cast in streaks of vermillion, blackened the sky, turned it to a void. They stretched fully across the eastern horizon, not mere clouds but a wall of pitch, an absence of light.

Refugees emerged from their tents in ones and twos, looking east to the tenebrous sky, shielding themselves from the rain. Jiiris stepped from the tent behind them.

She looked east as lightning flashed and the refugees gasped. Thunder rolled anew.

"That is not a storm born of nature," she said.

Cale agreed, and the shadows around him swirled in answer to the churning sky.

Abelar emerged, too. He held Elden tightly against him and put his other arm around Jiiris. She leaned into him and Cale thought that some wall between them had fallen. Faith had been supplanted by something more earthly.

Cale thought of Varra, the last woman he had held in his arms. A similar wall had stood between them and he'd never been able to breach it. Faith, or fate, seemed to leave little room for ordinary needs.

"Wizardry out of Ordulin," Abelar said. "Battle will be on its heels."

"Look at it," Jiiris said. "All of eastern Sembia will be caught in it."

Jiiris was right, and the import of her words caused Cale to curse.

"What is it?" Riven asked.

Cale drew the darkness about him. "Varra."

Riven looked puzzled for a moment, then recognition lit his face. "Varra? The woman from Skullport?"

"Wait for me here," Cale said, and the shadows surrounding him deepened. He pictured in his mind the cottage where he and Varra had spent a year, the cottage in which he'd left her behind, the cottage that was or soon would be within the magical storm.

"Cale, we stay together," Riven said. "I will come with you. Cale!"

Cale hesitated for a moment, nodded, and extended the darkness to Riven.

Abelar stared at Cale, at the darkness, his expression thoughtful.

"Return if you can," Jiiris said. "We will need you here."

Cale nodded as the shadows whisked them across Sembia.

Rain drizzled from the dark sky. The low rumble of thunder from the east promised a still heavier downpour. The smell of Saerb, reduced to damp ash, still hung in the air, or perhaps simply lingered in Reht's memory. The smell of Saerb's dead, thankfully, did not.

Reht pulled up the hood of his cloak and sloshed through the camp. A few stubborn bonfires tended by equally stubborn soldiers smoked and sizzled in the wet. Eyes watched him pass and he left murmured questions in his wake.

The men had already heard. Reht should have known. Stories went through camp faster than a plague of the trots, even in the dead of night.

He reached the center of the camp where a crowd of soldiers stood around Forrin's large tent. The pennons on the center pole snapped in the breeze. Lantern light poured out of the tent's open flap. Reht saw Enken and two others within. He pushed through the press, nearly slipping in the mud.

"They got the general, Reht," one of the men said as he passed.

"What are we doing about it?" said another.

Reht decided to take a moment to remind the men that they were and remained soldiers, whatever the fate of their general. He stopped, pulled back his hood, and stared into one face after another.

"What will be done about it is what your commanders order you to do. And that will be in due time. Meanwhile, if any man loitering here is supposed to be standing a post, I will personally string him by the balls for dereliction of duty. Saerbian forces are in the field and they could be mustering for a counterattack. Rain and darkness are not armor. Am I understood?"

A chorus of "Aye, sirs" and averted gazes answered his words.

Enken stood with Strend and Hess inside the tent. The rain beat staccato off the canvas. Enken nodded a greeting and

Strend and Hess saluted. Hess's moustache drooped as much as the man's shoulders. Strend, as barrel-chested as a dwarf, shifted uncomfortably on his feet.

At a glance, everything within the tent seemed in order. There was no blood, no items tossed about. It appeared as though General Forrin had simply stepped out to the privy.

"What exactly happened here?" Reht asked.

Hess and Strend hesitated, looked one to the other.

"Tell him what you told me," Enken said to Hess. "Neither of you is at fault here."

Hess eyed Reht and shook his head. "We heard a shout, Commander, and rushed in. We saw a man—"

"Wasn't a man," Strend said, shaking his head and crossing his arms over his chest.

"The Hells," Hess said. "It was a man, but not normal. He was dark, with shadows all around him. He saw us, the tent went dark, then he was gone with the general."

"Shadovar," Reht said. They had heard that forces out of Shade Enclave had allied with the Selgauntans and Saerbians.

Enken grunted agreement, pulled one of his many knives and ran his thumb across its edge. "My thoughts as well."

Strend looked nervous, eyed the dark pockets in the corners of the tent. "Shadovar. . . . I've heard things."

"Tales and naught else," Enken said, pointing his blade at the young soldier. "Shadovar bleed as well as any and better than some." He looked to Reht. "We could turn the clerics on to this Shadovar's scent. Follow him. They must have wanted the general alive or they would have killed him here."

"Agreed," Reht said.

Hess looked like he'd eaten bad beef. "He warned us not to follow."

Reht and Enken stared blades at the boy. "What? Who?"

"The Shadovar."

"And?"

"And . . . that is all," said Hess and looked away.

Enken grunted in disgust, took Hess by the back of his cloak, and shoved him toward the tent flap.

"You left your balls out in the rain, soldier. Get out there and find him 'ere I see you again."

Reht, Enken, and Strend chuckled at Hess's expense as Hess sulked his way out of the tent. The moment he stepped outside the questions from the loiterers flew as heavy as the rain.

"Lorgan has not reported back," Enken said. "That leaves the rank to you or me."

"Fight you for it?" Reht said.

Enken smiled, showing his chipped front teeth. He sheathed his knife. "I would, but we can't afford to lose you."

Reht chuckled.

Enken said, "You're longer in the Blades, anyway, known the general and the men longer. You take it."

Reht considered that, and nodded. While he had always been a tactician, a leader of small units, not a strategist, he could assume command until the overmistress replaced Forrin with another general.

"When Lorgan shows, he'll rank me and can have it."

"If Lorgan shows," Enken said. "His silence bodes ill. Meantime, keep a light around you. Shadovar seem to have a liking for anyone leading this army."

Reht smiled but it was forced. To Strend, he said, "Take Hess and get me Mennick and Vors, and the rest of the Talassans. Let's find out what happened here."

Strend saluted and started to bound from the tent.

"Wait," Reht said, and Strend stopped.

"Sir?"

"Bring the Corrinthal boy back with you, too. If Vors has a problem, you bring him to me."

Strend nodded and hurried out, and they heard him call for Hess.

"Vors," Enken said, and spit as if the name itself left a foul taste.

Reht thought that said everything that needed saying. He walked the confines of Forrin's tent, trying on his new rank, looking over Forrin's personal effects. Forrin had traveled light, still a mercenary footman despite his rank.

"Blade and armor are gone," Reht said to Enken.

"I noticed."

"Could be the general put up a fight before Hess and Strend entered the tent."

"Could be. But if so, it wasn't much of one."

"Bold, taking him out of his own tent," Reht said.

Enken nodded, his expression thoughtful.

Reht didn't have an eye for clues or a head for mysteries. He'd leave it to Mennick and the priests. He turned his thoughts back to his men, his army, things he understood.

"Extra discipline with the men for a time, to keep things in order while they stomach the news. We'll need to get word to the overmistress."

"Agreed to both," Enken said. "If she replaces you with someone political, I think the Blades will take it ill."

Reht nodded, listened to the patter of rain, and pondered his course. A third of his forces under Lorgan had not reported back. Likely they had been delayed by the weather or cut off by Saerbian forces. He knew a sizeable force of Saerbians had mustered on the shores of Lake Veladon. He suspected Endren Corrinthal was among them.

Reht was inclined to meet them in the field. He knew that Forrin's orders had been to raze Saerb and disrupt any potential muster of Saerbian forces. They'd razed Saerb but at least a partial muster had gone forward anyway.

"I am tempted to move against the Saerbians at Lake Veladon."

"The commanders will support that," Enken said. "Gavist

and I had been advocating as much with Forrin before . . . this."

"Well enough. It'll give the men a focus. Call the commanders together."

Enken saluted, grinning through his beard the while, and stepped out of the tent.

"Reht has command until further notice!" Reht heard him shout to the gathered men outside. "Pass the word."

They would assemble the army with the dawn and formally announce Reht's promotion with all the assembled commanders at his side. He expected no resistance. He knew he was respected, even liked. He'd led many of the men in the army personally, fought beside them, bled beside them. They would follow him for as long as he had command.

But in the privacy of his own thoughts, he felt himself smaller than the task, a halfling in a giant's boots. He did not have Forrin's nose for strategy. The weight of authority felt heavy on his shoulders. He'd have to rely on his commanders.

He found a bottle of Forrin's wine and two tin chalices in a small chest. Spurning the chalices, he pulled the cork with his teeth and took a long swallow directly from the bottle. It'd be the last he had for a time.

A commotion from outside the tent rose above the sound of the rain. Reht set down the bottle and started out but before he did Strend burst into the tent, dripping rain, breathless, his face red from exertion.

"Speak, boy," Reht said.

"They killed Vors, too," Strend blurted. "And the Corrinthal boy is gone."

"Damn it." Reht strode past Strend and out of the tent. The weight of two dozen gazes settled on him as he emerged. He stopped and looked his men in the eye. He kept his tone even but authoritative.

"Stand your posts, stay alert, and do your jobs. We will avenge all that has happened."

Nods and grudging acknowledgements from all around.

Reht saluted, was answered in kind by all the men in sight, and walked through the camp. As he passed, men saluted, hailed him as commander. Word had spread.

On the way to Vors's tent, he met Gavist, a skilled junior commander who could not yet grow a full beard. Gavist, too, saluted him.

"I am tired of that already," Reht said.

Gavist smiled.

Reht said, "The general is taken and Vors is dead."

Gavist's young face showed no emotion. "I heard as much."

"Anyone else?" Reht asked.

"Not that I've heard," Gavist said.

"Precise strike," Reht said.

They fell in together and marched through the camp. By the time they reached Vors's tent, they trailed two score soldiers in their wake.

Othel stood at the entrance to Vors's tent and greeted Reht and Gavist with a nod. Reht was thankful Othel didn't salute.

"Ugly in there, Commander," Othel said.

Reht stepped through the tent's flap and looked inside.

"Tempus's blade," he swore.

Vors lay on the ground in the center of the tent, his breastplate at his side. A spear impaled his guts, stuck out of his body like an oriflamme. His open eyes, glassy and swollen from a beating, stared upward at nothing. His mouth hung open in an unfinished scream of pain. Blood caked his lips, his beard. The pungent, sour stink of blood and worse hung thick in the tent.

Vors had died in pain, prolonged and deliberately inflicted. He would have taken a quarter hour or more to die with the spear in his belly.

Gavist chewed his upper lip, as if feeling for the non-existent moustache with his teeth. "Looks personal. And why take the boy?"

"The Shadovar are allied with Selgaunt and Selgaunt is allied with Saerb," Reht said. "The Corrinthals are important among the Saerbians. Rescuing the boy makes sense, either to earn goodwill or use as leverage." He nodded at the slaughter. "Not sure why the assassin would do it this way, though."

"Vengeance for the boy?" Othel said.

Reht thought it might be possible. "No one heard anything?"

Othel shook his head.

"What is it?" some of the soldiers shouted from outside the tent. "What happened in there?"

Reht made his expression neutral, stepped out of the tent to face them. They blinked in the rain. "Vors is dead. A spear through the gut."

Expressions turned angry, fists shook. No one had liked Vors except his fellow priests, but he had been one of their company.

"Someone pays for this in blood," boomed a voice from the crowd, and the four other Talassans in the army, their unkempt hair flattened against their heads by the rain, wild eyes glaring, elbowed their way through the press.

Reht stepped forward to meet them, cut them off from entering Vors's tent. The big warpriest almost bumped him. Almost.

"Agreed, Kelgar. But it happens my way, and only on my orders."

The tall warpriest's wild eyes fixed on Reht. Spit flew when he spoke. "And who are you to me?"

Reht eased forward into Kelgar's space, nose to nose. The men watching fell silent. The priest stood a hand taller than Reht, and a stone heavier.

"Your commander, which means you follow my orders. Understood?"

"A Stormlord is dead, murdered." More spit.

"He is. But in this army, you answer to me first, to your god second. Otherwise, you ride off now. Find the slaughter you seek somewhere else."

"You disliked Vors. We know what happened on the last raid."

"I hated him passionately," Reht said, eliciting a growl from Kelgar. "But he was a soldier in this army. My army. That is all that matters."

The Talassan stared into Reht's eyes, measuring him. Reht gave no ground.

Finally the priest smirked, stepped back, and nodded. No spit.

"Well enough . . . Commander."

Reht stepped aside and let them through. "We'll have a council with all the junior commanders in one hour. You are to be there."

Kelgar grunted agreement and entered the tent with his fellows. The moment they saw the carnage they shouted curses and blood oaths.

Gavist and Othel cleared out of the way and Reht stood in the tent's doorway as the warpriests honored their dead by howling over his body and destroying his possessions, overturning tables, shattering glass, slashing carpets and bedding. Reht had seen it before. Talos reveled in destruction and battle. So did his priests. The Talassans would pile up the wreckage and set it all aflame with a summoned lightning strike before dawn.

As if in answer to the funereal rage of the Talassan warpriests, the sky rumbled with thunder, a lasting peal that reached a booming crescendo.

"Double the men on guard duty," Reht said to Gavist, and the young junior commander nodded.

"You think the assassins might return?"

"I don't. Vors, at least, looks to have been personal. But we may as well take precautions. Taking Forrin could be a precursor to an attack."

Mennick, the army's most powerful wizard, strode through the men as the Talassans within the tent unleashed their own storm. Magic kept Mennick's dark robes and gray-streaked hair shielded from the rain.

"You've heard?" Reht asked.

Mennick's eyes clouded over. He'd known Forrin for many years. "Yes."

"Mages are at work in this," Reht said. "Shadovar mages. Do what you can to prevent this from happening again."

"I can raise some wards," Mennick said. "I should start with you."

"Fine. Inform the overmistress via sending, then find out who did this and where they are."

Mennick nodded and looked over and past Reht in thought, his brow grooved.

Lightning flashed and his eyes widened. He pointed at the horizon.

"Look at that."

Reht turned to see pitch devour the eastern sky, swallowing stars. Not storm clouds, but a churning fog of impenetrable night. Streaks of green lightning sliced through it at intervals. An uneasy murmur went through the gathered men as the darkness expanded.

"Not natural," Mennick said.

"Shadovar?" Reht asked.

Mennick shrugged. "Seems likely."

"Shadovar troops could be moving under cover of that storm," Gavist said.

"Possible," Mennick said. "They take Forrin, thinking to disrupt our command, then attack under cover of darkness."

Reht nodded, thoughtful. The storm was moving west

toward them, bracketing Reht's army between it and the Saerbian forces. He liked it little.

He decided he would not sit idle while his enemies determined the field of battle. He had thought to march against the Saerbians, but now he had a different target, one whose agents had attacked his camp.

"Sound the muster," Reht said to Gavist. "Get the men geared up. We're moving into that storm. We take the fight to them."

Gavist saluted, and headed off.

"Scouts forward with half hour reporting," Reht shouted to Gavist's back. "And double the scouts to the rear. I don't want the Saerbians taking us unawares. And get some scouts in the field looking for Lorgan."

A raised hand acknowledged the orders and the camp soon erupted in activity.

Reht walked among his men, watching the approaching storm. It was still hours away, given its slow advance. In his mind's eye, he imagined the Saerbian forces marching from Lake Veladon, thinking to catch Reht in a vise.

"No, no,," he said. He would engage the Shadovar as soon as possible. After defeating them, he'd turn and finish the approaching Saerbians. He had the forces to do it.

Behind him, the Talassans ignited Vors's body, possessions, and tent. Their roars of rage chased the smoke into the dark sky.

The next day would bring battle.

Once, the prospect would have lit a fire in his belly. Now, it kindled only a spark. A long life of soldiering had shaped Reht into a certain kind of man, and sometimes he tired of himself. He'd almost been apprenticed in his adolescence to a cartographer but the man had taken on another instead, a nephew. Reht had always loved maps, still did. He wondered what his life would have been like had he spent it as a mapmaker. Would he have married? Had children? Certainly he'd have had fewer scars.

He shook his head, rebuking himself for being sentimental. He had made his choice, had put aside maps for steel.

Donning his helmet, he put cartography and regrets out of his mind and saw to the preparation of his army.

# CHAPTER TWO

*1 Nightal, The Year of Lightning Storms*

Cale and Riven materialized in darkness as thick and black as a pool of ink. A cutting wind gusted from the east, and knifed through their clothes. Rain pelted them, and carried down from the black sky the musty smell of old decay. Tangible swirls of shadow turned the cool air thick, gauzy.

"Where is this place, Cale?" Riven asked over the wind.

"Home," Cale shouted in answer. "For a time."

It was also in the center of the storm. They stood in the meadow not far from the small cottage where Cale had lived with Varra. The sentinel elm, towering over them, whispered and creaked in the wind, sizzled in the rain. The furniture Cale had made from deadwood lay overturned in the grass. The wildflowers Varra had planted were browned and dead on the stalks. The window shutters and door of the cottage flapped in the gusts, all of them beating as if in anger against the cottage's walls.

"Varra!" Cale shouted. "Varra!"

His voice barely penetrated the howl of wind and rain. Lightning lit the meadow. The downpour and wind hissed against the trees in the surrounding forest.

"You feel that air?" Riven shouted, and drew his blades. "Same as in the Calyx."

Cale nodded, and drew Weaveshear. "Same as in Elgrin Fau." He rode the darkness into the cottage. "Varra!"

He found their old home empty, their bed unmade. The wind shrieked through the open windows and doors. Blankets, utensils, pails, and broken pieces of clay lamps lay strewn about the floor, dislodged by the wind. He tore open cabinets, trunks, piles of linens, looking for any sign of what might have happened.

"Varra!"

He cursed himself for bringing her out of Skullport, cursed himself for leaving her alone in an unfamiliar place. He had not merely left her alone; he had abandoned her. She could be wandering in the woods, lost in the storm, anywhere.

He tossed their room, found one of the smocks she sometimes wore in the summer, and decided to use it as the focus for a divination. He held his mask in one hand, the smock in his shadowborn hand, and intoned over the wind the words to a spell that would locate her.

The magic manifested and the shadows darkened before his face, forming a lens in the air. But he felt no connection to Varra. He poured power into the spell, willed it to show her, but the lens remained black, dead.

Cursing, he ended it.

He stood in the center of the ruins of their life together, wondering if she was dead. He hesitated for only a moment before making up his mind. He cast another spell that allowed him to commune with his god. The wind-driven beat of the shutters and door on the walls kept time with his heart.

"Is she alive?" Cale asked, his voice a monotone in the wind's wail.

The darkness swirled around him and the voice of his god whispered in his brain, She lives and is safe, far from you, but not in distance.

He exhaled with relief, tried to process the rest of the reply, but Riven's shout from outside carried over the shriek of the wind.

"Cale! Get out here!"

Cale cloaked himself in shadows and rode them back out to the meadow. He emerged from the darkness beside Riven, in Varra's garden. Lightning ripped the sky, cast the meadow in sickening green. The wind picked up, took on an odd keening that stood the hairs on his arms on end. It bent the trees of the forest, sent a barrage of leaves and loose sticks into the meadow.

"Up there," Riven said, and pointed skyward with one of his sabers.

Astride his mount, Reht crested a rise and looked at the edge of the crawling darkness. His commanders crowded around him. All squinted against the wind and rain. All cursed.

His army stood arrayed a spear cast behind them, cloaks drawn, shields held over heads to shelter them from the pounding of the rain. Dawn would break in a few hours, but Reht thought it unlikely they would notice once they entered the storm. It looked like ink.

"Gods," said Norsim, a towering junior commander with a reputation for good luck.

A wall of black fog lay before them, extending from the ground to the sky. Tendrils and spirals of pitch reached out of it, seemed to pull it along in dark billows. The fog cloaked the ground, sank into the hollows, and shrouded everything in its path. Its edge seemed to demarcate more than the border between light and shadow. The earth looked different under its shroud, foreign, deformed. They could not see more than a stone's throw within in.

Lightning flashed from time to time, turning the thick haze the greenish black of a bruise. Reht's horse neighed nervously, pawed the ground, tossed its head. Shifts in the saddle betrayed the concern of his commanders, though none spoke their fears aloud.

"Shadovar magic," Mennick said.

"Aye," Reht said.

Enken's horse tossed its head, blew a spray of spit. "There could be ten thousand men within it."

"Or there could be a few hundred," Reht said.

"Or none," Norsim said.

"Not even you are that lucky," said Enken.

Kelgar slammed a gauntleted fist against the lightning bolts on his shield. "Let us hope that it is ten thousand. The Thunderer demands blood for Vors."

Reht saw motion within the darkness. Forms separated from the murk and the shadows birthed the silhouettes of two men and horses. No one else seemed to notice. Reht still had his archer's eyes.

"Scouts are returning," he said.

"Where?" asked Enken, leaning forward into the rain. "Ah."

Othel and Phlen burst from the fog, trailing stubborn streams of black disinclined to release them. They shook their heads as they emerged from the fog, spotted Reht and his commanders, and raced toward them.

"Ten fivestars on Othel," Norsim said, though the offer sounded half-hearted.

No one took the wager.

Othel and Phlen, with Phlen in the lead, tore toward the gathered commanders and wheeled to a stop. Both of the men looked pale, the mud spatters that covered them dark by contrast.

"General," Othel said to Reht, as his horse turned a circle, neighed, and pawed the earth.

Enken tossed Othel a waterskin. The scout took a long draw then wiped his mouth.

"Report," Reht said.

"It is cool within the fog and grew cooler as we advanced," Othel said. "Visibility is poor but light can cut through it. I found it difficult to keep my sense of direction."

"As did I," Phlen agreed, nodding. Othel passed him the waterskin and he drank.

Othel said, "We rode in half a league and encountered nothing. It appears to be nothing more than an unusual storm. If Shadovar forces are within, they are farther back than we advanced."

Kelgar looked past the scouts to the storm. "The Shadovar are in there."

"Your spells tell you as much?" Reht asked.

Kelgar thumped his breastplate with his fist, over his heart. "This tells me as much. There's battle in there, General."

Reht made up his mind and spoke to his commanders.

"Put the men in a skirmish line, with three man teams scouting all sides. Mennick, use the darkvision wands on all the scouts and all senior commanders. Scouts are to return with word on the half hour."

Enken eyed the storm, and licked his lips. Lightning lit up the clouds. "I don't like it, Reht. Could be anything in there."

"Then you best prepare for anything," said Kelgar with contempt.

Enken edged his horse toward Kelgar's. "Close your hole before I fill it with steel, priest. Revenge for your dead fellow and Forrin's snatching is not reason to be rash."

The Talassans glared at Enken and snarled. Enken answered with his own glare, his hand on one of his knives. The other commanders took position near Enken, facing off the priests.

"Calmer heads, men," Reht said. "All of you. There's work ahead." To Enken, he said, "You think it rash?"

"Yes," Enken said, and tilted his head. "But I don't see many options. If we retreat before it, it will chase us into the Saerbian forces, which may be the intent. Even if it stops advancing it cuts us off from Ordulin and leaves us unsupplied. Moving south toward Selgaunt is not an option. I'd rather enter it and take our chances than sit on my hands." He smiled. "But that doesn't make it any less rash."

Reht chuckled. "Agreed. Sometimes rashness is a soldier's ally. That's why we keep Norsim and his luck at our side."

Norsim smiled.

Reht continued, "Let's keep the men sharp and see what we see."

"Aye," Enken said. He spat at the feet of Kelgar's mount. "Maybe these battle-happy fools can lead the advance, eh?"

"We've been leading since we arrived," Kelgar answered.

The men all laughed as the group dispersed back to their units.

"Remain," Reht said to Mennick, and when they stood alone atop the rise, he said, "What have you learned?"

The mage shook his head. "Nothing. Whoever took the general is well warded against scrying." He nodded at the storm as distant thunder rumbled. "And divinations reveal nothing about the storm. It's a void, Commander."

"Ordulin and the Overmistress?"

"I cannot make contact with anyone there. The storm may be blocking the magic."

Behind them, horns blew and men shouted, the army forming up.

Reht eyed the black wall before him, and the twisted look of the world under its shroud. He and his army were isolated in the field, with scant knowledge of their enemy, supply lines cut by the storm, and no instructions from their ostensible leaders in Ordulin. He did not like the courses open to him but had to choose one.

"Get yourself ready," he said to Mennick. "We go in. If the Shadovar are within the storm, we engage. If this is just a ruse or magic gone awry, we push through it, return to Ordulin, and regroup."

When the mage was gone, Reht whispered a prayer to Tempus, asking the Lord of Battle to strengthen his men.

Cale looked up into the dark sky. Above the tree line he saw thousands of tiny points of red light streaking toward the meadow. From a distance they looked like a swarm of fireflies, a swirling constellation of red stars. But Cale recognized them for what they were—eyes.

"Shadows," he said.

Riven nodded, and absently spun his sabers. "She's not here? Varra?"

Cale shook his head.

The air grew cooler as the undead approached. The wind pasted Cale's cloak to his skin. "This storm, the shadows. It's like the Calyx."

Riven nodded. "Kesson Rel is in Faerûn, His shadow giants cannot be far off."

Cale tried to count the shadows as they swarmed toward them but gave up. There were thousands. Cale remembered the pit under the spire in the Adumbral Calyx, the black hole that vomited newly formed shadows into the world.

"He has opened a gate," Cale said. "Or a rift."

Cale had seen something similar, long ago, when a portion of the Abyss had bled into the guildhouse of the Night Knives.

"Too many," Riven said, as the undead creatures closed. Hundreds of them descended into the forest, still flying for the meadow, and the soft glow of their eyes cast the boles and boughs of the trees in crimson. Riven bounced on the balls of his feet, slowly twirling his sabers.

"Too many, Cale."

Cale tried to imagine the scope of the deaths that thousands of shadows could cause, but it was too large. He thought of the Saerbians, Selgaunt. He sagged under the weight of his role in it.

"We did this," he said.

Riven stopped spinning his sabers. "No. Kesson Rel did this."

Cale tried to agree, but failed. "We freed him to do it when we killed Furlinastis. Kesson Rel played us, and now he is come to Faerûn."

"We didn't know."

"We didn't think. We just acted."

The shadows drew closer, the keening louder.

Riven looked over at Cale. "We aren't going to undo it here. There are too many."

Cale barely heard him. He thought of Varra, of his spell's verdict: She is safe, far from you.

Wasn't that true of everyone he cared about? He thought of Thazienne and the demonic attack that had nearly killed her, thought of Magadon and the archfiend who had torn his soul in half, thought of Jak, who'd died at the claws and teeth of a slaad who'd never paid, not in full . . .

"Cale."

He had failed everyone and now he had wrought the ruin of an entire realm.

"Cale . . ."

Cale pulled his mask from his cloak and donned it. Darkness leaked from Weaveshear; darkness leaked from Cale. He let divine power flow into him. He would cut his way to Kesson Rel or die trying.

"We aren't going to undo it," he said. "We're going to end it."

Huge forms materialized from the shadows at the edge of the meadow, ten gangly giants as tall as three men, the vanguard of the army of shadows. Darkness swirled in strands around their stooped forms, twisted around their gray flesh. Their long white hair whipped in the wind. Each wore a hauberk of dull gray links and bore swords in their hands almost as long as Cale was tall. Their black eyes took in the meadow, looking for prey. Their gazes fixed on Cale and Riven. They pointed.

"We are leaving," Riven said. "Cale, think."

"No," Cale said to him, his eyes on the shadows arrowing toward them, the giants stalking across the meadow. "I am finishing this."

He felt Riven staring at him, into him.

"No," Riven said.

The darkness around Cale whirled. "No?"

Riven's good eye narrowed. "No."

Four giants stepped through the shadows and materialized before Cale and Riven, huge blades held high.

Before Cale could brandish Weaveshear, he felt a flash of warmth as the magic of Riven's teleportation ring took hold. He tried to resist it, failed, and Riven transported them across Faerûn.

Three hours after Reht's army entered the storm, the rain turned to a downpour, the wind to a gale. The scouts stopped returning word back to the lines. Perhaps they had gotten lost.

The army was marching blind and the men were edgy. Reht could sense it.

Dawn had come but the storm put a blanket between the earth and sky. What little sunlight penetrated the swirling clouds and rain served only to gild the abnormality of the earth under the storm with a lurid glow. The wind pulled at Reht's cloak. His mount tossed her head and whinnied into the storm. He rode a little behind his men in the center of the line, bent against the rain, clutching his cloak closed, his mount sinking into the sloppy earth. The air seemed to pull at him. He felt his strength diminishing.

The line of his army extended a bowshot in either direction but even under the effect of a spell that granted him darkvision he could see little more than the score or so men to his immediate left and right. The shadows and rain swallowed the rest.

"Tighten up the line," he shouted at two of the runners who lingered near him. "Pass it to the commanders."

"Aye," the runners said. They saluted and galloped off, one to the left, one to the right, shouting to tighten up the line. The wind, rain, and darkness soon ate their voices and Reht lost sight of them.

"How can we fight in this?" Reht said to no one in particular. "The air itself is an enemy."

The line gradually tightened, the men crowding more closely together. Reht could see maybe three score men, all of them squinting against the rain and magical darkness. Many had blades drawn, though there was no visible enemy.

The cold seeped into Reht's bones. Mennick, Kelgar, and several more runners rode beside him. Reht looked at their shadowed faces and saw blue lips, pale skin, and uncertain eyes.

Lightning painted the fog green. Thunder boomed and their horses reared and neighed. Men cursed. He steadied his mount with effort.

"Steady men!" he shouted. "Steady!"

The darkness and rain played havoc with his perception. He frequently saw movement at the edge of his vision, ominous hints of creatures or men, but moving forward they found nothing. Shouts from his men sounded from out in the blackness, faint and distant. His men, too, were seeing ghosts, or becoming ghosts.

"The Shadovar cannot turn us back with wind and darkness," Kelgar shouted, though the shadows hollowed out his words. A few "ayes" answered the big warpriest, but most of the men continued forward in sullen silence.

"This is uncanny," said Mennick, though Reht barely heard his voice. Mennick pointed. "Look at the trees."

Stands of trees materialized out of the darkness. Leafless, skeletal, their limbs stuck out of the boles at twisted, agonized angles. Their dry boughs rattled in the wind. The men pointed and murmured.

Mennick steered his horse close to Reht's side and spoke in a tone only Reht could hear.

"Do you feel the air, Commander? It has changed. As the storm grows stronger, the air seems to steal strength. I find it hard to breathe. Do you feel it?"

Reht nodded.

"The deeper we move in, the worse it is becoming."

Reht looked the mage in the eye and saw concern there. The nervous seed in Reht's stomach sprouted leaves.

"We've made a mistake," he said.

The storm was not Shadovar magic. It was something else entirely, something not of Faerûn, and he had led his men right into it.

"Halt," he said, but his voice broke. He turned to the runners, cleared his throat, kept his voice steady. "Halt! We are calling a halt and turning around. Do it now!"

"Commander . . ." Kelgar said.

Reht threw back his hood and stared at the warpriest. "You see what this is as clearly as I. There are no Shadovar here, priest. This is something else and we need to get clear of it. Now, follow your orders."

Kelgar stared back, nodded. "Aye, General."

"I don't know if we'll be able to get out," Mennick said.

To that, Reht said nothing. He did not know either.

Word spread but slowly in the rain, in the darkness. The line stopped at last and reorganized for a march out of the storm. Horns sounded, their clarion strangely muffled.

"On the double quick!" Reht said to his runners. "Pass it on!"

"The scouts?" Mennick asked, his horse blinking in the rain.

They had not had word in hours. The scouts were either lost or . . . something else. Reht shook his head, refusing to give voice to his concerns.

"They will have to catch up with us."

Mennick nodded, and looked back into the darkness.

Orders carried through the pitch, the men prepping to move out on the double quick. The rain abated and some of the men cheered. The darkness, however, remained unrelenting.

Reht found the absence of rain more ominous than comforting. Black mist curled around the muddy ground, around the twisted dead trees, and around the nervous hooves of their horses, who pranced and neighed. For the first time, Reht realized that he had not seen a wild animal in hours. He stilled his heart and forced calm into his voice.

"On the double quick! Move!"

The wind at their backs swallowed the last of his order as it picked up, howled, and took on a strange keening. The line lurched forward as the cold deepened. Reht's teeth chattered and the hairs on his arms and the back of his neck stood on end. He felt eyes on him, looked over his shoulder, but saw nothing save the darkness. His instincts screamed at him to run, told him that something unforgiving out there in the darkness was coming for him. He saw the same sentiment reflected in the alarmed faces around him.

They were moving too slowly.

"On the double quick! On the double quick, damn it!"

"There!" someone shouted, the word nearly lost in the wind. "There!"

Shouts erupted along the line and carried through the black. Reht turned in his saddle to see thousands of coal red points of light floating in the darkness, as numerous as the stars.

Eyes.

The darkness was coming for them.

The keening sounded again, a mistuned longflute, and Reht realized it was not the wind. It was the creatures, shrieking at them, closing on them.

"Around and hold formation!" he shouted, and hated himself for the tremor in his voice. "Around and hold!"

The shouts of commanders carried through the darkness, echoing his words. Horns sounded again, making a cacophony with the keening.

The army scrambled into formation as the wind turned to a gale and the creatures sped toward them. A few men deserted, fled with their horses at a dead run. Reht cursed them for cowards.

Armor chinked, men cursed, and weapons were readied. Hundreds of crossbows and bows twanged. A swarm of bolts and arrows flew into the darkness at the eyes, veering wildly in the wind. The creatures wailed again, apparently unharmed, and closed. Soul deadening cold went before them.

Reht drew his blade, readied his shield. His magically augmented vision allowed him to distinguish the creatures as they neared, but barely. Vaguely humanoid in shape and composed of living shadow, they rode the wind and flew like arrow shots through the night. Red eyes glowed with malice.

"Shadows!" Kelgar shouted, and clanged his blade on his shield.

The darkness deepened as the throng of shadows closed. Some darted into the earth and disappeared. Others flew high and circled around the army. Still others flew directly for them. There were still more behind the initial wave, so numerous they blotted out the storm. They seemed unending, filling the air with their cold, their shrieks, their hate.

They hit Reht's army and men and horses began to scream. Beside Reht, Kelgar roared a battle cry and galloped into the shadows. A lightning bolt shot from the war priest's outstretched hand as he charged the undead. Two other Talassans followed him, whooping battle cries.

"Hold your ground, dammit! Hold!"

The darkness prevented a large-scale organized response and the battle turned into a series of isolated melees. Shadows darted in and out of Reht's field of vision, merging with the darkness in the air. Red eyes flashed past him, around him, over him, under him. He slashed and stabbed at any within reach, heard the men near him do the same. His horse reared, kicked, whinnied.

He and a dozen other men formed a circle, but it proved useless. The incorporeal shadows moved as freely through the earth as through the air. He and his men were attacked from all sides no matter their formation. The cold hand of panic gripped some of the men, more.

Magical globes of light formed in the darkness but lasted only moments before the shadows blotted them out. Screams sounded from all directions, muted shrieks, all of it an eerily beautiful symphony for the dying.

Reht's mount neighed and bucked as a throng of shadows burst from the ground under it. The movement threw Reht, and he hit the ground in a clatter of steel. His mount wheeled, nearly trampled him, and darted off in a panic.

Reht scrambled to his knees, to his feet, slashing, shouting. Men fought and died beside him, around him. The shadows nearest him focused their dead, glowing eyes on him and in the otherwise blank holes of their faces he was able to distinguish features.

"Lorgan?"

His fellow commander's expression wrinkled with hate. Reht saw other faces he recognized and understood what had happened to Lorgan and his men.

And what would happen to Reht and his.

"Find peace, old friend," Reht said, and charged Lorgan.

Lorgan shrieked and his features dissolved again into indistinguishable darkness. Other shadows darted in close, reached through Reht's shield and armor, cooled his flesh, diminished his soul. He screamed, and slashed at Lorgan. His enchanted blade bit Lorgan's shadowy form and sent streamers of deeper darkness boiling away into the air, but Lorgan reached into Reht's chest and nearly stopped his heart. Reht staggered backward, gasping, his vision blurred.

In the distance, he heard the sound of chanting, the Talassans calling upon the power of their god to fight the undead. Reht glanced around, saw men and horses dead and dying all around him. He heard their shouts, screams, and whinnies, but he felt isolated, alone in a cyst of darkness warring against his own personal shadows.

The surrounding sounds diminished then went silent. He heard only his own labored breathing, his grunts as he swung his blade, and the sound of his own heartbeat keeping time in his ears. He slashed, backed away, stabbed, twisted, stabbed again. Shadows emerged from the ground and passed into and through him. Others flew, heedlessly, at and through his blade, reached into his chest to his lungs and heart, stole his breath, his strength. He staggered, still breathing, still fighting. He looked around for a mount, any mount, saw none. He tripped over a corpse and fell on his back.

Shadows swarmed him. He felt so cold he could not breathe, felt his heart slow. He saw Lorgan's face in one of the shadows over him, Enken's on another, both of them caricatures of the living men they once were.

They reached for him. He felt himself drifting, floating. He reached for the maps at his side, thinking of his father, and the cartographer to whom he should have been apprenticed, the life he should have led. Cold filled him and he gasped. He could not see anything but red eyes and darkness.

He died thinking of maps and regrets.

He rose thinking of hate.

# CHAPTER THREE

*2 Nightal, the Year of Lightning Storms*

Cale and Riven materialized on the Wayrock, outside the Temple of Mask. Sunlight, alien after the darkness of the storm, cast the temple's shadow out before it. Cale and Riven stood within the column of darkness. Rain dripped from their cloaks.

Both men turned and looked back toward Sembia but the Shadowstorm was too far away to see. Cale saw only the rocky ledges of the Wayrock and the boundless blue-gray of the sea. White clouds dotted the sky. There was no indication of the black lesion spreading across Sembia, across Faerûn.

Still staring into the distance, Cale said to Riven, "Never do that again."

Riven, too, stared over the sea. "I do what needs done, Cale. Get clear on that. I'll do it again next time, and the time after that. You don't get to give up."

The truth in Riven's words stung. Cale faced him. "I wasn't giving up."

Riven said nothing. He didn't need to.

Cale sighed, looked away. He was tired and did not understand how Riven was not.

"How do you keep fighting, Riven? Why? Not for Sembia."

Riven made a dismissive gesture. "No. Not for Sembia."

"Then?"

Riven tapped the holy symbol he wore around his neck, the black disc. "This is why. Mask wants Kesson Rel dead and his divinity returned to him. That is enough of a why. Should be enough for you, too."

Cale stared at the disc, at Riven's face. "It's not."

"Then find something that is. This is a long way from over."

Cale shook his head. "You don't understand. You can't."

Riven stared at him for a moment. "You're tired. I see that."

Cale looked Riven in the eye, grateful for even that little bit of shared understanding.

"Yes. I'm tired."

Riven's face did not change expression. "It's a lot of weight."

"It is."

"Bear it. We can only see this through together. You see that, yes? Find a way to stay with it." When Cale said nothing, Riven went on, "Cale, you didn't kill Jak. You didn't. And you didn't take Magadon's soul, and you didn't make that Uskevren boy join with the Shadovar. You're carrying weight that is not yours to bear. No damned wonder you're tired."

Cale heard the words, heard the sense in them, but they did nothing to ease the burdens he bore. *Safe, far from you.* That was what his god had said to him.

"Let's go," he said and started up the drawbridge.

Magadon stepped out of the darkness of the temple's interior and appeared in the archway. The mind mage looked as thin and dried out as an old stick, wan, with circles the color of bruises under his eyes.

"Mags," Cale said, and tried not to wince at Magadon's appearance.

Riven's two dogs bolted through the archway past the mind mage and for their master, a blur of brown fur and wagging tails. Riven knelt to meet them, rubbed heads and sides. They growled playfully and jumped on him.

Magadon walked up to Cale, wavering in his stride like a drunk. He looked even paler in the light.

"You all right, Mags?" Cale asked.

"I want off this island, Cale," he said. "Now."

Each time Magadon said "Cale" instead of "Erevis," Cale felt it like a punch in the stomach. He and Riven shared a look. Riven stood and pointed at the temple.

"Go on," he said, and the dogs darted back inside. To Magadon, he said, "You don't look well."

"That's because I'm not."

"Then why leave the island now?" Riven asked. "Stay. Get better."

Cale saw anger in the crease between Magadon's eyes, quickly suppressed.

"My own affair," Magadon said.

"Is that right?" Riven said.

Cale reached out to touch Magadon's shoulder. The mind mage recoiled but Cale persisted, taking his thin shoulder in hand.

"Listen, Mags. Kesson Rel is here, in Faerûn. He opened a rift. The Calyx is pouring through. It's rolling across Sembia."

A spark touched tinder in Magadon's white eyes and something kindled there. Cale decided to take it as hope and was pleased to see it.

"Where? We've got to kill him, Cale. I can use the Source to . . ."

He stopped, white eyes wide, perhaps realizing he'd said too much. He took a step back, and his gaze darted about, as if looking for an escape.

"The Source?" Cale and Riven said in unison.

Magadon licked his lips, steadied himself.

Cale spoke softly. "What are you talking about, Mags?"

Riven did not speak softly. "We nearly died taking you out of the Source. The Hells if you're using it for anything again. The Hells if you're leaving this island. You're not yourself. You'll wait—"

Magadon's face contorted with rage. He emitted a roar and bounded forward for Riven, hands reaching as if for the assassin's throat.

Riven put a short, sharp kick in Magadon's gut and the mind mage doubled over at his feet, gasping, coughing, retching.

"Damn it," Cale said to both of them.

Nayan and Vyrhas materialized out of the shadows in the archway of the temple.

"It's all right," Cale said to them, and waved them back. "Go, Nayan. It's all right."

The shadowwalker looked at Magadon, at Cale, then at Riven. He nodded, bowed, and melded back into the darkness.

Magadon recovered his breath and rose to his knees. He glared at Riven and an orange glow formed around his head, rage leaking from his skull.

Riven had a blade at his throat in a breath.

"I feel a tingle in my head, Mags, and I open your throat. I mean it."

Magadon, his pale face flushed, stared fury at the assassin. The orange glow faded.

"You're an addict, Mags," Riven said. He lowered but did not sheathe his blade. "And I know a lot about addicts. And you're damaged. You're no use to us until you're well."

Magadon coughed, started to stand. Cale tried to help him but Magadon shook him off irritably.

"I'm worse than that," the mind mage said, standing. He burst into a giggle and the sound made Cale uneasy. "Much worse. And I'm never going to be well."

He wobbled on his feet and Cale put an arm around him, held him upright. His shadows coiled around the mind mage, supporting him.

"We will kill Kesson Rel," Cale said, trying to ignore how light Magadon felt in his arms. "Take what he took, give it to your father, make you whole. We'll do it, Mags."

Magadon grabbed a fistful of Cale's cloak, the gesture one of desperation. When he spoke his voice cracked but he sounded more like himself. "I need myself back, Cale. I'm falling so fast. You cannot understand . . ."

Riven started to speak but Cale silenced him with a glare. To Magadon, Cale said, "We will see it through, Mags. But Riven is right. This is not your fight, not like this. You'll be a problem for us, not a help. You know that. If we need you, we'll come for you."

Magadon pulled away and looked Cale in the face. "And if I need you?"

Cale shook his head. "I don't understand."

"I mean if you can't do it, if you can't take back what Kesson Rel stole, then I want you to kill me. I need you to. I can't do it myself but I can't go on this way. Either of you. Hells, get Nayan to do it. He's been watching me and thinking the same thing." Magadon ran a hand through his hair, over his horns. "My thoughts, Cale. I don't know what I might do. I can't continue this way."

It took Cale a few moments to produce a reply. "Mags, it won't come to that."

"If it does."

"Mags—"

"If it does!" the mind mage said, and tears glistened in his eyes. He looked at Riven, at his blade. "You're both killers. I know it. You know it. Tell me you'll do what needs done."

Cale just stared, his throat tight, his mouth unable to work.

Riven sheathed his saber and looked Magadon in the face. "I always do what needs done, Mags."

Magadon stared at Riven, his breath coming fast. He nodded once, turned, and walked back into the temple.

"Come, Nayan," he said to the shadows as he passed under the archway.

When he was gone, Riven said, "What's next?"

Cale stared after Magadon, his thoughts racing. "What?"

"What's next, Cale?"

"With Mags?"

"No. With Kesson Rel. The Shadowstorm. Hells, Mags too. It's all the same."

Cale shook his head, still unnerved. "I don't know."

"You don't know?"

Cale turned to face the assassin. "That's right. I don't know. I need some time."

"I doubt we have much," Riven said, eyeing the archway into which Magadon had disappeared.

Cale nodded, stuck his arm outside of the shadow of the spire and into the sun, melting away his hand. He stared at the stump.

"No. Not much."

Tamlin sat in his father's walnut rocker, in his father's study, among his father's books, books Tamlin had never read. He'd spent his life in the shadow of his father, in the shadow of his father's things.

That was over now.

Selûne had set and no lamps illuminated the darkness. Cool night air and dim starlight bled in through the open windows. He sat alone, thinking, the creak of the rocker on the wood floor eerily similar to Vees's screams. Tamlin smiled.

Vees had been false to Tamlin, false to Shar. He had deserved death on her altar. Tamlin recalled with perfect clarity the cold hard feel of the dagger's hilt in his palm, the warm, sticky feel of Vees's blood on his hands. He recalled, too, the golden eyes of Prince Rivalen, aglow with the approval Tamlin had never received from his father or Mister Cale, approval that he no longer craved.

He was his own man, and all he'd had to do to become so was give himself to Shar.

Holding in his hand the small, black disc that Prince Rivalen had given him as a meditative aid, he confessed to Shar in a whisper what would become his Own Secret, a truth known only to himself and Shar.

"I have never felt so afraid, or so powerful, as I did when sacrificing Vees."

Clouds blotted out even the minimal starlight, and darkness as black as ink shrouded the room, closed in on him, pressed against his skin. A chill set the hair on his arms and the back of his neck on end, raised gooseflesh. His breath came fast. He felt the caress of his new mistress, as cold and hard as the dagger with which he had killed Vees.

"Thank you, Lady," he said, as the pitch lifted and starlight again poked tentatively through the study's windows.

Tamlin's conversion to Shar had birthed not only a new faith but ambition. He wanted to be more than a servant to Shar, more than his own man. He wanted also to equal then surpass Mister Cale, to transform his body into that of a shade. And he wanted to surpass his father by ruling not merely a wealthy House, not even merely a city, but an entire realm.

He nodded to himself in the darkness, still rocking. He was not his father's son. If he was born of anyone, it was Prince Rivalen and the Lady of Loss.

" 'Love is a lie,' " he said, reciting one of the Thirteen Truths that Prince Rivalen had taught him. " 'Only hate endures.' "

Footsteps carried from the hall outside the parlor. A form stepped into the doorway. Even in the darkness Tamlin recognized the upright posture and stiff movements of Irwyl, the Uskevren majordomo.

"My lord?" Irwyl called. "Are you within the parlor?"

Tamlin stopped rocking. "Yes. What is it, Irwyl?"

"Were you speaking just now, my lord?"

"To myself. What is it, Irwyl?"

Irwyl peered into the darkness, unable to pinpoint Tamlin's location. "There is news from Daerlun, my lord. A missive from High Bergun Tymmyr about your mother."

Tamlin felt little at the mention of his mother. She would not understand what he had done, or why. Perhaps she would even condemn him for it. No matter. He served another mistress, now.

"What are its contents?" Tamlin asked. Irwyl had permission to open and read all documents sent to Tamlin in his official capacity.

Irwyl cleared his throat, shifted on his feet. "High Bergun Tymmyr has made your mother, sister, and brother his personal guests. He asks that you allow him to offer them sanctuary in Daerlun until events in the rest of Sembia resolve themselves. He promises to show them the utmost hospitality."

Tamlin understood the message behind the message. Daerlun had declared its neutrality in the Sembian Civil War. No doubt it had promises from Cormyrean forces to aid it should battle be brought to its walls. Cormyr had long coveted Daerlun and Daerlun, on the border between Cormyr and Sembia, was in many ways more Cormyrean than Sembian. So the high bergun, having heard of Selgaunt's victory over Saerloon's forces, wanted to inform Tamlin that his family would be held hostage to ensure that Daerlun be left out of the conflict to pursue its alliance with Cormyr. For the time being, that suited Tamlin. He had other concerns. Daerlun could wait.

"Acknowledge receipt and understanding, Irwyl. Thank the high bergun for his kindness and let him know that I will repay it in kind. Use both my official and my personal seal."

"Yes, my lord."

Irwyl lingered.

"What is it, Irwyl?"

"Will my lord be retiring soon? The hour grows late."

Tamlin leaned back in the rocker. "I think not. I am enjoying the darkness."

Irwyl cleared his throat. "As you wish my lord. May I retire, then?"

"Yes, but before you do, please send for Lord Rivalen and inform the gatemen that he is to be given entry. I need his counsel. He will be awake."

Tamlin knew that the shadowstuff in Rivalen's body obviated his need for sleep.

"Yes, Lord. Anything else?"

Tamlin glanced around the parlor, at his father's detritus. It was time to make Stormweather his, then Selgaunt, then Sembia.

"Tomorrow I want the parlor emptied of my father's things. New furnishings, Irwyl, for a new beginning."

Irwyl said nothing for a time and the darkness masked his face. Tamlin wished that he were a shade, that his eyes could see in darkness as well as daylight. He felt betrayed by his mere humanity.

"Very well, Lord," Irwyl said, his tone stiff. "A good eve to you."

"And to you," Tamlin said.

Irwyl left him alone with the night, with his goddess. He found the solitude and the darkness comforting but could not shake the chill.

Rivalen sat alone in the darkness of his quarters, his mood as black as the moonless sky. The broken pieces of his holy symbol lay on the table before him.

The requirements of his faith had declared war on the needs of his people. The priest was at war with the prince. He needed to resolve the situation, satisfy both.

Shadows boiled from his flesh.

For millennia Rivalen had kept his faith and civic duty in an uneasy truce, the needs of the one separated from the demands of the other by the gulf of time. Rivalen knew the world eventually would bend to Shar and return to darkness and cold, but he had believed he had many more millennia still, that he could accomplish his goals, and those of his people, before Shar reclaimed the multiverse. Oblivion seemed always in the future.

But synchronicity had disabused him of his delusion. The Shadowstorm was happening now, devouring the realm needed by Shade Enclave to secure its future and resurrect the glory of Netheril.

He must choose his faith or his people.

"Mustn't I?" he said. He held a Sembian raven in his hand. Tarnish blackened the silver.

"Obverse or reverse," he said, turning it in his fingers, seeing the late overmaster's profile on one side, the Sembian arms on the other.

Hope had been his transgression, he realized. He had hoped to resurrect the Empire of Netheril and return his people, and Faerûn, to glory. He had hoped—later, much later—to summon the Shadowstorm that would herald the beginning of the world's end. Events had proven him a fool. The Lady of Loss spurned hope and expected her Nightseer to do the same. Rivalen had learned the lesson but wisdom had come too late, and its tardy arrival did nothing to assuage his bitterness, his rage.

Shar had chosen others for her instruments. A priestess he had thought to use and discard had betrayed him, stolen *The Leaves of One Night*. And a mad heretic, once a priest of Mask but now a servant of Shar, had brought forth the Shadowstorm and lurked in its dark center as it devoured the realm Rivalen had thought to annex for his people.

Rivalen had murdered his own mother for his goddess, but his goddess had kept from him a profound secret—he was not to be the cause of the Shadowstorm; he, and his hopes, were to be its victims.

And he sensed deeper secrets still, corpses buried in the fetid earth of Shar's darkness. They would rise when she saw fit, but not before.

He tried to accept matters, but failed. The shadows around him whirled, filled the room, poured forth through the shutter slats and into the night.

"I will not have it," he said, turning the coin more rapidly.

A soft buzzing sounded in his ears, grew in volume, clarified. A sending. He almost countered it but decided against it.

In his mind he heard the voice of his father, the Most High.

*Faerûn's powerful will not stand idle for long while this Shadowstorm darkens Sembia. End it, Rivalen.*

The Most High's imperious tone pulled at the scab of Rivalen's already wounded pride but he kept his irritation from his tone.

*I will do what I can, Father.*

*Hadrhune's divinations have revealed the possibility of a Sharran at the root of the storm. Perhaps you are not equipped for this task?*

The mention of the Most High's chief counselor, a rival to Rivalen, rankled.

*Hadrhune's understanding, as always, is limited. The Sharran behind the storm is a heretic. I will see to him and it. Meanwhile, please remind Hadrhune, and yourself, that I have raised Sakkors, shattered Saerloon's forces, and given you Selgaunt. Soon I will add to it all of Sembia.*

*There will be nothing to give if the Shadowstorm is not stopped. End it, Rivalen. Soon. Other matters in the heartland proceed apace. This is a distraction.*

*Other matters?*

The connection ceased. Apparently his father, too, had secrets.

Rivalen swallowed his irritation and decided to interpret his father's sending as a sign. Kesson Rel was a heretic. And Rivalen would not allow centuries of planning to unravel so that a heretic could serve the Mistress and destroy the realm Rivalen had thought to make. The Lady wanted the Shadowstorm. She had it. But Rivalen wanted more time, and Sembia. He would find a way to have both.

He put the silver raven on the table and set it to spinning on its edge. A word of minor magic kept it upright and whirling. He watched it, obverse to reverse to obverse to reverse.

"I choose both," he said. "Faith and city."

He would contain the Shadowstorm and claim what was left of Sembia. And if that made him a heretic, then so be it. The Lady knew his nature when she had chosen him as her Nightseer.

He held his palm over the pieces of his holy symbol and spoke the words to a mending charm. Tendrils of shadow spiraled around the disc, pulled them together, made them whole.

"If Kesson Rel is your true servant, then let him be the victor. If not, then let it be me."

Outside, darkness obscured the stars. Rivalen nodded.

"Thank you, Lady."

The enspelled raven continued to spin, obverse, reverse.

❧ ❧ ❧ ❧ ❧

Abelar and Jiiris stood in the rain and watched the ink of the distant storm digest stars, its lightning casting the world in ghastly viridian. Abelar surmised Elyril's involvement, Shar's involvement, and felt the Calling in his soul, the same Calling that had pulled him in his youth from a life of privilege to one of service to others. He thought of his son and denied it.

"There are dark forces there," Jiiris said and put her hand to the rose of Lathander she wore at her throat.

"Yes," Abelar said. He had no holy symbol to hold so he put his hand in hers and found it offered equal comfort.

She smiled at him but the expression faded when her eyes fell on the empty chain around his throat, where his own holy symbol had once hung. She looked away as if to spare him the embarrassment of staring at a scar.

"There is always atonement," she said softly, not looking him in the face.

"There is nothing for which I must atone," he said, surprised at the sharpness of his tone.

She looked at him, saw him. He saw the concern in her expression.

"You worry for me," he said. "You should not."

"No?" Her eyes showed disbelief.

"No. I am free now, Jiiris."

"I did not realize you had been bound."

"Nor had I."

Seeing her confusion, he smiled softly and led her back into the tent. "Come. You will be soaked."

After they entered, He glanced at Elden to ensure he was still asleep—he was—then drew Jiiris to him. She did not resist and he brushed her cheek with the back of his hand.

"I have loved you a long time."

She flushed but held his gaze. "And I you. But . . ."

"But?"

She looked away and he saw the jaw muscles working under her cheeks as she masticated whatever she intended to say. "But we cannot do this now. I cannot do this. You are . . . hurting. You almost lost your father, your son, and have turned from the faith that has sustained you for—"

His anger rose at the mention of his faith and his words came out in a rush, a flood through the ravine of his rage.

"Lathander's church is presided over by heretics who stood idle while this, all this, happened. He still grants spells to them. Did you know that? Why would he do that?"

She shook her head, her eyes welling. "He has his purposes."

Elden stirred, groaned in his sleep, and Abelar quieted his voice. He didn't want to wake Elden, didn't want to hurt Jiiris.

"His purposes? How often must we assume that events will work out to his purposes? Why should we be the playthings to him? How much am I to endure in service to the Morninglord? At what point does service become base servitude? At what point am I to say, 'enough'?"

She winced at the words, placed a hand on his chest, as if to keep him from proceeding further.

"When it is my son, Jiiris. That is when it is enough. When my wife died in childbirth, I praised Lathander for the life he had brought forth even in death. When my father was imprisoned, I fought in Lathander's name the forces of she who had imprisoned him. When darkness fell across Sembia and the priest who trained me in the faith did nothing to stem its tide, I thanked Lathander for the chance to be a light in the darkness. But when my son was taken and tortured . . ." He looked into her face, at the rose at her throat. "That is too much. If that is his purpose, then his purpose can burn."

She blanched, but stood her ground and defended her faith, the faith that had once been his.

"You sound like the heretics you've often condemned. How often have I heard you admonish them for waiting for the Morninglord to do their work for them? He does not reveal himself to us that way, Abelar."

Perhaps she had thought to strike him hard, but he did not perceive even a glancing blow. He took her by the arms.

"Have I been waiting, Jiiris? Have I been idle? I have taken the fight to evil my entire life and have been rewarded with one calamity after another. Through it all I have been steadfast, but . . ." he looked past her to Elden, sleeping in a bed of furs, ". . . he has gone too far. And I am tired of being tested."

"Faith is not a test—"

"It can be nothing else!" He found himself shaking her gently, and released her with surprise. Elden stirred, rolled over onto his side, but did not awaken. Abelar spoke in an intense whisper. "What it cannot be is a hole into which I pour everything and from it receive nothing. That is not faith, Jiiris. I renounce it. I renounce him."

She looked as if she had been struck hard. Saying the words aloud rather than merely thinking them crossed some indefinable barrier, put a chasm between his present and his past that he would never be able to cross. He hoped it had not put a chasm between he and Jiiris.

"Listen to me," he said gently. "I see clearly now for the first time in a long while. There is light even where Lathander is absent. Who saved both my father and son? Who, Jiiris?" She simply stared and he answered his own question. "Servants of Mask. There is light in them."

Jiiris shook her head. "No, Abelar. Saving Elden was a good thing, a wonderful thing. But I saw into those men when they stood in this tent. They are not good men. Not like you."

"You judge them harshly. We are what we do, Jiiris."

"No. We are what we are and sometimes that shows in what we do. But sometimes it does not. Hear this, Abelar. Before

Elden fell asleep, he told me a bad man saved him from the other bad men. Do you hear? Children's eyes see clearly."

Elden rolled over in his furs and opened his eyes. His bleary eyes focused on Abelar.

"Papa?"

To Jiiris, Abelar said, "We will talk more of this later. For now, assemble my father and the leaders of the company. We must see the refugees to safety. There are not enough men here to stand against Forrin's army and whatever storm Shar has brought to Sembia. Tell them to begin preparations."

Jiiris's eyes widened at his words. "But I thought . . ."

He took her by the shoulders. "I have turned from Lathander but not from the people of Saerb, not from you. I am the same man I was two days ere."

She looked into his eyes and nodded.

"Papa?"

Abelar went to his son, sat beside him. Elden reached up a small hand. Abelar took it between his.

"I am here," he said. "And I am not leaving again."

Elden studied his face. "You diffent, Papa."

Abelar nodded, felt his throat tighten. The eyes of children saw clearly, indeed.

Rivalen watched the coin spin, and pondered. He would have to kill Kesson Rel, but he did not know if he could do so.

Rivalen knew some of Kesson's history. He had been a servant of Mask who later converted to Shar. After becoming one of Shar's most powerful servants, being invested with a shard of divine power, he had succumbed to insanity and embraced heresy. Eventually the Lady of Loss had banished him to an isolated pocket of the Plane of Shadow, the Adumbral Calyx. There, he'd been left, forgotten.

Until now. Now he had emerged from his exile and brought the Calyx with him, threatening the delicate plans Rivalen had spent decades cultivating.

"Why now, Lady?" Rivalen asked the darkness. "Why here?"

Rivalen studied his remade holy symbol, noted the ghost of the fracture still visible on its surface. The line dividing his symbol reminded him of the divisions in his faith. Shar tolerated heresy, rewarded the heretic. Why? The answer was hidden in the dark folds of the Lady's secrets.

He placed the holy symbol in an inner pocket and decided that he did not need to know. But he did need information about Kesson Rel.

He activated the magic of his amethyst ring and thought of his brother. He felt the connection open.

*Rivalen?* Brennus asked.

*I need you to learn all you can of Kesson Rel. Everything there is to know. He must die, Brennus.*

A long pause, then, *Very well. I have already learned that he is quasi-divine. Did you know that, Rivalen?*

*Yes.* Rivalen did not know how or why Shar had infused Kesson with divine power, but he knew it had been done. *Continue your attempts to locate Erevis Cale. Kesson Rel served Mask before turning to Shar. I do not see coincidence. There's a knot here. We must untie it.*

*Agreed.*

*What have you learned of Cale's woman?*

Another long pause. *Nothing of her. She is gone but not dead. I cannot make sense of it.*

Rivalen sensed reticence through the connection. *Is there something else, Brennus?*

*No.*

Rivalen knew Brennus was lying but did not press. Brennus, too, was entitled to some secrets.

*Inform me when you learn anything, Brennus. We will need to face Kesson Rel, and soon. Much turns on your success.*

*I know.*

The connection closed and a knock on the door of the study brought Rivalen's mind back to his surroundings.

"Speak," he called.

"The Hulorn has requested your presence at his family's estate, Prince."

Rivalen knew the time to be two hours or more past midnight. Apparently the Hulorn did not find sleep appealing. Rivalen understood why. After murdering his mother in Shar's name, Rivalen had feared his dreams and slept fitfully for months. Tamlin had murdered a onetime friend. His sleep would be troubled for a time.

"Inform the Hulorn that I will attend him directly."

The doorman announced the arrival of Prince Rivalen and Tamlin stood as the prince's dark form filled the parlor's doorway. Rivalen's body merged with the darkness, the boundaries of his form indeterminate from the night. Glowing golden eyes hovered in the ink of his face, the two guiding stars of Tamlin's new life.

"Prince, thank you for coming."

"Of course, Hulorn. Sleep eludes you?"

Tamlin shook his head. He knew Rivalen could see the gesture clearly. "Not at all. I am . . . energized. And I am enjoying the darkness."

The shadows around Rivalen swirled slowly. The darkness carried him into the room.

"So you are."

The Shadovar prince glanced around the wood-paneled study, at the books and scrolls that filled the shelves. Tamlin would have offered him a chalice of wine, but he knew Rivalen did not partake.

"An impressive collection," said the prince.

"My father's. Sit, please."

Rivalen sat at the small table with the chessboard atop it, before black. Tamlin took the seat opposite. He had sat across the same table from his father many times, usually to receive this or that admonishment for one failure or another. He felt more comfortable with Rivalen than he ever had with his father.

"Do you play, Prince?" Tamlin asked.

"I did. Long ago. I gave it up after my mother died."

He picked up the black king and the shadows shrouding him enveloped it.

"I am sorry," said Tamlin.

"Thank you. My interest in chess waned when I realized that it is a transparent contest where one can see an opponent's forces and their movement. Life is rarely so clear."

"Truth," Tamlin said, nodding. "Myself, I was never a skillful player. My father and Mister Cale played often."

"Mister Cale," Rivalen said softly, and the shadows around him churned.

"I am going to be rid of it tomorrow," Tamlin said. "All of it. The books, the furniture. All of it."

Rivalen's eyes flared and he placed the king in the center of the board, exposed.

"I understand completely."

Tamlin had no doubt the prince did. He rose to pour himself a drink, navigating the study in the darkness. When he reached the sideboard, he said, "The high bergun has taken my family into custody. He hopes thereby to ransom Daerlun's safety."

Rivalen looked up from the board, his golden eyes veiled. "They could be retrieved, Hulorn. Shall I arrange it?"

Tamlin realized that something of import turned on his answer. He found a glass, a bottle of wine, and poured. He tried to determine the vintage from taste—Thamalon's Best Red, he thought. At least four years old.

"I am grateful for your offer, Prince. But the presence of my family would be a distraction to me just now."

"Indeed," Rivalen said again, the comment half question, half observation. "Families are sometimes a . . . distraction."

Tamlin returned to the chess table, chalice in hand. "You and your brother seem to complement one another well."

"We Tanthuls have had two thousand years to learn to work together," Rivalen said. He picked up the queen, studied it, a frown playing at the corners of his mouth. "But we, too, have had our . . . disagreements."

Tamlin smiled, thought of Talbot and the arguments they'd had over the years.

"Have you shared your secret with the Lady?" the prince asked as he replaced the black queen.

Tamlin nodded, running a fingertip over his holy symbol. "I have."

"That is well." Rivalen leaned back in his chair and his tone lightened. "I would like a coin from the treasury, minted this day. Is that possible? You've recently started minting your own coins, yes?"

A request so ordinary from the prince surprised Tamlin. "A coin? Of course. May I ask why?"

"I am a collector of coins, particularly those minted on or stamped with dates significant to me. They help me keep track of history." Rivalen eyed him across the chessboard, looking so unlike Tamlin's father. "And today is one such date."

Tamlin took the point, raised his glass in a salute. He wanted the night to last, wanted the pristine coldness of the moonless hours to continue forever, wanted the discussion with Rivalen to go on and on. He felt at home, comfortable in the study for the first time he could recall. He leaned forward. "Tell me more about the Shadowstorm. How should we deal with it?"

"Brennus is examining it, but we have determined that the Shadowstorm is the creation of an ancient being, a one-time servant of Shar who holds the same heretical notions as those held—once held—by Vees Talendar."

Tamlin felt a small pit open in his stomach at the mention of his one-time friend. Darkness filled it.

"As for how we deal with it," Rivalen continued. "We use it."

"Use it?"

"It began in Ordulin and is moving west toward Saerb and Archendale. It does not yet reach farther south than the mid-point of the Arkhen. It will, but we have some time. For now, Ordulin is gone and what remains of its army near Saerb will disband, surrender, or be consumed by the storm."

Tamlin was vaguely disturbed by the obliteration of Ordulin but found comfort in the cold, hard touch of his new goddess.

"The Saerbian forces, too, stand in its path."

Rivalen nodded. "True. But where was Saerb when Saerloon's elementals shattered Selgaunt's walls?"

"Defending its own holdings, I presume. Do you imply something else?"

"Hulorn, do you wish to rule all of Sembia?"

The question shocked Tamlin into silence.

"Do you?"

Tamlin re-gathered his nerve. "You know that I do, Prince Rivalen."

Rivalen nodded. "Endren Corrinthal is a respected leader. He commanded the loyalty of many on the High Council before the overmistress dissolved it. Perhaps he would not look kindly upon your ascension. Perhaps, for the moment at least, the Saerbians should be left to their own devices. They are, after all, of no military use to you. It will not be an army that halts the Shadowstorm."

Tamlin's hand went to his holy symbol and ambition annihilated conscience.

"I take your point and agree with your recommendation."

"Excellent," Rivalen said. "And that returns us to Saerloon. Lady Merelith rules a city without an army. She broke it on these walls. She knows she must negotiate a peace. She may suspect the Shadowstorm to be a weapon unleashed by us against Ordulin. Before she learns otherwise, we should make Saerloon bend its knee to Selgaunt. And after Saerloon has surrendered, after the Saerbian forces are addressed, who will stand against Selgaunt's consolidation of the realm?"

"Perhaps Daerlun," Tamlin said, and sipped his wine. "But no other."

"Not even Daerlun," Rivalen said. "The high bergun is strengthened by the wall of a friendly Cormyr at his back. That wall will soon show cracks."

"Prince?"

"Many matters are afoot, Tamlin. I ask you to trust me. Do you?"

Tamlin had come too far to hesitate. "I do."

"Then soon Sembia will name Selgaunt its capital and you its leader."

"But the Shadowstorm?"

"We will halt it ere it reaches Selgaunt."

"How?"

Rivalen looked across the table at Tamlin, irritation in his eyes. "Leave that to me, Hulorn."

Tamlin could not bear the weight of Rivalen's gaze. He felt, of a sudden, the way he had so many times when sitting across the table from his father. He looked into his wine chalice. The darkness turned the red wine black, made its depths limitless.

"I will obtain a Selgauntan fivestar for you, Prince," he said, and disliked the boyishness in his tone. "From the mint, and made this day."

"You are gracious, Hulorn," Rivalen said, and Tamlin ignored the hint of condescension he heard in the tone.

Rivalen soon returned to his quarters and Tamlin did not sleep, could not sleep. He continually found himself rubbing his right hand on his trousers, as if to remove something offensive.

The morning brought a griffon-mounted messenger from Saerloon. Rivalen had been a prophet. The messenger bore a missive from Lady Merelith, requesting terms for the peaceful turnover of her city. Tamlin's hands shook has he read it.

Let the hardships of the Sembian people end, she wrote. Let Saerloon and Selgaunt advance into the future in brotherhood.

Tamlin had heralds read the surrender on street corners and declared a holiday. The bells and gongs of Shar's new temple rang all morning.

Tamlin composed a response with the advice of Prince Rivalen. He agreed to an end to hostilities, required that Lady Merelith and her court publically abdicate, that Saerloon accept a regent appointed by Tamlin, and that the city allow a garrison of three hundred Selgauntan and Shadovar troops barracks within Saerloon's walls to ensure the peace.

"She will not accept these terms," Tamlin said to Rivalen.

"She will," Rivalen answered. "She has no choice. Choose as regent a trusted member of the Old Chauncel, perhaps one with mercantile ties to Saerloon. I will arrange the Shadovar contingent of the garrison."

Cale wandered the island as the setting sun ducked under the horizon and painted the shimmering surface of the Inner Sea in red and gold. The cries of gulls gave way to the steady heartbeat of the surf on the shore. Night crept out of its holes and hollows and slowly stretched its dark hand over the island, a sea-beset, solitary dot of rock.

He eventually found himself atop the low hill where they had buried Jak. A few of the stones marking the grave had fallen from the cairn. He replaced them, missing his friend, missing . . . many things. To one side of him the night-shrouded sea stretched out to the limits of his vision, black and impenetrable; the other side, the shadow-wrapped spire of Mask.

He crouched with his forearms on his knees and stared at Jak's grave. Patches of grass dotted the soil and poked up through the loose rock. Shadows curled around Cale, languid and dark. The wind blew and he fooled himself into thinking he smelled tobacco from Jak's pipe rather than sea salt. He felt eyes on him and looked to the temple. The Shadowwalkers congregated there on the drawbridge, in the shadow of the spire, watching him. He did not welcome their regard.

They thought he was one thing; he was striving to be something else. He feared their reverence would root him in place, make him what they wanted.

Desiring privacy, he enshrouded himself in shadows and sank into their dark coils. He thought of his friend and sought words, found them, and confessed.

"I am trying to keep my promise, little man, but it is hard."

The rush of breakers sounded in the distance. He had murdered the Sojourner to the same sound. Murder came easy to him, easier than it should for a hero. He felt saturated by darkness, permeated by it. There was no separation between him and it. He looked at his shadowhand, a tangible reminder that he would always exist fully only in shadow, complete only in the night. He reached into his pocket, felt there the small river stone the halfling boy had given him.

"You told me once that what we do is only what we do, not what we are. I think you were right, little man, but I wish you had been wrong."

He shook his head, looked through the shadows with his shadesight, out across the dark, inscrutable sea.

"You would smile at the things I've done, Jak. But I feel . . . nothing. Something in me has changed, is changing, and what I am would not make you smile."

Shadows boiled from his skin, swirled. He imagined it to be whatever was left of his soul, squirming from his flesh to flee the corrupted vessel in which it was forced to reside.

Looking back over recent months, he saw that he felt only anger with any acuteness. Other feelings were faint, blunt, sensed as if through a haze. He had loved Varra, but only from afar— love without passion. He had saved the halfling boy from trolls, saved Abelar's son, tried to save Varra, was still trying to save Magadon, but all of it felt false, deeds done more out of duty than a genuine sense of compassion or love.

He was becoming more and more shadowstuff with each day, more inhuman. His promise to Jak was the only thing that tethered him to the humanity of his past.

"I am not a hero. It's not in me, Jak."

There were other things in him, darker things, things that good deeds could not efface, things that graveside confessions could not expiate. The shadowstuff was not merely part of him; it was consuming him. He saw in Rivalen Tanthul his own future—thousands of years lived in darkness.

"I'm tired," he said, and meant it.

Around him the shadows took on weight, substance, presence. The hairs on the back of his neck rose and he felt only mild surprise when the darkness whispered in his ear with the mocking voice of his god.

"Tired? Already? But things have only just gotten started. Try running for thousands of years. Then speak to me of tired."

Cale did not turn, did not rise, refused to bow. His heart raced but he stared at Jak's grave and kept a tremor from his voice.

"You are not welcome here, not now."

"Why? Because you are communing with your dead friend instead of your god?"

"Yes. You are unwelcome."

"So you said, but you called me. I heard you."

Perhaps Cale had. He did not know anymore. Perhaps his soul whispered to the darkness in a voice the rest of him could not hear.

"Since when do you answer my call? You are a liar."

Mask chuckled. "Quite so." The god's tone changed, took a threatening cast. "And speaking of liars. You have been a naughty priest, talking with archfiends."

Cale's breath caught. His heart lurched. The darkness around him roiled.

"You thought I did not know? Tut, tut. I see clearly into darkness and there's no darker place than your soul."

The words mirrored Cale's own thoughts, but he summoned what defiance he could. "Then you know what I promised him and what that means for my promise to you."

The shadows darkened, tightened around him, their embrace a restraint rather than an embrace. Mask spoke with a voice as hard and sharp as a vorpal blade.

"Those promises are yours to keep, priest. I will hold you to your word."

Cale managed a half turn of his head, but saw only shadow, darkness. "You are a bastard."

"Yes"

"I hate you."

Mask chuckled. "It is not me that you hate. I understand your true feelings all too well."

Cale refused to follow the words where they led. Irritation made him rash. "Do you still have that hole I put in your armor? Show yourself and I'll give you another."

Mask's chuckle faded. "I keep it as a souvenir of our meeting. Do you still have that hole I put in you?"

Cale tensed. "What do you mean?"

"You know what I mean."

Cale did. The shadows were hollowing him out, turning him into a shell of a man.

"I'd do it again, too."

"That's why you're a bastard."

"Among other reasons," Mask said. "Some men in your situation would be grateful to me. What I gave you allows you to save those you want to save, to harm those you want to harm. I made you more than a man."

But I can't save myself, Cale wanted to scream. His anger boiled over, exploded out of him in a burst of words and darkness.

"This," he fought through the restraints and held out his arms as the shadows roiled around his flesh, "has not made me more than a man. It's made me less."

Mask said nothing for a moment, then, "You understand that much sooner than I did."

The words startled Cale. He started to stand but the shadows solidified, held him still, a penitent before Jak's grave.

"Who are you?" Cale asked. "What are you?"

Mask sighed. "I am what I am. Once a man, then a god, then a herald of something . . . awkward. But always a thief and a debtor. Same as you."

Cale did not feel up to parsing the words of his god. "I am tired."

"So you said."

"You are, too, yes?"

Mask said nothing.

Cale continued, "Tell me what is happening."

"The Shadowstorm is come. Our debts are coming due. You understand well about debts. You're as Sembian as anyone actually born there."

"What kind of debts? Who pays?"

Mask spoke softly. "Old ones. And we all pay. It is not for me to break the cycle. Perhaps another will, in another place, another time."

"What do you mean?" Cale asked.

"You keep your promise to me, priest, or the Shadowstorm will swallow all of Sembia. So complain to your dead friend, then go to what used to be Ordulin."

"Used to be?"

"See it through, priest. Things are almost at an end."

Cale's anger forced shadows from his skin. He picked up a stone from Jak's cairn, balanced it in his palm. He held Aril's stone in one hand, Jak's in the other.

"I will see it though. But not for you."

He felt Mask at his side, felt the god's breath on his cheek.

"I know. That is why I chose you for this. I want to tell you something, something I have said too rarely to those I've . . . harmed."

Cale froze, fearful of what would follow. Shadows leaked from him in pulses, an echo of his racing heart.

"I'm sorry," Mask said.

Cale heard sincerity in the words. He tried to turn, but failed.

"You said you were a herald? Of what?" A thought crossed his mind, then, an awful possibility. "Do you . . . serve her?"

But the moment was lost. Mask was already gone. The sound of the distant surf returned. Cale remembered to breathe. It took him some time to recover and when he did, he put a hand on Jak's grave.

"I will do what I can, little man."

When he dissolved the shadows around him, he found the Shadowwalkers no longer on the drawbridge. He stood and rode the shadows into the temple. He turned his form to shadow, invisible to ordinary sight, even that of the Shadowwalkers, and walked the halls seeking Magadon. He found the mind mage alone in a small, stone-walled meditation chamber, balled up in the corner. Faint starlight shot through a high, narrow window and divided the cell in half, light and dark, a line separating Cale from Magadon.

Stress lined the mind mage's face; his hands were fists. A vein pulsed in his temple, the visible manifestation of the storm raging behind his closed eyes. He murmured to himself. Cale could not understand the words.

Cale shed his shadows, turned visible.

"Mags."

Magadon shook his head, murmured louder, wrapped his arms more tightly around his legs, as if trying to hold himself together.

"Magadon."

"Leave me alone!"

"Mags, it's me. Erevis."

Magadon opened his eyes, the movement so slow his eyelids could have been made of lead. The whites of the mind mage's eyes glowed in the darkness.

"Cale."

The mind mage's voice sounded far away, and Cale wondered in what far realm his thoughts had been wandering.

Cale stepped into the cell, across the spear of starlight, and kneeled beside his friend. Magadon smelled of old sweat, a sick room. Cale put a hand on Magadon's shoulder.

"Are you all right?"

The black dots of Magadon's pupils pinioned Cale. "No."

"I'm sorry."

"I know."

Cale stood, extended a hand to Magadon. "On your feet."

Magadon took his hand, rose.

"I'll fix this, Mags. I'm going now."

Magadon licked his lips and blinked away sleep. "I want to come with you. I should be part of it."

"You know you cannot be there. But I want you to link us and keep us linked. Can you? Or is it too much?"

Magadon consulted his will, nodded. "I can do it."

"If you need me, if anything happens, if you . . . start slipping, you tell me."

Magadon held his eyes for a moment then nodded.

"No farther, Mags."

Magadon smiled, and Cale saw in it the last bit of hope wrung from the husk of his deteriorating mental state.

"There's not much farther to fall, Cale," Magadon said.

"Do it," Cale said.

Magadon closed his eyes and furrowed his brow. He winced as a red glow flared around his head. Cale felt the irritating itch root behind his eyes, the effect of the opening mental connection.

*It will need to be latent most of the time,* Magadon projected.

Cale noted that Magadon's mental voice sounded deeper than it had previously, more like his father's voice.

*If you need me,* Cale said. *Tell me and I'll come.*

Magadon nodded. Cale squeezed his shoulder and left him with his thoughts, with the war in his skull. The moment he left the cell, he felt the connection go latent.

Cale sought Nayan, found him sitting alone in a dining hall lit only by the two thin tapers melting away into their holders. Looking upon him sitting there, Cale decided that the Wayrock Temple had become a mausoleum, where the dead and dying sat alone in dark stone rooms.

The small man wore a loose shirt and trousers and a sense of purpose. He stood as Cale entered. A plate of bread and cheese sat on the table before him. Cale was distantly pleased that Nayan had not heard him approach.

"Sit," Cale said. "Eat."

Nayan tilted his head in gratitude. His body sat but his eyes never left Cale's face.

"The Shadowlord visits you in physical form," Nayan said.

"Sometimes."

"You are blessed."

Cale chucked. "So you say. Nayan, I need you and the others to remain here and watch over Magadon."

Nayan's expression did not change, but the shadows around him surged. "You are leaving?"

"For a time. With Riven."

"We would accompany you. Serving the Right and Left hands of the Shadowlord is what brought us here."

"You will be serving me by watching my friend. He cannot be left alone. But he cannot come with me."

Nayan studied Cale's face, and finally nodded. "Where are you going?"

Cale thought about the answer for a moment. "To kill a god," he said, and exited the hall to find Riven. He found the assassin in the central hall on the second story, his two dogs in tow. They wagged their tails at Cale but did not leave their master's side.

A question lodged in the lines of Riven's brow, then smoothed into an answer.

"Found something, after all, I see."

Riven *could* read him.

"Something," Cale acknowledged, thinking of Mask, of Magadon, of Jak.

"What next, then?" Riven asked.

The shadows around Cale swirled. "We tell Abelar the nature of the Shadowstorm so he can get the refugees out of its path."

"Then?"

"We kill Kesson Rel. Or die trying. Mags is nearly gone."

Riven inhaled, nodded. "Plan?"

"Go to Ordulin. Find him. Kill him."

Riven chuckled through his goatee. "Must have taken you a while to come up with that."

Cale smiled despite himself. He still found the rare demonstrations of Riven's humor as incongruous as beardless cheeks on a dwarf.

"That double of him that we fought back in the Calyx," Riven said. "The real him will be stronger than that."

Cale nodded. "I know."

Riven looked away, nodding, finally bent down and pet his dogs, the gesture one of farewell. He stood.

"There's nothing for it. Let's gear up."

# CHAPTER FOUR

*4 Nightal, the Year of Lightning Storms*

Brennus held his mother's platinum necklace in his palm. The facets of the large jacinths caught the dim light of the glowballs and sparkled like flames.

"Pretty," said the homunculi perched on his shoulder.

He nodded. His father had given it to his mother thousands of years earlier, on the night she died. Her body had been found in her chambers that night, as though she had died in her sleep, but the missing necklace suggested something else—murder. Despite a magical and mundane search of first the palace then the city, the murderer and the necklace had never been found.

Until recently.

Brennus had found the necklace buried in the soft

earth of a meadow in a Sembian forest while he had been trying to determine the whereabouts of Erevis Cale's woman, Varra. Varra, pursued by living shadows, had inexplicably disappeared from the face of Faerûn. Brennus had scoured the meadow from which she'd vanished. He'd found no clue to Varra's fate, but had found one to his mother's.

The find unnerved him. He recalled Rivalen's words about the involvement of Mask and Shar in the events unfolding in Sembia. Like Rivalen, Brennus did not accept coincidence.

He turned the necklace over, eyed the inscription on the charm, the words of another age resurrected from a shallow Sembian grave: For Alashar, my love.

He had mentioned the necklace to no one, not Rivalen or his other brothers, not his father. The necklace had torn open the scab of long forgotten grief, returned to him memories and feelings buried with his mother's body centuries ago. Perhaps that was why he had not shared his find with his brothers or father. He saw no reason to raise their grief from the dead.

He had cast numerous divinations on the necklace to ensure its authenticity, used it as the focus for other divinations, all in an effort to determine his mother's true fate, and all to no avail. Thousands of years had passed since her death. He knew the murderer was dead. But he still had to know the truth. He owed his mother that much.

He had been closer to his mother than any of his brothers. She nurtured his love of constructs, clapped with delight at the first gear-driven wood and leather automatons he had built as a boy. He mastered the art of divination only later, at his father's urging, to learn the truth of his mother's fate.

But the truth had eluded him then, as it did now, and now the inquiry must wait still longer. He needed to turn his Art fully to Erevis Cale, to Kesson Rel, to the Shadowstorm. He and Rivalen needed information if they were to fulfill the Most High's charge to annex Sembia and make it the economic workhorse of the reborn Empire of Netheril. To that end, they were to leave the realm only mildly scarred by war.

The Shadowstorm would leave more than mild scars were it not stopped soon.

He puzzled only a little over the religious implications of the fact that two of Shar's most powerful servants, Rivalen the Nightseer and Kesson Rel the Divine One, seemed at cross-purposes in Sembia's fate. Brennus's faith in Shar started and ended with nothing more than words, and those mostly to appease his father and Rivalen. Belief did not sink below the surface in him. Whatever conflict existed in the Sharran church, it was a matter for Rivalen to answer for himself. Though he would also answer to the Most High should he be unable to stop Kesson Rel.

Brennus put his mother's necklace in an inner pocket, near his heart. A sudden sensory memory struck him—the smell of her dark hair. The shadows around him swirled. He recalled her laughter, the crisp, unrestrained sound of it. . . .

"Home now?" his homunculi said in unison, bringing him back to himself.

"Yes," Brennus said. He pulled the darkness around him, pictured in his mind the circular divination chamber in his manse on Shade Enclave, and rode the shadows there.

He smiled when he felt the air change. Unlike the moist air of Selgaunt, rich with the tang of the sea, the cool air of the enclave bore the dense, aggressive aridity of the great desert over which the city flew, though it wouldn't be a desert for much longer.

Ephemeral ribbons of shadow formed and dissolved in the murk, the welcome tenebrous air of home. A domed ceiling of dusky quartz soared over the circular chamber in which Brennus performed his most challenging divinations. Dim stars peered down through the quartz, diffident pinpoints of light that barely penetrated the haze.

"Home," his homunculi said, their voices gleeful. They leaped from their shoulder perches and pelted across the polished floor of the chamber, sniffing at the floor and occasionally squealing with delight.

"Mouse turd," one of them said, holding a tiny mouse pellet aloft like a trophy.

Brennus smiled and shook his head at their foolishness. He intoned the words to a sending spell and transmitted a message to his seneschal, Lhaaril.

*I am returned to Shade Enclave for a short time to work my Art. In four hours I will take a meal.*

Lhaaril returned, *I will have it prepared. Welcome home, Prince Brennus.*

Brennus gave the homunculi some time to frolic then walked to the center of the scrying chamber where stood a cube of tarnished silver, half again as tall as a man and positioned to take advantage of the invisible lines of magical force that veined the world. His homunculi, having completed their olfactory reunion with their home, climbed his robes and resumed their normal place atop his shoulders.

He held an open palm before one of the cube's faces. His homunculi mimicked his movement, giggling. Shadows extended from his hand and brushed the cube. At their touch the silvery face took on depth. Black tarnish swirled slowly on its surface, a cloudy ocean of molten metal.

When the cube fully activated, Brennus began his inquiry. He cast one divination after another, scoured the past and the present, and the entire face of Faerûn. Shadows and sweat leaked from his flesh. He worked in silence and his homunculi soon grew bored and fell asleep on their perches, bookending his ears. Their snores did not affect his concentration.

Despite the comprehensiveness of his magic, Brennus's spells resulted mostly in frustration. He learned nothing of Varra; she remained . . . absent. And he learned nothing of Erevis Cale, his activities or location. The power that warded him allowed him to slip the grasp of any attempted divination. Brennus suspected that Mask himself might cloak Cale.

Brennus did learn of the world from which Kesson Rel hailed, a cold world of which Brennus's most powerful spells revealed little more than a name—Ephyras—and the promise of darkness as deep as the void. He pulled back before pushing his spells further. The hole felt too deep. He feared falling into it.

He turned his spells back to Faerûn and another series of divinations showed the swirling darkness of the Shadowstorm as it roiled across Sembia, deforming and transforming the life with which it came into contact. It grew in strength as it expanded. The currents of negative energy swirling invisibly in its midst could drain the life from a man in a matter of hours.

Within the storm, Brennus saw the ever growing army of shadows, their numbers legion. He saw the regiments of towering, pallid, shadow giants clad in gray armor and darkness, saw the spire of Kesson Rel's otherworldly abode hovering like an executioner's blade over the twisted, shadow-haunted ruins of Ordulin, and saw in the tortured sky a slowly turning maelstrom of shadow and dull viridian light, the rictus of the planar rift vomiting up the corrupting darkness of the Plane of Shadow. Repeated lightning strokes flashed between the clouds and the spire. The sight of it made Brennus dizzy. His homunculi stirred uneasily in their sleep, and one waved a hand before its face as if to shoo away a pest.

Brennus resisted the urge to turn the eye of his divinations to the interior of the spire. He didn't want to alert Kesson Rel to his spying, lest Kesson redouble his wards. Still, he heard Kesson's name in the dull thunder that rumbled within the Shadowstorm, and felt like an ache in his teeth Kesson's immense power, even through the scrying cube. Brennus knew that Kesson Rel was no longer a man. He was semi-divine, a godling, and what the Shadovar intended to conquer and use, Kesson intended to pervert and destroy.

Brennus watched for a short time longer then deactivated the cube. Sweat soaked him. His body ached. Fatigue dulled his mind. But he needed to know more. He knew that Kesson's divine nature would make killing him problematic.

Brennus occasionally relied on powerful extraplanar entities to assist his inquiries, immortal creatures whose knowledge and understanding sometimes exceeded even Brennus's. He would have to rely on such assistance again were he to be of assistance to his brother. Knowledge floated on strange currents in the lower planes, and powerful devils sometimes learned important snippets of information about gods and men. Such information was as much the currency of the Nine Hells and the Abyss as were mortal souls.

He strode to the far corner of the room where a large triangle surrounded by a circle had been inlaid with lead into the floor. His movement awakened his homunculi. They yawned, smacked their lips, noticed the thaumaturgic triangle, and sat up straight.

"Devil!" they said, and clapped with glee.

"Retrieve candles," Brennus said, and they jumped off his shoulders to perform their task.

In moments they returned with wrist-thick candles. Streaks of crimson spiraled around the otherwise ivory-colored shafts of the tapers. Brennus placed them so that their bases exactly straddled the three points where the triangle touched the circle that enveloped it. He backed away, lit them with a command word, and they birthed blue flames.

He cleared his mind and intoned the words to the summoning that would bring forth one of the most powerful devils in the Nine Hells, a fiend of the pit.

After the first stanza, the room grew cool His homunculi shivered and tried to wrap themselves in the loose folds of his cloak, chuckling nervously at the clouds their breathing formed. Ice rimed the lines of the thaumaturgic triangle. The blue flames burned steadily.

After the second and third stanzas, the air grew cold and a point of red light, a hole into the Nine Hells, formed in the air above the center of the summoning triangle. First groans then screams leaked through the hole, a tunnel that ended in a realm of suffering.

Shadows poured from Brennus as he voiced the words to the conjuration. Power coalesced in the room and concentrated in the air between his upraised hands and the summoning triangle. The air became frigid and frost formed on his fingers and palms, the cold like the bite of sharp teeth. He let nothing disturb his recitation of the arcane couplets.

After the fourth stanza the power of the spell peaked and Brennus pronounced the name of the devil he wished to draw forth.

"Baziel, come!"

The mention of the pit fiend's name concentrated the arcane power, gave it voice, and his call went forth into the Hells.

In answer, a cyclone of coruscating fire formed in the space over the summoning triangle. Darkness gathered in the core of the flames, a black seed of evil that began to expand into a doorway between worlds. The flames whirled around it, flared. Smoke churned above the circle and mixed with the shadowy air, obscuring his vision. The smell of brimstone polluted the room and Brennus thought something had gone awry.

A form materialized in the doorway amidst the smoke and flame, and slowly took on definition, features. Brennus recognized the towering, muscular, red-skinned frame and membranous black wings of a pit fiend. He ended his summoning with the final words of binding.

"You are called, Baziel and you are bound to answer my . . ."

The devil stepped through the doorway and into the triangle and Brennus's voice died. The fiend's face resolved not into the bestial, horned visage of Baziel, but into a handsome mien that could have been human but for the black horns that jutted from the brow, but for the pupiless white eyes that stared out of the cavernous sockets and pinioned Brennus to the floor of the chamber.

Brennus recognized the fiend—the archfiend—immediately. Shadows whirled around Brennus, the physical manifestation of the jumble in his mind. The archfiend gazed around the room with only mild interest. He seemed to take up too much space, to be too heavy for the floor, too real, too present.

The homunculi lost their stomach for the summoning.

"Wrong devil!" they squealed, and darted into the folds of Brennus's cloak, trembling with fear.

Brennus struggled to hold his ground under the weight of the fiend's gaze. He licked his lips, fought for calm, and called to mind the various defensive spells at his disposal.

None of them would be of any use. The archfiend was beyond him. His father, with assistance perhaps, could match the fiend on the Prime Material Plane, but no other in Shade Enclave.

Only the binding circle and the constraints of the conjuration protected Brennus from soul death.

Or so he hoped.

Mephistopheles showed fangs in a smile, as if reading Brennus's mind. His voice, deeper even than Rivalen's, resonated with power ancient even by Shadovar standards.

"What a pleasant locale," the archfiend said. With his clawed forefinger, he pulled a tendril of diaphanous shadow from the air, spun it around his finger, and watched it dissolve. "Shadows seem to be my lot in these days."

Brennus cleared his throat. "The summoning called Baziel."

He realized the stupidity of the words only after they exited his mouth.

"Baziel is in service to me, now, and resides in my court at Mephistar."

"I . . . was not aware of that, Lord of Cania. It was not so when last I summoned him."

The archfiend's features hardened, and when they did they reminded Brennus of someone, though he could not draw forth the name.

"You should have inquired, shadeling. By summoning him, you have offended me. I am here to receive your apology."

Two thousand years of co-rule in Shade Enclave rendered Brennus unused to demands. He held the archfiend's gaze with difficulty.

"I intended no offense, Lord of the Eighth." He waved a hand and released the binding. "You are released."

He expected Mephistopheles to dissipate, return to Cania. Instead, the archfiend remained before him, towering, solid, threatening.

"You are dismissed," Brennus said, and put power into his voice.

The archfiend drew in his wings. "I do not wish to leave. There are matters we should discuss."

The homunculi squeaked and tried to burrow farther into Brennus's cloak. Despite his trepidation, Brennus was intrigued by the archfiend's words.

"You wish—"

Words failed him as Mephistopheles reached through the magical field that encapsulated the summoning triangle and binding circle. The magic flared a feeble orange as the archfiend broke through, the whole of Brennus's binding mere cobwebs to the archfiend's power.

"First, apologize," Mephistopheles said.

Brennus backed up a step, activated the communication ring

on his finger. His heart slammed against his ribs. The shadows in the room darkened, churned.

*Rivalen, I am in my summoning chamber in the enclave. Attend me with the Most High. I have—*

"Your ring is not functioning," Mephistopheles said. He picked up one of the candles from the thaumaturgic triangle, and snuffed the flame with thumb and forefinger. "Apologize."

Brennus retreated another step, drew the shadows around him, and prepared to ride them to the mansion of the Most High where he would get aid to face the archfiend.

"Your spells will not serve you either, nor your powers over darkness," the archfiend said, his voice rising. He extended his wings, and dark power, deeper and blacker than shadows, haloed his form. "Apologize!"

The power in the archfiend's voice shook the manse, cracked the quartz roof of the summoning chamber, and dusted Brennus and the entire room in ice.

"My apologies, Mephistopheles," Brennus said, the humiliating words bitter on his tongue. He refused to bow, even halfway. "I intended you no offense. I merely wished to question Baziel on certain matters beyond my Art to answer alone."

Power retreated back into the archfiend's form and his voice returned to normal. He seemed to shrink, to shed some of the threat implicit in his mere existence.

"We understand one another now." He smiled and inclined his head. "I accept your apology, Prince of Shade. And the matters about which you wished to query Baziel are the matters that I wish us to discuss. Kesson Rel?"

Brennus looked up, his mind racing. He knew all fiends to be liars. If Mephistopheles wished to answer Brennus's questions, it was because his answer, whether true or false, served the archfiend's purpose. What stake did Mephistopheles have in matters in Sembia?

"Why make this offer?"

"It amuses me to see you correctly informed."

Brennus bluffed. "I have no questions."

Mephistopheles smiled. "You lie poorly."

The shadows around Brennus swirled.

"You bear an interesting trinket," the archfiend said, and nodded at Brennus's chest.

It took Brennus a moment to process the conversational detour. The archfiend meant his mother's necklace. He tried to keep eagerness from his tone. The necklace suddenly felt warm against his flesh. He could feel his heart pounding against it.

"You know something of it?"

"Now you have questions?"

"Do you?"

Mephistopheles made a dismissive gesture. "Perhaps."

Brennus took a step toward the summoning circle, the whiff of a revelation drawing him forward.

"Who murdered my mother?"

"Kesson Rel."

Brennus stopped short. "Kesson Rel?"

"We were discussing Kesson Rel."

Brennus shook his head. "No, no. We were discussing my mother."

"Were we?"

"Yes. Yes. Tell me about my mother!"

Mephistopheles crossed his muscular arms across his chest. "No. First things first."

Brennus realized he was breathing rapidly. The shadows around him whirled and spun.

"Kesson Rel," he said.

The archfiend nodded. "Continue."

"We want him dead."

"He is powerful, infused with the power of a god."

"A god? Not a goddess?"

Mephistopheles smiled. "Kesson Rel stole his power from the Shadowlord. Shar lays claims to it, now. Of course, how the Shadowlord came by it is . . . another tale."

Brennus processed the new information, and would ponder its implications later. He looked up at the crack in the quartz ceiling, at the dusting of ice that still rimed the room, back at the fiend. "Can it be done? Can Kesson Rel be killed?"

The archfiend beat his wings, once, stirring a breeze that smelled of corpses. "Everything dies. Even worlds."

Brennus did not understand that last. "How then, if he is as powerful as you say?"

Irritation wrinkled Mephistopheles's high brow, narrowed the orbs of his eyes.

"Because his power is not his own. He came by it as all faithless thieves do. By stealing it. He thinks to have locked it away, but the key yet remains. You will find it in Ephyras."

"The world from which he came?"

The fiend nodded. Smoke issued from his nostrils.

Brennus considered the information. "You want him dead, too, else you would not have come. Why?"

The archfiend's face was expressionless. "To collect a debt."

Brennus knew he would get nothing more. "Tell me how to do it. Then tell me of my mother."

Mephistopheles chuckled. "I will tell you one or the other. How to kill Kesson Rel or the identity of your mother's murderer. Which will you have answered?"

Brennus swallowed his anger, his frustration, struggled, and finally said, "Tell me how to kill Kesson Rel."

The archfiend smiled, and began to speak.

Lifelong habits died only with difficulty and time. As he had for over a decade, Abelar awakened before the dawn. He lay on a bed of wool blankets set on the cold, damp earth in his tent. Elden slept on the cot near him and the sound of his son's breathing, easy and untroubled, soothed Abelar's troubled spirit. After a short time, he donned trousers, cloak, and boots, kissed Elden on the forehead, and stepped out of the tent.

The rain had slacked and the faint light of false dawn painted the water-soaked camp in lurid grays. Coughs and soft conversation carried from here and there among the cluster of tents. The smell of pipe smoke carried from somewhere.

He looked east to the rising sun, but saw there only the swirling dark clouds of the magical storm, a black lesion marring the sky. It had grown during the night. It was coming for them, for all of Sembia.

Atop the rise overlooking the camp he saw the men and women of his company, servants of Lathander, gathered for Dawnmeet. His separateness sent an ache through him. He led them now only on the field, not in worship. They looked east, their backs to Abelar, facing the sky where the shadows masked the dawn sun. The sound of their voices carried through the morning's quiet.

"Dawn dispels the night and births the world anew."

The words resounded in Abelar's mind, the echo of the thousands of Dawnmeets when he had spoken the same words to his god. He recalled the first time—he had been a mere boy—when Abbot Denril had first taught him the liturgy. Said in the face of the Shadowstorm, the words seemed hollow.

"May Lathander light our way, show us wisdom," said his companions, their voices carried to him on the morning mist. His own lips formed the words, but he did not speak them aloud, would not, ever again.

"You should be among them," said his father's voice, turning Abelar around.

Endren wore his blade, a mail shirt, and a tabard embroidered with the Corrinthal horse and sun. He looked thin to Abelar, and the weight of recent events had turned his hair entirely gray. His ragged beard, untrimmed in days, gave him the look of a prophet, or a madman. The stump of his left hand, too, looked ragged.

Abelar shook his head. "I am no longer one of them."

"The symbol you wore was not what made you one of them."

Endren's soft words surprised Abelar. "You have never shown such respect for my faith before, Father."

Endren put his good hand on Abelar's shoulder. "I am not showing respect for your faith. I am showing respect for my son. The light is in you, Abelar. Isn't that what you say?"

Abelar felt himself color, nodded.

"Lathander did not put it there," Endren said. "And Lathander did not make what was there brighter. Gods know I did not put it in there. But the light is in you."

Abelar was not so certain but said only, "Thank you, Father."

Endren gave him a final pat as the Lathanderians completed the Dawnmeet.

"Elden is well?" Endren asked.

"Yes. Sleeping."

"That is well."

Father and son stood together for a time in silence, watched the light of the sun war with the storm of shadows, watched gray dawn give way to a stark, shadow-shrouded day.

"We will need to break camp as soon as possible," Abelar said. "Flee west. That storm grows uglier by the hour."

"West takes us to the Mudslide. The droughts have shrunk it, but this sky—" Endren indicated the clouds—"seeks to refill it."

Abelar nodded. "We will cross at the Stonebridge, continue around the southern horn of the Thunder Peaks and toward Daerlun. Maybe even all the way to Cormyr. There, we can reorganize, perhaps gain aid from Alusair or the western nobility."

Endren eyed the distant storm. Thunder rumbled. "That will be a long, hard journey for these people. They are not soldiers used to marching so far. And I expect we'll be adding refugees to our numbers as we go. No one outside of a protected city will willingly sit in the path of whatever magic summoned that storm."

"What do we know of the whereabouts of the overmistress's army?" Abelar said. "If we must leave a force to delay their pursuit . . ." Abelar almost volunteered to lead a rearguard but trapped his words behind his teeth. He would not leave his son again. "Regg will lead it."

Endren nodded. Perhaps he understood Abelar's stutter. "Scouts are in the field. I have not yet had word this morning. I will start to get the camp prepared. It may take a day or two to get all in order."

A scream from within Abelar's tent put a blade in his hand and speed in his feet.

"Elden!"

Abelar and Endren raced into the tent and found Elden sitting upright in his bed, brown eyes wide with fear, tears cutting a path through the layer of grime on his face. He saw Abelar and held out his arms.

"Papa!"

Abelar scanned the tent and the shadows, but saw nothing. His father did the same. Abelar sheathed his blade, hurried to his son's bedside, and took him in his arms.

"What is it, Elden? What's wrong?"

"My dreamed of bad men, Papa. Bad."

Abelar surrounded Elden with his arms. His son buried his face in Abelar's cloak. Tears shook Elden's small body and

Abelar's relief at finding no real danger to his son moved aside for a sudden stab of rage that caused him to wish he had prolonged Forrin's suffering. His son would have nightmares for years because of what Forrin had ordered done.

"It's all right," Abelar said, stroking his son's hair, speaking to both himself and his son. "It will be all right."

Endren put a hand on Elden and his stump on Abelar. After a time, Elden stopped crying. He looked up and Abelar wiped the tears and snot from his face with the sleeve of his cloak.

"You good man, Papa?"

The question took Abelar unawares, set his heart to running and stole his voice. He stared into his son's brown eyes, unable to find words.

"Papa? You good?"

Endren rescued him. "He is a good man, Elden. He's always been a good man."

Elden smiled at his grandfather and embraced his father again.

Abelar nodded gratitude at Endren, held onto his son, and wondered.

Brennus ate, rested for a time, then walked the shadow shrouded halls of his manse on Shade Enclave. He did not relish the coming conversation but nevertheless reached out to Rivalen through his ring.

*What have you learned?* Rivalen asked.

Brennus recounted what Mephistopheles had told him. *There is a world called Ephyras, a dead world, on which stands a temple at the edge of nothing, a temple that will soon be destroyed itself. Within is the Black Chalice, a holy artifact from which Kesson Rel drank to obtain his divinity.*

Brennus paused, hesitant to continue. He felt Rivalen's

impatience through the connection.

*And?*

*And a drink from the Black Chalice will transform the imbiber into a weapon who can take back what Kesson Rel stole, which appears to be a portion of Mask's divine power.*

Satisfaction, not surprise, poured through the magical conduit. *Well done, Brother.*

*You already knew that Kesson Rel's divinity has its origin in Mask and not Shar?*

*I did.*

Brennus was not surprised. Rivalen was as secretive as his goddess.

*Is there more?* Rivalen asked.

Brennus hesitated, steeled himself, and dived ahead. *Only a Chosen of Mask may imbibe from the Black Chalice. Any other will die. The artifact is holy to the Shadowlord.*

Silence. So Rivalen had not known that.

Brennus felt Rivalen's anger and understood it. A heretic of Shar threatened their plans for Sembia. To thwart him, it appeared they needed to beg the assistance of an enemy, an enemy who would profit in the bargain.

*Erevis Cale,* Rivalen said, the words hot with anger.

*So it seems. Since Kesson Rel stole a portion of Mask's divinity, it is not of him. Upon his death, presumably, it will revert to the Chosen of Mask who drank from the chalice.*

*We cannot allow that,* Rivalen said.

*Agreed,* Brennus said.

After a time, Rivalen said, *I will arrange for the assistance of Erevis Cale. Meanwhile, I have another task for you, Brennus.*

Brennus waited.

*When the power is freed upon Kesson Rel's death, I want it.*

The homunculi on Brennus's shoulders gave a start, leaned forward, and stared at one another across the intervening landscape of Brennus's face.

Shadows swirled around Brennus. *You want it?*

*Yes. Or I want it obliterated, though I think that likely impossible.*

*Does the Most High know of this?*

Rivalen's silence provided answer enough.

Brennus made the connections between what he had learned from Mephistopheles and what Rivalen had told him of Kesson Rel.

*Rivalen, the divinations suggest that the divinity can be recovered only by Mask's Chosen. If you—*

*I need you to find another way, Brennus.*

*Rivalen . . .*

*We must kill Kesson Rel to stop the Shadowstorm, but we cannot afford to elevate Erevis Cale in his place.*

*True.*

*There is a way. There must be. Find it. Whatever methods you used before, use them again.*

The homunculi squealed and darted into his cloak. Brennus shook his head, recalling the power and majesty of the archfiend. He did not relish another encounter.

*You do not know what you are asking,* Brennus sent.

*Do you see another option?*

Brennus shook his head. *No.*

*You divined that the temple at the edge of nothing would soon be destroyed. We have little time.*

*Yes.*

*Then I will expect prompt word of your success. I will not forget your assistance in this, Brennus.*

The connection went silent, leaving Brennus alone with his homunculi and his thoughts. Exhausted, he decided to take a meal. He strode the shadows to the dining hall and there found a platter of steamed mushrooms and braised beef awaiting him. A minor magic had kept it hot. His homunculi bounded from their perches and lingered over the mushrooms, inhaling the aroma. They did not need to eat, but enjoyed indulging their senses.

Dim glowballs cast the table in faint green. Thick shadows spun lazily in the air. A dying fire spat its last, defiant crackles from the large, central hearth. A framed portrait of his mother, formally posed, hung over the hearth. He loved the portrait; its laughing eyes and soft smile captured her perfectly.

She stood in a long, yellow gown, one hand on a side chair. Her dark hair, pulled up and tied with diamond studded silver wire, contrasted markedly with her pale skin. A diamond necklace hung from her neck, not the jacinth chain weighing down Brennus's pocket, weighing down his soul. The portrait had been made before Shade Enclave had fled Karsus's folly to the Plane of Shadow, before Brennus had abandoned shaping for divination. His life would have been different had his mother lived.

He owed it to her to discover the identity of her murderer. If he could learn how to kill a god, surely he could learn that. He *would* learn that. Mephistopheles knew the name of the murderer. Or purported to know.

He lifted a goblet of nightwine, drank, but barely tasted it. He held it before his face, shadows coiling around it, and studied it while he thought. His mind turned to the Black Chalice, and he tried to understand events and their implications. But matters were complicated, dark. He could not see through them to the endgame.

"Brennus."

The voice startled Brennus. His homunculi gasped, and looked up with mushrooms held limply in their hands. Shadows poured from Brennus.

His father, Telemont Tanthul, the Most High, emerged from the darkness at the far end of the table. His platinum eyes glowed in the dark hole of his face. The darkness in the room coalesced around him like iron shavings to a lodestone.

He glided forward, his legs indistinguishable from the cloud of shadows that moved with him.

Brennus sprung from his seat, bumping the table, spilling the wine, and startling his homunculi.

"Most High. This is a rare pleasure."

His father seldom left the palace. Plots and counterplots, and a quiet, ongoing spell war with Mystra's Chosen kept him occupied and in seclusion.

"It has been long since we have shared a meal, Brennus," the Most High said. His deep voice sounded most like Rivalen's among all the Princes of Shade. The two shared many traits.

"Please sit," Brennus said, and gestured at a chair opposite his.

Instead, the Most High stopped before the hearth and stared up at the portrait of his wife. The shadows around him churned, reached out to caress the portrait. The glowballs dimmed still further.

A voice to Brennus's right said, "The Lady Alashar was a rare woman."

Hadrhune, the Most High's chief counselor, stepped from the darkness. He bore his darkstaff in both hands and shadows played along the runes embroidered on his robes.

"Hadrhune," Brennus said, unable to keep the distaste from his voice. His homunculi made an obscene gesture at the counselor. Hadrhune pretended not to notice.

"Prince Brennus," the chief counselor said, inclining his head.

Brennus pointedly did not invite Hadrhune to sit.

The Most High turned from the portrait. His narrow face carried sadness in the eyes. Brennus had seen it only rarely.

"She was more than rare, Hadrhune. She was my life."

"Of course, Most High," said Hadrhune, and inclined his head.

"I think of Mother often," Brennus said.

The Most High and Hadrhune shared a look at his words. Both approached him and Brennus could not rid himself of the feeling of walls closing in.

"You are wondering why we have come," the Most High said, as if reading his mind.

The homunculi nodded in unison.

"Yes," Brennus said. "It appears more than a social visit."

The Most High took station across the table from Brennus, the portrait of his wife visible over his shoulder. Hadrhune stopped at the head of the table, his gaze alternating between Brennus and the Most High.

"You have been discussing with Prince Rivalen the manner in which Kesson Rel can be killed and the divine power within him taken," the Most High said.

Brennus felt only fleeting surprise that his father knew of his discussions with Rivalen. The Most High was, after all, the Most High. Still, shadows and sweat leaked from Brennus in abundance. His homunculi stood still as statues on the table, mushrooms held aloft.

"Yes," Brennus acknowledged and offered all he knew. "It appears that the power, once freed, can be taken only by a Chosen of Mask, but Rivalen wishes to take the power for himself. I am to find a way to make that possible."

Brennus expected the Most High to show anger, or at least concern, that Rivalen thought to arrogate divinity to himself. But the Most High seemed untroubled.

"Is it possible, Most High?" he asked.

"I believe it must be, but we will soon know for certain. You are to return to your summoning chamber and again call forth Mephistopheles."

Once more, Brennus found himself unsurprised by the depths of his father's knowledge. He started to ask why the Most High would not summon the archfiend himself but realized the answer before he uttered the words—Mephistopheles would answer Brennus, but he might hesitate to answer the call of the Most High.

"Come," the Most High said. "Let us make a second query of the Lord of Cania."

# CHAPTER FIVE

*4 Nightal, the Year of Lightning Storms*

Rivalen considered Brennus's information from all angles and no matter how the light struck it, he saw it the same way. He did not have much time. The Shadowstorm was spreading. He had to stop it or there would be no Sembia to annex. And he had to stop it soon, or Mystra's Chosen would take a hand.

He made up his mind, stepped through the shadows in the corner of his great room, and completed the stride by emerging in the foyer of Stormweather Towers, the Hulorn's family estate. Afternoon light filtered in through high windows, cross-hatching the carpeted floor with alternating lines of light and shadow.

A gasp greeted Rivalen's arrival. The major domo, Irwyl, stood two paces from Rivalen, his dull eyes wide, his hands on a medium sized wooden chest he bore.

"I have need to see the Hulorn," Rivalen said.

The gangly, graying Irwyl stood frozen, rooted to the floor, a creaky oak in a well-tailored shirt rolled up to his elbows.

Rivalen strode toward him and Irwyl looked as if he might bolt. The contents in the chest, whatever they were, audibly shook.

Irwyl stared at a point somewhere around Rivalen's chin. "I was clearing the study." He held up the chest as evidence, or to interpose a barrier between himself and Rivalen. "The laborers have not yet arrived, but I thought I should remove the small valuables before they did."

Irritation caused the shadows around Rivalen to swirl.

"Where is the Hulorn?"

Irwyl shook his head. "I believe he returned in the carriage to the Palace. He seemed not himself. He seemed . . ."

Rivalen rode the shadows in the hall across the city, to the foyer entry of the Hulorn's Palace. The helmed, spear-wielding guards looked startled at his sudden appearance, but only for a moment. They had gotten used to his comings and goings and the Hulorn had authorized his free movement throughout any part of the city.

"Prince Rivalen," the bearded sergeant said, and inclined his head.

Both the sergeant and the guards eyed with ill-concealed wonder the shadows that shrouded him.

"Where is the Hulorn?" Rivalen said.

"Is the Hulorn expecting you?" said a voice from the far side of the foyer.

Thristiin emerged from wherever it was that he laired and smiled his tight smile at Rivalen. His thin gray hair was neatly parted on his age-spotted pate and his clothing, down to the tufted shirt cuffs, looked freshly cleaned and donned.

"He is not," Rivalen answered, and walked across the tiled

floor to stand before Thristiin. "Do you suppose that means he will not see me?"

Thristiin sought a refuge for his gaze that did not include Rivalen's face.

"Of course not, Prince. He is in the map room. May I escort you so that I may announce your arrival?"

Thristiin led Rivalen through the wide, comfortably dark corridors of the palace. Thayan and Chessentan rugs dotted the floors. Tapestries bedecked the walls.

"Prince Rivalen of Shade Enclave," Thristiin announced, as he opened the door to the map room.

Tamlin stood with arms crossed over a large, rectangular oak table on which lay an unrolled map of Sembia, the Dalelands, and Cormyr. Chess pieces from the set that had been in the study in Stormweather Towers stood here and there on the parchment, denoting various locations. Rivalen smiled to see the white king positioned near Selgaunt. Tamlin still needed to think of himself as pure.

"Prince," Tamlin said. "I did not expect to see you until our customary repast after sunset."

"Forgive me, Hulorn, but I must speak with you on a matter of some import."

Thristiin took Rivalen's point. "If there is nothing else, Hulorn?"

"You may go," Tamlin instructed the chamberlain.

Thristiin bowed to each of Tamlin and Rivalen then exited the room, closing the door behind him.

Tamlin wore a thin blade at his belt. His holy symbol of Shar hung from a silver chain around his neck, open for all to see.

Rivalen stepped to the table, eyed the map. A black bishop was toppled on Saerloon, while the other stood on Urmlaspyr. A toppled white knight lay on Saerb. Black rooks stood on Daerlun and Yhaunn. Black pawns were arranged in an arc across northeastern Sembia. Rivalen assumed they denoted the leading edge of the Shadowstorm. The remaining pieces from the set sat in a velvet-lined coffer to one side of the map.

Tamlin took position beside Rivalen, close enough that the shadows around Rivalen brushed him.

"I brought my father's chess set from Stormweather Towers and you see my poor attempt to represent matters as they stand. This is all based on the most recent reports of our scouts as well as what divinations have shown. The Shadowstorm appears to be accelerating as it moves west."

"It grows in power as it consumes more life," Rivalen said.

Tamlin stared at him for a long moment. "Yes—" he cleared his throat—"well, it seems it is not yet spreading east. Yhaunn, so far as we know, remains untouched. But we must wonder for how long? I think we must stop it soon, Prince."

"You are correct," Rivalen said. He withdrew the black king from the coffer, placed it over Ordulin on the map. "Kesson Rel is the cause of the Shadowstorm. To stop it, we must kill him."

He toppled the king, though he knew perfectly well he could not stop the Shadowstorm. He would not even try. The Shadowstorm was Shar's will. He could only contain it. Perhaps.

"Sensible," Tamlin said and rubbed his hands together.

Rivalen picked up a black pawn, eyed it, and showed it to Tamlin.

"But to kill him, I require the assistance of Erevis Cale."

The words stopped Tamlin in mid-nod, froze his hands, flushed his skin. "Mister Cale? Why? Surely you and I can accomplish whatever needs accomplished."

Rivalen knew he had to trod with care. He played and would continue to play on Tamlin's sense of inferiority relative to Mister Cale, but he knew not to play too hard lest the strings snap.

"Ordinarily, I would agree. But this is a matter of a unique kind."

Tamlin shook his head, paced, then gestured at the map. "Look what we have done so far. How can Mister Cale be necessary?"

Tamlin spun on his heel, paced some more, and nearly spat his next words. "Mister Cale. Erevis Cale. What can require Mister Cale that I cannot do?" He stopped, eyeing Rivalen. "Is it because he is a shade? Then make me one. You know I want it."

"It is not because he is a shade. It is because he is a Maskarran."

"I do not understand. How is that relevant?"

The shadows around Rivalen churned with irritation, but he kept his voice patient. He did not wish to damage the relationship he had so painstakingly built.

"Kesson Rel is a divine being. A god. Quite minor, it is true, but divine nevertheless."

Tamlin's voice sounded small. "A god you say?"

Rivalen nodded. "Yes, but the unique circumstances involved in Kesson's ascension render him uniquely vulnerable. That vulnerability can be exploited only by a special servant of Mask."

"Mister Cale," Tamlin said, with surrender in his tone. He took another black pawn from the coffer, closed his fist around it until the knuckles were white. "He will not help us."

"Not willingly."

Tamlin looked up, eyebrows arched in a question.

"Brennus is unable to scry Cale directly, but he has learned that Cale has been of service to Abelar Corrinthal. Our spies among the Saerbian refugees—"

"You have spies among the refugees?"

"Do not interrupt me again or ever," Rivalen said, his voice rising with his ire. "Do you understand?"

Tamlin's mouth hung slack under his wide eyes. He nodded slowly.

"Yes," Rivalen said, more calmly. "We have spies. Not in human form, of course. But a few."

Tamlin, his face still red from Rivalen's rebuke, went for a wine chalice on a side table, and drank. Of late, Rivalen thought the Hulorn drank more than had been his custom.

"You will use the refugees against Mister Cale?" Tamlin asked.

"Mister Cale has an interest in their safety. We can use that to compel his cooperation."

Tamlin's expression showed pleasure at the thought of compelling Cale. "How?"

Rivalen took a white rook from the coffer, held it in the air over Saerb, beside the toppled white knight. He used a minor magic, released it, and it hovered in place.

"Leave that to me," Rivalen said.

"And afterward? What of Mister Cale? I would rather he not be involved in what we have built here. His presence will vex me."

Rivalen knew what Tamlin wanted to hear. He crushed the pawn in his fist, and let the pieces fall to the floor.

"Leave that to me, also."

Tamlin licked his lips. "I would participate in that."

Rivalen heard sincerity rather than bravado in Tamlin's tone. It both surprised and pleased him.

"Perhaps you will have that chance," Rivalen said.

"I would like a chance at more," Tamlin said. "Shadedom, as I mentioned."

Before Rivalen could respond, Tamlin went on. He must have rehearsed the words in the privacy of his mind many times.

"I have converted to Shar. Fully. I feel her here." He touched his chest. "A weight. But welcome. My soul is hers."

Rivalen nodded.

"I wish to complete my conversion. Make my body hers as well."

"You negotiate this with me as if it were just another contract between merchants. It is more."

Tamlin looked crestfallen. "I know that, Prince. I do not make the request lightly. I know it is more."

Rivalen eyed Tamlin, nodded, and the shadows around him swirled. He had done his work well.

"Understand, Tamlin, that becoming a shade does more than simply transform your body. You will no longer be human. You will live alone, with history as your companion. Your family will die, your friends, even elves die and you live on. Everything will crumble and you will continue. Imagine watching the world slowly surrender to its end, the end Shar's teachings tell us is inevitable. You will be a witness to the end. No peace of the grave for you. Perhaps this sounds appealing, but I assure you it is as much burden as boon."

"It is a burden I am ready to bear. I am already alone."

"Very well," Rivalen said. He gestured with a fingertip and a charge of arcane power disintegrated the prone black king nestled within the Shadowstorm. "But first things first."

Kesson Rel stood on one of the stone balconies that protruded from his spire. He had moved his entire tower from the Adumbral Calyx to Toril. It hung over the blasted, withered ruins of Ordulin like an accusatory finger, a black dagger driven into the heart of the city. The stink of Ordulin's dead hung in the air, as thick as the darkness.

Black clouds roiled in the sky as far as he could see, an expanding blanket of night that obliterated the sun, obliterated life.

In the distance, jagged bolts of green lightning knifed through the darkness, each bolt the byproduct of the energy gathered by the storm as it murdered Toril, each a conduit through which the energy was transferred back to Kesson's spire, where a continual stream of crackling bolts attached the spire's top to the sky like a hundred umbilicals. The spire transformed the gathered energy, focused it on a point in Ordulin below the floating spire. There, a small dark seed had rooted in Toril's reality. Out of its emptiness would grow the annihilation of the world.

Kesson touched the holy symbol embroidered on his robes, the black disc of Shar, and smiled.

Living shadows thronged the air around the tower, wheeled and spun like a cloud of bats, their eyes like coals. Regiments of shadow giants marched in the darkness. And still darker things roamed the outer fringes of the storm. Kesson felt every life within the growing darkness, mice and men, felt each of them die in turn.

He savored the taste of destruction, luxuriated in the bitter tang of death. It had been a long while since he had enjoyed it on so massive a scale. He had destroyed Elgrin Fau long ago, but only imperfectly murdered his world. Its slow demise continued even now, thousands of years after it had begun. He still could not return to finish what he had begun. He had failed Shar then and his failure had driven him to madness. His goddess had bound him in the Calyx as punishment for his failure, allowing him freedom to Faerûn only now.

He would not fail her again. And his atonement would be the end of Toril.

Rivalen left and Tamlin walked the halls of the Hulorn's Palace, his mind and body afire for his transformation.

His feet bore him up stairways until he stood on the highest balcony of the palace's northwest tower. These days he often retreated to the balcony when he wished solitude, a moment with his thoughts away from the burden of leadership.

The brisk wind carried the smell of fish off the bay and snapped the pennons atop the turrets above him. The high vantage afforded him a panorama view of his city, of Selgaunt Bay, of the floating mountain of Sakkors. From so high up Selgaunt and the water of the bay looked still, quiet, like a painting, the bustle lost in the lens of distance.

The forest of the Hulorn's hunting gardens stretched before him, a walled swath of green that fell away to reveal the towering spires, domes, and towers of Temple Avenue. The avenue was quiet, almost dead. No bells tolled the hour in Milil's Tower of Song, and no flames danced in the everburning ewers on the portico of Sune Firehair's House. No festive pennons danced atop the spires of the Palace of Holy Festivals. Temple doors up and down the avenue were closed, their priests and priestesses arrested or fled, their windows dark, pews and worship benches empty. Only the gray stone of Shar's temple had open doors and lit glowballs, and the Shadovar priestess Variance Mattick presided over the prayers to the Lady. Tamlin fancied he could hear the sound of the Thirteen Truths in the air. He touched his holy symbol and whispered them to the wind.

He looked past the tangle of Selgaunt's winding streets and broad thoroughfares, past the packed bunches of woodshingled and tiled roofs, past the turrets of the mansions of the Old Chauncel, and past the Khyber Gate, to where Sakkors hovered three bowshots up in the air on its craggy, inverted mountaintop. Shadows enshrouded it. It looked like a storm cloud, like he imagined the Shadowstorm must look. Not even the afternoon sun could defeat its fog of darkness. From time to time the breeze parted the swirl of shadows and hinted at a tiled rooftop, an elegant turret, a soaring spire, but the entirety of its appearance was a mystery, a secret. The patrol of shade-mounted veserabs had withdrawn into the city. It was soon to travel north and west in answer to Rivalen's will.

When it did, it would take with it the priests and priestesses of the other Selgauntan faiths, currently held captive in the Shadovar enclave. Tamlin suspected their quarters to be less than luxurious and the suspicion pleased him. He regarded them all as traitors, but could not yet bring himself to give the order to execute them. Some of them had headed their temples since Tamlin was a boy at his father's knee.

He began instead to let them drift into the background of his mind, let concern for their fate slip into the recesses of public consciousness. When they had adequately faded from the collective memory, he would do what needed done. Rivalen had told him it was necessary. Perhaps Tamlin would assure Rivalen that he was worthy of shadedom when he gave the order for their execution. He would have the order drawn up.

Meanwhile, only Shar's worship would be sanctioned in Selgaunt. And soon, Shar's worship would predominate across all of Sembia. Perhaps Tamlin would tolerate other faiths for a time, but only for a time. The Lady of Loss consumed rival faiths the way the Shadowstorm consumed Sembia, drowning them in her darkness.

A distant rumble of thunder sounded from the north, from the Shadowstorm. Tamlin's dreams of rule depended upon Prince Rivalen stopping it. He looked toward Ordulin and imagined he could see the advancing edge of the Shadowstorm.

"Goodbye, Mirabeta."

He hoped she had died in pain. She merited such a death.

His thoughts surprised him for a moment, but only a moment. He realized that his religious conversion had freed him to think openly about matters he once would not have considered, or at least would not have acknowledged. The self-realization pleased him. Shar and Rivalen had freed him from the shackles of his past, the shackles of an outdated morality. The old Tamlin had died the moment he plunged the sacrificial dagger into Vees Talendar. And Tamlin had buried the body of his past self in the depths of his worship.

An urge struck him, a desire to symbolize his death and rebirth. He knew how he would do it.

The diminutive of his father's name died with the old Tamlin. He was, after all, not smaller than his father. He was larger than his father could ever have hoped. He was not Tamlin, not Deuce, but Thamalon II, and would be from then on. Perhaps he would order a coin minted to that effect. He thought Rivalen would appreciate the gesture.

As the sun sank lower, roofed the sky in the crimson of blood, Sakkors began to move. Watching the monumental edifice, the whole of it as large as Selgaunt, fly through the air brought Shar's praises to Tamlin's lips. Rivalen would take it north, toward Saerb, and trap the Saerbian refugees between a Shadovar army and the onrushing Shadowstorm. He hoped thereby to force Mister Cale to assist him in destroying Kesson Rel.

Rivalen had seemed unsure that Mister Cale would accede, but Thamalon knew Cale would. Mister Cale still thought about morality the way Thamalon once did, the way Thamalon's father once had. Thamalon knew better now. The refugees were a tool to be used to achieve a greater end. Their individual lives were of no moment.

"Love is a lie," he recited. "Only hate endures."

He stood on the balcony for over an hour, watching Sakkors vanish into the night. His city came to life with nightfall. Link-boys illuminated the streetlamps. Shop windows glowed. He watched it all with a smile. He had fed his people in the midst of famine, defended them against an unwarranted attack instigated by an ambitious, lying overmistress. Saerloon was already his.

Urmlaspyr would soon follow, as would Yhaunn.

If anyone had the right to rule Sembia, it was him. He had earned it. He need only convince Prince Rivalen to share with him the secret of transforming into a shade. Then his rule would last for a thousand years.

He looked into the darkening sky. Selûne had not yet risen. The moonless twilight belonged to Shar.

"In the darkness of night, I hear the whisper of the void."

He found he was wiping his right hand on his trousers and could not understand why.

# CHAPTER SIX

*4 Nightal, the Year of Lightning Storms*

Cale and Riven materialized on a rise in the shadow of a stand of towering larch at the outskirts of the Saerbian refugee camp at Lake Veladon. The wind tore leaves from the limbs, showering them in debris. Iron-gray clouds roofed the sky directly above. Behind them loomed the Shadowstorm. Cale did not turn but he felt the weight of it between his shoulder blades, imagined in his mind the dark clouds sliding across the sky, a black curtain closing on Sembia's final act. Thunder growled like a beast, announcing the storm's hunger.

"We need to hurry," Cale said. He felt urgency down to his bones. He tried to contact Magadon.

No response. The connection remained dormant.

From their vantage point atop the rise, they saw the camp below bustling with activity. Wagons and mule-drawn carts were being arranged around the outskirts of the camp into a large caravan. Teamsters checked yokes, wheels, axles, the animals themselves. The horses, oxen, and mules endured their examinations with the passivity of the exhausted and underfed. Many gave starts or snorts with each roll of thunder.

The men and women of Abelar's company, their otherwise shining armor dulled by the wan light of a diseased day, supervised the organization of the caravan. Cale noted only a few score. He presumed the rest to be on patrol.

Several men stood knee deep in the lake, filling barrels and skins with water, then passing them on to pairs of youths who splashed out of the shallows and carried them to the wagons. Thin dogs darted around the camp, tails wagging, barking, excited by the activity.

"Breaking camp," Riven said.

"Wise," Cale said.

Behind them, the sky rumbled its disapproval.

"Come on," Cale said, and started down the rise. Riven's words slowed his stride.

"Abelar is as broken as Mags, Cale. He just doesn't know it yet. Remember that."

Cale considered the words, considered the man, and shook his head. "Not broken. Cracked. Both of them. But fixable."

Riven looked unconvinced but let it go. Together, they hurried down toward the camp.

The teamsters saw them coming, stopped their work, and hailed them. Children waved and smiled. Women and men packing up their goods took a moment to nod a greeting or utter a hail. Cale did not know where they found their resiliency.

"Tough folk," Riven said, taking the thoughts from Cale's head.

Cale nodded. He wanted to feel fondness for them but did not. He didn't know what he felt. He pitied them, understood their plight, but felt no connection, at least no *human* connection.

He was broken, too. Or cracked. And he was not fixable.

By the time they had reached the center of the camp, they had picked up a contingent of children and young men. Cale did not need his darkness-enhanced hearing to hear the frequent mention of the words "hero," "shadows," and "Mask."

Two of Abelar's company directed them to Abelar and shooed the children back to their duties.

They found Abelar standing among a stand of trees at the shore of the lake, away from those gathering water, arms across his chest, staring out at the still waters as if he had lost something in them. Cale and Riven navigated down the riverbank.

"Abelar," Cale said, and his voice pulled Abelar around only reluctantly. Cale noted the lack of a holy symbol, the new breastplate that did not feature an enameled rose.

Abelar smiled a welcome, stepped forward and clasped hands.

"Erevis, Riven, well met and welcome. I am pleased to see you returned. How did matters fare within the storm? Your woman?"

Cale shook his head.

Abelar put his other hand on Cale's shoulder. "I am sorry, my friend."

"Thank you," Cale said.

Abelar's eyes grazed Riven's holy symbol, moved away. His jaw tightened and a tic caused his left eye to blink.

"We came to warn you about the storm," Cale said, nodding back at the growing blackness. "Seems you scarce needed it."

"We thought it dark magic out of Ordulin. It seemed best to stay out of its path."

"It did not originate in Ordulin," said Cale. "But in the Plane of Shadow, with Sharrans."

"Sharrans," Abelar said, the word a curse. His eyes again returned to the surface of the lake.

"I fear Ordulin may be . . . gone," Cale said, thinking of his conversation with Mask on the Wayrock.

Abelar turned to him, a stricken look on his face. Cale envied him his empathy.

"There are tens of thousands of people there," Abelar said. "And the Dawn Tower? Gone? What magic is this?"

Before Cale could answer, a voice from atop the bank carried over the rain.

"Papa! Papa! Rain coming! Hurry!"

The three men looked up to see Elden appear at the top of the riverbank. Exertion reddened his round face. Labored breaths came from his mouth, still somehow slack even in a smile. But his eyes shone with . . . something. Cale thought it insight or perhaps unfiltered love. He found he envied Elden, too.

The boy's expression fell when he saw Cale and Riven. He looked uncertain, eased back a step, and looked over his shoulder.

"Grandpapa."

Endren appeared behind him and his reassuring hand on Elden's shoulder seemed to steady the boy. Endren, dressed in mail and with a blade at his belt, nodded at Cale and Riven, crouched, and said something in Elden's ear. The boy visibly relaxed.

"The healers have done well by my son,," Abelar said, waving to Elden. He smiled at his boy, though the fate of Ordulin still haunted his eyes. He took Cale and Riven each by the shoulder and turned them around. "Come."

They started up the rise and Elden's eyes grew wider at Cale and Riven's approach. He looked like he might bolt, but Endren kept a hand on his back and the boy held his ground. Father and son both had nerve, it seemed.

"These are the men who brought you back to us, Elden," Endren said, loud enough for them all to hear.

"My knows," Elden said. He slid behind his grandfather and peeked out from behind his legs like an archer through an arrow slit.

They gained the rise. Cale and Riven nodded a greeting at Endren, at Elden. The boy avoided eye contact.

"It rain again soon, Papa," Elden said to Abelar, avoiding eye contact with Cale and Riven. "Hurry to tent. Hurry."

"First, a dragon grab," Abelar said. He knelt, arms out, and the expression he had carried when looking at the lake—the look of having lost something—disappeared entirely. Instead, he looked like a man who had found something.

Elden smiled and braved his uncertainty. He charged Abelar and leaped into his embrace. Abelar roared like a dragon, nuzzled the boy's neck, and Elden giggled uncontrollably.

Cale could not help it. He chuckled, too. The boy's laugh was as contagious as plague. Even Riven smiled.

Abelar stood, his son under one arm.

"Elden, these are Papa's friends, Erevis and Riven. Do you remember them?"

The boy didn't look at them. He pointed at the sky. "It going rain."

"These are the men that saved you," Abelar said to him. "They returned you to me."

A cloud passed over Elden's face, a personal Shadowstorm. He put his cheek on Abelar's shoulder.

"Rain, Papa."

"It's all right," Cale said to Elden, to Abelar. He could imagine how he must appear to some children. He would not have made much of a father.

Abelar kissed his son and placed him in the ground. "Grandpapa will take you back to the tent. I need to speak to Erevis and Riven. I will be along soon."

Elden nodded and hugged his father again. He turned and actually looked at Cale and Riven, studying them. The peculiar vacancy of his other features contrasted markedly with his eyes, which looked as sharp as daggers.

"Tank you," the boy said.

Cale kneeled down, forced the shadows leaking from his flesh to subside. "You are welcome, Elden."

"Watch this, boy," Riven said.

The assassin produced four small, painted wooden balls from a belt pouch.

Elden eyed them with curiosity. "What you do?"

"Watch," Riven said. He tossed them into the air one after another and juggled them with facility.

Elden grinned and clapped with delight. "Him juggle!"

Cale thought that of all the sights he had seen in his life, none had been as incongruous as Riven entertaining a child by juggling painted balls. Riven caught the balls one after another, finished with a flourish, and held them out to Elden.

"These are for you. Practice when you have time. Next time I see you, you can show me what you have learned."

Elden, still smiling, took the painted wooden balls, his reticence around Riven forgotten.

"Run and play with Grandpapa," said Abelar. "I will be along."

"Come, Elden," said Endren.

"Tank you," Elden said to Riven, who smiled in return.

To Endren, Abelar said, "They have brought news. I will share it with you later."

Endren nodded and he and Elden walked off, the boy tossing and dropping the balls as he went.

"You spend time with a troupe in a fair?" Cale asked Riven, smiling.

"Something like that. In Skullport. Long time ago." Riven spit, looked away.

Cale lost his smile. "Sorry, Riven. I didn't mean—"

"As I said, long time ago, Cale. No harm in your words. I

carried those around . . . Hells, I don't know why I carried those around." He reached into another pouch. "I need a smoke."

While Riven found, tamped, and lit his pipe, Cale told Abelar what they knew. As he spoke, droplets of the rain Elden had prophesized started to fall, as thick and heavy as footsteps on the leaves, the trees, the surface of the lake. They took shelter under the canopy of an elm and Cale told Abelar of the Shadowstorm, of Kesson Rel, of Selgaunt's alliance with the Shadovar, of Rivalen Tanthul, servant of Shar.

"Shar is everywhere in this," Abelar said, and his gaze went back to the surface of the lake. He looked uncertain.

"Not everywhere," Riven said, and exhaled a cloud of smoke.

The three stood under the elm, isolated from the rest of the camp in a bubble formed of the sky's tears.

"You are part of this now," Cale asked Abelar. "Do you want to hear it all?"

Abelar didn't look at Cale. He looked out at the lake, the surface boiling in the rain, and nodded.

Cale told him of lost Elgrin Fau, the dead who haunted it, and his promise to them. He told him of their role in freeing Kesson Rel, of Furlinastis, and of Magadon and Mephistopheles.

When he finished, Abelar shook his head. "You have done a lot of good."

Riven chuckled and blew out smoke.

Cale said, "No. We've done what we had to do."

"I understand that," Abelar said. He looked Cale in the face, cleared his throat. "What turned you to your god, Erevis?"

The question took Cale aback; he struggled for an answer, felt Riven's eyes on him, too. "No one thing, I suppose. It's been a process, gradual, like it . . . unfolded."

"Like the events of your entire life had been arranged beforehand to bring you to faith," Abelar said, nodding.

"Yes."

Abelar turned away. "Strange that one moment, one thing, can entirely undo a choice born in a multitude of moments across a lifetime. Is it not?"

Riven answered before Cale. "You've got to live with yourself before you have to live with your faith, Abelar. Your son needed to be avenged. There's nothing more to it. You made the right choice." Riven looked at both Cale and Abelar and spoke slowly. "You made the right choice."

"I made the only choice," Abelar said, and shook his head. "And there is the problem."

Riven blew a cloud of smoke. "Not the way I see it."

Abelar turned back to them, smiling through his pain. "But then you've only one eye."

Riven smiled around his pipe but his tone was serious. "And you've only one son. Remember that."

Abelar lost his smile. He glanced back at the lake, the surface vibrating under the onslaught of rain. He looked back to Riven and said, "Truth."

Cale realized that Abelar was not broken, or cracked. He was torn. Like Magadon between devil and fiend. Like Cale between past and present, human and . . . inhuman.

"What will you do now?" Cale asked.

"Stay with my son. See these people to safety. What will you do?"

Riven chuckled and extinguished his pipe.

Cale said, "Go kill a god."

Brennus stood before the thaumaturgic triangle, incanting the summoning. Shadows and arcane power whirled slow spirals around him, around the room. The thrum of gathering energy formed the dark seed over the triangle, expanded into a window on the Hells. Screams and stink poured through the opening. Brennus called the name of the archfiend over the tumult and his voice boomed across the planes.

Mephistopheles answered. The shadow of his muscular, winged form appeared in the planar window. Brennus gagged at the charnel reek. The power peaked and Mephistopheles manifested within the circle. His white eyes fixed on Brennus, narrowed. Unholy power rippled from his glowing red flesh.

"You presume to summon me again, shadeling? For that—" He stopped, sniffed the air, and frowned. His mouth split in a fanged smile. "You are not alone."

Telemont, Hadrhune, and five archwizards of Telamont's court let the shadows around them fall away.

"No, he is not alone," Telemont said.

As one, the shadow mages incanted words of power. Mephistopheles roared, and grew in a heartbeat to the size of a titan. A three-tined iron polearm longer than Brennus was tall appeared in his hand, sheathed in a black cloud of unholy might.

He stepped from the circle, piercing Brennus's binding with ease. He held out a hand and a bolt of black energy arced from his palm, struck one of the archwizards, and reduced him to a pile of twitching gore.

Telemont, Hadrhune, and the remaining archwizards completed their spell and chains of shadow squirmed from the floor at the archfiend's feet, shackling him at ankles and wrists. Telemont made a cutting gesture with his hand and a final chain, thicker than the rest, sprung from the floor and ringed the archfiend's waist.

Mephistopheles beat his wings, pulled against his bindings, but the chains, composed of the stuff of Shade Enclave itself, rattled and held him fast. He glared at Telemont and viridian beams shot from his white eyes. They struck the Most High and shadows exploded around him. He groaned, staggered backward, but kept his feet. Telemont shouted a word of power, held a hand before him palm out, and the chains on Mephistopheles tightened.

Mephistopheles exhaled a cloud of power at Telemont but it stopped a few paces from the fiend's face, dissipating into the dark air.

"The shackles suppress your power now," Telemont said, his voice strained.

Mephistopheles roared, beat his wings, and pulled in a frenzy against his bindings. Brennus backed away, his heart racing.

Power seethed around the archfiend, a black cloud shot through with lines of crackling green power. Veins and sinew looked like ropes in his straining muscles. He roared again and chunks of quartz from the dome above rained down, shattering on the floor into hundreds of jagged shards. He lurched from side to side and yanked against his bonds. The whole of Shade Enclave bucked and rolled. Brennus fell and the shards of quartz skittered across the floor.

Telemont and Hadrhune merely watched, their eyes aglow.

"You have him, Most High," said Hadrhune.

After a time Mephistopheles ceased his struggles. Huge breaths expanded his mammoth chest and his lips peeled back to show his fangs.

"You cannot harm me, shade," he said to Telemont. "Even on this plane, in this form, I am well beyond you. And you cannot hold me here forever. Yet forever is how long I have." He nodded at the archwizards and pulled at the shadow chains. "How long before one of your lackeys errs and these chains weaken? I forget and forgive nothing, Tanthul."

Brennus stood, remembered to breathe. The shadows around him churned in time to his racing heart.

"You speak truth," Telemont said. The Most High glided forward until he was nearly within reach of the archfiend. Dark power shrouded them both, though Mephistopheles towered over Telemont. "But your realm will suffer in your absence."

Mephistopheles snarled. "And your realm will suffer in my presence."

Telemont inclined his head, conceding the point.

"We will free you if you tell me what I wish to know."

Mephistopheles's eyes flashed cunning at the mention of a deal.

"Ask and I will decide whether to answer you with truth, lies, or not at all."

"Kesson Rel's death will free the Shadowlord's stolen divinity. I wish to divert it before it returns to the god or enters another of his Chosen."

The statement seemed to surprise the archfiend. Behind the white eyes, Brennus saw the complicated workings of an ancient, powerful intelligence calculating.

"It cannot be done."

The shadows around Telemont swirled. He glided forward another step and said, "A lie. I can detect them even from you."

Mephistopheles pondered for a moment, perhaps considering Telamont's claim.

"Can you?" he murmured.

Telemont waited, saying nothing. The archfiend looked past him to the archwizards, to Hadrhune, to Brennus, where his gaze lingered for a moment. Brennus again sensed the fiend's mind working through possibilities.

"Perhaps Baalzebul has noticed your absence already," the Most High said. "Perhaps he prepares a move against Mephistar while you scheme in your chains."

At the mention of one of his rivals, Mephistopheles's eyes narrowed. His flesh brightened to crimson and smoke exited his nostrils.

"Very well, shadeling. It can be done."

"Tell me how."

Brennus listened with interest as Mephistopheles told them the series of spells and the focus necessary to do what they intended. They would have little time once Kesson Rel was dead.

Afterward, Telemont nodded, and backed away. "My thanks, Lord of Cania. You are free."

The Most High gestured and the shackles opened, though the chains remained near Mephistopheles, ready to re-bind him should he do ought but leave. Power sizzled in the air around the archfiend. The shadows in the room darkened.

The archfiend began to fade. Before he did, he pointed a finger at Brennus.

"You wish to know the name of he who murdered your mother?"

"My Lord!" Hadrhune said, stepping forward.

Telemont gestured as if to cast a spell but did not complete it in time.

"Your brother," Mephistopheles said. "Rivalen Tanthul murdered your mother to seal a pact with Shar."

With that, the archfiend vanished in a cloud of smoke and brimstone.

Silence expanded to fill the room. The dead or nearly dead archwizard made wet sounds.

Jumbled thoughts bounced around inside Brennus's skull. The shadows around him whirled and spun in response. He grabbed hold of the thought that Mephistopheles was a liar, that he had, in fact, lied. But the archfiend would also know that Brennus could use his spells to determine the truth of the claim.

Why lie, then?

Hadrhune breezed past Brennus to Telemont. "He says nothing out of pique, my lord. He plans to seize the power, too. This complicates matters."

Telemont nodded. "It does. But we must trust in the Lady, Hadrhune. Events will be what they will be."

Brennus could not understand his father's indifference to the fiend's words.

"Did you hear his accusation, Most High?"

Telemont shared a look with Hadrhune, with his arch-wizards. The latter bowed and vanished into the shadows after teleporting the gore of their fellow from the room.

The Most High and Hadrhune turned to face Brennus and their somber expressions told Brennus all he needed to know.

It was true. Rivalen had murdered his mother.

And his father had known.

"You knew?"

The Most High looked away and Brennus flew at his father. Hadrhune interposed himself but Telemont moved him aside with a hand. Brennus grabbed his father by the cloak, shook him, stared into the thin, dark face. The light of his platinum eyes did nothing to illuminate the blackness in the hollows of his cheeks, the circles under his eyes.

"You knew and did nothing? For how long? For how long?"

The tears wetting Brennus's face embarrassed him but he could not stop their flow. The betrayal drained him of strength. He released his father.

Hadrhune said, "The Most High learned of it long after—"

"I asked you nothing, lackey!" Brennus spat. "This is a family matter."

Hadrhune's eyes flashed but he inclined his head and took a step back.

Telemont put a thin hand on Brennus's arm. "Shar revealed it to me more than a century after the enclave fled Karsus's Folly for the Plane of Shadow."

"Shar?"

Telemont nodded. "And in doing so she forbade my punishing him." He shook his head. The darkness around him roiled like boiling water. "But I do not know if I would have even if she had allowed it. By then, Rivalen had proven himself invaluable to me, to us. He headed her church and her church preserved our people in those darkest of days in the Plane of Shadow. We owe him much, Brennus."

Brennus remembered well the war with the malaugrym, the constant challenges facing the enclave after the Fall. But none of it justified what his father had done.

"To the Hells with her church, her faith. She is the reason my mother is dead."

"She saved our city and people when the other enclaves fell from the sky. Through her a new Netheril will be born on Faerûn. Matters are . . . complicated, Brennus."

"Complicated? Complicated? My mother is dead. Your wife."

Anger fired Telamont's eyes and Brennus knew he had gone too far. Telemont grabbed Brennus, shook him with a strength that should not have been contained in his thin body.

"I know the price I pay for this, boy! Do not think to lecture me on grief! You are a child in such matters!"

Brennus stared into his father's face, his mouth open but wordless.

Telemont released him, regained control. "Forgive me, Brennus."

Brennus knew he would not. He tried to understand, but could not. "Rivalen should be made to pay."

The shadows around Telemont churned. "He will."

"How? You would allow him to become a god. He will be beyond our ability to punish if he succeeds."

"The power he seeks, once gained, is punishment enough."

"I do not understand."

"You would not. But I have looked into the void, Brennus. I stand on its edge each day but do not enter. Rivalen will embrace it and live with it the rest of his existence."

"It is not enough. He murdered my mother."

"What is enough is not for you to say. You will obey me in this as in all things. Assist Rivalen as you have been. He loves you, Brennus, in his way, considers you as much friend as brother. But he cannot know that I know. Not ever. And if you betray me in this, I will kill you."

Brennus looked into his father's eyes and knew he spoke truth. He did not give his father the satisfaction of more tears.

"You are not a man, Father."

Telemont regarded him with an odd expression, both sad and defiant. "No. Not for a long time, Brennus."

"All this for empire, Most High?"

Telemont looked puzzled at the question. "What else is there?"

# CHAPTER SEVEN

Cale and Riven took a meal with Abelar, Regg, and Endren then assisted the refugees with their preparations. Meanwhile, the sun continued its westward course across Faerûn's sky and by late afternoon it broke out of the leading edge of the Shadowstorm like it was newly born. Light penetrated the rain cloud and blanketed the refugees' camp. Spirits visibly lifted as the refugees went about their work. Cale stood in the light, his hand disincorporated, his powers diminished, and tried to feel human.

The rest of the Lathanderians moved among the refugees, assisting and encouraging them. Abelar, Endren, and Elden prepared a covered wagon for their transport. Regg approached, sloshing through the muck, the rose on his chest mud-spattered.

"The scouts report no sign of Forrin's army," Regg said to Abelar. "The entire force has vanished."

Cale looked out at the expanding, lightning-veined blackness of the Shadowstorm and guessed at what had happened to them.

"Darkness eats its own," said Abelar. "The storm has them, I'd wager."

"Agreed," said Regg. "I only regret that we were not able to avenge their attack on Saerb ourselves."

"Aye," Abelar said, and loaded a pack into the wagon. Elden climbed over barrels and bags, whooping as some tipped and he rode them down.

"Be mindful, Elden," Abelar said, and Elden paid him no heed whatsoever.

Regg said, "The camp is prepared, Abelar. I have Swiftdawn ready for you."

Abelar looked in the wagon to Elden, back to Regg. "I will ride in the wagon for a time, Regg."

Regg kept his face expressionless, though his body stiffened some. "Well enough."

"Our paths part here," Cale said. He embraced Abelar and Endren then clasped Regg's hand. Riven did the same.

"We will see you again in Daerlun," Abelar said.

"In Daerlun," Cale agreed.

Riven peeked into the wagon. "You show me what you can do with those balls when I see you again, yes?"

"Yes," Elden peeped.

Riven returned to Cale's side. Cale stood in Riven's shadow, intensified the darkness, stared at the distant Shadowstorm, and felt for the shadows within it. Strangely, the contact eluded him. As it had been with Elgrin Fau, the darkness in the storm did not answer to him easily.

He felt instead for the edge of the storm, the point at which his ability to feel the correspondence ended. As the darkness closed on them, he heard Abelar call to them, "Good hunting."

"Aye, that," said Regg.

The shadows transported them across Sembia, to the edge of the Shadowstorm.

Brennus sat at his dining table. His mother looked down on him from her portrait and he saw accusations in her eyes. He took her necklace from his pocket and set it on the table. Shadows poured from him. Grief poured from him. He had lost his mother and been betrayed by his brother and his father. He had heard the truth only from an archfiend.

His homunculi sat on the table facing him, their legs crossed, their chins in their palms.

"You sad, Master?" one of them asked.

Brennus reached out and scratched the creature's head, eliciting a growl of pleasure. The other, jealous, inched over to receive a scratching of his own. The creatures made him smile, made him think of his mother.

"I wish she could have seen you two," he said.

His constructs had amused her endlessly. The homunculi were simple creations for him now, hardly representative of his Art, but their antics would have brought her delight.

"They are wondrous, Brennus," she would have said in her clear voice, and he would have beamed.

His memories of her were so clear. It seemed only a day since he had last spoken with her, not two millennia. For some reason, he associated her memory with sunlight. He was pleased she had not lived to flee to the Plane of Shadow with them. She had been too bright for it.

He did not understand his father, nor did he forgive him. Shar had demanded the sacrifice of his mother's body. Now his father demanded that Brennus sacrifice his memory of her, poison it with inaction.

He could not do it. He would not.

He drew the darkness to him and pictured his makeshift quarters on Sakkors, now hovering over northern Sembia, and rode the shadows there.

Cale and Riven materialized at the edge of the storm. Rain poured from the pitch above, softening the ground, soaking their clothes, chilling their bones. Green lightning split the sky, cast the air in smears of vermillion and black. The wind gusted and swirled. Dead and dying vegetation covered the darkened plains before them. Trees shook in the wind, their twisted forms testament to the transformative powers of the Shadowstorm. The leading edge of the storm pulsed and lurched grotesquely as it shrouded the land.

The mental connection between Cale and Magadon flew open, startling him.

*He is in there, Cale*, Magadon said in his mind.

Cale nodded. He tried again to feel the correspondence between where he stood and the darkness within the Shadowstorm. The feeling was there, but it was distant, alien. The darkness in the storm was foreign to him. His inability to connect to it fully struck him oddly. It had been a long while since he had not been one with the darkness. It made him feel more himself.

"Ready?" Cale said to Riven.

The assassin fiddled with the teleportation ring on his finger. "We could use the ring, Cale. Go directly to Ordulin."

Cale shook his head. "We do not know what we will find there. Things would get ugly if we appeared in the midst of a score of shadow giants."

"Ugly for them," Riven said.

"We can cover ground less rapidly by stepping from shadow to shadow, but we'll at least see what we're in for before appearing neck deep in it."

Riven inclined his head. "That's sense."

"Let's move," Cale said.

"No need," Riven replied.

The leading edge of the Shadowstorm lunged forward like a predator, covering them in its darkness. Sound deadened. Color faded. It was as if a veil had been drawn across the land, as if they had been submerged in murky water.

"The air is different than last time," Riven said.

As if to make his point, the grass under their feet curled, browned, withered, and died. Trees and shrubs near them cracked and split as the Shadowstorm remade them into twisted, thorny versions of themselves.

Cale nodded. "It's getting more powerful as it grows."

The air in the Shadowstorm felt charged, powerful. The coolness seeped into Cale, pulled at his warmth, at his essence. They would need protective wards or they would soon be drained of warmth and strength.

"Hold a moment."

He held his mask and intoned the words to a prayer of protection. When he finished, he touched a hand to himself then to Riven. He felt its effect instantly as the Shadowstorm released its hold on his essence.

"Better," Riven said.

"It will last for a few hours," Cale said. He followed with the words to a prayer that would ward him and Riven against the chill. When he completed the spell, he let the warmth of the magic flow into him, touched Riven's arm, and did the same.

"Best be moving," Riven said.

Cale nodded and chose a spot within the Shadowstorm at the limits of his vision, a rise under a deformed oak. He stepped through the darkness and they appeared under the oak. The gusting wind drove the rain so hard it felt like a hail of nails. Lightning lit the transformed landscape. Thunder rumbled.

"Which way?" Riven asked.

"East until we reach the Dawnpost road. We take it all the way to Ordulin."

Riven nodded. "Which way is east?"

*Magadon?* Cale sent.

*Cale?*

*We need to head east, but we can see nothing in the storm.*

Cale felt a twinge in his mind, as if Magadon had pinched his brain.

*Turn an arc*, Magadon said. *You will feel it as a pull.*

Cale looked out across the Sembian plains, the sea of dead grass, the skeletal shapes of deformed trees. He pivoted his body, felt a pull at a certain point.

*I feel it.*

*That is east.*

Only after they had started moving again did it register with Cale that Magadon had used his powers through their connection. He had not known Magadon would be able to do so through an ordinary mindlink. Then it occurred to him that Magadon might have linked them with something other than an ordinary mindlink.

*Mags . . . ?*

*Cale?*

Cale could think of no way to ask the question without it coming across as an accusation. *Forget it.*

*Hurry, Cale*, Magadon said, and the connection went quiet.

Together, Cale and Riven shadowstepped through the storm. They covered a bowshot at a stride and the leagues fell behind them. The storm worsened as they penetrated farther into it.

Swarms of shadows thronged the darkness, on the ground, in the air. They flocked in groups numbering as few as a score to gatherings in the hundreds. There seemed no end of them. When Cale and Riven saw the red eyes of the undead break the otherwise uniform blackness of the air, usually they simply sheltered under trees, boulders, or shrubs, and blended into the shadows. Other times they shadowstepped past or around the creatures. They were an island within an ocean of the creatures. Cale did not know how long they could go undetected. One slip would be all it took.

"Stay sharp," he said. Fatigue would take its toll on Riven before it would him.

"Do not worry over that. No giants, yet."

"Not yet," Cale said.

A few hours in, they stepped into a copse of twisted larch. The limbs of the trees, jutting at odd angles, reminded Cale of mace-broken bones. The needles hissed in the rain and wind, whispered indecipherable threats in ominous tones. Cale looked out of the copse and stared out into the storm.

"What in the Hells?"

Riven stepped to his side. "What is it?"

"Bodies."

A long bowshot before them, the remains of a battle littered the plains. Bodies, weapons, and shields lay scattered over the ground.

Cale eyed the immediate area, the sky, and saw no sign of any shadows. He wrapped the darkness around him and Riven and shadowstepped to the battlefield.

Desiccated bodies dotted the plains. They looked like skeletons wrapped tightly in flesh. None showed any wounds from weapons. Horse carcasses, too, lay scattered across the grass, their abdomens bloated, ready to burst.

"Shadows did this," Cale said, and Riven nodded.

Shrunken, withered faces stared out of helms and mail coifs, the sunken eye sockets as black as the sky. Lips drawn back by tightening skin offered them mocking smiles. Skeletal hands still clutched blades or crossbows. The soldiers wore rain-soaked tabards that featured the golden wheel of Ordulin. The Shadowstorm had already started to drain the color from them.

"The overmistress's army," Riven said, lifting one of the tabards with a blade.

Cale nodded.

They walked the carnage for a time. The bodies of horses and men covered a wide area, faced his way and that. The battle appeared to have been a confused affair.

"Look," Riven said, and pointed past Cale with a saber.

Cale turned and saw a single horse standing on the battlefield. It appeared so unlikely that Cale thought it the leftover remnant of a spell, or a hallucination.

"How can that be?"

He and Riven hurried toward the creature, but slowed as they neared. The horse was real enough.

"It's all right," Cale said, but sounded insincere. He had never been comfortable around horses.

Riven whickered, approached more assuredly. "Steady, girl. Steady."

The horse—a muscular brown mare—stood on three legs over a corpse, perhaps that of its rider. It held its other leg off the ground, bent at the knee, and Cale saw a shard of bone sticking through the flesh above the hoof. The horse trembled with cold, with terror, with woundshock. Wild eyes watched them approach. It snorted, shifted on its feet, stumbled, and nearly fell.

"Steady," Riven said in a calm tone. "Steady, now."

The assassin moved forward slowly, took the horse by the reins. He rubbed its neck and nose, making soothing noises. The horse blew out an exhalation and its trembling subsided somewhat.

"She should not be alive," Cale said. Curious, he cast a minor spell that allowed him to see dweomers. The horse's saddle glowed a faint red in his sight.

"Saddle is enchanted. It must shield her from the effects of the storm."

"Tymora smiled on you," Riven said to the mare. He kneeled, eyed the fracture just above the fetlock. The mare eyed him warily.

"She needs to be put down," Riven said.

"We could heal her."

Riven shook his head. "Then what? There are shadows everywhere. Better to die by the blade than those things."

"They haven't bothered her yet."

Riven considered, shook his head. "No. She's freezing. And how will she find her way?"

Cale felt his anger rising, but could not articulate why. "I can shield her against the cold. And animals find their way. Give him a chance, Riven. You are too damned ready to put down whatever you cannot save for certain."

Riven stood, eyed him through the rain. "Him? Are we still talking about a horse?"

Cale realized that he was not and he understood his anger. He calmed himself. "A chance. Yes?"

Riven relented, shrugged. "Well enough." He pulled darkness around his hands, used it to gently wrap the horse's leg, temporarily hiding the fracture. The horse whinnied, and Riven jumped back to avoid a kick. When the shadows dissipated, the wound was healed. The mare put her weight on the leg, gently at first, then more confidently.

Cale approached her from the side, whispering soothing words. He placed a hand on her flank and intoned the words to a spell that would ward her from cold, at least for a few hours.

Riven faced her in the direction they had come and removed her bit. He smacked her on the flank and shouted. She neighed and bolted away at a dead run. Cale wished her well. They watched her until she vanished into the darkness and rain.

"She's got a chance," Cale said.

"Maybe," answered Riven.

"So does Mags," Cale said.

"Maybe."

They stared at each other a long moment before the roll of thunder ended the moment.

"Let's keep moving," Cale said.

Magadon's voice sounded in Cale's head. *How close are you, Cale? Matters are . . . difficult for me here.*

*We're moving fast, Mags. Not long now.*

Still dodging red-eyed shadows, Cale and Riven made their way east over the dead landscape. Soon they reached the Dawnpost. The winding, packed earth ribbon of the road stretched east, impaling the darkness. Marker stones lined its length at intervals. They reminded Cale of grave markers.

Using the darkness as stepping stones, they ate up the leagues. The storm continued to worsen as they moved toward Ordulin. The landscape itself grew more and more like the Plane of Shadow—drained of color, twisted, cold.

Wagons and carts stood abandoned along the Dawnpost here and there. Dried out corpses or animal carcasses sometimes lay near the deserted vehicles. They checked for survivors, found none, and kept moving.

Ahead, the land started to drop away, sinking toward the River Arkhen. The Dawnpost led toward a cluster of buildings that crowded the river's banks. A mid-sized stone wall enclosed the center of the town, but dozens of buildings appeared to have spilled outside the wall. Most were one story and composed of mortared river stones, but a few two and three story structures deeper in the town peeked over the walls—the villas of the rich.

"Archenbridge," Cale said.

Cale had been to Archenbridge only once, years before, escorting Thamalon while the Old Owl negotiated a caravan contract. That day seemed to have happened a hundred years before, on another world.

The town appeared abandoned. Cale hoped the inhabitants had fled north into the Dales and not been caught up in the storm. He picked the next spot into which he would shadow-step when movement drew his eye. He put a hand on Riven's arm, pointed.

Four shadow giants appeared, walking the streets of the town outside the walls. They ducked through doors and shouted to one another over the thunder. Mail shirts covered their muscular, stooped forms and shadows bled from their pale flesh.

One of the giants emerged from a building with a chest in his hands. He shook it, grinned, and shouted to his companions. The other three giants materialized from the shadows near their fellow, one of them bearing another chest. The giants tossed both chests to the street and they broke open, spilling coins. The giants crouched down on their haunches and set to counting, speaking amongst themselves.

"Looting," Riven said.

Cale nodded. Greed was universal, he supposed.

Riven looked over at Cale. "Storm seems not to affect them. They warded, too?"

Cale doubted it. "They are native to the Calyx. Maybe that renders them immune."

"Well, they aren't native to Sembia," Riven said. "And if they're the only four. . . ."

"Risky," Cale said, and studied the buildings and streets nearby. He saw no other giants, no shadows. "But doable, though none can escape."

"None will."

"I've got the two on our left."

Riven nodded. "Well enough. I'll use the ring. On a three count. One, two, three."

Cale stepped through the shadows, appeared behind one of the crouching giants, and drove Weaveshear through the creature's throat. Blood spattered the giant's comrades, and scattered the coins. Shadows exploded from the giant's form. The towering creature tried to stand but collapsed before getting out of its crouch. Cale jerked Weaveshear free.

Riven appeared behind the giant across from Cale and put a sabre into the creature's back. It started to stand, roared, and turned. Riven slit its throat before it gained its feet and it fell, bleeding, leaking shadows and gurgling.

The other two giants lurched to their feet, scattering coins, and pulled their blades, but Cale and Riven were already upon them. With one saber Riven deflected a wild stab by a giant, with the other he opened a gash in the creature's chest. The giant stumbled backward, slipped in the mud, and fell. Riven drove both sabers through its chest and heart.

Cale lunged forward at the last giant, feinted low, drew the creature off balance, and drove Weaveshear through its mail and into its gut. He jerked the blade free as the giant roared with pain, bent double. A two handed slash to the exposed neck separated its head from its body. Weaveshear leaked blood and shadows.

Riven and Cale went back to back as the corpses spasmed, watching the darkness for more giants, shadows, anything.

"Nothing," Cale said.

"Nothing," agreed Riven.

Both relaxed.

Riven spit on the corpses and said, "We keep moving."

The rain had already washed most of the giants' blood into the ground, but did nothing to clean the earth of the invasion the giants represented.

"We walk through the town, first," Cale said. "Ensure there are no survivors. Besides, someone needs to bear witness to this."

"Yes," Riven said, wiping his blades clean on a giant's trousers.

They left the corpses of the giants behind them and walked the streets of Archenbridge. Shutters and open doors banged open and closed in the wind. Murky water overflowed catch barrels and horse troughs. Plazas stood empty, forlorn, haunted only by the past.

Hints of a rapid evacuation littered the streets—loose sacks lay strewn about. Stacked barrels, coffers, chairs, divans, and other household furnishings had been left outside on the walks but never loaded onto carts, all of it a testament to lives disturbed, changed forever. A cooking pan lay half submerged in the mud of the street; Cale could not take his eyes from it.

They found no survivors but also no human bodies, though the carcasses of dogs and cats haunted doorways, curled up as if the creatures had fallen asleep and never awakened. Perhaps they had scratched at the doors for owners long departed before the life-draining storm had finally taken them.

Riven noted each dead dog, his eye hard, and Cale imagined him keeping a count in his mind, a ledger for which he would ultimately hold Kesson Rel to account.

The buildings of Archenbridge struck Cale in a way that the twisted plains had not, in a way that the bodies back on the Dawnpost had not. The empty structures represented not just a loss of life, but the loss of a way of life. The areas affected by the Shadowstorm would never be the same. Emerging from the wind and rain and darkness like the gravestones of titans, the buildings seemed like monuments to a lost world. By the time they reached the edge of the town and the graceful stone arch that spanned the Arkhen, Cale felt exhausted. Archenbridge was Sembia, was all of Faerûn, if they did not stop the storm. The realization weighed on him.

They passed the bridge's toll gate and walked the arch side by side, saying nothing. The churn from the storm had turned the Arkhen's waters brown. They seethed under the rain's onslaught. Hundreds of dead fish floated in the current, gathered in the shallows.

Halfway across the bridge, a flutter in Cale's stomach stopped him. His mouth went dry and he found it hard to breathe. The shadows around him roiled.

"Feel that," he said to Riven.

Riven tried to speak but failed, and nodded instead.

Both of them slid their blades free and sank into the darkness on one side of the bridge. With an effort of will, Cale deepened the shadows around them.

"Kesson?" Riven asked.

Cale shook his head. He didn't know.

The dread grew palpable, thicker and more oppressive than the rain. It weighed on Cale's chest, stole his breath, and set his heart to racing. Shadows boiled from him, from Weaveshear. Beside him, Riven looked as tense as a bowstring.

*What in the Nine Hells is causing that?* Riven signed with a shaking hand.

Both of them peered out over the bridge, across the water, into the darkness. Even with his shadesight, the rain prevented Cale from seeing much on the other side of the river.

The dread intensified, rooted in Cale's mind. Tremors shook him. He stared across the river for the source, unable to move, unable to blink. He knew it was supernatural fear, that he had to fight it, but it overwhelmed his will.

A barrage of lightning flashed in the distance and Cale saw the source of his feeling, saw its silhouette framed for an instant by the sickly vermillion of the lightning bolts.

"Gods," Cale said.

In form it had the shape of a man, but stood as tall as three shadow giants, looming over even the tallest buildings in

Archenbridge. The blackness that composed its immense body was more than mere darkness; it was a hole, the night brought to life. Cale knew it was not Kesson Rel. It was instead the embodiment of fear, terror made manifest.

It stalked silently along the riverbank with the slow, methodical stride of a predator that had nothing to fear from other creatures. Supernatural terror leaked from it the way shadows leaked from Cale.

Cale held his breath as the creature paused before the bridge. It turned a featureless black face toward Archendale. Its head bobbed as if it were sniffing for spoor.

*Prepare yourself,* Cale signed to Riven, and the prospect of a battle helped clear his mind. His heart slowed. His breath came easier. He put both hands on Weaveshear's hilt, and readied himself.

The creature put a foot on the bridge, seemed to think better of it, and turned and continued its path along the riverbank. Cale and Riven watched in relieved silence until it disappeared into the darkness.

"Dark and empty," Riven said.

Cale agreed. There were darker things stalking the Shadowstorm than mere shadows and giants.

"We need to get to Ordulin," he said.

# CHAPTER EIGHT

*4 Nightal, the Year of Lightning Storms*

Following the road, avoiding shadows and an increasing number of shadow giants, they made their way east toward Ordulin. The land became bleaker as they neared the provenance of the storm. Trees, grass, and shrubs had not been merely twisted, but many of them had been transformed entirely by the planar influx. Oaks and elms had been changed to black-barked trees with fat, spade shaped leaves. In place of larch there stood thin conifers with warty trunks and black needles. Malformed animals stalked the plains. Shadows dripped from the creatures' mangy fur and they skulked away with growls and howls when Cale and Riven materialized in their midst. Some might have once been raccoons or foxes, but Cale could not tell for certain.

"It is like the Plane of Shadow," Riven said, and Cale nodded.

They passed a road marker stuck in the embankment along the Dawnpost. It told them Ordulin was two days by wagon. The marker struck Cale as ridiculous, the artifact of an ancient, lost civilization. An abandoned horse cart lay in a ditch not far from it.

"How much farther?" Riven asked above the wind and thunder. The assassin could not read.

Cale estimated the time, based on the speed they had been moving.

"Two days by wagon. That puts us hours away."

The assassin nodded, and glanced back the way they had come. "I wonder if she got out."

At first Cale didn't know what Riven was talking about. "The mare?"

Riven nodded.

"She got out," Cale said, and thumped Riven on the shoulder. "Let's move."

Patrols of shadow giants grew more frequent, but they avoided them as they had been, and ate up the miles until they reached their destination.

Several bowshots away, Ordulin rose from the plains. Even from afar, Cale could see the black spike of Kesson Rel's spire hovering over the center of the city, as if about to stab it through the heart. A continuous onslaught of green lightning bolts shot out of the churning sky and struck the top of the spire. With each strike, a tremulous line of energy raced along the spire's length, from top to bottom, as if the spike were a conduit for the power, directing it to something or somewhere beneath it.

"Ordulin," Cale said.

Even in the steady illumination from the continuous lightning, the walls and buildings of the city looked like featureless rectangles of black, shadowy tombstones marking the deaths of tens of thousands. Darting clots of black plagued the sky around the city, around Kesson's tower.

Shadows. Thousands of them.

A great, swirling column of shadows spiraled around the tower for a moment, then perched on its side. A boom of thunder dislodged them, sending them spiraling into the air again.

"He will be in the tower," Riven said. "Has to be."

Cale nodded. "We need to get in and get out. Unless his death will destroy the shadows, we can't linger."

"We find him. We kill him. We leave."

Cale drew the darkness around them, chose a tall building within Ordulin's walls not too far from Kesson's tower, and rode the shadows there. They materialized on the flat roof of what once had been a two story storehouse.

The wind and rain died. Ordulin sat dry, dark, and still in the eye of the Shadowstorm. After hours in the violent weather, the calm unnerved Cale. Everything seemed too loud, even his breath.

Energy suffused the air, drew up the hairs on his arms, and caused his skin to tingle. The lightning striking Kesson's spire seasoned the air with the tang of acrid smoke. Calle moved forward to the edge of the building to see what was beneath the tower. Riven followed.

"Dark," Cale said.

The rings of power traversing the spire fed a black void beneath its bottom. The hole yawned in the center of the plaza, a doorway into an abyss of darkness. The spire discharged the energy of the lightning into the void and with each pulse of power the void's edges trembled, expanded incrementally. And as it grew larger, it devoured whatever its edges touched.

Cale looked into the hole and saw in it Shar's will. Its emptiness made him nauseous, caused his temples to throb. Beside him, Riven heaved, vomited over the side of the building, and cursed.

Above, the clouds turned as one in a slow maelstrom around the black, lightning-streaked hole of the planar rift. Kesson's tower was the axle connecting the hole in the sky to the hole in the world. Shadows poured from the rift and fed the churning, expanding clouds of the Shadowstorm.

Around them, as far as they could see, the rest of Ordulin lay in ruins, a burst pustule of stone, wood, and flesh. The energies unleashed when Kesson Rel had opened the planar rift had caused otherwise solid substances to run like candle wax. Some of the buildings, rendered unstable by their deformities, had collapsed. Piles of rubble pockmarked the city's streets. Cale saw corpses everywhere, barely recognizable lumps of melted flesh and bone. Many bodies had run together with the stone or wood, creating grotesque amalgamations. Spheres of impenetrable darkness about the size of wagon wheels floated here and there. Several sections of the city's stone wall had collapsed and large cracks veined them where they still stood.

"We gear up," Cale said softly.

Riven spat, nodded.

Cale cast a series of spells that increased his speed, his strength, warded both he and Riven against fire and lightning. Riven held forth his blades and asked Mask to empower them. The Shadowlord answered and the blades oozed shadows. Cale spoke the words to a spell that infused him with divine vitality, and the spell increased his size half again, making him stronger still.

"We hit him hard and fast," Cale said.

"Hard and fast," Riven echoed, bouncing on the balls of his feet.

Cale pulled the shadows around them and stepped from roof to alley to roof to roof, hopping across the city. The spire grew ever larger in their vision and they kept their eyes from the ruined bodies that dotted the streets and buildings around and below them. Cale could not see the growing void under the tower from their vantage atop a single story building, but he could feel it, a wobble in the rhythm of the world.

As they closed on the tower, Cale noticed the handful of metal balconies and archways that opened in its sides, apertures to a deeper darkness.

In the air above them, shadows streaked past. Cale kept the darkness close around them and they went unnoticed in Ordulin's gloom.

Kesson Rel felt the arrival of the Chosen of Mask, a faint tremor in the web of shadows that blanketed Ordulin. The divinity within him allowed him to feel the shadows within the city as if they were an extension of his body.

"What is it, Divine One?" asked Gobitran. The gnome toyed with her necklace of eyes with one hand. With the other, she pawed at his leather robe, fawned in his darkness.

"The Shadowlord's Chosen have come," he said.

She hissed with anger and remembered pain. The Shadowlord's Chosen had nearly killed her when they had entered the spire back on the Plane of Shadow, when Kesson had tricked them into freeing his essence from Furlinastis's shroud.

"What do we do?" she said, her voice a slightly higher pitch than usual.

"Kill them," he said.

He left off his dark pondering and strode for the nearest archway, Shar's power sizzling in his left fist, arcane energies bursting from his right.

Crouched in the darkness, Cale and Riven saw Kesson emerge from an archway halfway up the spire and step onto a balcony. Hundreds of shadows launched themselves from the sides of the tower and swarmed toward him.

"Do not move," Cale said. He deepened the darkness around them.

Kesson put his hands to the balcony's rail and leaned over. His gaze swept the city, and stopped when it was fixed on Cale and Riven.

Cale felt Kesson's regard like twin dagger stabs. He stood, and let the shadows fall away.

"He knows we're here. Ready yourself."

Riven cursed, stood.

Kesson leaped over the edge of the balcony, beat his wings, and launched himself into the air. The shadows fell in around him, a black tide swirling in his wake. The darkness around him crackled with power. A net of lightning lit the sky, struck the tower, and fed the hole. Distant thunder rumbled.

"Use the ring," Cale said, the shadows around him whirling. "You're left. Hard and fast."

Riven understood his meaning right away, and nodded.

"Return to this spot," Cale said.

Riven looked around to fix the location in his mind, whirled his blades, and said, "Go."

Cale and Riven leaped off the building. Cale stepped through the shadows and appeared in mid-air to one side of Kesson. Riven, using his teleportation ring, appeared on the other.

Cale stabbed with Weaveshear as he started to fall. A ward flashed yellow around Kesson and Cale felt as if he were trying to drive the blade through iron. The recoil from the impact set Cale spinning as he plummeted to the ground.

He heard Riven's sabers ring, heard the assassin curse, and heard Kesson speaking words of power.

Tumbling out of control, he plummeted through one undead shadow after another. The wards that had protected him against the life draining energy of the Shadowstorm also protected him from the negative energy of the shadows, but he felt their cold as his body passed through them. He caught alternating, disorienting glimpses of the city below, the tower, Kesson, the city again.

He concentrated on the darkness, felt it around him, and rode it to the top of the building from which he and Riven had leaped. Riven appeared next to him in almost the same instant.

Both looked up to see Kesson Rel streaking toward them, arms outstretched. Four fist-sized balls of flame exploded from his right hand and roared toward the building. From his left, a line of fire streaked toward them.

Cale and Riven cursed, and dived in opposite directions. Neither the balls of fire nor the jet of flame hit either of them directly but the spells slammed into the rooftop and it exploded in flame. The power behind the flames burned through Cale's protective ward and the inherent resistance of his body to magic, and seared his flesh. He felt it blister, char. He screamed, and heard Riven doing the same. Shadows coalesced around him as his regenerative flesh began to heal the damage.

Meanwhile, the impact from the spells shook the already unstable building. It groaned under Cale's feet and rumbled with the beginnings of a collapse.

Cale jumped up, clothes smoking, and sped toward Riven while the burning building cracked apart under them. Red-eyed shadows swarmed around him, reaching for him, through him, but his wards shielded him from their touch. He channeled Mask's divine power as he ran and it exploded outward from him, obliterated half a dozen shadows, and caused another handful to flee.

Riven sprung to his feet, his cloak and face blackened by flames, blades and body spinning a deadly circle. His enchanted sabers sent shadows boiling away into oblivion. He saw Cale, looked past him, pointed with one of his blades behind him, his one eye wide.

"Cale!"

Cale whirled and looked back just in time to see Kesson hovering over the burning rooftop. A forked bolt of green lightning shot from his right palm, while he empowered himself with energy from his left. The fork of lightning split halfway to Cale and sent separate bolts at Riven and Cale.

Cale lurched sideways while interposing Weaveshear. The bolt struck the blade but Weaveshear did not absorb the magic, merely deflected it, bleeding shadows, and drove it sizzling into the already burning rooftop. A cloud of splinters shot into the sky. The other bolt hit Riven in the thigh and sent him spinning, knocking him prone. Shadows swarmed him. If not for Cale's ward, Riven would have been dead. The assassin recovered almost instantly and even from the ground his blades stabbed and slashed. Shadows keened and died.

Cale ignored the shadows harassing him and intoned the words to a spell as he hurried to Riven's side. In answer to his words, a column of flame formed in the air above Kesson and bathed the First Chosen of Mask in searing orange fire. The heat and flame washed over Kesson to no visible effect. He beat his wings, smiled a mouthful of fangs, and rapidly intoned another spell.

"We go at him again," Cale said, and started to draw the darkness around them.

Kesson completed his spell before Cale could transport them and Cale felt the magic turn Weaveshear's hilt warm, felt the buckles on his armor and scabbard start to heat up, but the magic resistant shadowstuff that composed his form resisted the spell and the metal returned to normal temperature.

"We need to bring him out of the air," Riven said, sheathing his sabers. Thin streams of smoke issued from his belt, several places on his cloak, and his scabbard. He was not resistant to Kesson's spell and his metal gear was growing hot.

Cale took his point, and sheathed Weaveshear. He grabbed

hold of Riven's cloak and they stepped through the shadows to appear again beside Kesson Rel.

Darkness met darkness.

Cale grabbed Kesson around the waist and tried to bring him down with his weight. He tried to get a hand on a wing, hold it still, but could not. Riven grabbed one of Kesson's arms, and wrapped one of Kesson's legs with his own.

"You have not the strength," Kesson said, wings beating rapidly as he incanted another spell.

"We'll see, bastard," Riven said, and freed one hand to retrieve one of his punch daggers. Meanwhile, Cale began his own spell.

Shadows whirled all around them, keening, reaching for them, into them, but Cale's ward held. Still, it would not resist the onslaught much longer.

Kesson finished his spell first and a blast of unholy energy went out from his body in all directions. As it passed through Cale, it tore open wounds in his flesh, hammered organs, loosened teeth. Cale tasted blood but endured the pain and kept the thread of his own spell.

Riven screamed, spraying spit, blood, and at least one tooth as the energy of Kesson's spell tore open his skin and ripped at his body. The assassin lost the grip of his legs on Kesson but swung them back into place before he fell. He pulled a punch dagger from a sheath at his back and drove it into Kesson's stomach, once, twice, again, again. The hilt of the dagger smoked in Riven's hand and the assassin screamed, but whether with rage or pain Cale could not tell.

Kesson winced, grunting with each blow Riven dealt him. The beat of his wings slowed and they started to descend. Hope rose in Cale and he finished his spell. Dark power gathered in his hands, already gripping Kesson's robes. He let it flow through him to Kesson but it was as if the spell had struck a wall. Kesson's body resisted magic, the same as Cale's.

Cale cursed and reached for a dagger as his regenerative flesh worked to heal the damage he had suffered, closing gashes, repairing organs. Kesson's flesh did the same where Riven had stabbed him.

The First Chosen of Mask steadied himself in flight, nearly shook Cale and Riven loose, and held his position in the air. They were not going to ground.

Kesson began another spell.

Riven, his clothes and armor smoking, stained dark with blood, reared back for another blow, but the punch dagger glowed red hot in his hand. He screamed and dropped it. His clothes caught fire where other metal implements on his person reached almost to their melting point—buckles, snaps, knives, caltrops. Cale could see the teleportation ring on Riven's finger glowing orange, could see the flesh around it turning black and curling. Riven screamed, a prolonged, stubborn wail of agony, but refused to release his grip on Kesson.

Cale grabbed at Riven, put a hand on him, and rode the shadows to a nearby rooftop.

The moment they appeared, Riven, roaring with pain, tore off or cut off the metal buckles, clips, and other items burning on his person. A rain of implements pattered on the rooftop. He tried to get the teleportation ring off his finger but could not grip it to pull it.

"Cale," he said through the pain, and held out his ring finger.

Cale drew one of his daggers, pried the ring loose from a finger that looked like a burned sausage. Riven hissed with agony. The ring, made malleable by the spell, split from the force of Cale's dagger.

"Damn it," Riven said, cradling his hand.

Cale hurriedly intoned a spell of healing, put his hands over Riven's, and let the energy flow into the assassin.

Riven winced as the wounds closed. "I put that dagger in his gut four times, Cale. I don't think I hurt him."

"My spells did nothing either," Cale said, and turned to scan the sky.

Kesson was gone. The shadows, too, were not in sight and their keening had fallen silent. Lightning lit the city.

Both men drew their larger blades. Shadows boiled from Cale's flesh.

"Where is he?" Riven said.

"Here," Kesson answered from behind them. His spell of invisibility ended when he put a clawed hand on each of them, and a surge of magical energy poured through Cale's resistance and into his flesh. The magic pulled at the wards and other spells that enhanced Cale's size, strength, and speed, ripping all of them away, and to judge from the sudden increase in Kesson's size, transfered them all to Kesson. Meanwhile, Riven screamed as baleful energy poured into his body, searing his flesh from the inside out.

Cale twisted free of Kesson's grasp and stabbed low with Weaveshear while Riven knocked Kesson's hand from him and slashed high with his sabers. But Kesson bounded backward with frightful, magic enhanced speed. The holy symbol of Shar he wore on a chain at his throat bounced with each beat of his wings.

Cale and Riven stalked after him but he backed off and kept his distance.

The keening of the shadows broke the silence behind them and Cale whirled to see hundreds of the creatures swarming toward them up from the ground, red eyes aglow.

His wards were gone. So were Riven's.

"We leave," Cale said.

Magadon's voice screamed in his head. *Do not leave, Cale. Do not. Kill him.*

Riven threw three daggers in rapid succession at Kesson's chest. All struck an invisible field of force around him and fell to the rooftop.

"My ring is gone," Riven said.

"You will not be allowed to leave, shade," Kesson said, and emitted a green beam from his eyes. Cale could not dodge it. It struck him, warred with the magic resistant shadowstuff in his body, overcame it, and haloed him in a soft green glow.

"Such paltry vessels the Shadowlord has chosen in this age," Kesson said.

The shadows closed from behind and Kesson stopped retreating. He intoned words of power, and darkness gathered in his hands.

Cale drew the darkness around Riven and himself, and imagined the point along the Dawnpost where they had seen the road marker for Ordulin. They could regroup, plan another attack . . .

He did not feel the correspondence.

Shadows leaked from his flesh, and mingled with the green glow of Kesson's spell. He tried to use the darkness to step through to a nearby alley, but felt nothing.

The shadows shrieked. The power grew in Kesson's hands. He strode toward them, half again as tall as Cale, fire in his black eyes.

"Cale?" Riven said, and twirled his blades, his gaze moving between Kesson and the onrushing shadows.

*Kill him, Cale,* Magadon projected. *You promised me!*

Cale ignored Magadon's pleas, felt around the edges of Kesson's spell, probed for weakness, found a spot, and tried to slip around the interference. The green light shrouding him winked out and he rode the shadows to the Dawnpost.

But instead of the Dawnpost, they instead appeared in the middle of one of Ordulin's streets, a short distance from the building on which they had stood moments before. The green glow reappeared, flashing intermittently.

The shadows thronged the top of the building, whirling around it in frustration. Kesson rose into their midst and eyed the area.

"What in the Hells, Cale?"

Kesson's gaze fell on them.

Cale shook his head. "His spell is affecting my abilities."

The shadows turned like a flock of birds on the wing and darted toward them. Kesson followed them, a great dark bird of prey with holes for eyes. The power in Kesson's hands formed black flames around his fists.

Cale and Riven sprinted for a nearby doorway, leaping rubble, dodging corpses.

Black fire exploded behind them, blew them off their feet, turned the rubble into projectiles. The fire seared Cale's flesh; shards of stone knifed into him.

He pulled Riven to his feet, the shadows around him swirling, and ran for the building.

*I cannot let you leave, Cale,* Magadon said. Cale felt a tingle in his limbs, suddenly felt separate from them.

Before he reached the building, Magadon stopped him, turned him around.

*Fight, Cale. Gods damn you to the Hells. There may not be another chance. And I am out of time.*

Riven grabbed Cale by the shoulder. "What are you doing? Come on!"

"It's Mags," Cale said through gritted teeth, and his body tried to shake free of Riven's grasp.

Riven cursed, kicked Cale behind his knee, knocked him down, and dragged him toward the nearby building.

"Let him go, Mags!" Riven shouted.

*Stop, Mags,* Cale said. *Stop. We will try again.*

He fought against Magadon's control, but the mindmage's hold was too strong.

*Mags, if you don't release me, Riven and I will die here, now.*

"Walls won't stop the shadows," Riven said, and plucked pieces of rock from the flesh of his face.

*Help me, Erevis,* Magadon said, and freed Cale's body.

*I will*, Cale said, but the connection went dormant and he was not sure that Magadon heard him.

He put it out of his mind and worked to get around Kesson's binding spell again.

The building started to shake. Beams of wood and slabs of rock fell from the ceiling.

"Cale," Riven said.

Outside, the keening of the shadows grew louder. Through an opening in the building's front, they saw a multitude of red eyes in a cloud of black forms.

"Cale!"

The ceiling groaned, and started to fall.

Cale again slipped Kesson's binding spell and the green glow flashed out for a moment. Once more Cale pictured the spot on the Dawnpost and rode the shadows away.

# CHAPTER NINE

*4 Nightal, the Year of Lightning Storms*

They materialized not along the Dawnpost but somewhere in the Shadowstorm. The echo of Magadon's rage and despair rang in Cale's mind like a temple bell. Rain thudded into their cloaks. Thunder rumbled. Flashes of green lightning illuminated the twisted landscape in ghastly glimpses. The Shadowstorm pawed at their unprotected souls, drained away their essence. Cale hurriedly intoned the words to the protective wards that shielded them from the life draining energy of the storm, touched a hand to himself, to Riven, and replaced what Kesson Rel had stolen.

"Dark and empty," Riven cursed. Smoke still rose from his charred armor. Blisters dotted the exposed skin of his seared arms and face. Slivers of rock were still embedded in the flesh of his cheeks and brow.

Cale shared the sentiment. The faint green glow of Kesson's spell flashed in and out, warring with the shadows that cloaked him. His regenerative flesh collected the darkness around him and filled his wounds with it. He winced as burns healed, gashes closed.

*You failed me, Cale,* Magadon said in his mind, and the calm pronouncement hit him as hard as a maul.

Cale was too tired to argue.

Moving gingerly, Riven spun a hand in the air, wrapped his fingers in shadows, and patted them into his wounds, the way he might a healing loam. The magic pulled the slivers of stone from his flesh, healed some of his blisters, but did not heal his wounds entirely. Cale placed his palms on him and intoned a healing spell to Mask. The assassin breathed easier, and nodded thanks.

"Where are we?" Riven asked, looking around.

Cale shook his head. "Not where I intended. This—" he indicated the intermittently flashing green glow around him— "interferes with my abilities even when I'm able to slip it."

Riven paced a circle, his hands on the hilts of his sabers. "He's more powerful than the Sojourner."

"Maybe," Cale said.

Riven stared into Cale's face, a look in his eyes, then he resumed pacing.

"Something you want to say?" Cale asked.

Riven stopped pacing and looked off into the darkness. "I don't know, Cale. I don't."

The sense of Riven's sentence echoed in Cale's head: *I don't know if we can stop Kesson Rel.*

"There has to be a way," Cale said.

*Oathbreaking bastard,* Magadon said in his mind.

Cale shook his head, as if he could shake Magadon loose from his thoughts. In handcant, he said to Riven, *Mags is almost gone.*

Riven stared at Cale a long while before he signaled back, *Then we keep our promise to him.*

"No." Cale shook his head. "No."

"You see another way?" Riven asked, then signed, *He almost killed us both.*

They stared at each other through the rain, the funeral of their friend suspended in the dark between them.

*What are you discussing?* Magadon asked.

*It's a mercy killing,* Riven signed.

Cale signed back, his gestures sharp and cutting. *For who? And we are not there yet.*

*Not yet,* Riven signed. *But soon. Get your head around it. He's a risk. We've seen what he can do. He's in your head, Cale. He took control of you.*

Cale could not deny it. Anger boiled up in him and he shouted it into the sky. "Dark!"

*Go back, Cale,* Magadon said in his mind. *Please go back. Do what you promised.*

The shadows around Cale boiled.

"Damn it, Mags, I will go back! I will kill Kesson! But we need another way."

*I have no time for another way,* Magadon said, the voice more his own. Before Cale could answer, the connection went quiescent. Cale still felt the uncomfortable itch of mental contact deep in his skull, but it was as though the door through which he and Magadon communicated had been left ajar only a sliver. Only Magadon could reopen it. Cale could not.

Riven exhaled a change of subject, shook the fatigue from his arms. He looked around, squinting in the rain. "Kesson will be coming. As long as we're in the Shadowstorm, he'll be coming."

"He will have to find us first," Cale said. He cast a series of wards to shield them against scrying and divinations, but had his doubts they would work against Kesson. "I can try to get us out, back to Lake Veladon . . ."

Riven was already shaking his head. "Not with that spell on you. We could end up anywhere—back in Ordulin."

Riven looked at his right hand, as if pondering the absence of the ring Kesson had slagged with his spell.

"We walk, then," Cale said, and threw up his hood.

"So we do," Riven said with a nod. "Bad things in this storm, though."

Cale remembered the looming, dark creature whose presence they had fled on their way in.

"Nothing for it," he said, his mind on Magadon. "We have to find another way. I am not putting Magadon down. Get *your* head around that. The horse got out, yes?"

"Cale, if we have to—"

Cale stopped, turned, and stared at Riven. "We are not giving up on him."

"I can offer another way," said a voice to their right, a voice that put Weaveshear in Cale's hand and Riven's sabers in his.

Rivalen Tanthul's golden eyes appeared to float freely in space until the Shadovar disengaged from the darkness. He bore no visible weapon. The shadows hugged his form, blurred his borders.

Cale and Riven fell in side by side, weapons ready. Cale scanned the darkness around them, but saw no one else.

"I am alone," Rivalen said. He held his hands at his side.

"All the worse for you," said Riven.

Cale put his free hand on Riven's shoulder to prevent him from charging. "He could have attacked already," he said. What Cale did not say was that Rivalen had mentioned another way and Cale was prepared to grasp at anything to save Magadon, even the words of a Shadovar.

Rivalen eyed Cale, inclined his head.

The tension went out of Riven. Somewhat.

"You wonder why I am here," Rivalen said. He advanced a few steps and stopped, perhaps eight paces from Cale and Riven.

"You are a Sharran dog and Kesson has your leash," Riven said.

Genuine anger flashed in Rivalen's eyes before he hid it behind a mask of calm.

"Your words are those of a fool," the Shadovar said.

Cale held onto Riven as his mind hurried through possibilities. He did not think Rivalen was delaying them for his fellow Sharran. The Shadovar prince could have simply watched them from afar, and brought Kesson whenever he wished. They had not known Rivalen was near. And had the Shadovar wanted to attack, he could have. They would not have seen it coming.

"This makes no sense," Cale said. Shadows leaked from his body, from his blade.

"That is because you think Kesson Rel and I are allies because we both serve Shar. Not all who serve the same god are allies."

Cale understood that well. He and Riven had started in service to Mask as rivals.

"Kesson Rel is a heretic," Rivalen said. "I want him dead, the Shadowstorm stopped."

In answer to his words, the wind gusted and thunder rumbled.

Riven scoffed. "That's a dungpile."

Rivalen's eyes flared, and the shadows around him whirled.

"Why?" Cale asked.

Rivalen smiled. "He is destroying Sembia, and Sembia is an ally of the Shadovar."

"Another dungpile," Riven said, and Cale agreed. If Rivalen was offering even a little truth, there was much more to the matter than he was sharing.

"Stop him, then," Cale said. "You will find him in Ordulin."

"I know where he is but I have learned that I cannot stop him alone. It will take a Chosen of Mask."

The shadows around Cale spun. "Learned? How?"

"I am willing to lay our past differences aside . . ."

"I'm not," Riven said.

Rivalen continued, ". . . to rid Sembia of this threat. Our interests coincide. We both want the same man dead."

"He's not a man," Cale said.

The shadows around Rivalen churned. "No. He's not. But we can end this, and him, together."

Cale considered. He wondered if Rivalen, too, sought what Kesson had stolen from Mask. He reminded himself that Rivalen had kidnapped Magadon, bonded him to the Source. That had been the beginning of Magadon's descent. Rivalen Tanthul was a bastard, not to be trusted.

"To the Hells with him, Cale," Riven said. "We do it our way."

"Agreed," Cale said reluctantly. "No."

Riven sneered. "You fly away now, little shade. And the next time we see you, our discussion will be a little different."

Rivalen never lost his mask. He showed no anger, did not even raise his voice.

"I believe I can make you reconsider."

Drizzle sank through Abelar's armor and caused the leather and padding under the steel to chafe. After spending several hours riding with his father and son in the wagon, he rode on Swiftdawn at the head of the column of Saerbians. His father and Elden rode in the body of the caravan.

Behind them, the Shadowstorm expanded, devouring the sky and casting Sembia in darkness. The roiling black thunderhead, streaked through with flashes of lightning, was gaining on them.

"We need to move faster," he said to Regg. He kept his eyes from the rose enameled on Regg's breastplate.

His friend looked back at the storm and nodded. "We may have to abandon the wagons. There are not enough horses for all, but we would move faster afoot."

"Not with the children and elderly," Abelar said. "And they would all be exhausted in a few days."

Regg surrendered to Abelar's point and grunted agreement.

Abelar looked on the long column of men, women, children, and wagons that snaked out behind him. Oxen and horses, heads lowered against the rain, stubbornly pulled their burdens through the muck. Mothers cradled children, and tried to shield themselves from the rain with blankets and cloaks. Men walked beside wagons and helped push when they bogged down in the soft earth. They were moving at a crawl. If the storm continued its present course and speed, they would be caught in mere days.

A sharp roll of thunder from behind elicited gasps and turned heads. Dozens of lightning bolts lit the ink of the Shadowstorm.

The Lathanderians of the company rode up and down the caravan, offering encouragement, spell-summoned food, or a prayer of blessing. Smiles and grateful nods greeted their passage and the Lathanderians kept flagging spirits from sinking into despair. But Abelar knew that blessings and food would mean little if they could not outrun the storm.

"We continue west to the Mudslide," he said. "Then south to the Stonebridge and on toward Daerlun."

"The race is on," Regg said softly, and patted Firstlight.

Hours later, the caravan reached the Mudslide, a murky flow that ran south out of the Thunderpeaks, then hooked east, back toward the River Arkhen and the Shadowstorm. It made a triangle out of Sembia's plains, with the river on two sides and the Shadowstorm on the other. Ordinarily not a very wide river, the recent rains had swollen its width.

The men, women, and children dismounted wagons and horses, plodded through the muddy shallows, and re-filled waterskins. The pack animals were unyoked and watered. Abelar released Swiftdawn to drink and forage.

To Regg, he said, "Roen and his fellow priests should summon as much food as they can. Let's put a hot meal in everyone's bellies. We eat quickly and press on."

"What are you going to do?"

"Check on my son."

Regg nodded and rode off, calling Roen to his side.

Abelar walked through the caravan on his way to the small, roofed wagon in which his father and son rode. He kept his eyes off the sky, off the storm. The refugees smiled at him, nodded, but he saw the questions in their eyes, the confusion. He did not bear his shield. He did not display a holy symbol. Returning greetings and smiles, he offered no explanation for their absence and went to his son.

He found Elden and Endren standing in the rain outside the wagon. Elden was smiling and petting the muscular side of the ox yoked to the wagon, perhaps in preparation for unyoking it. Endren stood with one hand on the boy's shoulder.

Elden saw Abelar approaching. Rain pressed his hair to his scalp. "Papa!"

His exclamation startled the big animal and it lurched. Abelar's heart jumped in his chest but Endren pulled Elden backward and the ox, too tired for much exertion, calmed immediately.

Abelar hurried forward and glared at his father. "Mind his safety."

Endren lost his smile, looked surprised, then hurt, then angry. "He was in no danger."

"My all wight," Elden said.

Abelar scooped him up, put his body between Elden and Endren. To his father, he said, "The caravan is taking a meal then continuing onward. Get some food in you."

Thunder rumbled.

"How do matters stand?" Endren asked.

"Morale is holding. We make for the Stonebridge. But the terrain and weather work against us. We are moving too slowly."

Endren nodded. He understood the implication, though he would not say it in Elden's presence.

"If the storm does not change course, I want you to take Elden on Swiftdawn and ride for Daerlun. We'll mount as many as we can. The others will . . . remain behind with me and some others to guard them."

Elden clapped at the prospect of a horseback ride. He loved riding Swiftdawn.

"You come, too, Papa?"

Endren and Abelar stared at one another.

"You should go, too," Endren said.

Abelar started to shake his head but stopped. Duty to the refugees did battle with his paternal instincts. He did not want to leave his son but was not sure he could abandon the refugees. He remembered the words Riven had said to him—You have to live with yourself first. He was not sure he would be able to live with himself whatever his choice.

"We will discuss it again if it comes to that," he said to Endren.

Thunder rumbled.

Elden put two fingers on Abelar's throat, where he would ordinarily have worn his holy symbol.

"Where flower?"

Where indeed, Abelar thought, but said only, "Gone, Elden."

"Bad men take it?"

Abelar smiled. "No, son. It's just . . . gone. I . . . I gave it away."

"You get back, Papa."

To that, Abelar could think of nothing to say.

"Let us eat," Endren said, and took Elden from Abelar.

Abelar took his father by the arm. "I am sorry I snapped at you."

"It is nothing," Endren said. "Come, Elden."

They headed off to where the priests were summoning meals.

Abelar stood alone in the rain, thinking of flowers and choices. He resolved to speak to Regg about contingencies.

The caravan took the meal quickly, in a drizzle, and started moving south along the rapidly flowing Mudslide. Abelar and Regg took their position at the front.

As they started off, Abelar said to Regg, "If matters become dire, I want you and the company to double up with as many of the women and children as possible and go ahead. Without the wagons to slow them, the horses will outrun the storm."

"You speak as if you would not come."

"I won't. But I would want you to take Elden."

"You ask me to do something you would not?" Regg smiled, and thumped Abelar on the shoulder. "You know I cannot do that. None of us can. None of us will. We will find another way or we will give our horses to the refugees. They can ride in twos. That gets more than four hundred to safety."

"They cannot be left unguarded."

"Then a small force will accompany them. But I think we will have to draw lots to determine who leaves. None of the company will want a spot in a saddle better filled by a refugee. You know this. You made us, Abelar."

Abelar nodded.

"The light is in you, Abelar. Rose or no rose. I see it."

Abelar looked off into the rain. He did not feel the presence of his god in his soul but he did feel something. The sensation puzzled him.

"What is that?" Regg said, squinting into the rain.

Abelar followed his friend's gaze into the southern sky. The rain and twilight reduced visibility, but he saw what had caught Regg's eye. At first he thought it a cloud, but that could not be.

"It moves against the wind."

"Aye," said Regg, pulling Firstlight to a stop.

Abelar did the same with Swiftdawn and studied the sky.

Behind them, the caravan slowed, then stopped. Above the patter of rain, above the constant low roll of thunder, Abelar heard the murmur of questions turn to cries of dismay.

The object continued to close, looming larger, darker.

"It is immense," said Regg.

"Get Trewe to sound the muster and form up."

Regg spun Firstlight and rode back into the caravan. The clarion of Trewe's trumpet sounded. The company began to assemble around Abelar and all eyes watched the sky.

A floating, inverted mountaintop closed the distance. A pall of shadows enshrouded it, leaked from it like fog. Hints of buildings—towers and spires—poked here and there from the swirling darkness. Winged forms wheeled awkwardly about its craggy, conical bottom. Abelar marveled at the power that must have been needed to keep an entire city afloat.

"Shadovar," he said, as much puzzled as alarmed.

The caravan huddled in the plains, exposed, caught between a Shadovar city before and the Shadowstorm behind.

The city stopped a few bowshots distant, on the other side of the Mudslide.

"They are near the Stonebridge," Regg said.

Abelar nodded. The Stonebridge provided the only means of crossing the Mudslide for leagues.

The rain continued. Eyes moved back and forth from the Shadowstorm to the Shadovar city. The tension thickened.

The city hovered ominously in the air, hovered ominously in their future, a lesion on the sky.

"What do they want?" someone shouted from the caravan.

"We cannot just remain here," shouted another.

"If they meant us well, we would have heard already," Regg said. "Let us go knock on their door."

"I won't leave Elden," Abelar said, and felt Regg's gaze on him.

"Then we wait a while longer," Regg said softly. "After that, I will take a party forward."

The sun sank low on the horizon and night crept over the plains.

Regg turned to the company. "I want twenty swords to ride forward to the city. Volunteers?"

Most everyone in the company indicated a willingness and Regg started ticking off names.

As he did, the darkness ten paces before them started to swirl and deepen. Abelar grabbed his friend by the bicep and turned him around.

"Regg."

Swords rang from scabbards. Shields were unslung. The soft sound of spell casting carried through the rain, Roen asking for Lathander's blessing.

The darkness expanded and eight or nine score Shadovar warriors materialized from the darkness. They wore archaic black plate armor that featured points, studs, and spikes in abundance. Their large, oval shields, enameled in black, showed no heraldry and looked like holes. Helms with nose guards obscured most of their faces, but the gray skin Abelar could see reminded him of a corpse. They bore bare swords in their fists, the blades made of black crystal. Shadows leaked from all of them. They seemed part of the darkness.

"Shades," Abelar said. Like Erevis Cale.

Leather creaked. Horses whinnied. The two forces regarded each other across the grass, the rain thudding off of armor.

One of the Shadovar took a step forward and in that single stride moved from the darkness in which he stood to within a few paces before Abelar and Regg. Firstlight and Swiftdawn did not buck. Abelar and Regg did not start.

The Shadovar removed his helm to reveal a bald head and black eyes.

"By order of the Hulorn, ruler of Sembia, you are prohibited from crossing the Mudslide River."

A rustle went through the company, the murmur of anger. It took a few moments for Abelar to reconcile the words with reality.

"The Hulorn does not rule these lands," Regg said. "His power extends to Selgaunt and its environs. No farther."

"You are mistaken," said the Shadovar.

"The Hulorn and Selgaunt are allies of Saerb," Abelar said.

"If it were otherwise," the Shadovar said, "you would all be dead already."

Regg, on Firstlight, took a step forward. Abelar stopped him with an arm across his chest.

Regg said, "You should hope your blade is as sharp as your tongue, shade. Should it come to that."

The Shadovar did not take his gaze from Abelar. "Matters are as I have stated. You will not be allowed to cross the Mudslide. Go back. Stay. Neither is of any moment to me. We will prevent with force any attempt to cross the Stonebridge or otherwise ford the river."

The company murmured angrily.

"Force?"

"Prevent?"

Horses inched forward. The tone grew uglier than the weather.

Shouts carried to them from the caravan.

"What does he say?"

"What is happening?"

"Have they come to aid us?"

"We must cross," Regg said. "Whatever the Hulorn may say."

Following the Mudslide would hook the refugees back in the direction of the Shadowstorm. And mountains blocked them to the north. Their only hope was to cross.

Abelar dismounted and approached the Shadovar. The shadows around the shade swirled.

"Look behind us, man," Abelar said, working to keep his voice calm. "These people cannot be caught in that storm. We must get across the river. We are trapped against it. I will answer to the Hulorn for you allowing us passage."

The Shadovar looked past Abelar and into the sky, to the Shadowstorm. When his gaze returned to Abelar, Abelar saw no pity or understanding in it, just darkness.

"You have heard my words."

Growing anger put an edge on Abelar's tone. "My son is in this caravan."

Shadows spun around the Shadovar. "The more pity you."

Day after day of constant tension had drawn Abelar's emotions taut and they snapped at the Shadovar's words. Sudden rage stole his sense and he punched the Shadovar in the face with a gauntleted fist. Bone buckled and the man's nose exploded blood. He fell to the ground, groaning, shadows whirling. Abelar drew his blade and advanced.

"The more pity me, you say? The more pity me?"

Ten Shadovar appeared around their fallen commander, blades bare. Arms closed around Abelar from behind, lifted him from the ground, and turned him around. His entire company looked ready to ride the Shadovar down. Trewe's horse reared. Others whinnied and tossed their heads.

"Calm heads!" Regg shouted. It was he who had hold of Abelar. "Calm heads! Think of the refugees!"

Regg was right.

"All right," Abelar said to him. "All right."

"All right?" Regg asked.

Abelar nodded and Regg set him down and released him. Abelar turned to see the entire Shadovar force had stepped through the shadows and assembled before their commander in a bristling arc of steel. The bald Shadovar rose, and as Abelar watched, his nose stopped bleeding and the broken bones squirmed back into place. The Shadovar sniffed loudly and spit a glob of blood and snot.

"Attempt to cross the Mudslide and you all die."

The shadows engulfed him and his troop and they disappeared into the darkness.

Curses made the rounds of the company. Lightning ripped the sky behind them.

"Gods damn it," Abelar said.

"What the Hells is going on here?" Regg asked.

"How do you mean, 'reconsider'?" Cale asked Rivalen.

The Shadovar prince approached them, but stopped short of the reach of their blades.

"A dimensional tether," he said, nodding at the green glow that flashed around Cale. "Kesson tried to prevent your escape."

"He failed," Riven said.

"Did he? Why are you still within the storm, then?"

To that Riven said nothing.

"You had something to say," Cale said. "About us reconsidering."

"Yes. By now Sakkors and an army of Shadovar have intercepted the Saerbian refugees retreating before the Shadowstorm."

"What?" Cale asked. The shadows around him churned. Those around Rivalen swirled in answer.

"They will not be allowed to cross the Mudslide and continue to Daerlun. Instead, they will sit with the river to their backs and Kesson Rel's Shadowstorm closing in on them."

"You are a liar," Cale said.

"No. I will take you to them."

Riven took a step forward and spoke in a low voice. "There are children in that caravan."

"A solution is before you," Rivalen said, giving no ground to Riven. "Assist me in destroying Kesson Rel. When he dies, so, too, does his Shadowstorm."

Cale and Riven looked one to the other.

"Let them pass and we will help you," Cale said to Rivalen. "You have my word."

"Your word means nothing to me, priest. And while we debate and haggle, the Shadowstorm draws closer to the Saerbians. Their deaths will be on your head."

The shadows around Cale roiled. Weaveshear bled darkness. "You are a bastard."

"I am trying to save Sembia. Your intransigence leaves me little recourse."

"A show of good faith, then," Cale said, and indicated the glow of Kesson's spell. "Get this off of me."

Rivalen considered. "Very well."

Riven stepped to Cale's side. Shadows poured from his sabers. "You try anything other than a counterspell, you'll find me less than helpful."

Rivalen smiled, and took in his hands a holy symbol of platinum and amethyst. He intoned the words to a counterspell and shadows went forth from his outstretched hand and engaged Kesson Rel's spell.

Cale felt the power of the two spellcasters charge the air around him. Green sparks shrouded him, flared, flashed.

Riven tensed and Cale held up a hand to head off the assassin's attack on Rivalen.

"I am all right," he said.

Rivalen's face showed strain, then surprise.

His counterspell ended. The sparks of magical battle died. Kesson's spell did not.

"You cannot counter it," Cale said, not a question.

"No."

Riven sneered. Rivalen glared at him, the shadows around him roiling.

"It will expire in time," Rivalen said, his brow furrowed.

"How long?"

"An hour. No longer. When it does, verify my claims. I will meet you at the shores of Lake Veladon at midnight tonight. Then we can begin."

"Begin what?"

"Go see that what I say is true. When you come to me at midnight, I will tell you what you need to know."

Cale had no choice but that did little to mitigate his anger. "When Kesson's dead, then it's you and us, Rivalen. You have my word on that, too."

Rivalen smiled, showing fangs. "As I said, priest, your word means nothing to me."

A stab of pain behind Cale's eyes caused him to wince, his eyes to water. Hate sizzled in his consciousness.

*Kill him, Cale,* projected Magadon. *He is at the root of all of this.*

*He offers a way to kill Kesson Rel.*

*He lies, like my father.*

*Mags—*

*Kill him!*

Magadon tried again to control Cale, to control his weapon arm and lunge at Rivalen. Cale thought of the Saerbians, and resisted.

To his relief, the shadows swallowed the shade prince, extinguished his golden eyes, and he disappeared.

Magadon's attempt to control him ended.

*Do not do it again, Magadon. Never again.*

*You are a liar, too. You are all liars. To the Abyss with you,* Magadon said, and the connection closed.

Riven must have seen the mental exchange on Cale's face. "You all right?" the assassin asked.

"Magadon," Cale said, and the darkness around him roiled.

Riven stared at him a moment, then paced the dead grass. "There's more to all this than that Shadovar is telling, Cale."

"Agreed, but he wants to kill Kesson. He's gone through too much to just set us up. Agreed?"

"Agreed."

"After we've done that, after we've saved Mags, we'll deal with whatever comes."

Riven seemed to accept that. He stopped pacing. "Says something, him coming here by himself."

"It does," Cale said. It said Rivalen was not afraid of them.

They spent half an hour huddled against the rain, back to back, watching the darkness for the creatures that prowled the Shadowstorm. Cale felt like the green glow of Kesson's spell made him a beacon, but they encountered nothing. After a time, the glow winked out and stayed gone.

"Spell has ended," Cale said, and stood.

"Let's move," Riven said.

Cale smeared shadows into a lens, cast a minor divination, sought Abelar, found him, and caused the shadows to take them there.

Whether waking or sleeping, I dream of the Source. Cale has betrayed me, so the Source must be the tool of my revenge, my salvation. Remembering the feel of its power in my mind, the touch of its ancient intelligence, I feel a hole of longing open in my mind, an absence that needs to be filled.

I find myself standing near the hole, a gaping, jagged aperture in the mindscape of my mental domain. The stink of rot rises from it. I creep forward, peer inside, hoping to plumb the depths to which I have sunk.

Veins as thick as my wrist wind a jagged path along its sides, pulse like a nest of vipers. Its depth extends as far as I can see, the bottom lost in darkness, like me.

A voice whispers from within the hole, echoing up its sides. The veins throb when the voice speaks. It is my father's voice.

"Cale cannot kill Kesson Rel. He has already failed once."

I shake my head, trying to dislodge despair. "He will try again and succeed. I have seen him do things that no ordinary man could do. He will keep his promise."

My father chuckles. "His promises are shit. He promised his god to return his divinity. He promised the same thing to me. He will say anything, yet he means nothing. Now he allies with Rivalen Tanthul, who tortured you. You cannot trust him. You must save yourself."

I hear my own thoughts in the words and protest. "You lie."

"No. You lie. To yourself. Soon the Shadowwalkers will leave the Wayrock. They intend to leave you here. No one will ever return for you. They wish you to die, alone on this island as you are in your head. It is Cale's doing."

The words strike at my fears. I lean forward, start to speak, lose my footing, and nearly fall into the hole. I jerk myself back, heart racing, breathing rapidly.

The veins that line the hole are pulsing.

"Be mindful," says my father. "You are starting to slip."

He laughs. I curse. Staring into the abyss, I realize that Cale cannot save me. He does not want to save me. I must save myself.

"You want revenge on those who damaged you—"

"*You* damaged me!"

"The Source offers everything you want."

The ache for the Source's comfort wells up in me, accompanied by the beginnings of a plot. A hear a sound at the bottom of the hole, as if something ancient has stirred to life after sleeping for ages. I lean over the edge. Something is moving down here, deep in the darkness.

I lean too far, scream as I fall. My father's laughter rings off the walls as I plummet.

# CHAPTER TEN

Drawn blades and an alarmed shout of "Shades," met the arrival of Cale and Riven. Cale held up his hands. Riven already had his sabers clear of their scabbards.

"We are friends," Cale said.

"Hold!" Abelar shouted, his eyes on Cale.

Abelar, Regg, Jiiris, Roen, and a dozen other members of Abelar's company stood in a circle on the shore of a river Cale assumed to be the Mudslide. The Lathanderians relaxed, and sheathed their weapons. Apologies and greetings followed. Abelar embraced both Cale and Riven.

"I am pleased to see you both. We could use your blades and talents."

Downriver, Cale saw the inkblot of Sakkors hovering in the air. Opposite that, he saw the charred, churning clouds of the Shadowstorm as they ate the sky. Between them sat Abelar's company and the Saerbian refugees, just as Rivalen had said.

"Our blades and talents did nothing against Kesson Rel. We failed, Abelar."

The Lathanderian kept his expression neutral. "But you live, still. We will find another way."

"We may have found one. We need a word in privacy. You and Regg."

Abelar looked to Regg and Regg nodded and said to his company, "See to your duties. Get everyone near the river. No closer to that city, though. Summon food. Keep everyone as warm as possible."

Nods and murmured assent, then they moved off.

"Jiiris," Abelar called, and the red haired warrior brought her horse over. She nodded to Cale and Riven, though Cale saw distant hostility in her eyes. Perhaps she blamed them for Abelar's turn from Lathander.

"You do not have to ask," she said to Abelar. "I will see that Elden eats."

He smiled at her. "Thank you."

When the four men were alone, Cale said, "Ordulin is in ruins, as we suspected. Its people have been consumed by the storm and raised as shadows serving Kesson Rel. The storm transforms Sembia as it moves."

"The Morninglord's light," Regg oathed.

"He is more powerful than we thought," Cale said.

"Much more," Riven added.

Abelar shook his head. "Darkness grows. You see our straits." He nodded at Sakkors. "The Shadovar will prevent us from crossing the river on orders of the Hulorn. I misjudged Tamlin Uskevren badly. He did not seem a man to countenance this. When I met the two of you, I thought it you I should worry over, not him."

Cale smiled at that, recalling their first meeting. "Tamlin is desperate to prove himself and easily steered. I misjudged him as well. It is . . . unfortunate."

He could think of no better word. He was just pleased Thamalon had died before seeing his son sink so far.

" 'Unfortunate' understates his culpability should something happen to these refugees," Regg said.

Cale took the point. "The Hulorn is not behind this. Prince Rivalen of Shade Enclave is. Tamlin—the Hulorn—is just a tool."

"What does he hope to gain, this Shadovar prince?" Regg asked. "These are ordinary folk."

"Our assistance," Cale answered, and the shadows around him spun.

Regg and Abelar's expression formed questions, waited for answers.

Cale and Riven told them of their encounter with Rivalen, of the deal he offered if Cale and Riven helped him with Kesson Rel.

"He makes hundreds of innocent people the stakes in his play," Regg said.

"He is a Sharran," Abelar said simply, and Regg grunted in agreement.

"I am sorry," Cale said, and the darkness around him crowded close. "We did not intend for your people to be caught up in any of this."

"You are not at fault," Regg said, but Cale felt otherwise.

Abelar nodded at Regg's comment. He looked to Cale. "I have seen you use the shadows to move yourself and others from place to place. Can you take the refugees through the darkness, remove them to safety? Avoid this Sharran plot all together?"

Cale considered. Once, he had attempted to transport an entire ship and its crew across the Inner Sea. Instead, he had inadvertently taken the ship from Faerûn to the Plane of Shadow. He knew he could not safely move the refugees as a group.

"In twos and threes, perhaps, but I think the Shadovar would learn of it and exact payment from those who remained behind."

"At least some would get to safety," Regg said. "Elden could go first, with Endren."

Cale watched the war in Abelar's head do battle in his expression. He shook his head. "No. We cannot put everyone else at risk to save a few. If matters become desperate and there is no other way . . ."

Cale said, "If we assist Rivalen, all of you will be granted passage."

"If he keeps his word," Regg said, his tone doubtful.

"He is a Sharran," Abelar said again, as if that were all that needed said.

"He wants Kesson Rel dead," Riven said. "I saw it in his face. Cale?"

"Agreed."

Riven withdrew his pipe, shielded it from the rain, and used a tindertwig to light it.

"Why?" Regg asked. "To dispense with a rival? Is this prince strengthened if Kesson is defeated?"

Riven shrugged.

Cale said, "We have few options. Kesson is more than a match for us alone. We were fortunate to escape at all."

Riven exhaled a cloud of smoke.

"You have another?" Regg asked, nodding at the pipe.

The question seemed to take Riven by surprise. He eyed the Lathanderian over his pipe, grunted an affirmative, found his spare wooden pipe, tamped it, and provided it and a tindertwig to Regg.

"My thanks," Regg said. He propped the stem between his teeth, lit, took a long draw, and exhaled with a satisfied sigh.

"Been a while since I've enjoyed a smoke. That's good leaf."

Riven nodded. "Grown east of Urlamspyr."

"Good soil there," Regg said, nodding. "Or was, before the drought. Good folk, too."

"Aye, that," Abelar said.

Silence fell, as if the folk of Urlamspyr were already dead in the storm and the four men were paying their respects in silence. Smoke, shadows, and worry clouded the air.

"You believe this Sharran, then?" Abelar finally asked Cale.

"Hells, Abelar, I rarely believe my own god," Cale replied. "I believe Rivalen wants Kesson Rel dead. He says he has a way to do it but needs us."

"Why?"

"I don't know but it seems he needs a . . . special servant of Mask."

Regg looked away, as if made uncomfortable by the statement, and blew out a cloud of smoke.

"You?" Abelar asked.

"Us," Cale answered, indicating he and Riven.

"How long will you be gone?" Abelar asked. "We have only a short time before the storm reaches us. We will have to do something before that."

Cale shook his head. "I don't know. We don't know where we're going, what we're doing."

"Then you are at the Sharran's mercy," Regg said.

"Hardly," Riven answered, and tapped the pommel of one of his sabers.

"When will you go?" Abelar said.

"We meet him at midnight," Cale answered.

"An hour holy to Sharrans," Regg said.

"And to Mask," Cale said, and Regg looked away.

Silence fell, and all eyes drifted to the Shadowstorm, all of them measuring the distance it would close between then and midnight.

"We will march into the storm if necessary," Regg said. "Gain you the time you need."

"Let us hope it is not necessary," Cale said.

Abelar changed the mood with a lighter tone. "A meal. And rest if you need it."

Regg blew out another cloud of smoke, snuffed the pipe, tapped out the burned pipeweed and held it out to Riven. "Your pipe."

"Keep it," Riven said. "Until we sit down together for another smoke."

Regg looked Riven in the face. He seemed to want to say something, but instead just nodded, and tucked the pipe in his beltpouch.

Darkness fell. So, too, did the rain. The refugees in the Saerbian camp settled in for sleep, nestled against the river between Sakkors and the Shadowstorm. Abelar and his company stood assembled at the outskirts of the camp, on the side facing the Shadowstorm.

At midnight, Cale asked the Shadowlord to provide him with spells and Mask obliged. Cale's mind filled with power.

"Ready?" he asked Riven, and the assassin nodded.

Cale pictured in his mind the one-time Saerbian camp at Lake Veladon. Riven drew his sabers. Cale drew Weaveshear.

Cale tried to reach through the dormant connection with Magadon.

*Mags, hang on. We have another way to kill him.*

No response. He toyed with the idea of returning to the Wayrock to check on Magadon but decided that he could not spare the time. Besides, he could do nothing there other than bear witness to Magadon's slip into the void. He served his friend best by finding a way to kill Kesson Rel.

A little apart from Cale and Riven, the Lathanderians appeared to be readying themselves for battle, for a possible march into the Shadowstorm. Cale caught Abelar's eye and raised a hand in farewell. Abelar returned the gesture. Meanwhile, the men and women of his company checked and rechecked straps, secured shields, and donned helmets.

Cale drew the darkness around himself and Riven, left the Saerbians alone in the shadow of the Sakkors, and rode the shadows to Lake Veladon.

They appeared in darkness and rain. The remains of the Saerbian camp littered the lake's shoreline, the flotsam of war. Broken wagon wheels, a shattered axle, fire pits, buckets, a few sacks, a slashed waterskin, a tent that had been left behind, the snap of its flap in the wind like the crack of a whip.

The front edge of the Shadowstorm, a black shroud darkening the land, was within sight and drawing closer. The wind screamed. Thunder and lightning assaulted Faerûn, more intense than that experienced by Cale and Riven within the storm.

"It's growing stronger," Cale said.

Riven nodded.

With his shadesight, Cale watched the storm's darkness twist and wither the trees it engulfed, brown and curl the grass. A clutch of rabbits burst from their burrows and sprinted away from the storm. Squirrels and raccoons scrambled down trees and fled. To his right Cale saw deer and foxes, even a lumbering bear, bound past in the distance.

Sembia would never be the same. Sembians would never be the same. "Rivalen!" he shouted into the wind.

He and Riven stood side by side, blades out, awaiting the appearance of the Shadovar prince. Shadows leaked from Cale's flesh, from Weaveshear.

Rivalen emerged from the Shadowstorm, backlit by a flash of lightning. A stride through the shadows brought him to Cale and Riven's side.

"It is growing stronger and moving faster," Rivalen said. "We must hurry."

Odd, Cale thought, that two men could want the same thing but for such different reasons.

"Hurry to where?" he asked.

"We travel to Kesson Rel's world of Ephyras, where we will find a temple at the edge of nothing. Within is a weapon for a Chosen of Mask."

"Sounds like we don't need you, then," Riven said to Rivalen.

Rivalen showed his fangs. Smile or grimace, Cale could not tell.

"How did you learn all this?" Cale asked Rivalen.

"My secret," the shade prince said.

"What kind of weapon?" Cale asked.

The shadows around Rivalen churned. "I do not know."

"Dark and empty," Riven said, shaking his head and forcing a laugh.

Rivalen stretched out his hands and gathered the shadows to him as fauna streaked over their boots and the wind threw up a blizzard of leaves, twigs, and pebbles. The water of Lake Veladon seethed.

Cale found the shadows Rivalen gathered to himself, shadows shot through with the prince's power, surprisingly familiar. He caught a gleam in Rivalen's hand, thought at first it might have been the prince's holy symbol, but then saw it for what it was—a gold coin, a Sembian fivestar.

He had no time to puzzle over it before the darkness engulfed them all. Before they moved between worlds, Cale reached into his pocket and took his holy symbol, a silken mask, in hand.

Abelar and Regg stood side by side, watching the darkness grow in the night sky. Selûne, if she were not new, was curtained off from Faerûn by the Shadowstorm. The wall of black filled their field of vision, filled their world. It pulsed and lurched like a living thing. The severity of the thunder and lightning elicited a steady stream of gasps from the Lathanderians.

"They will have to return quickly if they are to stop it from reaching us," Regg said. He put his hand to the holy symbol he wore on a chain at his throat.

"Roen has used his divinations on the storm," Abelar said. "An intelligence guides it. Kesson Rel, I presume. It grows in power with each hour that passes. He tells me the very air within it will drain a man's life."

"We have wands," Regg said. "We can ward the company."

"Aye," Abelar said, "but what else is within that storm?"

"Shar is in that storm," Regg said softly.

"Aye."

Regg cleared his throat and said, "If Cale does not return before matters greatly . . . worsen, I think we will have to march on it, Abelar. If an intelligence guides the storm and the creatures within it, we can perhaps slow its approach by offering resistance."

Abelar suspected that there would be no returning from such a battle. And he knew Regg thought the same thing.

"Light will battle against darkness," Regg said. "Lathander's servants will face Shar's. It is fitting that we face it so, I think."

"I do not think it will come to that," Abelar said.

"If it does," Regg said. "I say we march."

Abelar winced inwardly at the word "we." He could no longer hold his peace. He faced his friend. "If we march, you will have to lead the company."

Abelar's words eroded the resolve in Regg's expression. "What . . . what do you mean?"

"I cannot leave my son, Regg. Not again. Not even for this."

Regg studied his face, and Abelar imagined his mind whirling behind the calm facade of his expression. Abelar saw no judgment in his friend's eyes, but neither did he see understanding.

"The sun rises and sets," Regg said. "So be it. I will lead."

Cale noticed the cold first, an unearthly frigidity that settled in his bones and chilled him to his core. Wind assaulted his ears, the sound the anguished howl of a trapped animal as it surrendered to death. He pulled his cloak tight as the darkness that had brought them dissipated.

"Ephyras," Rivalen said, glancing around.

They had materialized on the decaying corpse of a world. Black, barren earth with the consistency of sand stretched out in all directions for as far as he could see. Dry gullies cut deep, jagged lines in the dead earth but he saw no water to form them. The wind blew up dust cyclones here and there, little black spirals that frolicked on the grave of the world before losing their coherence and collapsing. If there had ever been vegetation on Ephyras, Cale saw no sign; it had long ago dried out and crumbled away.

The air smelled faintly of ancient decay, like the memory of rot. Long ribbons of shadow floated through the air, squirming in the wind like worms. A tiny, exhausted red sun hung in the sky, ringed by a collar of absolute black. Its wan, bloody light made no real attempt to light the world, merely colored it in a hue that hinted at slaughter.

As Cale watched, the darkness ringing the sun expanded slightly, reducing its glowing core to an even smaller circle. The darkness was choking off the sun.

"Dark," Cale oathed.

The dimness of the light allowed him to see stars twinkling faintly in the black-gray vault of the sky, appearing and disappearing behind the long columns of ink-black clouds that streaked across the heavens. Cale did not recognize any of the constellations. Lightning flashed now and then, long, jagged bolts of green that seemed to stretch from horizon to horizon, as if they ringed the world.

The sight of it all caused an ache in Cale's head, made him dizzy. He felt pressure building in his ears, numbness in his extremities, then realized of a sudden that his feelings had nothing to do with the sight of a dying world. Something was wrong.

He turned to Riven and Rivalen but his body answered him awkwardly and he stumbled and nearly fell to the black earth. He felt heavy, dulled. He grabbed at Riven's cloak, tried to speak, but found his mouth stuffed with cloth, his lips numb.

The expression on Riven's face suggested the assassin was experiencing a similar feeling. He staggered backward, out of Cale's grip, and slumped to the ground. Cale's legs failed him and he, too, fell. He hit the ground on all fours, collapsed, rolled onto his back in a bed of dead earth on a dead world looking up at a dying sun.

The shadows swirled around him, but neither they nor his regenerative flesh could combat the effect. He knew it for what it was. He and Riven had experienced it in the Shadowstorm. Ephyras's air drained life. He should have known.

Clutching his mask, he tried to invoke a protective ward, but his numb lips garbled the words. Rivalen appeared over him, golden eyes staring out of the black clot of his hood. The Shadovar appeared unaffected by the life draining effect of the air, of the world. He must have kept permanent wards on his person.

The shadows around both of them roiled and touched. The

prince reached down for him, took him by the arm, and pulled him easily to his feet.

"You need to ward yourself," Rivalen said. "I assumed you had."

The prince intoned a spell and energy flowed into Cale, enough to let him stand on his own feet. He shook off the prince's touch, wobbled, gathered himself, and managed to mouth the words to a ward before Ephyras again stole his strength.

The moment the spell took effect, the numbness began to leave him. He felt his heartbeat return to normal, inhaled a deep breath. He pushed past Rivalen to Riven, kneeled, and cast the same ward on the assassin. Riven's wide eye cleared. He blinked, breathed, sat up with a grunt, and spit.

"Negative energy," Cale said. "Same as the Shadowstorm."

A thought tugged at him, but flitted away before he could pin it down. He stood, pulling Riven to his feet after him.

"How can there be a temple here?" Riven said. "No one could survive."

"It must have been different here, once," Cale surmised. He looked at Rivalen, who surveyed the world as he might his own domain. Shadows leaked from him in long strands.

"Rivalen?" Cale asked. "What happened here?"

Rivalen seemed not to have heard him.

Cale started to ask again, but Rivalen spoke, awe in his tone.

"Another Shadowstorm is what happened here."

The words took Cale unawares. He and Riven shared a look.

Rivalen's hand went to the black disc at his throat, a symbol not unlike the one Riven wore, a symbol eerily reminiscent of the dying sun and the black collar choking it to death.

"In the darkness of night," Rivalen said. "We hear the whisper of the void."

Cale felt chilled. "How can there be another Shadowstorm?"

"There are many worlds," Rivalen said, his voice distant, the shadows around him dark. "Ephyras is older than Toril. Here, the Lady has already triumphed."

"Triumphed?" Riven asked.

Cale thought of Sembia, of Faerûn, of all of Toril. "You're telling us that the Shadowstorm withers a world, and kills its sun?"

"And more still," Rivalen said, his voice the disconnected utterance of a man in a trance. "Nothingness is the end. Soon Ephyras will be gone entirely. Annihilated."

Cale echoed the word, said it softly, the way he might a blasphemy. "Annihilated."

He found himself looking at the dust, the death, the darkness, wondering if there were still more worlds that Shar had killed. He supposed there must be. She was responsible for the deaths of millions.

"There were people here," he said, not a question.

Rivalen made no comment, though the shadows around him whirled.

"Dark and empty," Riven oathed. "A whole world? A whole world."

"All words die in time," Rivalen said. "In time, all existence ends."

"How can you look upon this and offer prayers?" Cale asked. He took the prince by the shoulder, pulled him around to face him.

Rivalen's eyes flashed. He took Cale by the wrist, for a moment they tested one another's strength, but determined nothing. They released one another and Rivalen stared into his face.

"How can you not feel awe as you watch a sun die?"

The shadows around Cale swirled. "Death does not awe me. Death is easy."

"You are broken, Shadovar," Riven said, contempt in his words. He advanced to stand beside Cale.

Rivalen stared at Cale, at Riven. "I acknowledge the truth that the fate of all worlds, of all of existence, will be the same as Ephyras. Is that broken?"

"You don't acknowledge it," Cale said. "You elevate it to an article of faith. You worship it."

"*That* is broken," Riven said.

The shadows around Rivalen whirled, as if stirred by the wind. "We are here because I wish to stop the Shadowstorm on Toril. To prevent this." His gesture took in Ephyras.

"And I cannot figure that out," Cale said.

Riven eyed the Shadovar, and said to Cale. "I trust him about as far as his blood will spray when I cut his throat."

Rivalen leaned forward, his golden eyes ablaze. He towered over the assassin. "If I wished you dead, you would already be so. Do you think there is anything that I would do that you could thwart?"

Riven had both sabers free in a heartbeat. "Why don't we find out?"

Cale shook his head. "Why stop it, Rivalen? This is what your goddess strives for."

Cale's question diffused the tension between Riven and Rivalen. The Shadovar prince stepped back and said, "My reasons are my own."

"Not good enough," Riven said.

Cale asked, "You can live forever but worship annihilation?"

"I do not worship it. I told you. I simply acknowledge its inevitability."

"You seek rule over a realm whose fate is dust and death," Cale said. "Why?"

"I forge meaning for myself in the face of ultimate meaninglessness."

"But nothing you do will matter."

The darkness around Rivalen whirled and he tilted his head to acknowledge the point. "In time."

And all at once Cale understood Rivalen. "In time" was the crux of Rivalen's life, the fulcrum that balanced meaning and meaninglessness. The prince wanted to control the pace of approaching annihilation. He wanted it to happen tomorrow, never today.

"You don't want to stop the Shadowstorm on Toril," Cale said. "You want to delay it, have it happen when you want it, on your terms."

Rivalen regarded Cale for a long while. "You also must struggle with meaning, Maskarran."

"Can the Shadowstorm be stopped?"

The prince stared into his face.

"Can it?"

Rivalen's eyes flared. "No."

Cale could find no words. Riven did, all of them curses.

"But it can be delayed," Rivalen said. "Delayed for a time that is long even to Shadovar high priests. For the moment, that aligns our interests."

"For the moment," Riven said, and glared at Rivalen.

Rivalen kept his gaze on Cale. "Perhaps we should seek the temple lest Toril experience Ephyra's fate sooner than any of us would like."

Cale considered that and nodded. There was nothing for it.

Brennus felt the magical ring on his finger open a connection between him and his brother.

*We are on Ephyras. It is a dying world. The Lady's will is manifest here. The time is drawing close, Brennus. You must determine how to capture Kesson Rel's divinity once it is freed.*

Brennus listened to the words, heard the hint of exaltation in his brother's tone, and seethed. He wished he could reach through the connection and choke Riven to death, hear his stilted, dying gasps, leave his corpse to end in nothingness with the rest of Ephyras.

*Brennus?* Rivalen asked.

*I am still seeking after the answer, Rivalen. You will know when I know.*

# CHAPTER ELEVEN

*5 Nightal, the Year of Lightning Storms*

The storm moved inexorably toward the refugee encampment. Wide eyes watched the growing darkness, exclaimed at the thunder, and recoiled at the lightning.

Abelar, Regg, and Roen stood at the far edge of the encampment, drenched in rain, in darkness, watching time drain away.

"They are terrified," Roen said, nodding back at the refugees.

"The storm is nearly upon us," Regg said. "We can wait no longer."

"Agreed," Roen said.

A void opened in Abelar's stomach. "Regg, hold until the last possible moment. If Cale and Riven have not returned. . . ."

But Regg was already shaking his head. "You know we cannot wait, my friend. We march on the hour. And by our lives we will purchase as much time as we can for the refugees. We do not have wards enough for men and horses so we will leave the mounts behind. If Cale and Riven do not return, rush the Stonebridge. Dare the river."

Abelar mined for words in the earth of his mind but found none. He nodded, a fist in his throat.

"Gather the company," Regg said to Roen, and the tall priest nodded. "Tell them mounts stay. And volunteers only. Any who wish may remain behind with Abelar and the refugees."

Abelar knew that all would volunteer. Only he among the company would remain behind.

Only he.

Roen embraced Abelar before he left to pass the word. The priest's long arms engulfed him.

"I am honored to have followed you into battle, Abelar Corrinthal. The light is in you still."

Abelar's tears mixed with the rain. "And you, Roen."

The priest jogged off toward the camp, his mail chinking, shouting as he went. Regg and Abelar stood alone in the rain. They didn't face each other, but stood side by side and faced the Shadowstorm, their enemy, as they had so often in previous battles.

"We have known each other a long while," Regg said, his voice choked.

"I am the better for it," Abelar said.

"As am I."

They clasped hands, and held onto each other for a moment.

"I always thought that if we fell in battle, we would fall together."

The tightness in Abelar's throat made his words stilted. "As did I."

"We stand in the light," Regg said softly.

"You do, my friend," Abelar said.

A shout from the gathering company below turned their heads. Jiriis ran toward them, her face stricken, as red as her hair.

"I will leave you," Regg said, and headed toward the company.

Jiriis ran past Regg to Abelar, stopped before him, her breath coming fast.

"You will not lead us?" Her green eyes swam in tears she refused to let fall.

"It is Regg's company to lead."

The space between them seemed much larger than it was. Abelar bridged it. He stepped forward, and took her arms in his hands.

"You could stay with me," he said.

She looked up at him and he saw her consider the offer, but then she shook her head. "You know I cannot. Come with us."

"You know I cannot."

Both clung to the other as if they could delay the inevitable if they hung on hard enough. At last he released her.

"I love you," he said. But he loved his son more.

"And I you."

He kissed her, passionately, fully, and both of them knew it was the last kiss they would share. He let himself fall into the moment, into her, the taste of her, the smell of her skin and hair. When they parted, neither looked the other in the eye and both were crying, tears born in the regret of what might have been.

"Go do what you were called to do," he said to her.

"And you do what you were called to do," she said, and left him.

Abelar stood alone in the rain, thinking of his son, his life of service, wondering what it was that he was called to do. He was unmoored.

❂ ❂ ❂ ❂ ❂

Ephyras's wind gusted, blew up a blizzard of black sand. The shadows around Cale and Rivalen deflected the particles. Riven, without any such protection, kept his hood up and his cloak drawn tight.

Cale tried to pry open the mental door Magadon had left ajar in his mind.

*Mags?*

He received no response and his worry manifested in a swirl of shadows.

"Which way to the temple?" Riven asked, as lightning bisected the sky.

Cale and Rivalen held their respective holy symbols, and both intoned the words to a minor divination.

"That way," Rivalen said, pointing.

"Agreed," Cale said, when the magic of his divination pulled at his body.

The prolonged rumble of falling stone sounded in the distance, the thunder of collapse. The ground vibrated under their feet and for a moment it felt as if the entire world were about to crumble.

"Over there," Cale said, and pointed.

In the direction they were to travel, a cloud of dust rose into the dark sky, the only landmark of any significance for as far as he could see.

"Magical transport will be dangerous," Rivalen said.

"We do not have time to walk," Cale said, thinking of the Saerbians, thinking of Magadon, thinking of Ephyras's death throes.

"You serve no one if your body materializes underground or in a stone. The currents of magic are wild here. You do not feel them?"

Cale did not, and had to rely on Rivalen's word. "Let's move, then."

The three men melted into the darkness and started out on foot, moving fast. The earth felt brittle, hollow under Cale's feet. The tremors that shook it from time to time nearly knocked him down. He imagined the entire world to be as hole-ridden as a sea sponge, ready to crumble into pieces were too much pressure applied to it.

He sweated despite the cold. They saw nothing of interest for a league and the flat, featureless landscape made distance hard to estimate. The sound of still more collapsing stone and the ever present cloud of dust ahead kept them roughly oriented.

Time weighed on Cale. He pressed the pace until all three men were soaked in sweat and gasping.

Ahead, mounds dotted the landscape like burial cairns. Eventually the mounds took shape and Cale recognized them for what they were—crumbling structures poking from the dried earth, ghostly hillocks lit by lightning flashes and covered in the dust of a destroyed world. Little remained, but he discerned partially collapsed domes, crumbling arches, hollow columns.

"Your goddess is a bitch," Riven said to Rivalen.

Rivalen said nothing, merely eyed the wreckage of a ruined world. A minor divination fell from his lips and, presumably led by its pull, he stopped from time to time to pick at this or that in the black sand. He finally lifted what he had sought—a coin of black metal, the markings upon it nearly worn away entirely.

"You collecting trophies, Shadovar?" Riven asked.

"Reminders," Rivalen said, and the coin vanished into his shadows.

The dying sun made its way across the dark sky as the three men made their way across the dark world. The ruins grew more frequent as they progressed and Cale thought they might have been moving through the remains of a city. The skeletons of some buildings remained standing here and there, lonely, hollowed out testaments to the remorselessness of time and Shar.

Holding his holy symbol in hand, Rivalen whispered imprecations and Cale could not tell if the prince was awed or appalled.

Bones appeared in the dust. First just a few—a thighbone jutting from the earth, a skull leering from the ruins—but then more and more. Soon they couldn't take a step without walking over remains.

"This place is a graveyard," Riven said.

It was as if an entire city had been murdered at a stroke and the bodies left to rot in the open. Cale could not help but think of Ordulin.

"Keep moving," he said.

The wind kicked up, moaned.

"That's not the wind," Riven said, his eye narrowed.

The three men stopped and closed the distance between them. Shadows swirled around both Cale and Rivalen.

The moans, prolonged and agonized, sounded distant, muted, as if heard through thick stone walls. Cale looked around, up, and down. He stared at the black ground beneath his feet.

"Dark," he said.

"Ready yourselves," Rivalen said, his holy symbol dangling on its chain from his left hand. "Not all life is gone from this place. Not yet."

As if summoned by his words, the spirits of the dead rose from the corpse of Ephyras. Hundreds, thousands of gray, translucent forms floated out of the barren earth all around them and filled the sky. Their forms were humanlike, though slighter, with elongated heads and tiny ears. Their overlarge eyes were as dead and hollow as their world. Despairing moans issued from the holes of their mouths.

They were everywhere.

"Spectres," Rivalen said, and started to cast a spell.

Haunted, despair-filled faces fixed on the three men. The specters' miens twisted with hate and the moans turned from agonized to rage-filled.

Cale reached through Rivalen's shadows and grabbed him by the cloak, interrupting the casting.

"We cannot fight this many. We hold them at bay and keep moving. The temple is why we're here."

Rivalen's eyes flashed with anger for a moment before he nodded.

Cale held his mask in a sweaty hand, and the shadows around Rivalen's flesh curled around it. Riven empowered his blades until they bled shadows. The specters swarmed forward from all sides, a fog of dead souls so thick it obscured their vision.

Cale held Weaveshear forth in both hands, called upon Mask, and channeled divine power through the blade. Shadows poured from it, expanded, and formed a hemisphere of translucent darkness around the three men, under their feet.

Cale braced himself as the specters crashed into it by the tens, by the hundreds. He staggered under the onslaught and the sphere began to collapse inward. The moans and wails grew louder.

One of the specters stuck his hand through the sphere, tore open a gash about as long as a short sword, and started to squirm through. Hundreds of others lined up behind him, screaming, clawing at one another to get through.

Rivalen bounded forward, blades whirling. He caught the specter halfway through, and slashed it across the arms and shoulders. He dived under its incorporeal touch, drove both sabres up through its chest, and it dissipated with a dying moan. The other specters tried pushing through the hole.

"Rivalen!" Cale shouted, and held out his left hand, his shadow hand.

Rivalen took it in his own, called upon Shar and joined his power to Cale's, to Mask's. The sphere darkened and the gash resealed, severing in twain a specter caught halfway through the opening.

"Keep moving!" Cale said. He tried to ignore the unexpected kinship he felt with Rivalen. The divine power they each channeled meshed comfortably, much more so than Cale had ever felt when joining his power with Jak's. Cale chose not to ponder what it might mean.

The specters thronged around the hemisphere. Their moans drowned out the wind and their forms nearly blotted out visibility. Twisted faces, malformed mouths, and dead eyes pressed against the barrier. Cale had to peer through and past their translucent forms to keep his bearings. The intermittent flashes of lightning helped.

They moved as rapidly as they could, attracting more and more specters as they went. Sweat beaded Cale's brow and dripped into his eyes. Rivalen said nothing, merely gritted his teeth, held his holy symbol aloft, and joined his power to Cale's. Shadows poured from both of them to replenish the hemisphere as it weakened here or there.

The press of the undead caused Cale's head to ache. His body weakened with each step. His breath came hard. He felt like he was yoked to a wagon.

"I am failing," Cale said.

Riven pulled threads of darkness from the air, spiraled them around his fingers, and touched them to Cale. Healing energy poured into him, refreshed his mind, renewed his strength.

"Holding?" Riven asked.

"For now."

Cale looked at Rivalen, who also looked strained.

"Do what you can for him, too," Cale said.

"The Hells with him," Riven said softly.

"If he dies, we die. I cannot do this alone."

Riven frowned, went to Rivalen's side, and touched the prince with healing energy. He didn't wait for thanks or acknowledgement, and Rivalen offered neither.

The hemisphere shrank incrementally as they moved across a desert of bones and ruins. The moans of the specters wormed through Cale's ears to his skull, causing his temples to pound. The ground vibrated with the distant rumble of collapsing earth.

"What the Hells is that?" Riven asked, bracing himself against another tremor.

Cale could hardly see through the strain, the sweat, could hardly hear through the wind and moans. "How close are we, Riven? We cannot hold this much longer."

As if to prove his point, one side of the hemisphere collapsed, pressed in like a squeezed waterskin. He and Rivalen both groaned, sagged, channeled what power they had left.

The specters swarmed, but the border of divine power held—misshapen, failing, but intact for the moment. The moans of despair turned to wails of frustration.

Riven moved to the edge of the barrier and peered through the darkness, through the specters. Only the veil of Cale and Rivalen's power separated the assassin from hundreds of undead. The specters, driven mad by the proximity of their prey, scrabbled against the hemisphere, moaning desperately.

"I see it." Riven gave a start, went pale. "Dark, Cale. The world is disappearing behind it."

Again the ground shook under their feet. Cale had no time to ponder Riven's words. "We're out of time. We use the shadows. I will take us. Rivalen, hold as long as you can. I need only a moment."

Shadows churned around Rivalen but he nodded. Darkness poured from his holy symbol, supporting the shrinking hemisphere.

Cale ceased lending his power to the support of the barrier. The release elicited a strained grunt from Rivalen. The hemisphere shrank in on them. The specters pounded against it like mad things.

Cale peered through them, looked in the direction Riven had indicated.

He saw it in a depression below them—a temple.

The whole of it was composed of smoky quartz streaked with veins of black. A dome capped the structure. Spires stood at each corner, just more bones of the dead jutting from Ephyras's dust. Long threads of shadow weaved in an out of columns, arched windows, statues. Closed double doors faced toward them. Cale was surprised to see the temple intact. The fact that it stood whole on an otherwise dead world struck him as somehow obscene. Magic—or something else—must have preserved it.

Beyond it, he saw what Riven had seen. The earth fell away. A black hole several bowshots in diameter yawned in the earth, a void in the world. The ground immediately around the hole slowly turned, like the flow of water around the edge of a maelstrom. It cracked, crumbled, sent up a cloud of dust, collapsed into the hole that was eating the world. It was getting larger as it fed.

He wondered if there were other such holes on Ephyras, other voids devouring the world.

"Transport us!" shouted Rivalen.

Cale pulled his eyes from the hole and drew the darkness about them. For a moment, he considered leaving Rivalen behind. He looked back, met Rivalen's gaze, and saw in the Shadovar's golden eyes that he realized what Cale was thinking. Cale saw no fear there.

Cale included Rivalen in the shadows he gathered. They would need him to defeat Kesson Rel. The darkness deepened around them as Rivalen shouted, fell, and the sphere collapsed entirely. The specters swarmed them, arms outstretched. Their touch reached through armor and flesh, cooled bones, slowed hearts, stole life. They filled the air, turned the already cold breeze frigid.

Cale held his focus in the midst of the chaos and rode the shadows to the temple, Riven and Rivalen in tow.

Regg mounted Firstlight so that his company could more easily see him. She remained calm despite the rain, thunder, and the onrushing Shadowstorm. Regg turned his back to the darkness to face his company, knowing as he looked upon them that all of them would die in the darkness and some would rise again as shadows. In the distance, Sakkors hovered in its cloak of ink.

Regg did not shout. He did not draw his blade. He spoke only loud enough to be heard over the rain. As he spoke, Roen and the priests moved from soldier to soldier, using spells and wands of pale birch to ward the men and women against the life draining power of the Shadowstorm. A flash of soft rose-hued light denoted the wards taking effect.

"Turn and look," Regg said to his company. "See the men and women and children you are bound to protect."

As one they turned, looked down on the Saerbian refugees huddled in their wagons and blankets against wind and rain, against evil and darkness.

"That is why we fight," Regg said. "They need time. It is their only hope. We must give it to them."

He patted Firstlight's neck and dismounted.

"Go," he told her, and swatted her flank. "Bear someone to safety."

She nuzzled him then trotted off to rejoin the rest of the company's horses.

Regg nodded at Trewe and the young soldier sounded his horn to signal the march. Heads emerged from wagons, tents, and carts. Hope animated the gazes of the refugees, though fear lurked behind it. Shouts carried over the rain—well-wishes. A small boy stood at the back of his cart, soaked by the rain, one hand in a trouser pocket, the other raised in farewell. He didn't wave, just held a hand aloft, as still as a statue.

Regg returned the gesture, turned, and led his company on foot toward the darkness.

"That is why we fight," Trewe said from beside him.

The lightning framed the silhouette of a horseman on a rise to the right of the company—Abelar on Swiftdawn. He held his blade in hand and with it, formally saluted them.

Thunder boomed.

Every blade of every man and woman in the company came from its scabbard and returned the salute as they passed and marched into darkness.

Abelar sat his saddle in the rain and watched his company march on the double quick toward the Shadowstorm. He felt drawn after them, pulled by the faith that had been his companion for years. But his love for Elden tethered him to the camp. He could not abandon his son again. Elden couldn't take it. And neither could Abelar.

But he feared he could not take abandoning his company either.

He watched the company until darkness and the rain began to swallow them. They looked tiny, insignificant as they marched into the black wall of the Shadowstorm. He tried to catch their silhouettes in the frequent flashes of lightning but eventually lost them to the smear of night.

The Shadowstorm roiled and churned, as if eager for their arrival. Abelar had his doubts that mere men would be able to slow it. But he had no doubt that they had to try. He would hold out hope.

He dismounted Swiftdawn, took her to the outskirts of the

camp where the company's other horses gathered, heads low, whickering in the storm. He rubbed Firstlight's nose. The other horses neighed, pranced nervously. Perhaps they smelled coming battle in the wind.

"Keep the rest of the horses calm," he said to Swiftdawn and Firstlight. "We may need them yet."

Both horses tossed their heads and neighed.

If he had to, Abelar would do as Regg had sugggested. He would put every refugee he could on the company's mounts and charge them over the Stonebridge. The Shadovar would resist, but perhaps some would get through.

After seeing to the horses' needs, he left them and walked through the rain among the Saerbians, asking after their spirits, calming them with his presence. They smiled gratefully for his attention and asked Lathander to bless him. He looked off in the distance, in the direction of his company, and felt unworthy of blessings.

A young mother with a child at her breast looked up at him from out of a rain soaked tent. Rain pressed her brown hair to her head. Tears streaked her thin, wan face.

"Will we make it to Daerlun, Abelar Corrinthal?"

Abelar looked at her, at the suckling child, and found that his throat would not dislodge words. He nodded, forced a smile he did not feel, and turned back into the rain.

Frustration bubbled up in him, needing release. He wanted to shout his anger into the sky but held it in for fear of alarming the refugees. Instead, he walked the camp with clenched fists and clenched jaw, until he regained control of himself.

When he had, he fixed hope on his face and returned to his covered wagon, found Endren and Elden within. Elden's brown eyes brightened when Abelar entered.

"Papa!"

He hugged Elden while Endren looked a question at him. Abelar shook his head in answer. Endren sagged.

"You all wight, Papa?"

"I'm all right," Abelar said to his son, and cradled his head.

But he was not. Nothing was all right. His body was with his son but his thoughts kept returning to his company.

Cale, Riven, and Rivalen materialized in a dust-choked courtyard. The ground shook and Cale imagined the earth upon which the temple stood cracking, crumbling, falling into the annihilating hole devouring the world.

"All right?" he asked Riven, and the assassin nodded.

"As am I," Rivalen said, though Cale had not asked.

They did not have much time. In the distance, he heard the moans of thousands of specters. The undead would find them, if the world did not end first.

A sculpture of glistening black stone dominated the courtyard. It depicted a tall, faceless woman in flowing robes. A circle of tarnished silver, ringed in amethysts, adorned her breast.

Before her in a fighting crouch stood a shorter male figure, a man clad in a long cloak. Leather armor peaked from under the cloak and he held a slim blade in each hand. A black disc adorned his chest.

The three men stared at the statue a long while, the implications freezing them in place. Shock stole anything Cale might have wanted to say. He heard his heart in his ears. Riven and Rivalen, too, seemed dumbfounded.

The shaking ground and the roar of a collapsing world roused them from stupor.

"How?" Riven said. "Is that . . . ? That cannot be right."

Cale just shook his head, staring at the statue, seeing in the male figure the form of the god he had faced in an alley in Selgaunt.

It could not be what it appeared to be.

Rivalen glided forward to the statue, and the shadows around him stilled. He stared at the sculpture for a time then whispered a prayer. Kneeling, he brushed dirt and dust away from a pedestal of silvery metal to reveal engraved words, weathered by age. He waved a hand over the letters, mouthed a couplet, and his magic undid the weathering. The writing appeared clear against the stone.

Cale didn't recognize the jagged script and didn't want to know what it said. The statue was enough. The affinity between his power and Rivalen's was enough. He needed no more, wanted to know nothing more. He held his mask balled up in his hand. Shadows leaked from between his fingers.

"Do not," he said, knowing what Rivalen intended.

Rivalen looked over his shoulder, his golden eyes afire.

"How can I not? We must know."

Cale remembered his discussion with Mask on the Wayrock, remembered what the god had left unsaid.

Do you serve her? Cale had asked.

He didn't want an answer.

"Why must we know?" Cale asked.

Rivalen smiled, showing fangs. "You know why."

He cast a spell that Cale recognized as one that would allow the prince to understand any written words. The ground shook as the magic took effect and the Shadovar prince read aloud.

"The Mistress of Night and the Shadowlord, her . . . herald."

The word hung in the gloom, the three men processing the import. Like Ephyras itself, Cale's world shook, circled the edge of a bottomless hole. The shadows around him whirled and spun.

"Herald?" Riven asked.

Cale tried to keep his feet, his bearings. He clutched his mask so hard it made his fingers ache. "We've been played," he said finally. "Mask and Shar are not enemies. They are allies."

Riven stared at him, mouth partly open. "No."

"Riven . . ."

The assassin shook his head. "No, Cale. No. There is another explanation."

"What explanation?" Cale said, and darkness shot from his flesh. "We freed Kesson Rel. Kesson Rel caused the Shadowstorm. Mask wanted it all the time. We've been duped. He is her herald. Her *herald*, Riven."

Riven paced a circle, agitated. He glared at Rivalen as if it were the Shadovar who had betrayed them. "No. Freeing Kesson was an accident. We were supposed to kill him."

"So we thought," Cale said. "But Mask knew. He always knows."

"It's too much, Cale," Riven said. "Even for a god. No."

Cale made a gesture that took in the dead world around them. "This is what we've wrought. Look at it. We killed Toril."

Saying the words placed the weight of what they had done squarely on Cale's shoulders. He sagged, wanted to sit down, to sleep. He had been trying to become a hero. Instead, he had unwittingly ended the world.

Riven stopped pacing, took a deep breath, a deliberate calm. "I don't believe it. We're not seeing something—something fundamental."

"We see it," Cale said. "It's just ugly."

"We don't," Riven insisted. "And stop giving up, damn it. You aren't what Fleet wanted you to be so you want to quit. To the Hells with Fleet."

Anger caused the shadows around Cale to whirl. Shame caused his face to warm. He advanced on Riven but his anger faded before he had taken two steps.

"I am not giving up. I just . . . this is the opposite of what I've been trying to do."

"There is something you have not considered," Rivalen said, his deep voice cutting through the space between Cale and Riven.

Cale had almost forgotten the Shadovar was present. They looked at him, waited.

"Kesson Rel is a heretic," Rivalen said. "Shar tolerates him but he does not serve her. She wants me to stop him. If Mask is allied with her, then he wants you to stop him, too."

Cale nodded at Rivalen's holy symbol. "How do you know he's the heretic? Maybe she only tolerates you and it's Kesson who serves her. Maybe you've been played, same as us."

Rivalen tilted his head to concede the point. "We'll know soon enough. I intend to drive back the Shadowstorm. He intends the opposite. Which of us prevails is the true servant of the Lady. To succeed, I need you."

Riven clutched at Rivalen's words, nodded as if he and the Shadovar were blood brothers. "He's right. And there's more to this, Cale. We cannot see it all, but we need to keep faith."

"Faith," Cale said, the word bitter and dry in his mouth.

Riven nodded at Rivalen. "He wants to stop the Shadowstorm. You want to stop it. That's enough. We see it through."

Cale heard in Riven's statement an echo of Mask's words to him back on the Wayrock.

See it through.

Perhaps there *was* something he could not see. He decided to think so. He had no other course. The alternative was calamitous. To do nothing was to allow the Shadowstorm to spread across Toril, to turn it into Ephyras.

"Faith, then," he said to Riven, and uncurled his fingers from around his mask. He held it up, looked through the empty eyeholes. "I hope we're right."

"We are," Riven said.

Cale gathered himself, licked the dust of Ephyras from his lips and asked Rivalen, "The weapon we came for is in the temple?"

"Yes, but I do not know where exactly," Rivalen said.

"Describe it. Or name it."

With either a description or a name, Cale could divine its location.

The ground shook again. The rumble of crashing earth sounded close. Too close.

"The Black Chalice," Rivalen said.

Cale and Riven shared a look as the walls of Fate closed in a little closer. The spirit of Avnon Des had told them of the Black Chalice back on the Plane of Shadow, had told them Kesson Rel had drunk of it in defiance of his god.

"The chalice is a weapon?" Cale said.

Rivalen hesitated long enough for Cale to conclude that he either didn't know or was about to lie.

"A drink from it transforms a Chosen of Mask," Rivalen said.

Cale had been transformed enough already. "Into what?"

Rivalen stared into his face, finally shrugged. "I do not know."

Riven cursed. "You don't know? How can you not know?"

Cale held up a hand to forestall anything further. "Doesn't matter." They had no choice. He held his mask in hand and spoke the words to a divination. When the spell reached its apex, he spoke the words of the item he sought.

"The Black Chalice."

The shadows spiraling around Weaveshear coalesced into a single, thick stream and flowed toward the temple. The weapon tugged at his hands, pulled him along. Cale felt like a fish who had just taken the bait.

"Follow me," he said.

The rain grew worse as Regg and the company approached the border of the Shadowstorm. Lightning veined the sky. Thunder shook the earth. The wall of black loomed, churned, spun. The Shadowstorm became Regg's world. He could not take his eyes from it.

"Dawn follows night," he said to himself. "Always."

Animals fled before the storm as though it were a forest fire—birds, rabbits, deer, foxes. The creatures broke around the company, howling, chittering, squeaking.

Regg said nothing to his company. He didn't need to. None wavered. They served the Morninglord and feared no darkness.

The wall of the Shadowstorm loomed before them, tangible, a black veil that hung across the world, separating the before from the after. It pulsed and expanded as they watched, lurched forward like a serpent, gulping the land. The grass and trees writhed at its touch, twisted into bleak caricatures of themselves.

"Light!" Regg shouted, and Roen and his priests withdrew wooden wands capped with ivory and held them aloft. Light blazed from the wands' tips. Magical daylight defied the darkness.

Thunder boomed.

Regg spared a look up and down his line. Men and women faced the darkness with blades and shields bare, light above them, light in their eyes.

"Onward," he called.

So illuminated, two hundred and fifty servants of the Morninglord breached the Shadowstorm, and Lathander's light did battle with Shar's darkness.

The wards on the members of the company shed motes of rosy light as the life-draining darkness of the storm eroded their efficacy. Darkness crowded close around the wands wielded by Roen and his fellows, dimming but not eliminating their luminescence.

Regg had no strategy other than to fight and survive as long as they could. He hoped to draw out the intelligence guiding the storm, give it pause, slow the storm's advance, and win the Saerbians some extra hours to wait for Cale and Riven to succeed.

The company walked through a rain soaked nightmare land of twisted, wind-stripped trees, and shriveled grass and shrubs. Nothing moved. It was only them and the storm. No one in the company spoke, except to give occasional orders. All had their eyes on the darkness around them.

"There," said Trewe, and pointed ahead.

Two dozen pairs of red eyes materialized in the darkness before them, rose up out of a copse of twisted trees. They started dim and distant, but grew bright as they closed.

"Shadows," Regg said.

Trewe's trumpet did battle with the thunder as two dozen living shadows streaked out of the darkness, red eyes bright with hate. They uttered a high-pitched keening as they closed, the sound enough to raise the hairs on Regg's neck.

"Roen!" Regg shouted. "Your junior priests with me!"

Four of Roen's junior priests rushed forward to Regg's side, their armor clattering.

The shadows shrieked, closed.

Regg held forth his shield, enameled with Lathander's rose, and the priests brandished their holy symbols. Regg waited until the shadows were within twenty paces.

"Now," he said.

He and the priests channeled divine power and their symbols luminesced. Power went out from them in a wave of pale light and hit the advancing shadows.

The shadows' keening died with them. The Morninglord's power turned all two dozen into stinking ribbons of black vapor dispersed by the wind.

"Perhaps they know we're here now," Regg said to the priests.

Thunder rumbled and lightning flashed. When the spots cleared from Regg's vision, he saw that his words had been prophetic. Ahead, so many pairs of eyes blinked into existence in the darkness that they looked like a clear night sky filled with red stars. There were thousands upon thousands.

"Gods," Trewe said, and faltered in his steps.

Regg did not know how much time the company's stand would earn the refugees, but he intended to acquaint the darkness with Lathander's light.

"Ready yourselves, men and women of Lathander!" he shouted.

# CHAPTER TWELVE

*6 Nightal, the Year of Lightning Storms*

Cale, Riven, and Rivalen left behind the statue of Shar and Mask and strode across the crumbling earth for the double doors of the temple. Octagonal gongs flanked the doorway.

Cale eyed Rivalen sidelong and reminded himself not to trust the Shadovar, shared interest or no. Cale's god might serve Shar, but Cale did not serve a Sharran.

"The doors are enspelled," Rivalen said. He held forth his holy symbol and incanted a counterspell without breaking stride. The doors, carved from a rich black wood and inscribed with writings in the same script as that on the statue, clicked and swung open. A lingering spell caused the gongs to sound a deep, funereal chime. Dry air carried the fading, distant smell of incense. Cale swore he heard whispers in the wind but they faded before he could make out any words.

Riven bounded inside, blades bare and leaking shadows.

"Nothing," the assassin called back.

Cale let Rivalen follow then fell in behind him.

Behind them, the moans of the specters grew louder. Cale looked back, saw the gray cloud of spirits rise into the sky and hurtle toward the temple.

"Quickly," he said.

Following the pull of his divination, Cale led them through a black-tiled foyer, vaulted halls, and darkened corridors. Shadows swam in languid spirals within the crystalline walls, or coalesced from nothingness in the air before them. For a reason he could not articulate, Cale thought of the Fane of Shadows.

They found all of the halls and chambers empty even of debris. The structure remained intact but it had been gutted, a mummified version of a temple with only a hint of a dark past to haunt its halls.

The floors groaned, buckled, and shook as more and more of Ephyras fell into the void outside. Dust fell from the ceilings. Cracks opened in the walls.

Paintings here and there repeated the iconography of the Mistress of Night and the Shadowlord, her herald. Cale could not long look at them. The images had a dreamy, surreal quality, as if produced in a fit of madness or a drug haze.

Eventually they entered the large central chamber under the faceted dome. The ceiling soared above them. A horseshoe shaped altar of black stone sat centermost. Inlaid stone formed images on the floor—a black circle bordered in purple and within it, offset from its center, another black circle, bordered in red—the Shadowlord's circle within Shar's circle, the one orbiting within the other.

Magic-sculpted shadows formed an image on the interior of

the dome above. A female figure, her face hidden in the shadow of her black cloak's hood, descended from a storm of roiling black clouds. Lightning presaged her approach. Already on the ground before her was a man, clad in black and steel, and cloaked in shadows.

The herald, preparing the way for the mistress.

Riven put a hand on Cale's shoulder, pulling him back to himself.

"Look there," the assassin said, and pointed with his chin at a small item sitting atop the altar—a tarnished chalice of silvery metal. Thin streams of shadows leaked from its contents, circled its rim.

The shadows leaking from Cale and Rivalen mirrored those emerging from the chalice.

"Is that it?" Riven asked. "It's just sitting here waiting for us?"

"There is no one else on this world to bother it," Rivalen said, his voice soft. "And Shar's temple will not fall until the world ends."

"Mask's temple," Riven corrected, and Rivalen smiled.

"Come," the shade prince said, and started forward.

Enshrouded on Sakkors in shadows and dark thoughts, Brennus felt the ring on his finger open the magical connection between himself and Rivalen.

*Brennus*, his brother said. *We have gained the temple but this world will soon end. Is there anything I must do to prepare for the freeing of the divinity in Kesson?*

Brennus stared at the amethyst and silver ring, his anger and the shadows around him seething. He wanted to tear the ring from his finger, never hear his brother's voice again.

*Brennus?*

*Take the chalice*, Brennus said. *I am still determining the rest.*

Rivalen's irritation was palpable. *Determine it faster. We will face Kesson upon our return.*

*Then delay the confrontation, Brother*, Brennus said, and said that last as if it were a curse. *Lie if you must. Dissembling is one of your strengths.*

*What did you say?*

Brennus had overstepped. *I am overtaxed, Rivalen. Listen to me. The sequence of spells you will need to cast upon the release of the divine power is nuanced. But you will need the chalice as a focus. Take it from the temple and keep it with you. I will contact you again when I am certain of the rest.*

He broke off mental contact before Rivalen could respond. He stared at his mother's necklace, into the face of the complicity he would feel if he did nothing to avenge her murder.

But doing something meant disobeying his father, perhaps sacrificing the possibility of a new Empire of Netheril.

He cursed, and slammed his fist on the table.

Cale, Riven, and Rivalen approached the altar in reverent silence. Outside, Ephyras quaked under Shar's onslaught and the moaning of the specters rose above the whistle of the wind.

The chalice—beaten, tarnished silver chased with tiny black gems that spiraled around its stem—sat atop a black altar cloth. Thin ribbons of shadow curled from its rim. The three men stared at it for a long moment.

"Such a small thing," Riven said, sheathing his blades.

But Cale saw into it, through it. The chalice was simply the doorway, a drink but a symbol. He placed Weaveshear in its scabbard, stepped forward, and reached for the chalice.

Riven grabbed his hand, staring a hole into his face. "Are you certain?"

"It is the only way," Rivalen said from behind them.

Cale nodded and Riven released him. Cale was walking in the steps of Kesson Rel, he knew, trailing him like a shadow. He put his hand, his shadow hand, on the chalice and found it cold, the cold of a grave. A jolt went through him, a charge from head to toe. He lifted it and discovered it weighed much more than it should.

Riven and Rivalen, perhaps involuntarily, crowded close. The shadows around Rivalen mixed with those around Cale, those of the chalice. Riven stood in the midst of their collective darkness.

Cradling the chalice in both hands, Cale held it close and looked within.

An oily, glistening liquid filled it to perhaps a quarter of the way. But Cale knew the chalice's depths went on forever, that the substance within, and the power it embodied, extended much deeper than the shallow depths of the cup. The darkness in the chalice reached back through time and worlds to the creation of the multiverse. He was looking upon the power of a god, the primal stuff of creation. Shadows leaked from it, and him, in languid ribbons.

The moans of the specters grew louder outside, the wail of the wind more pronounced. Ephyras continued to die, its corpse falling into oblivion. Its death throes rocked the temple, shook dust from the walls. Cracks like veins formed in the floor, spreading from wall to wall.

"Drink!" Rivalen said. "The end is coming."

Pieces of the dome cracked, broke, and fell in a rain of crystal to the floor. Riven and Rivalen shielded themselves with their cloaks. Cale stood in the midst of the ruin, untouched, transfixed by the chalice. The wind screamed through the openings in the dome, carrying with it the hateful, desperate moans of the specters. Dust and darkness swirled.

"Cale?" Riven asked.

"If this goes wrong," Cale said to Riven, and nodded at Rivalen. "Kill him."

With that, he lifted the chalice, let the cool, greasy liquid touch his lips, and drank.

Brennus lived in the space between the betrayal of his mother and the betrayal of his father. He could not long hold that ground. Either he honored his mother's memory by exacting payment from her murderer, or he did as his father instructed.

He didn't know if he could live with himself if he did nothing to avenge his mother.

But if he acted, Sembia could be lost and his father would kill him.

He ran his fingertips over his mother's necklace, the necklace that had been brought to him as if by providence. He recalled the moments he had shared with her, the joy. He had experienced little of either since her death.

He made up his mind, nodded to himself, and activated the communication ring.

*Rivalen, when Kesson Rel is dead, the divine power in him will flow to the empty vessel, Kesson's successor, the Chosen of Mask who drank from the chalice. Here are the sequence of spells you must cast, using the chalice as a focus, to take that essence for yourself.*

He recited a series of incantations and abjurations.

*Thank you, Brennus*, Rivalen returned. *You have done well.*

Brennus cut off the magic of the ring. The darkness around him deepened.

He had just murdered his brother. The spells he had named for Rivalen would not capture Kesson's divine power for Rivalen. They would cause the power to consume him.

He put his elbows on the table and his face in his hands. He didn't know how long he sat there before a tug on his cloak caused him to look up.

His homunculi sat on the table near him, the leathery skin of their brows creased with worry.

"Master sad?" one asked.

Brennus inhaled, sat up. The darkness around him was a shroud. "No."

Both of them smiled and held out their hands. "Treat, then?"

He smiled tiredly, took two paper-wrapped sweetmeats from his cloak, and handed them to his creations. They squealed with delight and ate with vigor.

His mother would have laughed. She would have said, *That is quite a family you have, Brennus.*

Indeed it was.

Power entered Cale, wormed its way through him completely, hollowed him out. In an instant he lost whatever humanity remained in him and became a shell, the temple at the edge of nothing made flesh, intact but empty.

And as much in danger of crumbling.

He dropped the chalice and fell to his knees. His scream mingled with that of the wind and the specters. The hole yawned in him, an emptiness that needed filled. His mind spun. Jumbled thoughts ricocheted around his brain.

He struggled to get his intellect around what had happened, what was happening. The chalice did not contain divinity. It contained revelation, realization, the *possibility* of divinity that skulked about in the silence of the human soul. But the possibility was so large, so consuming, that a mortal form awakened to it could not long bear the truth before it simply disincorporated.

Unless it realized its potential.

Shadows whirled around him, angry appendages of darkness lashing out at the world. He threw his head back in another scream and saw that the entire dome of the temple had not collapsed. A small portion remained intact—the black image of Shar, the Lady of Loss, looked down on him.

His scream died. His humanity died. And Riven was at his side.

"Are you all right?"

Cale clutched at Riven and shook his head. "No."

"What happened?"

"It gave me nothing," Cale said. "It just . . . prepared me to receive the power."

Riven cursed and looked back at Rivalen. "There's no weapon here!"

He started to rise, his hand on a saber.

Cale stayed Riven's hand, shaking his head. "This is not his fault."

Rivalen leaned forward, his eyes aglow, his brow furrowed. "What do you feel?"

"Empty," Cale said, and leaned on Riven as he stood. He felt heavy, thick, weighed down by what he might become. "We need to get to Kesson. We can separate him from the divinity, take it back."

"But we have to kill him to get it, Cale," Riven said. "We faced him already. You saw—"

"You did not have me with you, then," Rivalen said.

"Who are you again?" Riven spat at the Shadovar.

"We have to find a way," Cale said. "If we cannot kill him, and soon, this will kill me."

Riven cursed again.

"The Saerbians pass over the river," Cale said to Rivalen. "We have to help you now. You do not need hostages. Let them go."

Another tremor shook the temple. The far wall cracked, crumbled, collapsed.

"Let them go," Cale said again.

Rivalen eyed him, nodded, and specters poured in through the walls, the collapsed dome, all of them with arms outstretched, their translucent faces twisted by desperation.

Cale understood their language and read their lips.

*Help us,* they said, but the words only came out as moans.

"I cannot," Cale said. They were dead, along with their world.

Rivalen grabbed the chalice, whispered a word, and it vanished into his palm. He reached out and started to pull the shadows around them.

Above, another tremor shook the temple and the image of Shar in the dome broke loose, fell intact toward the floor, toward Cale. She would crush him, them.

The darkness grew deep and Cale felt the lurch of movement between worlds.

They materialized in the depths of the Shadowstorm, on the shore of Lake Veladon.

The storm bore down on the refugees. Abelar decided to take it as truth that Regg and the company had slowed it, that their sacrifice had given it pause. He stared at the darkness a long while, tried to pierce its veil through sheer force of will. He sought any sign of his company—a flash of light, the distant clarion of Trewe's trumpet—but he saw only the storm, heard only the rain and thunder.

A peculiar feeling had hold of him. He felt unsettled, foreign to himself, as if someone else were living through his body. He had never before stood idle when darkness threatened.

But he had no choice. Elden's safety was his foremost concern.

"I must live with myself."

The roll of thunder mocked his claim.

He turned and looked south toward the Stonebridge. Sakkors hovered in the air, dark, foreboding, only partially visible through the rain and shadows. Large, winged creatures flew in threes and fours in the shadow-shrouded air around the city, their Shadovar riders leaning over their saddles to eye the land below for any refugees who might try to cross the river or sneak across the bridge.

None would. The refugees huddled in their wagons, carts, and tents, awaiting their fates. Lightning bolts lit the sky and the relentless, hungry thunder of the storm hammered at the camp, eroded the refugees' spirits.

Abelar left off his self pity and walked among the refugees, peeked into tents, into carts, and offered words of encouragement. Again and again he saw the beginnings of surrender in their tired eyes. They did not have much time and they knew it. Fear polluted the air. They exhaled it with every breath.

"Darkness behind and darkness before," said an elderly woman shivering in a wool blanket in the rear of a wagon. Fever and fear had turned her pale. "What will we do, Abelar?"

"Endure," Abelar answered. They could do nothing else, at least for the moment. The word became the spell he incanted to all of them, though he knew it held no magic.

"Endure. Dawn follows night. Endure."

When he had no more to give the refugees, he slogged through the mud and rain to the covered wagon in which his father and son sheltered. He found Endren standing outside, braving the rain to eye the storm. Endren's weathercloak billowed in the wind. His moustache and beard drooped from the wet but Abelar saw no sag in his shoulders, no want in his spirit.

"Elden is asleep," Endren said, seeing Abelar approach and anticipating his question.

"How's he holding up?" Abelar asked.

"He's wearing thin."

"So are all the people," Abelar said. "This sky drains hope."

"Aye," Endren said. "How are *you* holding up?"

Abelar smiled wanly. "I am wearing thin, too. But I still have hope."

"As do I," Endren said, and put a comforting hand on Abelar's shoulder.

Together, father and son watched the lightning, the boiling black clouds. From a wagon nearby, audible in the small gaps between thunder, Abelar heard a woman's sobs. He did nothing because there was nothing he could do.

"The storm has slowed," he said to Endren.

"But not stopped."

"No, not stopped. I have no word from Erevis Cale."

"We have hours," Endren said.

"Perhaps not that long."

Lightning lit up the storm.

Endren turned to face him. "What will you do if the situation does not change?"

"I will mount the people double and triple on the company's horses and attempt to cross the river."

"The river is too fast for horse or man to swim."

Abelar nodded. "We will charge the bridge. I will lead it."

Endren stared at him but said nothing.

Both of them knew what a charge across the Stonebridge would mean for the refugees, should the Shadovar resist it. The refugees were not soldiers.

"Those who get over the bridge will disperse in hopes of avoiding Shadovar pursuit," Abelar said.

Endren looked off into the darkness. "Let us hope it does not come to that."

"Indeed. But we should prepare."

"I will assist you with the mounts."

"Someone must stay with Elden."

On another day, at another time, he could have asked Jiriis to mind Elden. He trusted her and she loved him and his son. But Jiriis had ridden with Regg and the company into the storm, where Abelar should have been.

"I will do it alone," Abelar said.

⊛　⊛　⊛　⊛　⊛

The shadows attacked in disorganized, chaotic swirls. Hundreds swarmed toward the Company, whirling frantically in an effort to get at the living. There were so many that Regg knew his company would be surrounded.

"Closed circle," he said to Trewe, who announced the order with his trumpet. To Roen, Regg said, "You and the priests stand within the ranks. You are to keep us lit throughout."

"Aye," said the tall priest, and he turned, shouting orders to his fellow priests.

Men and women hurried into position, splashing through the rain and the mud. They stood shield to sword in a closed circle. Roen and his priests stood in their midst holding incandescent wands aloft, an island of light against which an ocean of night would break.

Or so Regg hoped.

Thunder rolled. Lightning flashed. The shadows closed.

The junior priests chanted a prayer to Lathander and held aloft their hands. A rose-colored hue expanded outward from their palms and touched every man and woman in the company. The magic of the spell calmed Regg's heart and mind.

"The Morninglord has blessed our efforts," Roen proclaimed.

The shadows began to keen as they closed, a sound like the screams of the dying.

Roen and the senior priests chanted the words to more powerful spells, and beams of searing white light went forth from their outstretched hands. The scythes of luminescence knifed through the approaching shadows and burned away a score of them. Two score took their place.

"The Morninglord is with you all," Regg shouted, his voice as level as a planed board. He felt the heft of his sword and shield.

"And you," they answered as one.

Behind the swarm of shadows were more shadows, more. The line of their glowing red eyes seemed endless. Regg whispered a prayer to the Morninglord that infused his shield and sword with the Lathander's holy energy until both glowed a soft pink. Others along the line did the same, and flowers of rosy light bloomed in the darkness.

Beside him, he heard Trewe chanting in a whisper, not a spell, but a prayer nevertheless.

"We stand in the light. We stand in the light."

Regg bumped his shield into Trewe's blade. "Look under your feet."

Trewe peeled his eyes from the shadows to look at the dead grass underfoot.

"That is your world," Regg said. "One pace wide. You hold that ground."

Trewe nodded and turned his eyes back to the horde of shadows. They drew closer. Some dived into the earth, some darted above, some came directly at the line.

Regg turned to measure his line one final time. The men and women stood in tight ranks, blades, shields, and wills all hard and sharp. Roen and his eight priests stood spaced in the center of the circle, illuminated in blazing light, the roses on their shields and breastplates catching the light and twinkling like stars.

Roen shouted an order to his fellow priests and all of them intoned prayers to Lathander. When they finished their spells, a faintly glowing sword composed of magical force appeared and took station beside each of them. Regg knew the weapons would defend the priests, attack whom they directed, allow them to focus on keeping the company in the light and holding the shadows outside the circle.

Regg turned from the light to the darkness, and braced himself as the shadows ate the distance. The unnatural pitch of the dark creatures' keening stood his hair on end.

The undead swirled uncertainly as they neared the light of the company, but their hesitation lasted only a moment. Hundreds of shadows churned forward.

Moving into the light transformed the appearance of the shadows, sharpened the soft, dark borders of their forms and features. Regg caught glimpses of the men and women they had been in life. He saw shadowy ghosts of armor, weapons, and tabards featuring the wheel of the overmistress's army.

He knew then what had happened to Forrin's army. And he knew, too, that his company would have their chance to avenge Saerb after all.

"They wear the wheel of Forrin's army!" he shouted. "Forrin's army is come to face us at last."

"For Saerb, then!" Trewe shouted, and others took up his call.

Red eyes grew large in his sight and Regg readied himself.

The company's mounts stood in a group on the outskirts of the camp, heads lowered against the rain and thunder. They sheltered from the rain as best they could under a stand of three maples but the chill had many shivering. Firstlight and Swiftdawn neighed a greeting to Abelar.

Abelar moved among the horses, whickering, stroking flanks, and making soothing sounds as he saw to their tack and checked saddle straps. He stripped them of saddle bags and other unnecessary weight.

Firstlight and Swiftdawn followed him as he moved from horse to horse. Both nudged him with their noses and looked east to the storm, tossing their heads. Both knew battle was in the darkness.

"I know," Abelar said, rubbing their noses. Like him, they were bred to fight darkness. Like him, they felt uncomfortable with idleness.

Presently he had the mounts ready to go. He stepped out from under the maples, eyed first Sakkors, then turned to the Shadowstorm. They had perhaps an hour and it would be upon them. He recalled the verdict of Roen's divinations—the very air within the storm would drain a man of life, blacken his spirit, and raise him as an undead shadow. Abelar would not let his people, his son, die that way.

He imagined the members of his company fighting in the darkness, dying, arising to feed Kesson Rel's black army. He feared that if the storm caught the refugees he would see faces he knew in the shadows that came to kill them, faces wearing judgment and screaming accusations.

*You should have been with us*, they would say. *You could have made a difference.*

"Perhaps," he murmured, and ran a hand along Swiftdawn's side. "Perhaps."

He walked back to the camp, went to each wagon, to each cart.

"We ride within the hour," he said to them.

Hope fired in their eyes but he quenched it with his next words.

"Bring nothing but a weapon. We must fight our way across the river."

By the time he had completed his round of the camp, the refugees had emerged into the rain. Some sobbed, holding their children close. Others bore resigned looks on their faces and notched swords in their hands. Some carried farm implements that could double as weapons: axes, small scythes, hammers. A few bore hunting bows. Others fashioned clubs from wagon axles.

In pairs and small groups they made their way through the storm to the horses. Abelar cradled Elden in one arm and walked among them. He could not shake the feeling that he was leading them all to the gallows.

The rain worsened. The thunder and lightning grew more intense. Sakkors hovered in the distance, threat and promise. The horses whickered and stomped nervously in the storm. Abelar lifted Elden onto Swiftdawn.

"You come, Papa," Elden said, and patted the saddle.

Abelar touched his son's hand, but looked to Endren.

"Stay with him," he said, and his father nodded.

Abelar walked among the refugees, assisted them into the saddle, and gave brief instructions to those with little experience on horseback. As he did, as he looked into their faces and saw the hope and trust they put in him, he knew that he would not be able to ride with Elden on Swiftdawn. He would have to leave his son after all. The realization put a hole in his stomach, but warmed his spirit.

When he had them all mounted, he stood on a toppled log and faced them. The darkness made their expressions hard to distinguish. He was pleased he couldn't see them. He knew what he would have seen.

"Do not try to have your mount swim the river," he said above the thunder. "It's too wide and fast. We ride hard for the Stonebridge. I will lead you in this. The Shadovar will try to stop us. They will have steel and magic."

Sobs interrupted his thoughts.

"Do not stand and fight," he continued. "Flight is your best hope. If—" He stopped himself, cleared his throat. "When you cross the bridge, run away from the storm, as fast your mount will bear you."

He saw men and women nod and firm up, saw others wilt and hug each other.

He hopped off the log and walked through them, back to Elden and Endren.

"You ride Swiftdawn with Elden," he said to Endren.

"You come, Papa," Elden said. "With me."

Abelar blinked back tears, took his son from the saddle, and hugged him.

"I am coming. I'll ride Uncle Regg's horse. You take a ride with Grandpapa."

He kissed his son on the head and gave him over to Endren.

"If you gain the bridge, give Swiftdawn her head," he said to Endren. "Not even the Shadovar's flying creatures will catch her."

Endren nodded. "I've seen her run."

Father and son embraced. Together, they lifted Elden into the saddle. Endren hopped up behind the boy.

"Are you afraid?" Abelar asked Elden.

He shook his head. "No, Papa."

"Nor I," said Abelar, rubbing Swiftdawn's face. He leaned in close to Swiftdawn and whispered in her ear, "You are his, now."

She eyed him, neighed, nuzzled his face. He turned and walked back through the refugees to Firstlight. He found his eyes drawn back to the Shadowstorm, where his company was fighting and dying. He regretted that he would not die with them.

He leaped into Firstlight's saddle, feeling light for the first time in days. He turned her, drew his blade, and prepared to give the order to ride.

A hole of darkness formed in the middle of the group. Women screamed, horses reared, everyone backed away.

"Shadovar!" someone screamed.

From the darkness emerged Erevis Cale, Drasek Riven, and a third man blanketed in shadows—Rivalen Tanthul, Abelar presumed.

Rivalen's eyes glowed golden. Cale's glowed yellow.

# CHAPTER THIRTEEN

*6 Nightal, the Year of Lightning Storms*

The identity of the three newcomers registered with the refugees, manifested in hopeful whispers.

"The Maskarran."

"Erevis Cale has returned."

None of the refugees dismounted, none shouted for joy, none closed ranks around Cale and his companions. They held their seats in the saddle, watching Cale warily, as if moving too fast would cause him to return from whence he had come. An empty space separated the refugees and their ostensible saviors.

"Erevis," Abelar said, and fairly leaped off of Firstlight.

"The dark men are back," Elden said as Abelar passed.

"Everything's all right," Abelar said, reaching up to pat his son. He pushed through the horses and broached the empty circle in which Cale, Riven, and Rivalen stood.

Up close, Abelar could see that something in Cale had changed. He looked more clearly defined, more substantive, as if the world were a painting and he its viewer. He stopped short of embracing Cale and Riven. A hush fell over the refugees.

"Something has happened to you," Abelar said.

"Something has happened to you, too," Cale said, his voice hollow.

"Kesson Rel is dead?" Abelar asked.

Cale shook his head. "Not yet."

Abelar eyed Rivalen. "These people are crossing that bridge, Shadovar, and if—"

"Tell him," Riven said to Rivalen.

The shadows around the Shadovar churned. "You and your people may pass. You will remain safe while in Sembia."

The words hung there, alone in the air for a long moment before the first of the refugees cheered. Abelar blinked then sagged with relief as fists and weapons rose into the air, as shouts of joy, for a moment at least, overwhelmed the thunder.

"But you said Kesson Rel still lives," Abelar said to Cale and Riven.

"We've made other arrangements," Riven said.

Abelar did embrace Cale and Riven then. "Thank you, my friends."

Presently, Endren was shouting orders, getting the group ready to move, not for a death charge across the Stonebridge, but for a gallop to safety.

"I knew you would save us," a women called to Abelar.

"It was not me," Abelar said, "but these men."

"Regg and the company?" Cale asked.

The words squelched Abelar's joy. He nodded at the Shadowstorm. "Within the storm."

Endren, atop Swiftdawn with Elden, led Firstlight by the reins to Abelar.

"It seems the Corrinthals owe you yet another debt," he said to Cale and Riven. "My thanks."

Cale inclined his head. "You should get them across the bridge and keep moving." He looked back at the storm. "This is far from over."

"Aye," Endren said.

"If there is anything I can do for Regg and your company, I will do it," Cale said to Abelar. "But Kesson Rel is our first priority."

Cale's words stuck with Abelar. *Your* company. They *were* his company.

Endren held out Firstlight's reins for Abelar. "Abelar."

Abelar looked at them, looked up at his father, at his son, and did not take the reins.

Endren read his eyes. He let the reins fall from his hand. "You aren't coming."

Elden looked down, alarm on his face. "No. Papa coming."

Abelar looked back at Cale, Riven, and the Shadovar. "Can you take me with you? To my company?"

The shadows around Cale swirled. He shook his head. "Our fight is with Kesson Rel. You don't want to accompany us there, Abelar. But . . ."

"But?" Abelar prompted.

"Papa," Elden said.

"I can provide you with a mount to take you."

"I have a mount," Abelar said. "And no horse runs like her. But even that is too slow."

"I mean a different kind of mount, one that doesn't run at all."

Abelar looked a question at him and Cale said, "Get everyone out of here, first."

"Time is short," Rivalen said. "We must locate Kesson Rel.'"

"We know time is short, Shadovar," Cale snapped.

Elden's voice pulled Abelar around. "Papa?"

Abelar turned, his heart in his mouth, and lifted his son from Swiftdawn. The boy looked wet, vulnerable. Abelar placed him on the ground, kneeled down, pressed his brow to Elden's.

"Papa is going to find Uncle Regg. You go with Grandpapa now. Everything's all right. Do you understand?"

Elden nodded and smiled uncertainly. "Uncle Regg lost?"

Abelar smiled. "Yes, he's lost."

Elden's face twisted as he processed the reply. "Uncle Regg sad, then."

Abelar's resolve almost crumbled. Tears fell. "Yes, he is sad. As is Papa."

"Why?" Elden said, and took his hand.

Abelar tried to give his thoughts words. "Because Papa has not lived up to his view of himself."

Elden frowned. He didn't understand. "My still want you to come with us, Papa."

"I know, but Uncle Regg needs me."

He wanted to tell Elden that he was who he was, that he had to live with himself and that he could not be the father or man he thought himself to be if he didn't stand and fight. He had tried to stand idle but he couldn't.

Elden cleared his throat and eyed him with a bright, clear gaze. "You good man, Papa."

Perhaps he understood, after all.

Abelar cried, took his son in his arms. "I love you, Elden."

"My loves you, Papa."

Abelar stood, lifted and held his son, reluctant to let go.

Endren hopped down from Swiftdawn, hugged them both, thumped Abelar's back, sniffed back tears.

Abelar handed him Endren. "Go now. Now."

Endren and Elden mounted.

"We will see you when you return," Endren said.

Abelar nodded. "Hurry. The storm is almost upon you."

"Bye, Papa," Elden said, and smiled. "Find Uncle Regg."

Abelar touched his son's hand, could not speak.

He kept his composure as the group of refugees rode off. The Saerbians thanked him and Cale and Riven as they passed.

"Bless you. Bless you all. Lathander watch you all."

Endren led the refugees at a gallop and soon they were nearly lost to the night.

"A good end for them," Abelar said. "You both have my thanks."

"Don't thank us yet," Cale said.

Riven spit. "Ends aren't likely to be good for everyone."

Abelar stepped close to Rivalen Tanthul, reached through his shroud of shadows, and took him by the cloak.

"Look at them, Shadovar," he said, and nodded at the refugees. "Those are the women and children you would have murdered."

The shadows cloaking Rivalen coiled around Abelar's hand and forearm. The Shadovar looked into Abelar's face, eyes hard, took him by the wrist—

Cale and Riven had blades free and pointed at Rivalen's chest.

"Easy," Cale said, shadows leaking from his black blade, from his pale flesh.

Rivalen forcibly removed Abelar's hand from his cloak. The strength in the Shadovar's grip might have cracked bone had Abelar's mail not protected him.

"I would have looked each of them in the eye and killed them myself should it have been necessary to ensure a weapon against Kesson Rel," Rivalen said.

"You disgust me," Abelar said.

Riven kept his blades leveled at Rivalen's chest. "The prince here doesn't think like you, Abelar. He thinks it's all for nothing, so worrying over anything is pointless."

"You saw Ephyras," Rivalen said to Riven, and Riven said nothing.

Abelar stared into the darkness of Rivalen's face. He knew the Shadovar prince was beyond him. He didn't care.

"You are empty, Shadovar. All that power, yet you remain a hole."

Rivalen's golden eyes flared. A long moment passed. "Your regard is of no moment to me, Saerbian."

Abelar's arm twitched but he restrained the desire to punch Rivalen in the face. He turned to Cale. "You spoke of a mount?"

"It is a creature of shadow. Does that deter you?"

Abelar thought of Regg and his company assailed in the storm. "No. I have seen light even in shadow."

Cale nodded, moved away from Riven and Rivalen. He stood in the grass, drenched in rain, shrouded in shadows, lit by lighting, with the Shadowstorm at his back. He drew the darkness around him, let it expand outward until it covered all four men then a swath of the plains as wide as a spear cast. They stood in a black fog.

"Furlinastis," Cale called into the shadows.

Time passed and Abelar realized he was holding his breath. He heard only the hiss of the rain and the drum of thunder.

"Furlinastis," Cale called again, louder.

A pungent organic stink filled Abelar's nostrils, faint at first, but then stronger, the smell reminiscent of mud, of life, death, decay. A reptilian hiss sounded in the blackness. Movement stirred the shadows. Abelar had the impression of an immense form moving in the darkness but he could see nothing. He leaned forward . . .

A dragon materialized out of the darkness, its body a mountain of black scales and muscle. The scales shimmered a faint purple around the edges when the wyrm moved. The vertical slit of its reptilian eyes fixed on Cale, Riven, Rivalen, and Abelar. It spread its wings and they blotted out the sky, sheltering them all from the rain.

Abelar met and held the dragon's gaze, though the power and age implied by the dragon's form made him feel tiny.

Its tail slid over the plains behind it, knocking over trees. Its claws, each as long as a short sword, sank deeply into the earth. It oozed toward Cale, silent despite its size. Shadows hung from its form, swirled, blurred its borders.

The dragon's voice was soft, sibilant. "I have heard and answered, First of Five."

Cale inclined his head. "My thanks, Furlinastis. You have kept your promise."

Streams of shadow leaked from the dragon's nostrils.

Cale pointed at the black wall of the Shadowstorm. "Kesson Rel's forces stalk the darkness of that storm."

The dragon hissed at the mention of Kesson Rel.

"My company battles them there," Abelar said.

"Bear him into the storm," Cale said, indicating Abelar. "Fight Kesson Rel's creatures as you wish."

"My promise was to serve you," he said to Cale then swung his head toward Abelar, "not to bear your lackeys."

Abelar took a step forward. Furlinastis's breath, as foul and damp as a swamp, moistened his face. "I am no lackey, wyrm."

The dragon's lips peeled back from his teeth in snarl, showing fangs as black as tarnished silver and longer than a dagger. The shadows around the creature swirled, engulfed Abelar.

"You serve me by bearing him to battle," Cale said. "You owe your life to me, dragon. I ask little in return."

Furlinastis hissed, exhaling twin streams of darkness from his nostrils. "I am—"

"My time is short, dragon!" Cale snapped. "Keep your promise to me."

The slits of Furlinastis's pupils narrowed. He swung his head from Abelar to Cale, sniffing the air as if sampling the shadows around Cale.

"You have changed since last we met, First of Five."

"Yes. Will you do this, dragon?"

They stared at one another for a long moment.

"How will you ride?" Furlinastis said to Abelar.

Abelar eyed the creature's body. The ridges along his neck would provide stability.

"Upon your neck, just above the wings. I need only a rope."

"Do it," the dragon said.

Riven produced a rope from his pack and he, Cale, and Abelar fitted the wyrm as they best they could. Riven's use of rope would have bested even a lifelong sailor. Abelar tested the knots.

"A good harness," Abelar said.

"I will not save you if you fall," Furlinastis said, and lowered his head to allow Abelar to mount.

Abelar climbed into position, secured his thighs with the sling knots they had improvised, and took the makeshift reins in one hand and wrapped them around his wrist.

"I have ridden since I could walk, wyrm." He shifted, testing his range of motion, his comfort with his perch. It was no saddle, but it would do. "I haven't lost my place in a saddle since I was a boy. Not even so mighty a creature as you can throw me."

Furlinastis snaked his neck around to look at him and Abelar thought he saw mirth in the creature's eyes. "We will see."

"You need to be warded against the storm," Cale said. He held his velvet mask in one hand, intoned the wards to a ward, and placed a charged hand on Abelar then Furlinastis.

"Thank you, Erevis," Abelar said. He held a hand out. "I am glad that we met, both of you.

"As am I," Cale said, clasping hands.

"And I," Riven said, doing the same.

He leaned down in the saddle and spoke in a conspiratorial tone. "Do not trust the Shadovar."

"We don't," Cale said. "But we need him. And he needs us. That is enough for now."

Abelar accepted that. War made for strange allies. And this war more than most. He looked Cale in the face.

"There is a haunted look in your eyes," Abelar said to Cale.

"I have seen what happens if we fail, Abelar."

Abelar studied his face. "Then do not fail."

Cale smiled softly and nodded. "Farewell, my friend."

"Fight well," Riven said.

"That I will. Fly, dragon!"

Furlinastis tensed, extended his wings, and leaped into the dark air.

The dragon's graceful form receded rapidly and soon melded with the darkness. Cale lost sight of him. The emptiness in him yawned. He needed to fill it or it would consume him.

*I know now what you endured*, he projected to Magadon. *Magadon, do you hear me?*

The mindmage did not respond.

"I should check on Mags," he said to Riven.

"No, you shouldn't. If he's out of your head, leave it that way. He's a distraction now. You holding up?"

"I'm losing myself, sinking."

Riven nodded and put a supportive hand on his shoulder, his expression thoughtful.

Rivalen's golden eyes burned dimly in the void of his face, twin echoes of Ephyras's dying sun. "We should prepare before we seek Kesson Rel."

"His counterspells steal for himself any wards or enhancements we might place on us," Cale said. "We've seen it."

The shadows around Rivalen roiled as he considered Cale's words. "You're suggesting we face him unprotected?"

"I'm telling you your protections benefit him, not you."

"You afraid, Prince?" Riven said with a sneer.

Rivalen stared at Riven. "Are you?"

"Yes," Riven said. "But not of death."

"He casts spells faster than anyone I've ever seen," Cale said. "And he's resistant to magic."

"Yours, perhaps," Rivalen said. "He will find mine much harder to deflect. And even if he can steal spells, magical devices should still work. Use them if you bear any."

Cale had only one. He drew Weaveshear. Riven withdrew the spell-absorbing stone he'd taken from the Sojourner and tossed it into the air in front of his face, where it took up orbit around his head. He drew his sabres.

"We should scry him first," Rivalen said.

"He cannot be scried," Cale said. "We've tried."

"Not by you, nor even me," Rivalen said, "but he can be scried by my brother."

Abelar looked ahead at the roiling black wall of the Shadowstorm and felt an echo of the feeling he'd experienced when he'd first answered Lathander's call in adolescence. His blood rose; he felt light.

He leaned over the dragon's neck, looked back and down, and saw Cale, Riven, and Rivalen standing together on the receding plains. They weren't looking at him. They had already turned their minds to Kesson Rel. He looked back farther, tried to spot the Saerbians under Sakkors, and thought he caught a blurry glimpse of motion atop the distant Stonebridge. Perhaps they were crossing even then. Love for his son and father warmed him, but love for Regg and Jiriis and his company drew him onward into darkness.

He drew his blade and faced the darkness of Shar's Shadow-storm. Lightning shot out of the sky to trace green lines in the clouds around them. The air stank of char, as if the sky were afire. Thunder vibrated in his ears. The wind pulled at him.

"Faster, dragon!"

Furlinastis beat his wings, extended his neck, and shot like a fired quarrel through the air.

The magical ring on Brennus's finger warmed. The mental connection with his brother opened.

*Brennus, I need you to scry Kesson Rel. Tell me where he is, and what you see. We are nearly at an end.*

Brennus sat at a table in an otherwise unfurnished room on Sakkors. The darkness embraced him. His homunculi wrestled on the floor, tumbling and squeaking. He sometimes thought of them as his family, but they were not. They were devices, nothing more. His family was his brothers and his father.

*Brennus.*

"I have killed you," Brennus said to the ring, his tone uncertain.

*Brennus.*

*It will take some time,* Brennus projected to Rivalen.

*We have little time, Brother. You must hurry.*

*Very well.*

Brennus cut off the connection. He lifted his mother's neck-lace, watching his homunculi frolic.

"Family," he said, and wondered if he had done the right thing.

He intoned the words to the first in a series of divinations.

⊛ ⊛ ⊛ ⊛ ⊛

"We must wait a short time," Rivalen said to Cale and Riven.

"A short time is all we have," Cale said to him.

Rivalen leaned forward, his darkness mingling with Cale's. "What does it feel like?"

Cale saw no reason to lie. "Like I am hollow. Like I will crumble soon."

Rivalen nodded and leaned back, his expression preoccupied.

"Give me the chalice," Riven said to the Shadovar.

The shadows around Rivalen swirled in agitation. "Why?"

"Give it to me or we will not help you."

"A lie."

"*I* will not help."

"What are you doing, Riven?" Cale asked.

Riven looked at him, one hand on his holy symbol. "You could fail. I am your second. *His* Second."

Cale understood immediately what Riven intended. "Do not. If we succeed, only one of us can be saved."

Riven stared at him, nodded. "It's sense, Cale, and you know it. It's why I'm here."

Cale shook his head. "You don't know how it feels. You're making a mistake."

But he wasn't sure Riven was making a mistake.

"This is mine to do, Cale." Riven held out his hand to Rivalen. "Give me the chalice, Shadovar. I saw you take it."

Cale eyed Riven and thought of Ephyras. He didn't know if he would hold on; he was sinking, fast. "Give it to him, Rivalen."

The shadows around Rivalen slowed, spun lazy streams about his form. "You must return it to me. We may yet need it."

"For what?" Riven asked.

"Give it to him," Cale said.

Rivalen spoke a word and the tarnished chalice, still leaking shadows over its rim, appeared in his hand. He handed it to Riven.

"Heavy," the assassin said.

"Yes,' Cale said, and knew they weren't talking about the chalice.

Riven looked at Cale, at the contents of the chalice, and drank.

Then he began to scream.

Furlinastis devoured the distance. The border of the Shadowstorm drew closer, larger, the wind and rain more intense. In moments they had reached the edge of the storm. A wall of churning black clouds and green lightning stretched from the plains to the heavens.

Abelar leaned forward, clutching his blade, as the dragon breached the dark wall.

The wind and rain did not abate. Lightning and thunder still shook the sky. But the darkness deepened, deadened sound, and dulled senses. Abelar felt the storm's life draining power testing Cale's ward. A vibration shook Abelar's body. It took him a moment to realize that the dragon's growl had caused it.

"The air stinks of Kesson Rel," Furlinastis said.

"I feel Shar in it," Abelar answered.

"The one is the other," the dragon said, and beat his wings.

Abelar leaned over the dragon's neck, searching for his company.

"Wide arcs," he said to the dragon. "As fast as you can. We are looking for a company of men and women, over two hundred strong."

The dragon lowered his altitude and angled left and right as he flew ever deeper into the storm.

"There," the dragon said above the wind.

"Where? Where?"

"Ahead," Furlinastis said.

Abelar heard the battle before he saw it—the high pitched keen of shadows, the shouts of men and women.

And then he saw them, a light in the darkness.

His company stood shield to sword in a circular formation. Thousands of shadows swirled in the air over them, before them, around them. Light flared here and there within the circle—no doubt Roen and the priests—but swarms of shadows pounced on it, tried to extinguish it. But for every light the shadows extinguished, the priests lit another. Abelar heard the clarion of Trewe's trumpet over the thunder and his heart soared.

"Let them know we are here Furlinastis," he said.

The dragon drew in a breath and expelled it in a roar that overwhelmed the thunder. Heads turned to look up. The red eyes of shadows glared out of the black.

Wanting the company to know it was him atop the dragon rather than another enemy, he struck a sunrod on the dragon's scales and the tip of the small device flared to life. The glow caused Furlinastis to growl as they streaked over the battlefield.

"I am with you!" he shouted but didn't know if they heard him.

Trewe's trumpet sounded another clarion. He looked back and saw blades raised, heard cheers. They'd heard him.

And so, too, had the shadows.

Ahead, behind, above, and below, he saw scores and scores of black, red-eyed forms arrowing toward them. Furlinastis roared and angled upward. The darkness extinguished the sunrod.

"Abelar is with us!" Regg shouted, and drove his illuminated blade into the chest of a shadow, one of Forrin's former soldiers.

The blow extinguished the creature's eyes and it boiled away, shrieking, into a cloud of foul vapor.

"The light is in you all!" Roen shouted from behind as another globe of white luminescence burst into being above their formation.

Shadows thronged the air all around the formation, darting past, streaking down from above. The presence of so many undead turned the already chill air frigid, and Regg's breath formed clouds in the air as he slashed, stabbed, butted with his shield.

The keening of the shadows filled his ears, but so did the comforting calls and shouts of the men and women of his company. Beside him, Trewe exclaimed in pain and fell to his knees. Three shadows reached into his chest. Trewe's mouth opened but no sound emerged.

"Down to whatever hell will take you!" Regg shouted. He brandished his shield, showed them the rose of Lathander, and let some of his soul move through him and into the rose.

A wedge of rose-colored light flared from the shield, vaporizing the three shadows attacking Trewe. A backhand crosscut slew another shadow and he grabbed Trewe with his shield arm, pulled him to his feet, and let healing energy flow into the young warrior.

"Well enough?" Regg asked.

"Well enough," Trewe answered.

Both men turned and eyed the horde of shadows that filled the air so thickly it was nearly impossible to separate one of the creatures from another. Black bodies clotted the sky, made the air impenetrable. Hundreds of them veered high to engage Abelar and his dragon. Regg didn't stop to consider how Abelar might have bent a shadow dragon to his service. He didn't care. He cared only that his friend fought with them. They couldn't hope to hold for long, but they would hold as long as they could and hope their sacrifice meant something for the Saerbians.

"Keep us in light, Roen!" he shouted, and slashed another shadow. "Hold this ground, men and women of Lathander!"

Riven fell to his knees, his head thrown back in a scream. The sky seemed to echo his agony with booms of thunder and flares of lightning.

Cale knew what Riven was feeling, the emptiness that accompanied revelation. He knelt beside the assassin, let his shadows cloak him, comfort him.

Rivalen watched them both intently, golden eyes alight, the Black Chalice already recovered from where Riven had dropped it and returned to the extra-dimensional space in which the Shadovar stored it.

"It will pass," Cale said to Riven. "It will pass."

Riven gritted his teeth, hugged himself, writhed, and screamed again.

After a time the screams ended. He drew a shuddering breath and let Cale pull him to his feet. His good eye regained focus. He doubled over, vomited. When he was done, he looked up at Cale.

"It's that simple? It's been there all along?"

Cale nodded. "That simple."

They stared at one another for a long moment.

Both knew that one of them, at least, must die. Both if they failed to kill Kesson Rel.

"We need to know where he is," Cale said over his shoulder to Rivalen. "Now."

The shadows around Rivalen swirled. He cocked his head, consulting his brother through some unseen magical means.

"Kesson Rel is not in Ordulin," Rivalen said, his tone mildly surprised.

"Then where in the Nine Hells is he?" Cale said.

Brennus communicated Kesson Rel's location to his brother then cut off the connection. He closed his hand around his mother's necklace and placed it in his pocket, where he would keep it forever.

He couldn't murder his brother. Murder itself didn't trouble him, but murdering his brother did. The consequences were too great.

If he betrayed Rivalen, his father would kill him. His other brothers would wonder what had happened, would eventually learn of it. Sides would be chosen and his family would splinter. The revived Empire of Netheril would die stillborn.

He couldn't do that to his family, to his people. He would bear the knowledge of Rivalen's deed alone, just as he would bear his mother's necklace.

But he would not do nothing.

# CHAPTER FOURTEEN

*6 Nightal, the Year of Lightning Storms*

Abelar gripped the makeshift harness and steadied himself atop Furlinstasis's back. Shadows poured from the dragon's purple and black scales. A cloud of ink stained the air around them and left a path of smeared black in their wake. The rain felt like sling bullets against his exposed face. The roar of the wind filled his ears, pierced only by the keening of the undead.

Living shadows thronged the air, swirled around him, a colony of red-eyed bats on the wing. They swooped and dived at him and the dragon. Furlinstastis wheeled, pulled up, bit at the undead within reach of his jaws. His teeth closed on three of the creatures and they boiled away into oblivion. His claws shredded several more into gossamer ribbons carried off in the wind.

Holding the rope harness with one hand, Abelar tried to anticipate the dragon's movements while he slashed and stabbed with his enchanted blade. A shadow darted in from his right, arms outstretched, and his blade tore through the space between its head and body. Its red eyes winked out as Furlinastis beat his wings rapidly and wheeled right to avoid a throng of the undead. A shadow swooped in and passed a hand through Abelar's chest. His heart rebelled, constricted. Cold sank into him. Grunting, he stabbed the shadow through the back as it streaked away. He felt the slight, tell-tale resistance that indicated the magic of his blade had found purchase in the incorporeal flesh. Whipping around, he saw another shadow streaking for him from the right. A reverse cross-cut slashed it into a dissipating cloud of foul-smelling smoke.

The dragon roared, reared, and slashed at a score of shadows congregating around his head and neck. His jaws killed several, but more streaked in to replace the dead.

"Down!" Abelar shouted at the dragon.

Furlinastis dived, leaving the shadows and their keening behind. Abelar bent low and held on.

On the plain below he saw his company between the breaks in the cloud of shadows, a circle of white light holding their ground against a swirling army of shadows. He saw flashes of rose colored brilliance, holy power channeled through priests and those given over to Lathander, saw shadows turned to vapor before it.

In the pauses between thunder, lightning, and the dragon's roars, he heard the shouts and chants of his company, the men and women who stood in the light. He raised his blade, hacked at a shadow that came within reach, and watched some of its form boil away into the darkness.

Furlinastis pulled up and wheeled, sending Abelar's stomach into his throat. The dragon swooped through a group of shadows.

Claws, teeth, and Abelar's sword destroyed half a dozen of the undead as the dragon streaked through and past.

Thunder boomed, rolled, and lightning ripped the sky and struck the earth near the battlefield. Abelar turned to look and saw several trees burning on the plain.

From the right, a throng of shadows, a hundred or more, flew like arrows at Furlinastis. More streaked toward them from the other side.

The dragon roared, beat his wings, and angled upward.

Nearly unseated, Abelar held on, feeling the tendons in his forearm stretch. He cursed and kept his wits enough to wave his blade at a nearby shadow, but missed. Another appeared from nowhere, passed through him. Cold settled in his bones, but Furlinastis's speed carried Abelar away from the creature.

The dragon veered again, swooped downward, and Abelar caught another glimpse of his company, of their light. Had he still stood in Lathander's light himself, he could have healed himself, could have turned his blade into a beacon, could have channeled the Morninglord's power through his body and soul and used its light to sear the shadows out of existence, could have rallied his company against even the Shadowstorm. But he had fallen, descended so far into shadow that he rode them into battle.

He shouted, slashed, stabbed, and killed. Shadows whirled around him, around the dragon. The sky was filled with them. They reached through his armor, tried to still his heart, tried to steal his life. He thought of his son, of his friends, and roared defiance. He slashed, cross-cut, and stabbed.

Furlinastis answered his shouts with roars of his own, the sound as loud as the thunder. The dragon wheeled through the sky, a Gondsman's engine of destruction. Great claws swept shadows from the sky like so many stinging insects. Teeth snapped up the undead by the half-dozen.

But the shadows were numberless, and Abelar knew that another would rise from the body of each man and woman of his company that fell to their life-draining touch. And as the storm moved across Sembia, it would add still more to its numbers.

He feared he was looking at the end of the world.

Furlinastis dived low, swooping over the company of Lathanderians. Abelar couldn't make out faces. He noted only the rise and fall of blades, shouts of pain and anger. Some had fallen. He saw their bodies flat on the black earth, spattered with mud and shadows.

Above the wind, above Furlinastis's roars, Abelar heard several of the men shout the battle cry of his company.

"We stand in the light!"

Growing despair made the words at first seem silly to Abelar, trivial in the face of a darkness that could not be slowed, a darkness that ate its victims and vomited them back up in a new form to serve it. But he found a kernel of hope in the words and grabbed at it. He realized that the only thing to do in the face of darkness was stand and fight beside like-minded men and women. He had fallen into shadow, true, but there was light in him still.

Shouting, he slashed a shadow, stabbed another, another. One of the creatures struck him in the chest and arm, turned his sword arm numb. He waved his blade ineffectually as the shadow reached into his chest. His breath left him. His heart lurched.

Another abrupt dive by Furlinastis left the shadow behind and saved Abelar's life.

He gathered himself and looked back, expecting to see the shadow army in pursuit. Instead, he saw them peeling off, streaking in the opposite direction.

Below and behind, a cheer went up from the battlefield. Trewe's trumpet blew a victorious note. The dragon, too, roared.

Abelar watched the shadows wheel away, gather some distance away, and felt only dread. The shadows swarmed around a point perhaps two long bowshots away from the company. Their numbers stunned him. The swirling column of their forms seemed to reach from the ground to the clouds.

"So many," he said, marveling at their numbers.

Without warning the rain and thunder stopped. Trewe's horn and the cheers of the company went quiet. For a moment, all was silent, pensive.

Cold seeped across the battlefield, a deeper cold than that of the shadows. Supernatural fear accompanied it. It reached into Abelar, sent his teeth to chattering, stole his nerve. The dragon growled his discomfort. Abelar heard inarticulate whispers in his mind. He discerned no words he could understand but the sibilant tone touched something primal in him, set his heart to racing, lit his mind afire with terror.

A moan went up from his comrades below. He heard Regg shouting to the company, his old friend's voice on the verge of panic. "Hold! Hold!"

Abelar fought through the terror as best he could and scanned the darkness for the source of the cold and fear. He could see little through the impenetrable cloud of living shadows. He sensed something at the fringe of his vision, something large, dark, remorseless, terror given form and set loose in the world.

"What new evil is this, dragon? I cannot see!"

Furlinastis extended his neck to look behind them, hissed, and veered left.

"A nightwalker," the dragon said. "But I have never seen nor heard of one so large. Terror lives in its eyes, and death in its hands. This foe is beyond your companions, perhaps beyond even me. They are lost, human, as is the battle."

The cloud of shadows parted like a stage curtain and the nightwalker stepped between them. It towered as tall as ten men, looming over the field like a siege engine. It had the shape of a man, but hairless, featureless, its entire form smooth and black, like an idol carved from onyx by the jungle savages of Chult. The shadows broke ranks and darted around its massive form like flies around a corpse.

It regarded the battlefield, Abelar's company, and another wave of terror went forth from it. Thousands of shadows keened.

Abelar's company answered not with another moan, not with shouts of terror, but with the clarion of Trewe's trumpet.

"Back, dragon!" Abelar shouted. "Turn back!"

Furlinastis shook his head as he flew, completing his turn. "It is over, human. I will take you to—"

"Turn back! Now!"

"My service to the Maskarran does not extend to self-sacrifice. It is over."

From behind and below, Abelar heard Trewe's trumpet issue the order to form up.

Desperate, Abelar took his sword in both hands, turned as best he could in his makeshift harness, and put it in the divot on the dragon's back between his beating wings. He made sure Furlinastis felt the point.

"You will turn back or I will sink this to its hilt! They will not stand alone!"

The dragon's head whirled around, jaws open, streams of shadow leaking from his nose and throat.

Abelar pressed down on the blade. "Do not test me, wyrm!"

Furlinastis hissed in rage.

"Try to dislodge me or use your killing breath on me and I'll do it. It will take but a moment. You may not die, but you will not be able fly and you will face the nightwalker on foot."

Anger stoked the fire in the slits of Furlinastis's eyes

"How will you have it?" Abelar said, and pushed the point of his blade harder against the scales. "How? Decide!"

The dragon roared with rage, snapped his head forward, and started to wheel about.

"You are no servant of the Morninglord," Furlinastis shouted above the wind.

Abelar considered what he had done, knew that he would do it again if necessary.

"Perhaps not," he said softly.

Abelar looked over the dragon's wing as they came around and saw his company assembling not for a last stand but for a charge. Trewe's clarion rang out again, sounding the ready. Illuminated blades at intervals held the darkness of the Shadowstorm at bay. Dead men and women lay scattered about the field. Abelar presumed their souls, raised by the Shadowstorm, had already joined the army of shadows. He hoped that Jiriis was not among them.

The dragon continued its slow turn.

Regg stood at the forefront of the company. Abelar heard his voice but couldn't make out his words. He saw Roen and another priest moving quickly from soldier to soldier, healing with a prayer and a touch. The company answered Regg's words with raised blades and a shout.

The nightwalker held its ground, dark, ominous, surrounded by an army of shadows.

Trewe blew another blast, and Regg shouted, turned, raised his blade and lowered it. The company lurched into motion.

The shadows keened at their approach. The nightwalker watched them for a moment, then met their charge with one of his own.

Abelar cursed.

Each of the creature's strides covered a spearcast. The impact of its feet on the soft earth left deep pits in its wake, open graves waiting to be filled with Lathanderians.

"Turn, damn you!" Abelar said, striking the dragon with the hilt of his sword. "Faster, wyrm!"

The Lathanderians, a small island of light in the night of the Shadowstorm, charged to their doom. Regg led them, shield and blade blazing.

Trewe's trumpet sang. The nightwalker closed, hit the company's formation like a battering ram. Men and women screamed in pain, shouted in rage, light flared, winked out. The nightwalker crushed men and women under its feet or with its fists. Weapons slashed its huge form but seemed to do little. The company swirled around the nightwalker, surrounding it. The creature stood heedless in their midst, the black center of a whirlpool that drew into itself the light of the Lathanderians.

The dragon wheeled around at last and straightened. He roared and the beat of his wings propelled him toward the battle. The wind almost peeled Abelar from his harness.

He watched his companions, side-by-side, fighting, dying, aglow with Lathander's light. The nightwalker reaped a life with each blow of its maul-like fists, yet none of the company around it broke, none ran—not one—and their courage chased the despair lurking around the edges of Abelar's soul.

He understood them, then, in a way he had not before. They served Lathander, but fought and died for one another, for the men and women standing beside them. Abelar knew well the strength of feeling that bonded warrior to warrior, man to woman, father to son.

He thought of Elden, of Endren, recalled his father's words to him—*the light is in you*—and realized, with perfect clarity, that his father was right.

The men and women of his company did not stand in the light. The light was in them. Lathander was merely the reagent that allowed them to shine. *They* were the light, not their god. And they, and he, had not burned as brightly as they might.

The shadows saw the dragon's approach and a massive cluster of the undead peeled off from the assembled mass and streaked toward Abelar and Furlinastis.

Abelar readied his blade, and gasped when he saw the faint illumination that tinged its edges. Fallen from service, he should not have been able to light his blade. And yet he had. And he knew why. He knew, too, what he would do, what he must do, for Elden, for Jiriis, for Endren, for all those he loved.

"Ignore them, Furlinastis!" he shouted to the dragon. "Take me over the nightwalker."

The dragon looked back, eyed him sidelong, but obeyed. With each beat of Furlinastis's wings, the light in Abelar's blade grew, the light in Abelar shone brighter. Abelar's soul burned, fueled by epiphany.

He was the light. They all were the light.

Below, he saw more of his company fall, saw the nightwalker's darkness growing, devouring Lathander's light. The cloud of shadows, red eyes blazing, flew toward him.

Abelar watched the light in his blade spread to his hands, his forearms, his torso. It grew ever brighter in intensity. His light penetrated the shroud of shadows that wrapped the dragon.

The dragon turned to regard him, winced in the light, hissed with pain. "What are you doing, human?"

"Endure it for a time. We are soon to part ways."

The dragon roared as Abelar's luminescence flared and haloed them both in blazing, pure white light.

The shadows, heedless, swooped toward them, drawn to Abelar's radiance. Darkness and light sped toward each other, collided, and the darkness of the shadows' fallen souls was no match for the light of Abelar's reborn spirit. In the fullness of his light he saw the fallen souls for the pathetic creatures they were, saw on some the wheel of Ordulin, and smiled that he had avenged Saerb.

His light consumed the shadows utterly, dissolved them, shrieking, into a formless cloud of vile smoke through which Furlinastis streaked, roaring.

Abelar looked down, saw the upturned faces and raised blades of his comrades, saw hundreds more shadows take wing from their foul mass and fly toward him, and saw the nightstalker's featureless face turn its regard to the light in the sky.

The radiance bursting from his body shot beams of light in all direction, speared and destroyed dozens of onrushing shadows.

"The nightwalker," he said.

He slipped out of his harness, sat unrestrained on the dragon's neck, one hand griping the rope, as Furlinastsis swooped toward the nightwalker. Abelar's body, armor, blade, and soul blazed.

"My gratitude for your service," he shouted to the dragon. "Please forgive me my threats. For a time I lost my way. Now I am found."

He held his blade in both hands and leaped off the dragon's back.

White light veiled the world. He did not see things, he saw into them, through them, saw the nightwalker and shadows for the insubstantial entities they were. The souls of his comrades glowed, their light dimmed only by self-imposed restraints, restraints Abelar had shed.

As he fell, his body ignited with radiance, an apotheosis of light. For a moment, he felt himself motionless, suspended in space, as if he had become the light. He savored the time, thought of Elden, his innocent eyes, his trusting soul. He loved his son—forever.

The moment ended. He plummeted earthward toward the nightwalker.

The creature shielded its face with a forearm, cowered before Abelar.

Abelar's soul swelled. No regrets plagued him or tortured his final thoughts. His mind turned to those he loved, his wife, his father, his son. He laughed, shouted Elden's name as he descended, and his voice boomed over the rain, over the thunder, over the darkness.

The nightwalker melted in the heat of his radiance, disintegrated in the light, and Abelar, blazing, fell through the creature's dissipating form toward the hard earth below.

The sun sets and rises, he thought, and knew he would feel no pain.

❖ ❖ ❖ ❖ ❖

Abelar's voice boomed out of the heavens and shook the battlefield with its force.

*"Lathander!"*

Regg lowered his blade as the battle stalled. He shielded his eyes and watched, awestruck, as his friend's body transformed as it fell from glowing, to luminescent, to blazing, to a radiant dawn sun in miniature that chased away the darkness in the storm and in their souls. For a moment, the bleak, unending night of the Shadowstorm yielded fully to light. Beams of radiance shot in all directions from Abelar's form and annihilated the living shadows.

"Gods," Trewe breathed beside him.

The supernatural terror planted by the nightwalker in Regg's spirit, in all of their spirits, vanished, replaced by a surge of hope. And before that hope, before that light, the nightwalker, immense and dark, cowered.

"Abelar," Regg whispered.

The glowing form of his friend fell in and through the nightwalker like the sword of the Morninglord himself. The towering creature of darkness disintegrated in the luminescence, boiled away into harmless streamers of black mist, the groans of its dying a distant ache in Regg's mind.

Abelar slammed into the earth and lay still. His radiance diminished, ended.

For a long moment, the field was quiet, almost worshipful. Only the patter of the rain could be heard, the sky crying on Abelar's motionless form.

Jiriis's voice rang out, thick and broken with tears. "Abelar!"

Above, a small window opened in the churning black clouds of the Shadowstorm, revealing a flash of sky beyond, painted in the reds, pinks, and oranges of sunrise. Through the window a single beam of rose-colored light shone, cut through the darkness, and fell on Abelar's form. Bathed in the glow, Abelar's body looked whole, his expression peaceful.

The keening of the shadows turned to a groan that Regg felt more than heard. The multitude that remained flitted about in agitation, as if pained.

Regg's eyes welled and he fell to his knees, as did most of the men and women around him. The calm afforded by the light, the sense of hope, of awe, told him that the light was no mere light. It was a path to Lathander's realm, or the hand of the Morninglord himself. His friend had returned to his faith, and had brought faith back to all of them.

Abelar was sanctified. Regg smiled, cried for his friend.

The rose-hued light spread from Abelar to the company and its touched chased off fatigue and fear, closed wounds, reknit bones, returned strength, and planted a seed of hope in all their breasts.

The men and women of the company laughed, cried, and praised their god. The sky closed, the beam of light vanished, and Regg came back to himself, once more noticing the rain and the thunder.

As one the company rushed forward around Abelar, led by Regg and Jiriis.

Abelar's body looked unharmed, as if sleeping, despite the fall, but no breath stirred his breast. Jiriis stepped foward, crouched, stroked Abelar's hair, his cheek. Soft sobs shook hear. Tears smeared the grime of battle on her face. She sank to the ground, took Abelar's head in her lap.

"He smells of roses," she said, and wept.

"He is sanctified," Roen said. "His spirit will not rise in darkness."

Regg found his own eyes welling but he would have to postpone his grief. Many enemies remained. He still had a battle to fight. Lathander, through Abelar, had given them hope. Now they must use it.

"See her from the field," he said to Brend, indicating Jiriis. "Abelar as well. Roen, one of your priests lights their way."

With the help of two others, Brend and Jiriis carried Abelar through the company and away from the battle.

Regg, as well as every other man and women in the company, touched him as they passed. Regg felt a surge upon contact, and the hope planted in his breast blossomed. The light in him, the light he felt usually as a distant, comforting warmth, flared.

It was a sign.

"You are my friend," Regg said to Abelar, as Brend and Jiriis carried him away. A junior priest fell in with them, lighting his wand.

Then Abelar was gone. And darkness yet remained.

The silence over the battlefield ended with a roll of thunder. Lightning lit the sky. Rain fell anew. The keening of the remaining shadows—still a multitude—started once more. They swarmed in an enormous, whirling column.

"Form up," Regg said to his company. "We have been given a sign and the light is in you all."

"And in you," they answered, readying weapons, readying spirits.

A boom of thunder like the breaking of the sky rolled, shook the ground, knocked the men and women of the company to the ground. Lightning ripped the sky, again and again, until the coal-black clouds birthed a coal-black form that descended from the clouds, trailing darkness.

In size and shape it looked much like a man. Membranous wings sprouted from its back but did not flap as it gently descended to the ground. A robe of scaled leather draped its ebon-skinned form. Curving white horns jutted from its brow. Power seeped from the creature in palpable waves.

As surely as Regg knew his god had been present on the battlefield to bless them through Abelar, he knew at that moment that another god had taken the field. He was looking upon the creature that was the provenance of the storm, the origin of the darkness.

The sky again fell silent, the thunder and lightning but a temporary herald for Kesson Rel's arrival.

The column of shadows rendezvoused with their master in the sky, swirled around him as he descended. The moment he set foot on the ground, thunder rumbled and the earth shook anew.

Giant forms stepped out of the shadows to stand beside him, towering humanoids with pale skin and gangly limbs, encased in gray iron. They bore huge swords in their hands. Shadows clung to their flesh and their weapons. There were hundreds of them.

Regg knew the company could not defeat the shadow army and their master. But the hope Lathander had put in his breast would allow him no other course than to hold his ground. They had entered the storm to face the darkness. They would do so and they would die. Abelar was an example to them all.

Behind him he heard gasps from the men and women of the company, murmured astonishment. He turned to face them, to reassure them, and found that their surprise was not directed at Kesson Rel.

A clot of shadows had formed in their midst, a darkness the light of the priests did not illuminate, and Erevis Cale, Riven, and a Shadovar had stepped from it.

To Regg, Cale and Riven seemed weightier, somehow more defined than everyone else around them, save perhaps Kesson Rel himself. The men and women of the company seemed to sense the difference as well, for they parted around them.

All three looked past and through Regg, across the field to the shadow army and the dark god who commanded it. They strode forward and as they passed Erevis Cale put a hand on Regg's shoulder.

"Kesson Rel is beyond you, Regg. This is our battle now."

The growl of thunder broke the silence, low and dangerous. Shadows poured from Erevis Cale, from his dark blade.

Regg could find no words. He turned to watch them walk without hesitation across the space that separated three men from thousands of shadows, hundreds of giants, and the god who ruled them.

Regg realized he was not breathing.

Trewe appeared beside him, eyeing the trio as they strode into battle.

"This does not seem a field for ordinary men," said Trewe.

Regg nodded, thought of Abelar, and clasped Trewe by the shoulder. "It is well, then, that there are no ordinary men on it." He turned to his company and shouted, "Form up! Await my orders. The Morninglord's work is not yet done on this field."

# CHAPTER FIFTEEN

*7 Nightal, the Year of Lightning Storms*

Cale, Riven, and Rivalen spaced themselves a few strides apart. Ahead, the army of shadow giants assembled before and around Kesson Rel. Darkness bled from their pale flesh. The column of shadows—tens of thousands of the creatures—swirled in the sky over their master, their eyes like coals.

Looking upon Kesson, upon the power he held, the power he had stolen, Cale felt the void in him like an ache in his bones. The emptiness compelled him to fill it. He knew Riven must be feeling the same thing.

*Mags, I am keeping my promise to you. Right now. Do you hear me, Mags?*

No response.

Shadows swirled around Kesson. He held up a

hand and silence fell. Cale, Riven, and Rivalen stopped, the world stopped.

"I see the memory of a dead world in your faces," Kesson Rel said, his voice carrying across the field, filling the quiet. "The death of this world, too, is inevitable. Yet here you stand, a supposed servant of the Lady of Loss, and two servants of the God of Shadows."

He looked to the sky, to Furlinastis, who was turning an arc to return to the battlefield. "And you bring the dragon who served me in my youth. Let us see who is the stronger, shadelings."

"Let us see who serves the Lady in truth," Rivalen said softly, and shadows poured from him.

Shadows bled from Cale, too. He held his mask in one hand, Weaveshear in the other. Beside him, Riven channeled Mask's power and let it fill his blades. Thick, languid shadows dripped from the steel.

"We must waste nothing on his minions," Rivalen said.

"Agreed," Cale said.

"They will swarm to protect him," Riven said.

"Not if they are protecting him from someone else," Cale answered.

"Who?" Rivalen asked. "The dragon is not enough."

"*My* minions," Cale said, and quickly mouthed the words to a sending. The magic buzzed around him and he directed it to Nayan, back on the Wayrock.

*I need you and yours here. Battle is joined.* He paused, thought of Magadon. *Ensure Magadon is all right first. Then come. Be quick.*

The magic winged its way through the Weave for Nayan.

"Hold here," he said to Rivalen and Riven.

"Hold?" Riven asked. The assassin bounced on the balls of his feet, his eye on Kesson.

Cale nodded, and started to intone the words to a spell that would even the odds.

I awaken, gasping, from another dream of my father.

Opening my eyes, I find myself slouched against the stone wall of a meditation chamber. Drool wets my cheek. The memory of my father and the Source and falling forever is fresh in my mind. Sweat drenches my body. I stink enough to offend my own nose. I have not bathed or changed my attire in days. The stubble of a tenday old beard causes my cheeks to itch. I feel eyes on me.

Nayan stands in the shadow of the doorway. His form is one with the darkness, the lines between shadow and man blurred. I sit up, put my forearms on my knees. I am appalled by how thin they have become.

"We must go," Nayan says. He speaks in an even tone, but I see the urgency suggested by his stance, the clench of his fist.

"To Cale?"

He does not answer with words, but I read his face.

"Take me with you."

"No."

I expected the answer but still want to hollow out his head. I remember my father's words—*They will leave you here.* I squeeze a smile through my evil thoughts.

"Journey safely."

His eyebrows follow his thoughts downward. My words must have surprised him. I hold my smile and in the end he says nothing, nods, and melts back into the shadows.

The moment he disappears, I stand, find my mental focus. The exercise reminds me of the damage my father did, renews my desire to have vengeance. I avoid the broken mental connections, the sharp emotional shards, the gaps in cognition.

I reach out for one of the shadowwalkers I know by name. I put power into my words.

*Vyrhas, when the others leave, you are to remain.*

My suggestion worms its way into the regimented construct of Vyrhas's will. I feel him resist, feel the reinforcement of his training bolstering the mental walls. He is strong. I fear my plan may die stillborn.

All at once my power pierces his resistance and he is mine.

*Act as though you will leave for Cale's side with the others, but instead meet me in the dining hall.*

On the way to the dining hall, I retrieve my bow, my blade, my leather armor. When I reach the large dining chamber, I see no one.

"Vyrhas?" I say to the darkness.

The shadowwalker steps from the darkness along the far wall. He is taller than Nayan, leaner. His long black hair is tied into a rope that falls halfway down his back. Shadows curl around his hands, his head.

"Mindmage. The Right and Left have called. I remained only out of respect for our friendship."

My power has so scrambled Vyrhas's mind that he regards us as longtime friends, though we have rarely spoken before this moment. Still, his will is slippery. I must trod softly over his mindscape so as not to dislodge the compulsion.

"Cale and Riven called me, too," I lie. "They need you to take me somewhere."

Vyrhas looks relieved at the revelation. "Where?"

"I will show you. Open your mind."

Vyrhas opens his mind to me without hesitation. I picture in my mind the vaulted, hemispherical chamber deep within the floating mountaintop on which Sakkors stands. I picture the faceted stone walls, designed to reflect and amplify the Source's power. And floating in the center of the vault, slowly turning about its lengthwise axis, I picture the giant, crystalline form of the Source.

I push the image into Vyrhas's mind.

"There," I say. "I am to go there."

Behind him, Cale heard the Lathanderians assembling. Armor chinked, shields rung, and orders carried through the still air. Cale held his mask and continued his spell.

The shadows swarming the air behind and around Kesson began to keen, the discordant whine of doomed souls. The shadow giants, darkness bleeding from their forms, beat their swords on their shields, the sound like the heartbeat of the world.

Cale continued the spell, felt the power gathering, the borders between worlds weakening.

Above, Furlinastis completed his turn, roared his rage at the theurge who had forced him into service thousands of years before.

"Whatever you're doing, Cale," Riven said. "Do it now."

Kesson Rel rose into the air, raised his hands.

The keen of the shadows reached a pitch that hurt Cale's ears. The beat of sword and shield by the giants grew more rapid.

Kesson lowered his hand and thunder boomed. Hundreds of lightning bolts formed a green net in the sky. The rain resumed, poured from the black clouds. And Kesson's servants swarmed forward

The shadows formed a black cloud that swirled, parted in two. One half sped toward Furlinastis, one half toward Cale, Riven, and Rivalen. The shadow giants rushed forward, blades bare.

A clear, piercing note on a clarion sounded from the line of Lathanderians.

"The light!" they shouted as one.

Cale completed his spell, used Weaveshear to slice a gash in the veil between planes. He widened it and darkness streamed from the wound in reality. Beyond, he saw the Plane of Shadow and the haunted ruins of Elgrin Fau, once the City of Silver on Ephyras, now a wraith-haunted ruin. He saw the necropolis in its center, the dead core of a dead city.

Kesson Rel had bound Elgrin Fau's dead to the city's locale, but Cale knew the shadows of Elgrin Fau were the same as those of the Adumbral Calyx, and that those of the Calyx were the same as those of the Shadowstorm.

"You are unbound!" Cale shouted. "Emerge to face Kesson Rel!"

His words summoned moans through the rift. Black forms rose up from ancient graves, hundreds, thousands, the denizens of an entire city. Cold poured through the gash torn between planes. The wraiths' red eyes, so like those of the shadows', focused on Cale. He saw numbers to match those of Kesson's army of shadows.

"Come forth!" he shouted, and they did.

Thousands upon thousands of wraiths flew like arrows for the planar rift, poured through it like a black river. Their moans answered the keening of the shadows as they took to the air.

"It is for us and only us to slay Kesson Rel!" Cale shouted. "You must kill his army. Hear me, Lords of Silver!"

One of the wraiths peeled off, larger than the rest, its form twice the height of a man. Cold and power went forth from it.

"You are heard, First of Five," it said, and inclined his head. "Do what you promised."

Before Cale could answer, the wraith darted away and joined his fellows. Two hordes of undead flew toward each other, two clouds of darkness, a city of Kesson Rel's servants and a city of Kesson Rel's victims. Moaning and keening filled the air as the two forces clashed, intermixed, wheeled and swirled like enormous flocks of birds, dueling cyclones of shadow. Cale could not see the sky through the black cloud of their battle.

The ground vibrated with the charge of the giants. Hundreds of the huge creatures tore across the plains, their footsteps the drumbeat of war. The Lathanderians rushed forward to face them, broke around Cale, Riven, and Rivalen.

"Fight well," Regg shouted as he passed.

Shadows coalesced in the Lathanderians' wake and Nayan and the shadowwalkers emerged from the darkness to stand before Cale. All of them fell into a crouch at the sound of battle. Their impassive faces surveyed the scene at a glance, took in the undead armies warring in the sky, the shadow dragon wheeling through a cloud of still more undead, and the line of Lathanderians forming up to receive the charge of the giants.

"We are come," Nayan said to Cale.

Cale surveyed the field, watched Kesson rise into the sky behind his army. Other than Kesson himself, the shadow giants were the most mobile of their enemies.

"Assist them," he said, nodding at the Lathanderians, who had formed a line of flesh and metal to meet the charge of the giants. "Keep the giants occupied. Kesson is ours."

Nayan's face tightened but he nodded, turned to his fellows, and spoke hurried orders in his language. The shadowwalkers bowed to Cale and Riven, turned, and shadowstepped into battle, joining the line of the Lathanderians.

Cale looked up into the sky, trying to formulate a plan. He saw Kesson complete a spell and gesture with his right hand.

"Cover!" he shouted.

He and Riven dived and rolled as a column of flame engulfed the plains where they had been standing. Flame and heat soaked Rivalen but the Shadovar emerged unscathed. Cale assumed he had a ring or cloak or some other magical device that protected him.

Rivalen scowled, the shadows around him whirling, and answered with a spell of his own. He pointed a hand at Kesson and a black beam shot from his palm, through the undead warring in the skies, and struck Kesson in the chest. It was deflected harmlessly away.

"Spells are shite, Shadovar!" Riven shouted. "It's blades or nothing!"

Cale agreed, and both he and Riven leaped to their feet. Cale intoned the words to a spell that would empower his weapon, strengthening Weaveshear's already puissant enchantments.

Meanwhile, Kesson surveyed the field and gestured with his left hand not at Cale, Riven, or Rivalen, but at the ground near the Lathanderians who scrambled to meet the charging giants.

A twisting spiral of energy left Kesson Rel's hand, struck the earth near Regg's company, and caused the ground to ripple, rumble, shake, and knock Regg off his feet. Shouts went up all around him as other members of his company fell to the ground.

Meanwhile, the giants were closing.

The tremors gained intensity, rattled the plains, and the ground beneath Regg groaned, shifted, cracked. Chasms opened in the plains, hungry maws of stone and soil.

" 'Ware!" Regg shouted.

Men and women, already prone or off-balance from the tremors, fell into the holes by the dozen, screaming as the ground swallowed them. Regg, pulling Trewe with him, rolled away from a chasm that opened beside them.

"Get them out!" Regg shouted, and climbed to his feet on the unstable earth.

The men and women of his company climbed to their feet, extended hands down the gashes in the earth, or uncoiled rope. Shouts from the chasms told Regg that many of those who had fallen in still lived.

A great battle cry went up from the charging giants. Regg looked up to see hundreds of the huge creatures bearing down on them, bleeding shadows as they ran.

"Roen and the priests, get them out! The rest form up! Form up!"

The company scrambled to get back into line as the giants

closed. The ground went still for a moment, then the chasms started to close.

The Lathanderians trapped within screamed—panicked sounds that dug a pit in Regg's stomach.

Furlinastis beat his wings, his rage growing with each stroke. Darkness boiled around him, its agitated swirl a reflection of his rage. A cloud of Kesson Rel's shadows harried his flight, keened in his ears, and tried to take his vigor with their life draining touch.

Too slow to match his speed in flight, they swarmed the air before, below, and around him, trying to intercept him as he passed.

He snapped them up in his jaws by the half-dozen, shredded others with his claws. The beat of his wings dispersed the vapor of their remains into the wind. But some flew through his body as he passed, reached through his scales. The cold of their touch slowed his heart, coarsened his breathing.

Kesson Rel hovered in the air before him, facing away, his hands gesturing as he began to cast yet more spells.

Rivalen watched the energy of Kesson's spell evoke a localized earthquake. The Lathanderians screamed and fell as the ground shook but the tremors did not reach the ground under Rivalen's feet. He held onto Shar's symbol and shouted the words to another spell, a powerful evocation that caused the target to implode. He charged the spell with additional power, stretching its range, made a hammerfist with his two hands, and shot a pulse of the black energy at Kesson.

Kesson saw it coming, and deflected it with a casual wave of his right hand. Rivalen knew then that Riven was correct, that his spells would be useless against Kesson. He would have to engage the heretic face to face.

Irritated, he directed another blast of the implosive energy across the battle at one of the giants charging toward the Lathanderians. The wave of force hit the huge creature and it screamed as bones shattered and blood sprayed, the magic causing its body to fold in on itself again, again, again, again. . . .

Cale started to run toward Regg and the company, but Riven grabbed him by the arm.

"Let the shadowwalkers help them," the assassin said. "Kesson is our goal. Get us up there."

Cale nodded, looked through the storm of wraiths and shadows wheeling through the sky to Kesson, who had already begun another spell, and drew the shadows around him.

As he did, a huge form loomed out of the dark sky behind Kesson, a black cloud of teeth, claws, wings, and black scales. Hundreds of shadows flitted about Furlinastis's form but the dragon seemed not to care. The empty harness on Furlinastis caused Cale to think of Abelar. Cale hoped he had died at peace.

Furlinastis opened his mouth in a roar and Kesson whirled to face him.

Cale saw his opportunity. Gathering Riven within his shroud of shadows, he stepped through the darkness and into the sky behind Kesson.

Nayan would have preferred to have stood beside the Right and Left Hands but they had instructed him to do otherwise and he and his initiates would obey.

As one, they sprinted toward the line of the Lathanderians, their strides preternaturally fast. They kept their feet as the ground shook, and shadowstepped away from the chasms that opened in the earth to swallow the Lathanderians by the dozen. He was not even certain the Lathanderians had noticed him and his men.

*"Free them,"* he shouted to his men in their language.

A roar went up from the line of charging shadow giants and the shouted orders from the Lathanderian's leader had most of them rushing to meet the onslaught.

The chasms started to close, the ground groaning, screeching, rumbling. The men and women trapped underground screamed in panicked terror.

*"Quickly,"* he said, and stepped through the shadows to the bottom of a closing chasm. He materialized in the darkness of the hole, behind a Lathanderian shouting and trying to scramble up closing walls that offered scant purchase. Nayan's eyes, blessed by the Shadowlord, saw in darkness as though it were noon.

"Be still," he said to the woman.

The woman turned to face him and her brown eyes went wide. Sweat and rain smoothed her black hair to her scalp.

"Are you . . . Erevis Cale?"

Nayan shook his head and started to draw the darkness around them as the walls continued to groan closed. "His servant."

He shadowstepped back to the surface with the woman in tow. His fellows appeared at the same time, each beside a Lathanderian they had pulled from a chasm.

"Look!" said Trewe, and pulled Regg around.

Behind them, the shadowwalkers in service to Erevis Cale appeared on the torn, vibrating earth, each of them with one of the company in tow. Immediately they disappeared again into the shadows, reappeared in a heartbeat with another of Regg's company. They repeated the process again and again, appearing and disappearing as the chasms sealed, pulling dozens of the company from the closing mouths of the hungry earth.

Regg raised his blade in triumph. "There are no ordinary men on this field!"

Trewe sounded a blast as the line cheered and formed up.

The ground vibrated under the thudding tread of hundreds of giants. They loomed ever larger in Regg's sight. Their blades were as long as Regg was tall, their arms as thick as his legs, their legs like the trunks of oaks. But at least he would feel the bite of his blade into their flesh, and its edge would draw blood instead of shadows.

"At the ready!" he shouted as the creatures bore down on them.

Nayan repeated the process again and again, as did his fellow shadowwalkers. They pulled many from the closing chasms, but not all, and the grinding earth swallowed the screams of some. He winced as the screams died.

He did a quick headcount of his men, and realized that he was missing Vyrhas.

Vyrhas pulls shadows around us and I feel the lurch in my stomach that accompanies magical travel. The moment we reappear I notice the warm, rhythmic mental pulses of the Source's power, the gentle surf of my addiction.

The shadows dissipate from around us. We stand in the huge vault at Sakkor's core, the magical heart of the city. Light the color of blood bathes the chamber. No doors or archways offer ingress or egress. I remember that the Source's chamber is a cyst in the floating mountain, an abcess accessible only by magical transport.

The Source, its facets humming with power, hangs unsupported in the air, perpendicular to the floor, suspended only by its own power. It flares and pulses with the regularity of a heartbeat. I hold out my arms and let the power wash over me, into me, through me. My power is doubled in a moment. I find it hard to breathe, as if the air is too thick to squeeze into my lungs.

The polished planes fashioned into the walls and ceiling reflect the image of the Source a thousand times over, amplifying its power. The facets show my image over and over again, too, and I am struck with the thought that I do not look more numerous; I look shattered.

The shadows around Vyrhas coil protectively about him. He winces, as if the room itself were about to strike him. He clutches his brow, staggers. When he looks up at me, I see a trickle of blood leaking from his nose. He does not have the capacity to shield his mind from the incidental onslaught of the Source's mental energies.

"What is this place?" he says, and his speech is slurred.

"Go," I say to him, and my control over his will makes it an order. "There is nothing more for you to do here. Go to your comrades. Tell no one where you took me."

"Are you certain, my friend?" he says, as his other nostril starts to leak blood. "I could remain."

I admire his loyalty. "Leave. I will be all right."

Like many addicts, I prefer to engage in my vice in private.

Vyrhas nods, the shadows around him swirl, and he disappears into the black. I am alone with the Source.

The moment Cale and Riven materialized in the air behind Kesson, both drove their empowered blades through the shadows that shrouded him and into his flesh. Cale felt as if he were driving Weaveshear through dwarven plate armor, but the enspelled blade penetrated somewhat. Riven's blades, too, sank into Kesson's flesh.

Shadows boiled from all three men, intermingled, churned, the battle of Elgrin Fau's wraiths and Ordulin's shadows in miniature. Furlinastis's roar filled their ears. His body, streaking toward them, mouth open, filled their field of vision.

Kesson arched his back in pain, flapped his wings, but completed the final words of his incantation through gritted teeth.

His body turned incorporeal as Furlinastsis closed his jaws over him, narrowly missing Cale and Riven with his teeth. But the dragon's momentum carried him foward and he plowed into Cale and Riven like a falling wall of rock.

Cale managed to get a hold of Riven's cloak as the impact shattered bone and sent them both careening through the air.

# CHAPTER SIXTEEN

*7 Nightal, the Year of Lightning Storms*

The Source's power starts to fill the hole in my mind, rounds the sharp edges of my jagged mindscape, bridges the cognitive chasms. The jolt of power sends a thrill of pleasure through me.

I sense recognition from the Source. It knows me, and I it. We are old friends.

Shadows clot the air on the far side of the hemisphere, expand, and expel four Shadovar warriors cloaked in darkness and bristling with steel. They shout at me, point at me with their crystalline blades, and charge across the chamber.

I use what the Source has provided to reach into their brains. They feel the pinch of my mental fingers on the root of their minds, drop their weapons, and fall to the floor. I navigate the swirl of their pain and fear, and locate the unconscious mental mechanism that commands their hearts to beat.

I turn the mechanism off. As one they gasp, clutch their chests, die.

I know more Shadovar will come unless I prevent them.

I tap the well of power in my head, charge the walls of the chamber with a feedback matrix of mentally constructed corridors and walls, a labyrinth of the mind. Anyone attempting to transport into the chamber will find their physical form unmoved and their mind locked in an unending mental maze of their own making.

Alone and secure, I walk under the Source, formalize our mental connection. It welcomes me. I look up into the crystal and lose myself in its depths. Deep within the red sea of its form, flickers of light flash truths. I am already drifting. The pulsing in the Source increases. Perhaps it is addicted to me, as I am to it.

Rivalen rose into the air to face his trial. Hope did not pollute his spirit. Protective wards and contingency spells did not shield his person. He would rely on the Lady of Loss for his protection and he would prevail as her servant or he would die as her heretic. He took his holy symbol in his left hand, watched as the dragon closed its jaws over Kesson's form and Kesson, as insubstantial as a shadow, passed through and out the top of the dragon's head.

Furlinastis crashed into Cale and Riven and both men tumbled earthward, trailing shadows like dark comets. The dragon reared up, beat his wings, pulled up, turned his long neck to look back upon Kesson.

Dark energies burned on both of Kesson's fists. He pointed his right hand at the dragon.

The earth and sky alternated rapidly in Cale's vision as he and Riven spun uncontrollably toward the ground. He glimpsed Furlinastis, heard his roar, and used the shadows around him and Riven to transport both of them atop the dragon.

They appeared in time to hear Kesson Rel pronounce an arcane word and point his right hand at the dragon. Furlinastis tried to veer as he breathed a blast of life draining energy onto Kesson Rel.

Kesson stood in the midst of the killing breath, unharmed, and a churning mass of dark energy streaked through with crimson went forth from his hand, struck the dragon's wing, and in an instant, withered it to a nub.

Furlinastis roared, flapped his withered wing futilely, as he, Cale, and Riven spiraled toward the earth. Cale shouted the words to a healing spell as they fell, channelled the energy into the dragon, but it was not enough to repair the lost wing.

Rivalen recalled his own fight with the green dragon outside the walls of Selgaunt. He'd learned a lesson in that combat, one he intended to teach to Kesson.

A cluster of shadows streaked out of the sky toward him, arms outstretched, mouths open and shrieking hate. He held his holy symbol in hand, channeled Shar's power, and reduced them all to wails and vapor.

His eyes still on Kesson Rel, he traced a circle in the air with his holy symbol, spoke a long prayer, and reserved only the final, triggering word.

Furlinstasis spun wildly through the air and flapped his one wing frantically, but it only caused him to spin more rapidly. Cale and Riven held onto each other, onto the dragon's neck ridge, and watched the ground get closer and closer. Furlinastis roared with pain and frustration.

Shadows and wraiths whirled past them, brief flashes of red eyes and black forms. The air was thick with the vile vapor of their destruction. By chance, Furlinastis passed through some of the undead, as did Cale and Riven, and cold leaked into his bones.

"Leave him, Cale!" Riven shouted.

But Furlinstastis's uncontrolled descent was taking them toward the battlefield where the Lathanderians, many of them aglow with rosy light, fought an army of shadow giants.

"I can't," he said. "Look! Steer clear of them, dragon!"

But Furlinastis, lost in rage and pain, showed no sign of having heard Cale's words and his mountainous form plummeted toward the battle.

With nothing else for it, Cale tried to shadowstep himself, Riven, and the dragon to ground. He deepened the darkness around them, tried to eliminate their momentum while at the same time moving them safely down to the plains.

He felt the lurch of movement but they did not materialize on the plains. They appeared in mid-air, slowed not stopped, and immediately began falling at full speed again.

Cale cursed, tried again, but had the same result. He was stepping them down toward the ground, but doing little to change the dragon's trajectory or speed.

Rivalen stepped from the darkness around him to the darkness around Kesson Rel. Kesson grunted with surprise, but recovered quickly. He reached for Rivalen with his left hand, still charged with energy, still incorporeal. His hand passed through Rivalen's forearm, the energy discharged, and agony lit Rivalen. He felt his arm withering from the shoulder down, disintegrating into desicated flesh and hollowed-out bones.

Enduring the pain, he spoke the trigger word to the spell he had prepared and a field of anti-magic surrounded him, surrounded Kesson.

All of Rivalen's magic items went inert. All of the spells affecting both of them ceased functioning. Kesson turned corporeal. Rivalen grabbed Kesson's wrist with his one good hand and they fell together, leaking shadows.

Rivalen squeezed Kesson's wrist with all of his shadow borne strength, with enough force to snap the bones of ordinary men. But Kesson's bones did not snap, and he matched Rivalen's strength with his own.

"We will see who is the stronger," Rivalen hissed into his face as they flipped and tumbled earthward.

Flapping his wings, Kesson tried to right himself, but Rivalen's weight made it impossible.

Regg deflected a giant's slash with his shield, slipped on the wet grass, but managed to drive his blade into the huge creature's thigh. It roared, grunted, fell. Regaining his balance, Regg beat back an awkward thrust of the giant's sword and drove his blade into the creature's throat. It gurgled as he withdrew the blade, and it fell face down on the plains.

All around him men and women shouted, cried out in pain, roared. Light from Roen's priests kept the field awash in a rosy hue, preventing the giants from using the darkness to their advantage.

A roar from above drew his attention. He looked up to see Furinastis tumbling like a falling star toward the battle.

The wyrm's form filled the sky, a cloud of scales and shadows. Uncontrolled and roaring, the enormous creature was plummeting straight for the field where Regg's company fought the shadow giants. It winked in and out as it fell, tracing an irregular line through the sky.

Regg unleashed a flurry of blows on the giant attacking Trewe, managed in his fury to drive the large creature backward.

"Sound the retreat, Trewe! Now! Now!"

Trewe sounded a blast but it was too late.

Cale grabbed Riven and shadowstepped off Furlinastis's back the moment before the dragon hit the earth. They materialized off to the side of the battlefield and watched the dragon hit.

Men and giants saw the falling dragon, shouted, scrambled to get clear as the wyrm crashed to earth, causing the ground to shake as much as had Kesson Rel's earthquake, crushing men and giants, cutting a chasm in the plain and pushing huge, wet chunks of soil, grass, and trees before his huge form. Bones, metal, and scales shattered under the impact.

Kesson and Rivalen, clasping one another, twisted and tumbled earthward. Rivalen, with only one arm and surrounded by a field of anti-magic, could do nothing but hold on. Kesson shouted the lengthy incantation to a spell that could disjoin the anti-magic field, the only spell that could affect it, while with his free hand he tore at Rivalen's face with nails like claws.

Rivalen endured the pain, felt blood flow warm and sticky over his cheeks and jaw, and tried to maneuver Kesson underneath him. But there was no way to control their fall.

Through gritted teeth, he answered Kesson's disjunction by reciting one of the Thirteen Truths, spraying Kesson with the blood leaking into his mouth.

"Only hate endures."

They slammed into the ground before Kesson completed his spell.

Agony exploded in Rivalen as bones shattered, as ribs spiked organs, but he smiled through the pain—until he realized that Kesson, despite the fall, despite the damage he must have suffered, had not lost the thread of his spell.

Black veins form on the surface of the Source, ooze forth from its orange flesh. Eventually their ends detach from the Source and hang loose below it. I reach up, take them in my hand. They are warm, pulsing. I scream as they burrow into the flesh of my hands and forearms, but the pain vanishes quickly.

The Source's energy flows into me unadulterated and I scream with pleasure.

Cale and Riven watched the dragon bury men and giants under the mountain of its form. Furlinastis roared with pain. Cale presumed that the force of his impact had caused many of the weapons borne by the men and giants crushed beneath him to penetrate his scales. Shadows swirled around the dragon. Dirt and soil formed a hillock in front of him by the time his body came to stop.

Cale saw Regg shouting orders, ordering his men and women

to realign. Shadows churned around the surviving giants as they too tried to regroup. The shadowwalkers appeared amongst the Lathanderians, clots of darkness amidst their light.

Furlinastis lurched to his feet. Corpses and weapons impressed into his body dangled from the scales of his chest and abdomen. Blood leaked from a score of wounds, poured around a giant's sword that had been buried to its hilt in his chest. He extended his neck and roared his rage into the sky. He turned to face the giants. The Lathanderians rallied to either side of him.

"Where is Kesson Rel?" Riven said.

Before Cale could answer, a surge of unadulterated pleasure ran through him. He gasped, stopped, sought its source, found it in his mental connection with Magadon.

*Mags? What happened? Where are you?*

*It is wonderful, Erevis*, Magadon said, and his mental voice sounded as if it were floating. Power leaked into Cale's brain, images, memories, knowledge.

Cale shook his head to clear it, cursed.

"What is it?" Riven asked.

"Mags is at the Source. He's in Sakkors."

"What? How?"

Cale shook his head, blinking as his eyes started to water, as the tone of Magadon's mental impressions grew harsher. He grabbed his head in his hands, tried to hold it together.

*Mags, get away from the Source. Don't do it. Don't.*

When Magadon spoke again, his mental voice sounded deeper, harsh as a rasp. *Don't? You fear the power I hold. You are a liar and a betrayer.*

Cale endured the mental storm in his brain and said to Riven, "We have to get to him. He'll be lost."

"He's been lost a long time already," Riven said.

Cale glared at the assassin. "He's half a man. I'm not leaving him. If he were whole. . . ."

He winced as more and more mental energy poured into his mind. Magadon was awash in power and enough of it was leaking through their mental connection that it made the veins in Cale's temple throb.

"He cannot be whole unless we kill Kesson," Riven said. "That first, then we help Mags. Otherwise you, me, and everyone else here dies. Then Sembia. Then the rest. You know it, Cale. You saw Ephyras."

Cale knew Riven was right, but he feared that Magadon, in his mentally wounded state, would be irretreivable if they didn't get to him soon. Meanwhile, the emptiness within him beckoned, expanded, opened wider, ate at him. Riven must have been feeling the same thing. They had to kill Kesson Rel or die.

"There," Riven said, and pointed across the plain, where they saw Rivalen and Kesson rise on shaky legs and face off.

*Hang on, Mags.*

The Source awakens fully, then awakens me fully. The hole in me is filled, the emptiness bridged. My mind is magnified. My power is amplified. Knowledge fills me. I swim in the warmth of the Source's mind, my mind one with it, my will one with it.

But I am not content.

Rage burns like wildfire through my consciousness. It is born in the mind of the fiend and dwarfs everything else in my mindscape. Its fire consumes the weak barricades of conscience that try to stem its spread. What little of the man that remains in me flees before it. Bits of regret, guilt, love, leak out of the conflagration of my rage and flee my mind.

I am hate.

And I am power.

My mind reaches out into the world, senses the minds of other creatures, some of whom are responsible for what happened to me. My hate is indiscriminate.

With a slight effort of will, I cause Sakkors to move toward the Shadowstorm.

Kesson pronounced the last word of the disjunction and it shredded Rivalen's sphere of anti-magic. Rivalen rolled over, felt in the grass for his holy symbol, found it, and closed his hand over the cold metal. He climbed to his feet, hissing with pain.

Agony blurred his vision. His withered arm hung limp from his shoulder. The shadows enshrouding him had cushioned his fall, but the impact had still ruined his body. Shattered ribs stabbed into his lungs, filling them with blood, and his wet breathing bubbled. One ankle was shattered, causing him to hobble. A ringing sounded in his ears. Shadows spun around him as his regenerative flesh tried to undo the worst of the damage.

Across from him, Kesson, too, climbed to his feet, his dark eyes fixed on Rivalen. One of the bones of his forearm jutted from his dark skin. One of his white horns had broken at the halfway point. Blood leaked from his nose and mouth. His breathing was rapid, labored, his eyes glazed. No doubt he, too, had shattered ribs and a cracked skull.

Rivalen heard the sizzle of a triggered contingency and in an instant, all of Kesson's wounds healed. Rivalen cursed as Kesson spread his wings, glared at Rivalen, and mouthed words of power. Energy gathered in both his hands.

Rivalen stumbled backward, clutching the holy symbol of Shar, and incanted a counterspell. His words rose in opposition to Kesson's as he pitted his power against the burgeoning energies gathering in Kesson's hands.

The magical ring on his finger warmed, and the connection

opened. Rivalen felt anger pouring through the mental link. It filled Rivalen's mind, caused pressure behind his eyes, and broke his concentration on the counterspell.

*I know what you did to our mother,* Brennus said. *You murdered her in a meadow of flowers.*

The shadows spun around Rivalen. His thoughts spun similarly. He backed away from Kesson, backed away from Brennus's accusation, all while triggering a defensive ring, amulet, and necklace.

*Brennus—*

*Say nothing!* Brennus said. *I will not hear your denials, your rationalizations! You murdered my mother!*

The anger pouring through the connection turned to grief. Rivalen knew that Brennus was sobbing. He had no time for it.

Kesson advanced on him, wings drawn in, power in his hand.

Rivalen tried to gather his thoughts, cast his own spell, but his brother's words had scrambled his concentration better than anything Kesson could have said or done. He found it difficult to take hold of his thoughts. They raced around from possibility to possibility. He could pin none of them down.

*I wish you to die,* Brennus said.

*You may get that wish,* Rivalen said, and flew into the air.

Brennus seemed not to hear him. *But you are my brother and it will not be by my hand. The spell sequence I provided to you before will kill you if you use it.*

Rivalen had nothing around him but air yet he felt walls closing in on him, his plans unravelling before his eyes, the thread of his life being pulled from the weave of history.

*I will not cause your death but neither will I cause your deification. I will simply hate you forever.*

The words pained Rivalen faintly. He had felt closer to Brennus than other members of his family.

*I have not told the Most High,* Brennus answered. *Nor will I.*

*This is between us, Rivalen. And it will be between us forever.*

Rivalen understood Brennus's meaning. He had lost his brother. Soon he would lose his life. He was about to speak when a surge of surprise carried through the connection

*What is it?* he asked

*Sakkors is moving,* Brennus answered, and cut off the connection.

Rivalen glanced back and saw Kesson touch himself with his right hand as he completed a spell—an illusion, perhaps—that caused his form to shimmer for an instant, after which he extended his left hand at Rivalen and fired a line of orange energy that Rivalen could not avoid.

Rivalen screamed as his body exploded and he fell back to earth.

Broken bones and damaged organs caused Furlinastis to roar with pain. Blood poured out of him, fountaining around the giant's sword that spiked his chest. He was dying, vaguely aware of the Lathanderians forming up somewhere near him.

Unable to take revenge on Kesson Rel, he decided to take it on Kesson Rel's creatures.

Lurching forward into a mass of giants, he crushed two under his body, impaled another on his right claw, pulled the giant to his mouth, and bit him half. The blood and flesh fired his rage and he roared anew.

The giants shouted and bounded forward. Blades rained down on Furlinastis's scales. Giants shadowstepped atop his back, tried to drive their blades down into his spine. He lurched, throwing them off of him, crushed another under his body, and tore the arm off another with his fangs.

But some of the giants' blows penetrated his scales. Furlinastis leaked shadows and blood. He was slowing, weakening.

Cale and Riven stepped through the darkness and materialized two strides behind Kesson Rel, in time to watch Rivalen's
body burst in a shower of blood as veins and arteries exploded
outward from his flesh. The Shadovar prince fell to the ground
in a twitching heap of glistening gore. Shadows still streamed
from his ruined body.

"High," Cale said.

"Low," Riven answered, and both lunged forward, blades
bare.

Cale took a two-handed slash across Kesson's throat; Riven
stabbed his sabres in the middle of Kesson's back.

Their blades passed through him as if he were air.

"Illusion," Cale said, as the image disappeared. Riven cursed.

Kesson's voice, intoning a spell, carried on the wind from
somewhere to their right. They whirled, sought him, saw
nothing.

Holding his mask, Cale spoke a brief prayer and a circle
of force radiated outward from him in all directions to about
twenty paces, countering invisibility in its path.

Kesson appeared, hovering low over the plains, energy gathering in both his hands.

"I have Rivalen," Cale said, and winced as a wave of Magadon's mental energy caused a spike of pain in his head. "Go."

Riven nodded, and charged Kesson.

*I am power,* Magadon said in Cale's head, his voice an echo
of Mephistopheles's. *And I am hate.*

Riven threw one of his enchanted sabres at Kesson as he
charged. The curved blade, poorly balanced for throwing,
cut an irregular arc through the air and struck Kesson in the

shoulder. If the blade cut flesh, Riven couldn't tell. He could tell that it had no effect on Kesson's casting.

Kesson's dark eyes fixed on Riven. He flapped his wings, pointed both hands.

Cale shadowstepped to Rivalen's side and gagged at the stench. The Shadovar's body had been opened, as if his skin had been unbuttoned and the vitals pulled forth. One of his arms was little more than a withered stick.

Blood vessels, tendons, intestines all lay in a twisted heap on the ruins of his flesh. His eyes fixed on Cale, still aglow, filled with rage and pain. He opened his mouth to speak but nothing more emerged than a wet gurgle. Cale saw that Rivalen's hand still held his holy symbol, slicked with his blood. Perhaps the Shadovar's regenerative flesh would heal him in time. Perhaps not.

Intoning a rapid prayer, Cale cast his most powerful healing spell and fought back bile as the magic caused Rivalen's innards to squirm back into place and closed the flesh over them.

Rivalen, still slick and sticky with his own blood, inhaled in a gasp.

"Get up," Cale said, and pulled him to his feet.

Magadon's voice rang in his head.

*I am power.*

*Magadon!* Cale projected through the mental connection. *This is not you! Get control! Get out of the Source, Mags. Get out.*

*I have control*, Magadon answered, and began to laugh. *And I will never get out.*

Cale looked back the way they had come and saw through the darkness, through the raging battle of wraiths and shadows, a huge form moving through the storm, a floating city.

Sakkors.

And Magadon.

Riven dodged to his right as energy flew from both of Kesson's fists. A glowing orange ball of power streaked toward Riven from Kesson's left hand, while a line of green energy from his right hand coalesced in the air and formed itself around Riven into the shape of a large, barred cage. Riven slammed into its unyielding bars. He was trapped inside with the orange ball, which began to spin and hum.

Riven cut at the bars, but he might as well have been chopping at adamantine.

The ball spun ever more rapidly, emitting a high pitched whine. Riven backed away from it as far as the cage allowed. He looked over and saw Cale pull Rivalen, mostly whole, to his feet.

"Cale!"

The ball exploded, filling the cage with billowing black smoke shot through with burning streams of red-hot embers. Riven had nowhere to hide, no cover, and smoke and embers saturated him. He screamed as his flesh blistered, blackened, as his clothes caught fire.

Cale heard Riven's screams. Lines of burning embers snaked through a cloud of smoke, glowing runes of heat and agony traced in the air. The smoke leaked through the bars of a magical cage. Riven had nowhere to run.

"Forcecage," Rivalen said, and spit a tooth and blood.

Cale felt for the darkness within the cage, found it, held his breath, and stepped to it. Lines of fire wrote letters of pain on his flesh. He gritted his teeth, endured, and followed Riven's screams through the smoke. He found the assassin writhing on the ground, burning. Cale grabbed his cloak and rode the shadows out of the cage and onto the plains. He rolled Riven around on the the rain-swept grass as Cale's regenerative flesh healed the burns on his own skin.

Riven grunted with pain through bared teeth, as much angry as pained. His face and hands were blistered, blackened like seared meat. Blades of grass clung to the charred flesh from where Cale had rolled him on the turf. His hair was melted.

Rivalen stepped from the shadows next to Cale.

"Be still," Rivalen said, and held Riven still with his one hand. He chanted a healing prayer, the language not unlike that which Cale had used to heal Rivalen, and Riven's skin regenerated before their eyes. His breathing eased, though his hair and beard remained blackened and curled.

"Good?" Cale asked him.

"No," Riven said, and sat up. He drew a dagger to pair with his saber. He must have lost his other saber during the battle. He stood. "But that's not new. We cannot beat him, Cale."

Cale nodded. "I know."

Not even Rivalen protested.

"But we see it through," Cale said and looked across the plains to Kesson Rel. The First Chosen of Mask rose into the sky, energy in his hands. Kesson touched his hand to himself once, twice, presumably warding himself against attack.

Cale was about to speak when a blast of power soaked his mind, caused his nose to bleed, and sent him to his knees.

Sakkors, draped in shadows, floated over the battlefield.

*I am come!* Magadon projected.

Rivalen and Riven both covered their ears and groaned. Even Kesson grimaced.

And Cale realized what he must do. He rose to his feet.

"Spread out," he said. "And wait for my say so."

Blows rained down on Furlinastis's body. His good wing hung in shreds. He'd lost two teeth on a giant's breastplate. He could scarcely see and pinpointed his targets as much by sound and smell as sight. Roaring, he pinned a giant under one claw, pressed down, and felt the satisfying *crunch* of the giant's rib-cage collapsing.

A pair of giants slashed at his throat, opened huge gashes in his scales. He whirled, caught one by the leg in his jaws, and shook him until the leg came free. He gulped it down as the giant bled out on the grass.

Three giants to his left nocked arrows, drew, and loosed. All three sank to the fletching in his side. He whipped his body around, caught two of them with a tail lash, and shattered their knees.

But he was failing. A group of two score giants charged him. He reared up, roaring.

And a roar from behind joined his own.

The companions of Abelar Corrinthal charged the giants, breaking around and past Furlinastis, their numbers ablaze in magical light.

Regg and his company flowed around the dragon, shouting battle cries. The shadowwalkers, cloaked in darkness even in the midst of Roen and his priests' light spells, ran in the vanguard of the force.

The dragon roared as they passed, lumbered after. With the number of wounds the creature had suffered, Regg did not know how it even moved.

Trewe sounded a blast and the company hit the remaining giants like a maul. Regg sidestepped a giant's stab and hacked into the creature's knee. When it fell, roaring, he drove his blade through the back of its neck. A giant staggered into him, spouting blood from a throat wound, and knocked him down. Another loomed out of the battle, sword raised over his head for a killing blow.

The dragon's head shot out of the chaos of combat on his long neck and the giant vanished in a flash of teeth and spray of blood. Regg climbed to his feet and hacked about him until he could no longer feel his arms.

Cale and Rivalen shadowstepped away from Riven. Together, the three men formed a triangle around Mask's First Chosen, who flew in the air above them.

"You are not enough," Kesson said, and Cale knew he was right. They were not enough. To have any chance, Cale had to risk Magadon.

Rain drizzled from the sky. For a time, the four combatants simply regarded one another, each waiting for the other to begin the final act.

Cale tried to focus his mind, to push his thoughts through the blizzard of mental energy pouring through his connection with Magadon.

*Look through my eyes, Mags. Kesson Rel is here. We need you to help us.*

Kesson Rel began to cast. Rivalen did the same.

*Now, Mags. Look through my eyes! Now!*

A hand closed on Regg's shoulder. He whirled in a backhand slash, but a shadow-shrouded hand caught his forearm in a powerful grip and stopped the blow.

A shadowwalker.

Blood, rain, and sweat coated the small man. He had a

gash in one cheek and stood uneasily on his left leg. His face remained as impassive as ever.

"It is over," the shadowwalker said in his accented Common.

Regg surveyed the field and realized for the first time that it was raining again.

Hundreds of giants lay on the grass, their enormous bodies torn by fang and claw or slashed by blades. The rain drained their blood into the soil. Most of Regg's company lay dead on the field, too. He saw Roen and Trewe among a few score others start to walk among the bodies, checking for signs of life. When they found it, Roen or one of his fellow priests channelled Lathander's power into a spell of healing.

Regg caught Trewe's gaze, and held up his hand. Trewe, perhaps too exhausted to raise his own arm, merely nodded.

The ten or so shadowwalkers flitted among the giants' bodies, crushing the windpipes of any that still breathed. Regg was too tired to protest. Besides, he could take no prisoners.

The dragon, its enormous, shadow-shrouded form sprawled over the field, with bloody pieces of giants still clinging to his teeth and claws, inhaled a rattling breath. Regg staggered to his side, along his neck, noting the gashes, the spurting blood. The wyrm's eyes were open. Ribbons of shadow and ragged breaths leaked from his nose and mouth. The slits of his pupils dilated to focus on Regg.

Regg removed his gauntlet and put his hand on the ridge over the wyrm's eye.

"I have seen nobility in strange places this day."

The dragon's chest rattled, perhaps in a laugh.

"The one who rode me, Abelar, was at peace," the dragon whispered.

"I know," Regg said, and tears wet his face. "Be at peace also."

Regg stared into the dragon's eye until it closed.

"Dawn dispels the night and births the world anew," Regg said. "May Lathander light your way and show you wisdom and mercy. Today you were a light to others."

Shouts turned Regg around. The members of his company looked past Regg and into the sky, pointing with their blades.

"Sakkors!"

Regg looked up and saw the floating, shadow-cloaked Shadovar city emerge from the darkness.

Cale felt the tell-tale tingle behind his eyes, the displacement of his own consciousness as Magadon shared his senses. The mental energy racing through his brain surged, driving him to his knees. His mouth opened to speak but the voice was not his own.

"Kesson Rel!" Magadon screamed through him.

*Use all of the power in the Source, Mags,* Cale projected, cursing himself for the words. *Kill him if you can and we can save you.*

Cale knew that those words would stain him forever, that he might have just surrendered his friend to mental slavery to the Source. He vowed to himself that he would do whatever he must to save Magadon.

But first he had to survive.

*I am saved,* Magadon said. *But I will kill nevertheless. First him, then Rivalen, then you.*

*Kesson Rel!*

Regg heard the deep voice in his mind and felt as if his head must come apart. He gritted his teeth and groaned. Sparks exploded behind his eyes. Moans from the men and women of his company told him they were experiencing the same thing.

Beside him, Nayan stood with one hand held to his brow, his mouth fixed in a hard line, and his eyes half-closed as if against a storm.

"The mindmage," Nayan said

In the air above, the shadows and wraiths, bent on annihilating one another, wailed and keened.

The pressure diminished in moments, leaving only a dull throb in its wake. Regg watched in awe as a faint orange glow haloed the edifice upon which Sakkors stood. The air around him felt charged. His hair stood on end.

The entire company exclaimed as the mountaintop upon which Sakkors sat began to sink rapidly toward the earth, as if the power keeping it afloat had failed, or been diverted.

The power churning through Cale's head lit his body afire. The shadows around him spun wildly. Sakkors and its flying mountain flared with Magadon's power, glowing orange and red like a tiny sun as it sank toward the ground.

*I am hate!* Magadon shouted. *And I am power!*

Above them, Kesson's chanting gave way to a scream of agony. His horns shattered, and blood poured from his nose, his ears, his eyes. The shadows around him spun. He grabbed hold of his head, screamed again, and fell face-first to the ground.

"Now!" Cale said, and staggered forward, bent as if against a gale.

Riven and Rivalen, blades bear, did the same. Both men bled freely from their nose and ears.

Sakkors shined red and orange as it slowly sank, its light chasing the pitch of the Shadowstorm, overwhwelming the shroud that surrounded Sakkors. To Regg, it seemed an artificial dawn and he fell to his knees.

"There is light even in darkness," he said.

Lathander had provided him another sign. His work was not yet done. He stood and looked around the glowing plains.

Through the rain and darkness he saw four forms in the distance, and marked them as Erevis Cale, Riven, the Shadovar, and Kesson Rel.

He grabbed Nayan by the arm. "There! Can your men take us there?"

Nayan looked, saw, nodded.

"Roen, gather your priests!"

Cale, Riven, and Rivalen stumbled forward to execute Kesson Rel.

But Kesson, his head haloed in red light and bleeding from his eyes, ears, and nose, with pulsing veins tracing a throbbing web on his brow, rose to all fours.

"No!" he said, and made a cutting gesture.

*No!* Magadon shrieked, and Cale heard madness in the tone.

The red glow around Kesson's head winked out. Cale cursed, lunged forward, and raised Weaveshear high for a killing stroke across the back of Kesson's neck.

Kesson threw an arm out blindly behind him and power exploded outward from his form. Black energy slammed into Cale, Riven, and Rivalen. It blew all of them backward five paces, cracked bone, opened flesh.

Exhausted and bloodied, Cale rose to all fours, knowing they had missed their opportunity, knowing they were all going to die.

He found himself staring at a booted foot. Hands took him under his armpits and lifted him to his feet. Regg stood there, looking past him, through him, to Kesson Rel. Nayan stood behind the Lathanderian, his expression unreadable.

Cale glanced around and saw Roen and the priests of the company, ten in all, arrayed in a circle around Kesson Rel, who rose haltingly to his feet.

Warmth suffused Regg's body. The armor and shields of Roen and his fellow priests glowed orange in the setting sun of Sakkors' fall. He thought of Abelar, of faith, of friendship. The thoughts lit a fire in his spirit and he dropped to one knee, brandished his battle-scarred shield, and channeled the divine light of his god. The seed Abelar had planted in his soul bloomed fully.

"Dawn dispels the night and births the world anew," he began, and the rose on his shield began to glow.

Roen fell to one knee, held forth his own shield, his own rose, and joined his voice, and his light, to Regg's.

"May Lathander light our way, show us wisdom . . ."

The remaining priests fell to one knee, held their shields before them, and joined in the Dawnmeet prayer.

". . . and in so doing allow us be a light to others."

The shields of Lathander's faithful glowed with a brightness to rival a dawn sun. Regg's spirit soared to see their faith so embodied in the symbol of their god. He wept as the holy luminescence exposed the darkness of Kesson Rel.

Kesson, already weakened, screamed in the blast of light, fell to the ground. Their light burned away the shadows that shrouded him. He writhed on the ground as if he were afire, shrieking.

"Finish it," Regg said to Cale.

The light from the Lathanderians made Cale queasy but he endured. He watched Kesson fall, shriek, watched the darkness around Mask's First Chosen fall away. He took Weaveshear in both hands and stepped into the circle. Riven did the same.

The light stripped away the shadows that coated Cale, his shadow hand, and for the first time in a long time he felt human. He glanced at Regg and Roen, and thanked them for that with his eyes.

Still, the emptiness of his spirit, the hole dug by the Black Chalice, needed filled.

He and Riven stepped up to Kesson Rel. Riven stabbed him through the chest with a saber. Cale cut off his head, and his screams, with Weaveshear.

Power began to gather.

Rivalen watched blood and shadows pour from the stump of Kesson Rel's neck. His thoughts seethed, frustration burned. He clutched his holy symbol so hard in his good hand that it cut his flesh.

He had schemed for centuries only to watch it fall apart before his eyes. He didn't know the spells he needed to steal Kesson's divinity. Instead, he had to stand idle and watch Erevis Cale become a god.

He cursed Brennus, cursed fate.

Above, thunder rumbled. A lightning storm lit the sky. The Lathanderians rose, their light diminished, and backed away from Kesson's corpse. One of the shadowwalkers started forward, but the Lathanderian Cale had named Regg held him back.

The wind whipped. Darkness formed around Kesson's body, a cloud of impenetrable blackness. Cale and Riven eased back a step. The wind became a gale, tearing at their robes, turning the drizzle into a sizzling spray. Thunder and lightning lit the sky and shook the ground. Power gathered in the shroud around Kesson's body, the stolen divinity separating from its mortal vessel. It leaked into the air over his corpse to form a cloud that looked less like darkness and more like a hole. Rivalen saw in it the echo of the emptiness devouring Ephyras.

And in the emptiness Rivalen found revelation.

Brennus had told him that only a Chosen of Mask could safely partake of the Black Chalice, but Brennus had not known of the relationship between Shar and Mask. They were related, and so too were their servants. A Chosen of Shar, too, should be able to safely drink.

Cale and Riven fell to their knees as the power gathered. A hum filled the air, growing in volume. The clot of shadows continued to coagulate over Kesson, expanding.

Rivalen spoke an arcane word and summoned the Black Chalice from the extra-dimensional space in which he had stored it. It materialized in his hand, heavy with promise.

"I am your Chosen, or I am your failure," Rivalen said to Shar.

He drank, and screamed.

The hole in Cale's being yawned, and pulled at the dark power seething over Kesson. Cale heard a humming in his ears, the roll of thunder, a scream, and he could not be sure that it was not his. Shadows churned around him. The power gathering over Kesson expanded. The wind blew so hard it threatened to flatten him to the ground. A continuous boom of thunder shook the ground. Lightning shot from the sky, struck the inky cloud above Kesson, once, twice, again, again. The cloud roiled, seethed, the power within it gathering.

Cale braced himself. The hum increased in volume, the wind, the thunder.

A beam of darkness and power shot from the cloud at Cale, but not just at Cale. Another beam struck Riven in the chest. Another struck Rivalen.

All three screamed as a fraction of the stolen divinity filled their beings, overwhelmed their souls, transformed them from men to gods. Cale's senses felt afire. His nose burned. His eyes watered. His bones ached. He fell to all fours as his mortal soul recoiled, as divine power filled the hollow spaces in him.

Then it was over.

The wind died. The thunder and lightning relented.

"Are you well?" Regg called from behind, his voice uncertain. "Erevis?"

"Stay back," Cale said, and the shadows around him roiled. "Far back. Now, Regg. Hurry. You also, Nayan."

Cale heard armor and weapons chink as the Lathanderians and shadowwalkers backed away ten, twenty paces. He heard their every whisper.

"What just happened?"

"Kesson is dead."

"What are they?"

Cale looked up, over to Riven, and nodded. Riven nodded in return. Neither would have to die, at least not for lack of divinity.

He looked to Rivalen, saw the Shadovar rise, terrible and dark. Cale and Riven did the same.

Two gods stood to face one.

They stared at one another over Kesson's corpse. The rain fell.

# CHAPTER SEVENTEEN

*7 Nightal, the Year of Lightning Storms*

We stand with you," Regg called from behind. "You need only give us the word, Cale."

"As do we," Nayan said in his accented Common.

Before Cale could respond, a stream of wraiths—mere hundreds had survived the battle with the shadows—swooped down from the dark sky in a long ribbon and flew between the three gods, swirled in a cyclone over Kesson's form.

"Leave them," Cale said to Riven, to Rivalen, to Regg and the Lathanderians.

A towering wraith, one of the Lords of Silver, separated from the swirl and hovered before Cale. His red eyes flared. He leaned in close, as if catching a whiff of divine spoor.

"He is yours," Cale said, and the power in his voice

caused the wraith to recoil.

The wraith studied Cale a moment, bowed, and said in his whispery voice, "His corpse will rot in Elgrin Fau."

The Lord of Silver returned to the rest and the cyclone of undead whirled, their moans not despairing but triumphant. They lifted Kesson Rel's body and severed head from the ground and streaked across the battlefield, toward the rift Cale had opened.

After they'd gone, Cale, Riven, and Rivalen continued to stare at one another, their minds struggling to comprehend their new capabilities.

Cale knew a battle between them would turn Sembia into a wasteland, would destroy Sakkors, would kill everyone on the field. Rivalen had to know it too.

"A battle between us leaves nothing to the victor," Cale said.

Rivalen smiled, and energy gathered. "I disagree."

"Rivalen," Cale began, but a shriek from Magadon filled Cale's mind, filled the minds of everyone on the battlefield, the sound thick with power, incoherent with rage.

The Lathanderians and shadowwalkers fell to the ground, groaning with pain. Cale, Riven, and Rivalen winced. Pressure mounted in Cale's skull. He felt a warm trickle of blood leaking from one nostril. He tried to reach through the rage to Magadon.

*Mags, he's dead. Kesson is dead. I can save you now.*

But there was not enough of Magadon left to understand.

*I do not need to be saved!* he screamed.

Behind Cale, the Lathanderians began to scream, to die.

Power stormed in Cale's mind. His eyes felt as if they would jump out of his head. His thoughts grew confused. He tried to focus.

*This is how you pay for your betrayal of me,* Magadon said.

Cale staggered, felt blood drip from his ears.

"Your city is dying," he said to Rivalen through gritted teeth.

"So is your friend," Rivalen answered, and wiped the blood falling from his nose. His golden eyes, pained, looked as wide as coins.

Cale knew. Magadon had little time. If he could still be saved, Cale had to do something soon. He had already made a deal with one devil. He could make a deal with another.

"A bargain," Cale said.

Rivalen nodded, hissed with pain. "Speak what you will."

"The Saerbians settle where they wish and are left alone," Cale said, his voice punctuated by grunts of pain. "Magadon goes free and unharmed."

"Magadon is already dead."

"No," Cale said with heat. "Not yet."

Rivalen looked to Cale, to Riven. "Sembia belongs to the Shadovar."

Cale nodded, wiped the blood from his face. "Done. Now we need time. Do as I do."

Cale called upon his newfound power, trusting that Rivalen and Riven would recognize his intent as he began to cast.

The pressure in his mind mounted.

*Die! Die!* Magadon railed.

Rivalen and Riven recognized Cale's intent and their voices joined his.

Ignoring the screams of Regg and his company, the shadow-walkers, Magadon's rage, they drew on thier shared godhead and stopped time.

When they completed the casting, raindrops hung suspended in mid-air. A lightning bolt split the sky, frozen in place. Sakkors hung atilt in the air, still glowing, perhaps two bowshots from a collision with the ground. The Lathanderians and the shadowwalkers, light and shadow, were frozen in the moment on the wet ground, faces contorted with pain, blood pouring from eyes, ears, noses.

Cale had only a short time before time would resume, before Magadon would die. While the spell was in effect, they could affect no mortal beings, not directly. With no time to waste, Cale wasted none. He had already made up his mind.

"I am saving Magadon," he said to Riven and let the words register.

Riven nodded, missing his point. "Agreed, but how? We have only moments."

Cale looked him in the face. "There's only one way."

Riven looked up sharply. "You can't pay, Cale. It doesn't come out, except . . ."

His eye widened.

Cale nodded. The divinity could come out of him only when he died.

Riven's face fell. He shook his head, began to pace. "No, no, no. There's another way."

"This is the only way."

Riven stopped pacing and glared him. "We have this power, we can do something else. There's another way."

Cale knew better. Even if they could defeat Mephistopheles, they could not do so before he destroyed what he had taken from Magadon. "Riven, it's the only way. Riven—"

Riven held up his hands, as if trying to stop Cale's words from charging toward him.

"Just give me a damned moment, Cale. A moment."

Cale waited, felt the power of the spell draining away. He shifted on his feet.

Riven looked up, his expression hard. "No, you're giving up again, Cale."

Emotion flooded Cale but he could not determine if it was anger or something else. He stepped forward and grabbed Riven by the cloak. The shadows around him engulfed them both, spun and whirled.

"I'm not! I'm fighting all the way." He calmed himself,

spoke in a softer voice, releasing Riven. "I'm fighting all the way, Riven."

Maybe Riven understood, maybe he didn't.

They stared at one another a long moment. Riven's face fell.

"How can it be the only way, Cale? After all this?"

Cale shook his head, smiling softly. "How can it not? How else could it end?"

Riven looked away, down. "You're doing this for him?"

"There's nothing else," Cale said. "Just us. That's the reason for everything. Understand?"

Riven looked up, his face stricken.

Cale held out a hand. "You've been my friend, Riven."

Riven's lower lip trembled. He clasped Cale's hand, pulled him close for an embrace.

Cale took Weaveshear by the blade, handed it hilt first to Riven. The reality of his decision started to settle on him. His legs felt soft under him. His hand shook. Riven pretended not to notice.

"The fiend doesn't get this," Cale said.

Riven took it, nodded.

"I will keep my promise," Cale said. "You keep ours to him. You remember it?"

Riven's face hardened. He nodded again. "I remember it."

Cale turned to Rivalen. "Keep your word, too, Shadovar."

Rivalen's face was expressionless, his eyes aglow.

Faces and memories poured through Cale's mind but he pushed them aside and pictured Cania. He drew the darkness around him.

At the last moment, he changed his mind and pictured not the icy wastes of the Eighth Hell but the face of a grateful boy, the boy who had once invited him into the light. It suddenly seemed the most important thing in the world that Cale see Aril, a boy he had met only once.

"Good-bye," Cale said to Riven.

Riven didn't speak, perhaps he couldn't. Eyes averted, he signed, "Farewell" in handcant.

Aril slept on his side, peaceful in his small bed. Blankets covered him to the neck. His head, with its mop of hair, poked from the bedding. Cale stared at the boy for a time, thinking of times past, friends and enemies, all of them the scar tissue of a lifetime. Aril slept peacefully, contentedly. Cale found the moment . . . fitting.

A boy sleeping safely in his bed, free of fear, with his whole life before him. He realized why he had needed to see Aril instead of Shamur, Tamlin, or Tazi. He wanted the last person he saw on Faerûn to be innocent.

He put the back of his shadow-dusted hand on the boy's cheek and thought of Jak.

"I did what I could."

He hoped it made a difference for someone, somewhere.

He stepped through the shadows and into the darkness outside the small cottage. The quietude of the village seemed alien after the chaos of the battlefield. He had only a short while before time back in the Shadowstorm would resume.

The smell of chimney fires filled the cool air. He glanced around the village. Three score cottages sat nestled around a tree-dotted commons, quiet, peaceful, safe. The two-story temple of Yondalla, the lone stone structure among the log and mud-brick buildings of the village, sat near the common's edge and rose protectively over the whole, a shepherd to the sheep. Smoke issued from the temple's two chimneys, filling the glen with the smell of cedar, and home. The hearths burned fragrant wood and were never allowed to grow cold.

Cale inhaled deeply. He fought back tears born in realizations come too late.

He allowed that on at least one night not long ago the village owed its safety not to Yondalla, but to him. He had killed a score of trolls while he had answered to Jak's ghost, while he tried to climb into the light.

But there was no answering to the dead, and the light was not for him. Not anymore. Not ever.

He looked up into the vault of the sky, unplagued by the roiling ink of the Shadowstorm. The Sea of Stars twinkled above him, Selûne and her train of glowing Tears. He fancied he could see an absence in the celestial cluster circling the silver disc of the moon, the hole out of which one of the Tears had plummeted to Faerûn, the hole for which Jak had died, the hole mirrored in Cale's soul. He thought of the little man and his pipe, tried to smile, but failed. He had never filled the hole. And now he never would.

Power burned in him, cold, dark, near limitless. He could hear words spoken in the shadows on the other side of Toril, could rend mountains with his words. He knew more, sensed more, *was* more, than he could have imagined. His memories, Mask's memories, reached back thousands of years—before Ephyras even—recollections of deeds, people, and places long gone.

Melancholy shrouded him, wrapped him as thoroughly as the shadows. He understood Mask at last, but only now, at the end of things. He realized, too, that Mask had understood him, perhaps better than he had understood himself.

*You wish to transcend,* Mephistopheles had told him once.

Mask had said it to him, too, though not in words.

And Cale had wished to transcend, and so he would, though not in the way he had conceived.

He felt the connection to Riven back in Sembia, a connection that reached through time and distance. The assassin's grief, buried deeply but present, touched Cale. He swallowed the fist that formed in his throat.

They *were* friends, by the end. It had gone unacknowledged too long. He was glad they had said appropriate good-byes. The words had seemed small for so profound a moment. Cale would miss Riven, as he had Jak.

He reached into the pocket of his cloak and removed the small throwing stone Aril had given him. He had carried it for months, a reminder, a talisman of hope. The events involving Aril seemed ancient, something that had happened on another world, in another time. The smooth rock felt warm in his hand, solid.

"Shadowman," he whispered, recalling the name the half-lings had given him.

He placed the stone on the ground in the doorway of the cottage where Aril and his mother slept, a gravestone to mark his passing. The last thing his hand touched on Faerûn would be a river stone given him by a grateful halfing boy who had named him "Shadowman." He thought it fitting.

"Good-bye," he said, thinking not just of Aril.

He closed his eyes and readied himself. He did not lack for resolve but he still wanted the moment to stretch. An eternity passed between heartbeats. He savored the faint smell of pine carried by the westerly wind, the thrill of energy that permeated everything around him, all of Faerûn.

He had only seen it in full in that moment. He would miss it. He took comfort in the fact that he had helped preserve it, at least for a time.

Ready, he sank into the comforting familiarity of the darkness. It saturated him, warmed him. He knew the night now the way he knew his own skin. It was part of him. It *was* him.

He bade it good-bye, too, and stepped through the shadows, through the planes, to Cania.

The ordinary darkness of a Faerûnian night yielded to the soul-blighting darkness of the Hells. The reach of the time stop did not extend to Cania.

Cale sensed the cold of the Eighth Hell but his newfound power rendered him immune to its bite. But his enhanced senses and expanded consciousness made the horrors of the Eighth Hell more acute.

He stood on a wind-blasted plateau of cracked ice that overlooked a frozen plain cut by wide, jagged rivers of flame. Damned, agonized souls squirmed in the rivers, seethed in its heat like desperate, dying fish caught in a tidal pond. Others wandered the endless ice with empty expressions, dazed and frozen, their minds empty, their fates as cold and unforgiving as the air.

Towering, insectoid gelugons made playthings of the damned in the rivers, eviscerating, impaling, or flaying them as caprice took. Despair saturated the plane, a miasma as palpable as the cold and darkness. Shrieks of pain filled the wind, prolonged, agonized wails that Cale knew would never end. In the distance glaciers as old as the cosmos ground against each other and Cale felt in his bones the vibrations of their never-ending war.

The wind tore at his cloak, howled in his ears, and exhaled the stink of a charnel house, the reek of millions upon millions of dead who would spend eternity in pain. The suffering was eternal.

The darkness around Cale, the darkness that was Cale, swirled and churned. He felt the shadows of Cania, its deep and hidden places, its dark holes, but not as he felt them elsewhere. All shadows answered to Cale, but not to the same degree. Mephistopheles's power touched everything in Cania, tainted it, made it foreign even to Cale's divine consciousness. Cale forced Cania's darkness to answer his will and shrouded himself in its cover.

It was time to keep his promise.

Through their connection, Riven felt Cale leave Faerûn and move to Cania, felt the oppressive despair and unending suffering almost as strongly as if he were standing on its ice himself. He held Weaveshear in his hand, the weapon dripping darkness. He willed his lost saber back into its scabbard and it appeared there instantly.

Around him, as still as statues, stood the company of Lathanderians, a rose-colored glow still noticeable around the edges of their shields. Several lay dead on the ground, their ears leaking lumpy red liquid.

Furlinastis's huge, dark form lay sprawled across the plains, one wing gone, countless gashes open in his scales. The shadows and wraiths that had filled the sky were gone, returned to the Plane of Shadow.

Rain hung motionless in the air. A bolt of lightning hung in the darkness, splitting the sky, caught in mid-moment by the spell. Caught so, the Shadowstorm seemed almost tranquil, beautiful.

Sakkors, too, hung in the distant sky, barely visible behind its curtain of shadows. Magadon sat in its core, lost in the Source, lost in the damage his father had done.

Rivalen eyed him, golden eyes aglow, shadows burning with the same dark power that filled Riven, that filled Cale.

"I see it, now," the Shadovar prince said, his voice hushed, pained. "It is not what I thought."

"It never is," Riven said. "Keep your promise, Rivalen."

Riven left the threat unsaid.

The shade prince nodded.

Riven looked on the faces of the Lathanderians until he found Regg. Blood and mud spattered the warrior's bearded face. Dents dotted his breastplace. Links of his mail hung loose at the shoulder. Riven reached into his beltpouch and withdrew the small pouch of Urlampsyran pipeweed. He stuffed it into one of Regg's belt pouches.

"I do not think we'll get to share that smoke."

With that, Riven drew the darkness around him, the power, and rode it to his temple on the Wayrock. He materialized on the lowered drawbridge. The night sky above him twinkled with stars instead of the oppressive ink of the Shadowstorm.

His girls slept in the entry foyer, frozen by the time stop. He went to them, petted each in turn. He enjoyed the moment. He loved his girls. They were innocence to his transgressions.

He stood, thought of his task, and hardened his will.

He set down Weaveshear, inhaled, readied himself.

The wind gusted, pushed against Cale. He held his ground, drew on his power and let it fill his voice.

"I have come to keep my promise, devil!"

His words boomed across the plain, as loud as a thunderclap. The ground cracked, split under him. Chasms opened in the ice. Great shards of soot-stained snow and rock broke off mountains and fell in roiling clouds of ice to the plains below.

A million devils looked up and answered him with a bellow. The damned, spared their tortures for a moment, sighed at the reprieve. Somewhere, the halls of Mephistar itself rang with his words.

Within three heartbeats gelugons began to materialize around Cale, their white carapaces stained with soot, their vicious hook polearms painted with the gore of ages. Wet, greasy respiration came in pants from between their clicking mandibles. The opalescent surfaces of their bulbous eyes reflected Cale in miniature.

A dozen appeared, two score, a hundred. Their eager clacks filled Cale's ears. The ice groaned under the weight of their collective mass.

Cale stared at them in turn, let them see the power lined up behind his eyes, and their eagerness turned to uncertainty. The shadows around him roiled. They encircled him, claws scrabbling in the cracked ice, but none dared advance. They sensed what he was. He was not for them and they knew it. He stood in their midst untouched, an island of shadow in an ocean of diabolism.

"Inform your master—"

Mephistopheles appeared among them in a cloud of soot and power. They bowed at his arrival, the clack of their carapaces like the breaking of a thousand bones.

"I was aware of your presence the moment you dared set foot in my domain, shadeling."

The archfiend stood as tall as a titan, towering over his minions, over Cale. His black, tattered wings cast a shadow over the assemblage, over the whole of the plane. The heat from his glowing red flesh melted the ice and snow under his feet and sent up faint clouds of steam. The wind stirred his coal-black hair, tore dark smoke from his muscular form. He held his great iron polearm in one hand and lines of unholy power danced on its tines.

Cale truly saw the archfiend for the first time. Mephistopheles was nearly as old as the multiverse, his power and presence as rooted in reality as the celestial spheres. Shar was older, but not Mask. Cale understood the archfiend's full power for the first time.

Understood, too, that he was a match for it.

Perhaps.

The archfiend's pupilless white eyes, so like Magadon's, pierced Cale, saw within him.

"You have brought only a piece of what you owe."

Cale nodded.

"A piece satisfies my promise."

Mephistopheles considered, nodded. "So it does. And so is my plan brought to fruition."

Cale summoned Riven's sneer, laughed, and the sound cracked ice. "Your plan? You have been played, the same as me, the same as him, the same as all of us."

Mephistopheles frowned and the gelugons clicked, their uncertainty manifest.

"You are mistaken."

"No," Cale said. "You are."

Mephistopheles smiled. "And yet I will have what I covet, despite the machinations of godesses, gods, and archwizards."

"And I will have what I want," Cale said, and the pronouncement separated him from himself, split him in two. He felt outside his body, distant, an observer in events rather than a participant.

He found his mind focused not on the present, but on the past. Memories flooded him, the small, quiet moments he had shared with Thazienne, Varra, Jak, the mere hours he'd had with his mother, Tamlin, Riven, the bonds of his life born sometimes in laughter and embraces and sometimes in tears and blood.

"You are without your toy," the archfiend said, and nodded at Cale's empty scabbard.

Mephistopheles's voice seemed far away, a whisper, the faint calling of a fool in the night. Cale floated above the plain, above the devils, above himself, looking down on it all like a ghost haunting his own death. The image was blurred, as though seen through poorly-ground glass. His life, however, played out before him in clear, bright tones, the sequence of events that had brought him to this moment, here, now, when he would die.

"That is because I have not come to fight you," he heard himself say. "I have come to pay what I owe, and to collect what is due."

Riven sensed Mephistopheles's arrival, felt the sudden surge of power, malice, the eternal and unrepentant darkness. The shadows around him spun in slow spirals. Knowing what would come, what must come, Riven focused not on his sadness, not on the surprising sense of loss that turned his stomach into a hole, but on the job.

He was an assassin, as ever he had been. And he was working. He sheathed his grief, and put his hands on the hilts of his blades. He heard his heartbeat in his ears, as loud as a wardrum, each thump keeping time, counting down the moments left in Cale's life.

"To collect what is due," he said, echoing the words of his onetime enemy, now his friend, now his brother.

Mephistopheles stepped toward Cale, eyes blazing, bleeding power, malice, trailing gelugons eager to see a god's blood shed.

Cale, filled with power of his own, gave no ground, but increased his size until he stood eye to eye with the archfiend, until the gelugons were as children gathered for a story.

Dark power flared from Mephistopheles. Cale's shadows swirled in answer. The wind gusted, screamed. Glaciers groaned. The damned shrieked.

"There is only one way for it to come out of you," Mephistopheles said.

Cale knew. "I will pay what I owe."

Eagerness flashed in the archfiend's eyes, greedy hunger. He licked his lips, beat his wings once. The gelugons shifted on their clawed feet, clicked their fearsome mandibles in anticipation.

"First, what *you* owe," Cale said.

Mephistopheles blinked with surprise, as if he had forgotten, but recovered himself quickly. He smiled, showing pointed teeth. His eyes were as hard as adamantine. "Haggling like a Sembian to the last. Very well."

The archfiend backed up a step amidst the gelugons. He stopped, looked to Cale.

"You have what you have and yet are willing to give it up for my son, a man?"

Cale simply stared, but that was answer enough.

The archfiend shook his head. "I do not understand the minds of men. But here is the greater part of your friend."

The archfiend bent at the waste, put his hands on his knees, and began to gag, heave. Presently he vomited a gout of steaming blood and other unidentified lumps of gore onto the ice, turning it into a soup of carnage that smelled of tenday-old corpses.

Cale gagged and swallowed bile. The gelugons clicked in amusement.

In the center of the gore, slick with blood, lay the translucent remnant of Magadon's soul. It did not move.

"What did you do?" Cale said and took a step forward. The shadows around him whirled, ice cracked.

Mephistopheles eyed Cale sidelong, exhaled a breath of power on the soul. The delicate form quickened, stirred, turned, opened its eyes. When it saw the archfiend, its face twisted in despair, terror.

Cale ached for the suffering of his friend. He thought Magadon could be repaired, but never made whole. He would always have a crack, scars.

"But he is not broken," Cale said, and smiled.

Mephistopheles took the soul by the throat, lifted it high, and eyed Cale, the threat implicit. The soul squirmed and writhed, reaching desperately for Cale.

The power in Cale allowed him to see for the first time the power in the human soul, a power that transcended the trivial conventions of men, gods, and planes. Its beauty, *its light*, caused tears to well.

The archfiend sneered at his tears, spit, and wiped the gore from his mouth with the back of his hand.

"He is freed when I get what is mine."

Cale shook his head, let power leak from his form. "No. Free him first."

The gelugons crept closer but Cale had eyes only for Mephistopheles. Magadon's soul twisted in the archdevil's grasp, opened its mouth in silent pleading.

The devil's eyes flared. Power danced on the pointed tips of his polearm.

"Simultaneously."

Cale considered, nodded. There was no other way.

"There will be a moment after I release the half-breed's soul when I can snatch it back still," the archfiend said. "Should you renege, I will draw him back and destroy him utterly. Devour him before your eyes. Then I will find the rest of my son and cause him to suffer."

Cale was unmoved. "Should you attempt to take payment without releasing him, I will have a moment before it is done. I will fight you."

"You would lose."

"Perhaps," Cale acknowledged, "but you and everything in this plane would suffer a long while for the battle. Your rivals would know of it and come for you."

Mephistopheles smiled at Cale's point, though he showed no teeth, and there was nothing in it but malice.

"When I have what I want, my son will be of no matter to me ever again."

Cale believed him. "Let us conclude this business, then."

"Yes, let us."

The archfiend raised a hand in dismissal and the gelugons blinked out, teleporting away.

Cale held his hands at his side and let the power within him go dormant. The shadows subsided. Cale stood before the archfiend, alone, vulnerable.

"Do it," he said.

Riven calmed his heart, balanced his blades, and let the full scope of the power he had received manifest in his form. Darkness clotted the small room, as cold and unforgiving as his intentions. He stood in its midst, bouncing on the balls of his feet, hands fixed like vices around the hilts of his steel. He could not slow his heart, could not stop the clouds of shadow pulsing from his flesh.

Mephistopheles released Magadon's soul and it began immediately to disincorporate into sparkling motes of silver. The archfiend whirled on Cale, his weapon raised for a killing strike.

Shadows leaked from Riven's flesh, from his sabers, and coiled around him. He heard the exchange between Cale and the archfiend, sensed when Mephistopheles released Magadon's soul, knew when the archfiend raised his weapon to claim Cale's payment.

Riven released the time stop spell and reached out his consciousness for Magadon's mind.

*Magadon?* he projected.

*Riven?* Magadon answered in the groggy tone of a man who has just awakened. *Riven, what have I done?*

Riven heard gratitude in the tone, shame, and above all, grief.

He understood the feelings.

*Stop Sakkors's descent and get clear of there. That is the deal.*

*What deal? What are you saying? Where is Erevis?*

*Do it, Mags. Then get away from the Source.*

Cale stood his ground before Mephistopheles, eyes open, shadows swirling around him. He saw the hunger in the archfiend's eyes, knew it would blind him to everything else.

Like Magadon's soul, he, too, disincorporated, watched it all from afar. He felt light, free. For the first time in a long while he thought that he had done something out of love. For the first time since Jak's death, he felt like the hero he had promised he would be.

He felt a tickling under his scalp, behind his eyes—Magadon.

*Erevis, do not!*

*I must, Mags. Know that you saved me. You and Jak.*

Magadon's mental voice hit Riven like a punch.

*Riven, don't let him do it. Riven! Don't let him!*

But it was already done.

Mephistopheles's vicious weapon descended in a killing arc, the full force of an archfiend's power on its blades. Cale felt nothing as the first blow tore into his flesh. Instead, he smelled the welcome, familiar scent of pipeweed, Jak's pipeweed.

He fell to the ice, fell into his past, and realized that he had been mistaken.

He was not *all* darkness. There was light in him after all.

"Cale," said a voice.

"Jak?"

"There are so many things I want to show you . . ."

Riven winced, felt each blow of the archfiend's weapon, felt Cale's pain, thankfully distant, and counted them all.

One, two, three.

He shouted his rage as the blows fell. Darkness poured from him, covered Faerûn for a mile. His girls darted into the temple.

Riven would exact payment for each blow. He owed Cale as much. He owed Mephistopheles as much.

The shadows carried Riven between worlds. He materialized in Cania, a curtain around his new power, invisible to even the Lord of the Eighth. He felt but was untroubled by the blistering wind, the swirl of ice flakes as sharp as knives, the biting cold. The frigidity of the Eighth Hell could not diminish the heat of his rage. The wails of the damned burning in Cania's fiery rivers mingled with the howl of the wind but Riven paid them no heed. He focused only on the back of the archfiend who stood before him, the archfiend who had murdered his friend, perhaps the only friend he'd ever had.

Cale's bloody, crumpled form lay on the ice at the arch-devil's feet. A few stray ribbons of shadow lingered over his body before surrendering to the wind. Ice was already covering him, entombing him in the stuff of Cania. His eyes were closed, his arms thrown wide, his body torn open by the power of the archfiend's three-tined polearm. Cale's blood had turned the snow and ice near him to crimson slush. A few strings of shadow clung to the blood as if reluctant to abandon their maker, and held on despite the wind.

Mephistopheles slammed his polearm into the ice, impaling the plane itself. He shouted in ecstasy and held out his arms as a glistening, vaguely man-shaped cloud of black power exploded upward from Cale's ruined body—a portion of Mask's divine essence. It swirled around the archfiend, wrapping him in a shadowy helix. One end of the helix drove into his chest, eliciting a grunt, and the power of the rest poured in behind it.

"Yes!" Mephistopheles boomed, his voice a thunderhead.

He grew in size as the power merged with him. The red of his flesh darkened, the halo of unholy power shrouding him churned wildly. He roared with ecstasy and Cania trembled. The added power in his voice shattered glaciers, sent avalanches of ancient snow and ice sliding down the side of mountains as old as the cosmos, caused devils and doomed souls alike to wonder and cower. All of the Nine Hells rang with his victory.

"Tremble in your fortress, Asmodeus," the archfiend said, his voice heavy with the promise of things to come.

Having seen the debt paid in full, Riven unmasked himself. The dark fire of divine wrath boiled from his blades, streamed from his flesh, his fury made manifest. In a heartbeat he grew in size to match the archfiend.

Mephistopheles sensed him and started to turn, but too late.

"Let's dance," Riven said, as he drove his sabers into Mephistopheles's back. Power poured from the steel, coursed through the fiend's form. Mephistopheles howled with surprise, rage, agony. He arched backward, his wings flapping reflexively. Shadows swirled around them both.

Riven leaned into his blades, drove them through Mephistopheles's body until the tips of both sabers burst from the archfiend's chest in a spray of power and fiendish ichor. Mephistopheles fell to his knees and his impact caused the ice upon which they stood to vein, crack.

"You cannot kill me," the archfiend gurgled through a mouthful of ichor and bile.

Riven knew it to be true. He was perhaps a match for Mephistopheles, but only until the archfiend fully assimilated the power he had taken from Cale. Then, Riven would be vulnerable. He had little time.

He put a boot on Mephistopheles's back and kicked the archfiend flat to the ice while jerking his blades free. The heat from Mephistopheles's flesh sent a cloud of steam into the air. Riven willed a binding on the archfiend, preventing him from teleporting to safety.

"I cannot kill you," he conceded. "But I will hurt you. Hurt you so you remember it."

Mephistopheles roared, the wind gusted, and Riven slashed his empowered saber into the archfiend's head, cleaving one of his horns and sinking deeply into the skull. Thick, greasy fluid sprayed from the chasm in the devil's head. Riven funneled his rage through his blade, lit the archfiend afire with pain.

Mephistopheles screamed and tried to stand. Riven kept a foot on his back, and drove him face down into the ice of his own realm.

Somewhere in the distance, glaciers crumbled. Mountains fell.

"Those three, those are for the three you gave Cale." Riven eyed his friend's body, nearly covered in ice.

Mephistopheles groaned, said something indecipherable. The wounds Riven had given him were already closing.

He rocked his saber free from the archfiend's skull. "This one is for me."

Grabbing a fistful of Mephistopheles's blood- and brain-spattered black hair, he jerked back the fiend's head, exposing his throat. The archfiend grimaced, showing a mouthful of fangs stained black with blood. Riven put his saber edge on Mephistopeheles's neck and opened his throat. Blood that smelled like rot gouted from the gash. Riven held the flopping head in his hand for a moment before dropping it contemptuously to the ice.

Though not yet perfectly alloyed with the divine essence, Riven still sensed the arrival of two score gelugons as they teleported to the aid of their master. Their wet breathing was as a bellows in his divinely-enhanced hearing, the sound of their sudden weight on the ice like the crack of a whip.

He spun, and unleashed a cloud of viscous shadows that engulfed them all, binding them. They clicked and grunted with surprise and he sent a surge of power through the cloud to prevent any of them from teleporting out. With a minor exertion of will, he turned the thick cloud acidic.

The gelugons shrieked as the acid ate holes through their carapaces. They struggled against their bonds, hacked with their hooked polearms at the shadows that bound them, but to no avail. Foul, greasy black smoke and agonized clicks and screams rose from the slaughter. Riven put them from his mind and turned to face their master.

The gash in the archfiend's head was closing. So, too, the opening in his throat. Riven put a knee between his wings, leaned forward, and whispered in his ear.

"Step out of the Hells and I will be waiting. Everywhere other than here, I am your better."

Mephistopheles started to speak, gagged on blood, coughed, spit. He nodded toward Cale. "You will be back for him. And when you come, I will be waiting."

Riven looked over to Cale but could not see his friend's body. Perhaps the ice already had buried him, or perhaps . . .

For a moment, hope rose in him. But then he remembered that the archfiend was a liar, ever and always.

No, Cale was dead forever, his body encased in ice, and Riven could not spare the time to recover him. He figured Cale would understand.

"He is gone," Riven said, trying to believe his own words. "And I will not be back."

Mephistopheles smiled a mouthful of bloody fangs. "We will see."

Rivalen saw the glow around Sakkors dim, saw the city right itself as the mindmage released the Source and its power once more turned to keeping the city aloft. The echo of the mindmage's rage still rattled around his brain. His body ached, bled, but his regenerative flesh worked at closing the wounds and healing his bones. He would be able to regrow his arm in time.

*It is over*, the mindmage said, exhaustion and despair leaking through the mental emanation.

Rivalen shook his head and said softly, "No. It has just begun."

He pictured in his mind oblivion, the end of all, and pulled the shadows around him. He felt the rush of instantaneous movement and materialized among the shattered ruins of Ordulin.

Darkness shrouded the dead city. Long streaks of sickly blue and dull yellow vapor floated lazily through the polluted, stale air, the bruises left on Ordulin's corpse. Rivalen knew the acrid vapors to be poisonous but his new nature defied the weaknesses of a purely mortal form.

Walls of churning dark clouds surrounded the city, Shar's perpetual darkness taken root in Faerûn's Heartlands. Jagged streaks of vermillion lightning split the clouds. Ominous thunder rumbled.

But within the city, in the center of the storm, was stillness, vacuity. Only the wind stirred. It spiraled around him in insistent gusts, irritated breezes, and pushed at his back, driving him toward the core of the city and truth of Shar's plan.

He let his consciousness, divinely expansive, reach across the breadth of the city. It was entirely devoid of life. He knew the darkness outside the city proper teemed with twisted forms of life and unlife that fed on death and fear, but the city itself was a hole.

And he knew why.

Kesson Rel had failed; Shar had not.

But Rivalen had to see it for himself. He had to know.

He could have walked the shadows to the pit he would find in Ordulin's center but chose instead to walk through the destruction. He thought that someone living should bear witness to it.

The beat of his boots off the cracked and uneven streets were the moments recorded by a Neverwinter waterclock, dripping away the time left to Toril. He felt more and more lightheaded with each step.

Around him deformed buildings sagged on their foundations, drooped from the sides as if their stone and brick had run like melting candle wax, rounding edges, stretching shapes. The buildings leaned like drunks toward the center of the city, toward the hole in the world.

Thousands of corpses littered the city, lay in doorways, on balconies, flesh pale and drooping, twisted mouths open in dying screams. The wind tore at the rags of their clothing, Shar's victory pennons.

As he neared his goal, the deformation of the world increased. Eventually separation of melted flesh from melted stone was lost. Parts of bodies jutted from the sagging rocks and bricks. Torsos, heads, and limbs stabbed accusatory appendages at the black sky, the bodies trapped in the wreckage of crumbling reality, insects caught imperfectly in drops of amber. He did not avert his gaze at the grisliness. He took it in, tried to comprehend it, the shadows around him swirling.

"Your bitterness was sweet to the Lady," he said to the dead.

He felt reality, unreality, pulling at his form, trying to turn him first malleable, then unmake him all together. Only the divine power within him allowed him to remain physically and mentally coherent. He felt detached, as if watching himself in a dream.

Ahead, the street ended in a cobblestone paved plaza surrounded by a low stone wall. A bronze statue stood on a pedestal near the wall, a warrior with sword and shield. His features had flowed away, as if tears had melted his expression.

Rivalen walked past the statue and into the plaza. Kesson Rel's spire hung over the city, feeding the rift between planes that manifested as a gash in the sky. Rivalen put out his hand and a shadowy tendril extended from his palm to the spire, wrapping around its circumference again and again again. He let power surge through the tendril and Kesson's tower crumbled, fell to earth in huge chunks, each of them a monument to his failure. Then he intoned a stanza of power, and closed the rift. The Shadowstorm would retreat in time. Only Ordulin would remain in its shadows. Sembia would recover, mostly, and the Shadovar would rule it.

Rivalen picked his way through the rubble and there, in the center of Kesson Rel's ruin, he found Shar's victory.

A disc of nothingness, perhaps the size of a shield, hovered at eye height. It did not move but the border between it and the surrounding plaza blurred. Reality seemed to sag under the weight of its presence, as if the world were draining away in a wash basin.

Stillness reigned. Rivalen stared, awed, humbled.

The wind blew a ribbon of shadow into the hole and the shadow disappeared. Not consumed, Rivalen knew. Not disintegrated, but obliterated entirely, as would anything that fell into it, just as he had seen on Ephyras.

Rivalen held out his hand, his fingertips nearly touching the hole, his body the bridge between substance and nothingness. He looked into the hole, the lens through which he saw the end of all time and all things. He was looking at the end of the world, the unmaking of the universe. From an inner pocket, he withdrew the black coin he had taken from the ruins of Ephyras. It was cool in his hand, dead.

For the first time he understood, truly understood, the nature of his goddess, of her goals, of her needs.

She would end all things. He would be her instrument. He had murdered his mother, lost his brother, his father, his entire family, made a sacrifice of his soul, traded his faith for his humanity, and all of it for nothing. He closed his fingers over the coin, stared into the hole in the world, and wept.

Thamalon heard news of Rivalen's return to Selgaunt and awaited him in the map room of his palace. His gaze went again and again to the chess pieces he had placed on the map of Sembia, the black line of sword-armed pawns denoting the leading edge of the Shadowstorm.

He didn't know if the prince had succeeded in stopping Kesson Rel. He didn't know of Mister Cale's fate, of the Saerbians.

Impatience turned him fidgety. He paced the room, drank a chalice of wine, paced more, drank more, and still the prince did not come.

The glowballs in the room caused the chess pieces to cast shadows on the map. The pawns painted miniature shades across the whole of Sembia. Thamalon stopped pacing, stared at them, imagined himself able to step though darkness, to travel between worlds, to live forever.

He wanted what he had been promised, and wanted it badly. First things firstly, Rivalen had said, and Thamalon had accepted that, but the time had come. Thamalon rang for his chamberlain.

Thriistin's thin body and thin hair appeared in the doorway. His coat and collared shirt, as always, appeared freshly donned.

"Hulorn?"

"You have sent for Prince Rivalen?"

"Two runners, my lord. He is not in his quarters."

Thamalon stared at the map, at the shades, his fists clenched.

"Bring a carriage around."

"Yes, my lord."

Thamalon didn't bother with Rivalen's quarters. Instead, he instructed the driver to take him to Temple Avenue. The hunched teamster grunted an acknowledgment and snapped the reins.

The carriage rattled along Selgaunt's cobblestone streets and Thamalon took pride in the crowded thoroughfares, the bustle of commerce, the absence of food lines. His city was well-protected and well-fed, having weathered a war and a famine and emerged the stronger. Under his rule, all of Sembia would do the same.

The populace recognized his lacquered carriage and Thamalon returned salutes and waves as he went. He was the Hulorn and the people loved their Hulorn.

Squads of Scepters patrolled the streets afoot. Two or three Shadovar soldiers bolstered the ranks of each squad, their ornate armor an odd anachronism even on the diverse, cosmopolitan streets of Selgaunt. Thamalon realized that he had come to take the presence of the Shadovar for granted. The people had, too. He imagined that no one would think twice of it when Sakkors reappeared in the sky over Selgaunt.

The teamster shouted to his team and the carriage turned onto Temple Avenue. Thamalon leaned out of the window.

Few worshipers strode the avenue's walkways and no other carriages rode its cobblestones. The clatter of the carriage's passage disturbed the starlings that perched in the nooks of the statues and fountains. A cloud of them took wing as the carriage approached and Thamalon ducked back inside to avoid the rain of their droppings. The driver, with no roof to shield him, cursed the birds for fouling his coat.

As they moved down the avenue, they passed one dark, abandoned temple after another, the stone corpses of dead faiths. Stairs and halls once filled with worshipers stood as fallow and empty as had Sembia's once drought-stricken fields.

Soon Thamalon would formally outlaw all worship but that of Shar. Anything of value within the abandoned temples would be taken and placed in the city's treasury. He would order the temples torn down and use their stone to repair damage done during the war, a fitting use for the temples of traitors.

"Stop before the House of Night," he said to the driver, who nodded.

The temple of Shar squatted on its plot, all sharp angles and hard, gray stone. A single tower rose from the center of the two story temple, a digit pointing an accusation at Selûne. Only a few windows dotted its facade, and those the color of smoke or deep purple.

Once, Vees Talendar had tried to disguise it as a temple of Siamorphe, but all pretense had been shed. The black, lacquered double doors, standing open, prominently featured Shar's symbol—a featureless black disc ringed in purple. A large amethyst decorated the keystone of the doors' arch. In coming months, Thamalon would engage laborers to appropriately adorn the rest of the temple's exterior.

Without waiting for the driver to open his door, Thamalon let himself out and walked up the stone stairs to the doorway of the temple. He could not see within. Impenetrable magical darkness cloaked the entry foyer just beyond the doors, symbolically separating the church from the outside world. A congregant was forced to take his first steps into the temple blind, a moment of vulnerability to remind them of Shar's power. Within the darkness, the congregant was to confess a secret to the Lady.

Thamalon stepped out of the late afternoon sun and entered the darkness. Whispers plagued his ears, the combined babble of all others who had entered the darkness and made their confessions. He couldn't make out words but he heard Rivalen's deep voice among the cacophony, Variance's sibilant tone. For a moment he felt as if the floor had opened and he were falling, a vertiginous spiral into an unending void.

"I hated my father," he confessed through gritted teeth, and the feeling instantly ceased, the whispers subsided, and he knew his own secret had joined the babble.

The magic of the foyer tugged at the holy symbol of Shar he wore, lifting the symbol from his chest and pulling him by the chain. He followed its lead. In a few strides he emerged from the darkness to find himself face to face with Variance Mattick.

Shadows twirled around her in long, thin spirals. A scar along her cheek marred the dark skin of her round face. Her long, black hair melded with her shroud of shadows. She wore the purple robe of her office. He wondered if she, like Rivalen, was thousands of years old.

"Priestess," Thamalon said, inclining his head. "In the darkness of night, we hear the whisper of the void."

"Heed its words, Hulorn."

"I seek Prince Rivalen. He is not in his quarters, so I thought—"

"The Nightseer is within."

She made no move to step aside, nor offered further detail.

"May I see him?"

"He is at worship."

Thamalon looked past her, saw only the hallway and its purple carpet. "I think he will see me."

Variance smiled, the expression made sinister by the way the skin of her cheek creased around her scar.

"Remain here. I will inquire of the Nightseer."

Without waiting for an acknowledgement, she turned and walked down the corridor. She soon melted into the darkness of the windowless space.

Thamalon stood in the hall, irritated with the presumptuous manner in which Variance had ordered him to remain.

"As if I were a dog," he murmured.

His irritation only grew as the moments passed. He looked down the corridor, but saw nothing but the purple carpet and bare stone walls. Could she have forgotten him?

"Damn it all," he said, and started down the hallway after Variance.

"Hulorn," Rivalen said from behind him.

Surprise jolted Thamalon's heart. He turned to see Rivalen step from the darkness.

"You startled me," Thamalon said. "I did not see you."

Rivalen let the shadows fall away from him entirely. "Do you see me now?"

"I do," Thamalon said. "You look . . . different."

Rivalen stood no taller than he ever had, yet he appeared to Thamalon to fill the hall, to occupy more than mere space. The shadows enshrouding him appeared darker, like a bottomless hole. His exposed left hand was black, as if formed of coalesced shadows. The regard of his golden eyes made Thamalon uncomfortable. Thamalon had no desire to know what secret Rivalen had confessed to the darkness.

"You have disturbed my worship, Hulorn."

The incivility of the prince's words surprised Thamalon. Anger lurked in Rivalen's tone. Thamalon reminded himself that he was the Hulorn, soon to be ruler of all of Sembia. He and Rivalen were peers.

"I received word that you had returned, but had no word of the outcome of events. I expected to receive that from you."

Rivalen's eyes narrowed. "Expected? Why?"

Thamalon tried not to wilt under Rivalen's gaze. "Because I am the Hulorn."

Rivalen seemed to advance on him, though he did not move. "And what is that to me?"

"I . . ." Thamalon stuttered, swallowed, adopted a more deferential tone. "I should have said 'hoped,' Prince. I did not *expect* you to report to me. I *hoped* you would. We had kept close counsel previously and I . . . assumed that would continue."

"It will," Rivalen said, and something hid within the words. "We were . . . successful. The rift was closed. The Shadow-storm will retreat from Sembia, though Ordulin is lost to darkness forever."

Thamalon's heart surged at the news. "And what of Mister Cale? The Saerbians?"

Rivalen's brow furrowed, as if the question pained him. "Mister Cale is dead."

Thamalon could not contain a grin. He knew he must look like a gloating buffoon but he didn't care.

"Splendid news, Prince Rivalen! Splendid!"

Rivalen continued, "I allowed the surviving Saerbians safe passage through Sembia. They may settle where they will."

Thamalon lost his grin and his good humor. "*You* allowed?"

Thamalon regretted the emphasis the moment the words bid farewell to his teeth.

Rivalen stared at him, the shadows around him whirling. "Yes. I allowed."

"Of course," said Thamalon, forcing a smile. "You have the authority to act in my name."

Rivalen stared down at Thamalon, his mouth a hard line. "You will find that our relationship will change somewhat as Sembia is consolidated under Shadovar rule."

A small pit opened in Thamalon's stomach, a place for the truth to settle.

"I fear 'somewhat' does much work in that sentence, Prince."

Rivalen waved a hand in the air, batting aside Thamalon's point. "You will remain titular head of Sembia but you will answer ultimately to me and to the Most High."

Thamalon tried to keep the shock from his face and voice. "But I assumed we would rule as equals. I thought—"

"Your assumption was incorrect. We are not equals. You are an instrument of my will, and the Lady's."

Thamalon's mind spun. He struggled to keep his mental balance. "After all we have accomplished?"

"*We* accomplished nothing. I accomplished all. You are but the face of it to the outside."

Thamalon flushed. "But—but I worship the Mistress. I minted coins, Prince. I thought to become a shade, like you. I thought we were . . . friends."

Only after he had uttered the words did he realize how ridiculous they sounded, like the whines of a child. Embarrassment heated his cheeks.

"You will become a shade, Hulorn," Rivalen said. "I will keep my word. Promises are kept in these days."

"Thank you, Prince," Thamalon said, pleased at least by that, though he could not meet Rivalen's eyes.

"The transformation is prolonged and painful. Your body and soul are torn asunder and remade."

Thamalon backed up a step, eyes wide.

Rivalen followed. "The agony will plague your dreams for years."

Thamalon felt nauseated, and backed up another step.

"Your family and friends will die and turn to dust. You will linger, alone."

Thamalon bumped up against a wall. Rivalen loomed over him.

"But in the end, you will be hardened, made a better servant to the Lady, made a better servant to me."

"That is not what I wanted, Prince."

"It is exactly what you wanted. Power. You simply wanted to pay no price for it. But you are a Sembian, Hulorn. You should have known there is always a price. And the price will be pain and eternal loneliness."

Rivalen said it in the tone of one who knew that of which he spoke.

Thamalon gulped, imagined the pain of his transformation. He looked into his future and saw a friendless, solitary existence, feared and hated by those he ostensibly ruled. He did not want it, not anymore.

"Please, Prince. No. I abdicate. Here, now. To you."

"It is too late for that."

Tears leaked from Thamalon's eyes.

"What have I done?" he said, his voice soft.

Rivalen smiled, his fangs making him look diabolical. "Your bitterness is sweet to the Lady."

Mask manifested in a place that was no place, amidst the nothingness of cold and featureless gray. He manifested fully, not in one of the trivial, semi-divine forms he sometimes showed to worshipers.

He floated alone and small in an infinite void, the womb of creation. He marveled that the bustling, colorful, life-filled multiverse had been born from such yawning emptiness. He marveled, too, that the creation would one day return to the void. He was pleased he would not see it, though he knew he would have played his small role in causing it.

As would those who came after him and took his station.

Or perhaps not, if things went as he wished. He had planted his own seeds in creation's womb. Time would tell what fruit they bore.

"I am here," he said, and his voice echoed through infinity.

Fatigue settled on him all at once. He had been running a long while, delaying the inevitable. Surrender was not in him. He supposed that was why she had chosen him, why he had chosen his own servants.

His voice died as the feeling of nothingness, of endless solitude, intensified. He felt hollow, as empty as the space around him.

She was coming.

He held his ground and his nerve. The moment was fore-ordained. Within him, he carried all of the power he had stolen many millennia before, plus some—but not all—of the added power that he'd amassed since his ascension. And power was the coin she demanded in payment of his debts. The Cycle had turned.

"Show yourself. You owe me that, at least."

It had taken him a long while to accept that he would not be the herald who broke the Cycle of Shadows. He had stolen the power thinking he would. His hubris amused him. He found hope in the possibility that those he had chosen might break it, sever the circle.

"I see hope in your expression," she said, her voice as beautiful and cold as he remembered. "Hope is ill-suited to this place."

He swallowed and held his ground as the nothingness took on presence and he felt the regard of a vast intelligence that existed at once in multiple places, multiple times. She had seen the birth of creation. She would see it end.

"The Cycle turns," she said.

He felt her cold hands on him, felt the spark of divinity within him answer to its original owner's touch. She had taken her favorite form among many—a pale-skinned maiden with black hair that fell to her waist. The emptiness of the void yawned in her eyes. He looked at a point on her face below her eyes—he dared not look into those eyes lest he see his fate. The slash of her red lips against the paleness of her face struck him as obscene.

"I am come to pay my debt," he said, and bowed his head. He found his form quaking. In her presence he experienced the frailties he had not felt since his ascension. The experience pleased him.

She ran a hand through his hair, put her forehead to his.

"Your debt is long overdue. Mere repayment is inadequate recompense. Surely you know this, Lessinor."

He had not heard his birth name spoken in so long its pronouncement caused him to look up into his mother's eyes . . . and regret it.

He saw there the oblivion of non-existence, the emptiness that awaited him. He had not wished to see it. He had wished it only to happen, one moment existence, one moment non-existence. He did not wish to *know*.

The frailties endemic to his one-time humanity resurfaced. His body shook. He did not wish to end. He did not wish to know what "end" meant. All that he had done, all that he had been, for nothing.

Or perhaps not. This time, he kept the hope from his face.

"Ah," his mother said, and sighed with satisfaction. "You see it now, here, at the end of things."

He nodded.

"Interest is due on your debt, my son."

He nodded once more. He had expected as much and prepared. In the millennia in which he had been worshiped the faith of his followers had made him something greater than that which he had initially stolen from her. That she knew. But she did not know its scope, and that he had hidden some.

"I am come to pay that, as well . . . Lady."

He could not bring himself to name her his mother. She had possessed a vessel to birth a herald, nothing more.

"I know," she said, and drew him to her in an embrace. Her

arms enfolded him, cooled him. She stroked his hair, cooed. He put his head on her shoulder and wept.

Only then did he realize that he was cooling, that his power was leeching away, that the void he had seen in her eyes was coming for him. He gripped her tighter, closed his eyes, but could not dismiss the image of the end that awaited him.

"Shh," she hissed, and held him tightly.

He was sinking, disappearing in her vastness, entering the void. Non-existence yawned before him. He tried to speak, to rebel at the final moment, but could not escape her grasp.

Darkness closed in on him. He tried to enter the void with hope in his heart, recalling that he, the son of the Lady of Secrets, had kept a secret from—

# EPILOGUE

The ghosts of the past haunt my mind, specters of memory that manifest in sadness. I run an alehouse in Daerlun, now. It is a small thing but small things are all I find myself suited to now. My appearance startles no one in these days; most have seen creatures more exotic than me. I fill cups, tell jokes, hire bards, and try to brighten a few spirits in otherwise dark times. I call my place The Tenth Hell and the caravaneers and hireswords who stream through Daerlun seem to like the name.

The Tenth is my personal Hell, I tell them, and they think I am making a joke, given my horns and obvious fiendish lineage. But I do not mean it as a joke.

One hundred years have passed since Erevis Cale died. There have been other landmarks in my life since then, other tragedies, but his loss remains the most painful, the point that defines the "after" in my life. He sacrificed himself to save me when I did not merit saving. For that, I owe him what I am. And I owe it to him to be worthy of what he did.

There are still days when I tap a keg and convince myself that he is not gone, not forever. How can he be? I saw him do too much, survive too much, to be gone. I stare into the shadowy corners of my place, eye the dark alleys of Daerlun, looking for him, expecting him to step from the darkness, serious as usual, and call to me:

"Mags," he will say.

But he never does.

He is gone, forever I suppose, and no one has called me Mags in over ninety years. I do not allow it to anyone but Riven, and we have not spoken since two years after the Shadowstorm retreated.

He looked different when I saw him, darker, more *there*. Over a tankard of stout in the alehouse that I would buy seventy years later (it was called The Red Hen, then), he told me what he had become.

I believed him. I could see it in the depths of his eye, in the way the darkness hugged his form. He sat in the alehouse for several hours and I'd wager that only one or two patrons other than me even noticed him. He had become the shadows.

"Faerûn thinks Mask is dead," I said.

He took his pipe out of his mouth and exhaled a cloud of exotic smelling smoke. Shadows bled from his flesh, as they once had from Cale. He looked at me with an expression that did not belong to a mere man. His voice was a whisper, the rush of the wind through night shrouded trees.

"He is, but not forever. Let's keep that our secret, Mags."

I detected a threat in the statement, in the way the darkness around me deepened. I nodded, changed the subject.

Our conversation started with recent events and moved back through time. We spoke of Cale, Kesson Rel, Rivalen Tanthul, the Sojourner, Azriim the slaad, even our days in Westgate. I asked after his dogs, the temple. He did not touch his stout and when we parted it had the feeling of permanence.

"Take care, Mags," he had said.

I almost touched his arm but lost my nerve at the last moment. "Are we friends, Drasek?"

"Always, Mags."

I turned for a moment at the crash of a breaking tankard and the string of curses that accompanied it. When I turned back, he was gone. We spoke again only once more.

A few years later, in the Year of Blue Fire, the Spellplague ravaged Faerûn. Many people measure time from that point onward. Me, I still measure it from the day Erevis Cale died.

I was making my living as a caravan guide and roadman for the wagons streaming in and out of Sembia, working with the kind of men and women I now serve in The Hell. I did not learn the full scope of the changes wrought by the Spellplague until much later but I saw its effects in the Hen, when a wizard sitting at the table next to me looked up from his tea, wild-eyed.

"What is it?" I asked.

He opened his mouth to speak, managed only to utter the word, "Something . . ." then froze in his chair. His blood and flesh had turned to ice. I learned later that the Spellplague had turned the Weave to poison and caused havoc with practitioners of the Art. The magical surges and vacuums changed Faerûn forever.

I continued to work as a guide. Travelers from abroad told alarming tales around the campfires—some areas of Faerûn had sunk into the ground, replaced by chasms and lakes filled with dire, loathsome creatures from below. Seas had drained. Whole chunks of the world had simply disappeared, effaced from history and memory, replaced by parts of some other world that had bled in to fill the void. Thousands died, millions perhaps, including gods, and the world was transformed.

I found the tales hard to believe, and wanted to see for myself. Journeying across central Faerûn, I saw chunks of the world floating free in the air, eerie echoes of the Shadovar's floating cities. I saw twisted creatures rise from steaming pits to pollute nature with their presence.

And everywhere I saw fear and uncertainty in the eyes of Faerûn's people. Men and women of every profession and station gathered together in alehouses and taverns after night fell and shared whatever dark news they had heard that day. I saw the comfort they took in one another's presence, the importance of a common meeting place, and decided then that I would run an alehouse one day.

Wherever I went, no one seemed to know what caused the plague, though rumors abounded. My suspicions turned to the Shadovar and Shar, since Sembia, which had traded the darkness of the Shadowstorm for the darkness of Shadovar rule, went largely unaffected. To this day Tamlin Uskevren still rules Sembia, at least in name, though he answers to Rivalen Tanthul.

We all answer to someone or something.

Me, I answer to the past. Always will.

When I reached the dark shores of the Abolethic Sovereignty, with the hypnotic rhythm of its lapping waters, I turned back. Faerûn was different and I had seen enough. For the first time in my life I wanted to settle in somewhere, make a home, find another way of life. But I had one thing to do first.

I sought out Riven.

I hired a small ship out of shadow-shrouded Selgaunt and took it to the Wayrock. I told myself that I wanted to ensure that Riven was all right, that he had survived the Spellplague, but I think what I really wanted was to ensure that I was not the only one still living who carried the weight of our past.

I left the crew aboard ship and rowed a dinghy to the island. Mask's temple remained intact, the drawbridge lowered. I entered, walked its dark, empty halls, but found no one. Tears fell as I walked. I remembered the days I had spent in the temple, lost in fiend-spawned dreams, planning evil, harming my friends.

I hurried from that place, chased by self-loathing, and walked the island. Shadows filled the hollows and low spaces. The surf crashed; the birds squawked. I climbed the hill and visited Jak's cairn. It was well-tended still.

I thought at the time that Riven must have returned to the temple from time to time, but no longer resided there. Perhaps too many memories stalked its halls for him, too. I was wrong.

As I rowed back out to the ship, shadows coagulated around me. The boat pulled a deeper draft as additional weight settled on it. I tried to turn, but the darkness held me fast.

"Riven?"

Riven's voice sounded in my ear, as if he were sitting right behind me. His tone was one of surprise.

"Cale has a son, Mags."

"A son? How? Where? He lived through the Spellplague?"

"He was born afterward. He will be born afterward, rather."

"Will? What are you saying?" I set the oars and tried to turn on my bench, but failed. "How? Cale died in—"

"Mask pushed her forward through time to save her from the Shadowstorm, and from the Spellplague. I haven't yet located her."

"Why would he do that?" I asked.

"Why indeed," Riven said.

That was not the answer I had expected. "But . . . aren't you him? Don't you know?"

"I am not him, Mags. I just have some of his power."

"What does it mean?" I asked.

"Men have sons. Maybe nothing. Maybe it was just something he did for Cale."

I thought not, but held my tongue.

"He told me I would be back for him," Riven said.

"Who?"

"Your father."

I tried again to turn, failed. "Back for whom? Cale?"

But the darkness lifted and Riven was gone. I have not seen him since.

I returned to the ship, used my power to cause the crew to forget that they had brought me to the Wayrock, and returned to Daerlun. Years later I bought my place, my Hell, and here I reside.

My mind still bears the scars of my time with Riven and Cale. But they are healed. Mostly. The Source floats in Sakkors' core, one of the two floating enclaves that hover over the reborn Empire of Netheril, but I no longer feel its pull. I rarely use my powers at all. My father's voice no longer troubles my sleep. Only memories trouble my mind now, not addictions and archfiends. I hope my life is worthy of the sacrifice Erevis made to save it.

I still check the dark corners of the Hell, the shadowy alleys of Daerlun, but not just for Erevis. Also for his son. When I recall Riven's words to me aboard the dinghy, I think that Erevis's story may not yet have unfolded fully. Perhaps it can be completed only through his son. Perhaps that is why Mask spared him.

Time will tell.

# RICHARD LEE BYERS

The author of *Dissolution* and The Year of Rogue Dragons sets his
sights on the realm of Thay in a new trilogy that no
FORGOTTEN REALMS® fan can afford to miss.

## THE HAUNTED LAND

### BOOK I
### UNCLEAN

Many powerful wizards hold Thay in their control, but when one of them
grows weary of being one of many, and goes to war, it will be at the head of
an army of undead.

### BOOK II
### UNDEAD

The dead walk in Thay, and as the rest of Faerûn looks on in stunned horror, the very
nature of this mysterious, dangerous realm begins to change.

### BOOK III
### UNHOLY

Forces undreamed of even by Szass Tam have brought havoc and death to Thay, but
the lich's true intentions remain a mystery—a mystery that could spell doom for the
entire world.

Early 2009

### Anthology
### REALMS OF THE DEAD

A collection of new short stories by some of the Realms' most popular authors sheds
new light on the horrible nature of the undead of Faerûn. Prepare yourself for the
terror of the *Realms of the Dead*.

Early 2010

# FORGOTTEN REALMS®

# THE KNIGHTS OF MYTH DRANNOR

A brand new trilogy by master storyteller

# ED GREENWOOD

Join the creator of the FORGOTTEN REALMS® world as he explores the early adventures of his original and most celebrated characters from the moment they earn the name "Swords of Eveningstar" to the day they prove themselves worthy of it.

### BOOK I
## SWORDS OF EVENINGSTAR

Florin Falconhand has always dreamed of adventure. When he saves the life of the king of Cormyr, his dream comes true and he earns an adventuring charter for himself and his friends. Unfortunately for Florin, he has also earned the enmity of several nobles and the attention of some of Cormyr's most dangerous denizens.

### Now available in paperback!

### BOOK II
## SWORDS OF DRAGONFIRE

Victory never comes without sacrifice. Florin Falconhand and the Swords of Eveningstar have lost friends in their adventures, but in true heroic fashion, they press on. Unfortunately, there are those who would see the Swords of Eveningstar pay for lives lost and damage wrecked, regardless of where the true blame lies.

### Available in paperback in April 2008!

### BOOK III
## THE SWORD NEVER SLEEPS

Fame has found the Swords of Eveningstar, but with fame comes danger. Nefarious forces have dark designs on these adventurers who seem to overturn the most clever of plots. And if the Swords will not be made into their tools, they will be destroyed.

### August 2008

## FORGOTTEN REALMS®

### never been to the
### FORGOTTEN REALMS® world?

## SEMBIA:
## GATEWAY TO THE REALMS

Opens the door to our most popular world with stories full of
intrigue, adventure, and fascinating characters. Sembia is a land
of wealth and power, where rival families buy and sell everything
imaginable—even life itself. In that unforgiving realm, the
Uskevren family may hold the rarest commodity of all: honor.

But even the most honorable family is not without its secrets, and
everyone from the maid to the matriarch has something to hide.

# TRACY HICKMAN

PRESENTS

# THE ANVIL OF TIME

With the power of the Anvil of Time, the Journeyman can travel
the river of time as simply as walking upstream, visiting the
ancient past of Krynn with ease.

### VOLUME ONE
## THE SELLSWORD
**Cam Banks**

Vanderjack, a mercenary with a price on his head, agrees out of
desperation to retrieve a priceless treasure for a displaced noble. The
treasure is deep within enemy territory, and he must survive an army of
old foes, a chorus of unhappy ghosts, and the questionable assistance of
a mad gnome to find it.

### VOLUME TWO
## THE SURVIVORS
**Dan Willis**

A goodhearted dwarf is warned of an apocalyptic flood by the god
Reorx, and he and his motley followers must decide whether the
warning is real—and then survive the disaster that sweeps
through their part of Krynn.

**November 2008**

# JEAN RABE

## THE STONETELLERS

*"Jean Rabe is adept at weaving a web of deceit and lies, mixed with adventure, magic, and mystery."*
—*sffworld.com on Betrayal*

Jean Rabe returns to the DRAGONLANCE® world with a tale of slavery, rebellion, and the struggle for freedom.

### VOLUME ONE
## THE REBELLION

After decades of service, nature has dealt the goblins a stroke of luck. Earthquakes strike the Dark Knights' camp and mines, crippling the Knights and giving the goblins their best chance to escape. But their freedom will not be easy to win.

### VOLUME TWO
## DEATH MARCH

The reluctant general, Direfang, leads the goblin nation on a death march to the forests of Qualinesti, there to create a homeland in defiance of the forces that seek to destroy them.

**August 2008**

### VOLUME THREE
## GOBLIN NATION

A goblin nation rises in the old forest, building fortresses and fighting to hold onto their new homeland, while the sorcerers among them search for powerful magic cradled far beneath the trees.

**August 2009**

# EBERR⊙N

## Sword & sorcery adventure from the creator of the EBERRON® world!

### KEITH BAKER

### Thorn of Breland

A new war has already begun—a cold war, fought in the shadows by agents of every nation—and Thorn does all she can as a member of the King's Citadel. But her last mission has left her with gaps in her memory, and she'll have to work out what happened as she goes—after all, Breland won't protect itself.

### The Dreaming Dark

A band of weary war veterans have come to Sharn, hoping to find a way to live in a world that is struggling to settle into an uneasy peace. But over the years, they have made enemies in high places—and even places far from Eberron.

From acclaimed author and award-winning
game designer James Wyatt, an adventure
that will shake the world of EBERRON
to its core.

## THE DRACONIC PROPHECIES

were old when humans first began to forge their civilization.
They give meaning to the past, guidance in the present, and
predict the future—a future of the world's remaking. And now,
one facet of the prophecies is being set in motion, and all of
it revolves around Gaven, exiled from his house, thrown into
prison, and in the grips of a terrible madness.

**Book One**
*Storm Dragon*

**Book Two**
*Dragon Forge*

**Book Three**
*Dragon War*

**And don't miss James Wyatt's first EBERRON novel**
*In the Claws of the Tiger*
Janik barely survived his last expedition to the dark continent,
but when he finds himself embroiled in a plot involving the
lost wonders of Xen'drik, his one hope at redemption is to
return and face the horrors that once almost destroyed him.